THE DARK SIDE
OF
THE FYLFOT

A Mediaeval Fantasy

Andrew G. Lockhart

Magda Green Books

Publishing History

The Dark Side of the Fylfot was first published as a paperback in 2010
ISBN 978-0-9543923-4-5

It was subsequently published as an e-book in the same year
ISBN 978-0-9543923-5-2

E-book published with a new cover in 2018

This revised edition paperback 2021
ISBN: 9798502651448

Original cover photo by Julia Volk, courtesy of *www.pexels.com*

Prologue
1304 C.E.

In the Greek province of Magnesia, in the shadow of Mount Pelion and surrounded by the ruins of the ancient city of Demetrias, two women are walking on the shore.

It is evening, an hour or so before sunset. Away out to sea, dark clouds are retreating on the eastern horizon. The day has been too wet for the couple to take their daily walk, salvaging the flotsam and jetsam from passing ships or sifting through the wreckage of any vessel unfortunate enough to fall foul of the rocks on the headland. Now, whatever they find is placed in a hand-cart they have brought along for that purpose.

The older woman's name is Kolba; the younger is Tessera, her daughter and fourth child. Their skin is darker than that of the natives of Magnesia, their hair thicker and glossier. They are newcomers to this land, refugees who have recently arrived from Anatolia by way of the many islands that separate its coast from the Greek peninsula. Kolba's people have come a long way in the ten generations since their flight from persecution in India. They have crossed the salt deserts of Persia, the Zagros Mountains and the Fertile Crescent of Mesopotamia. Kolba's ancestors continued to Syria; others of their race turned south towards Egypt. They have their own language, their own history, their own dress and their own gods.

As far as Kolba and Tessera know, their clan is the first to set foot on Greek soil. Later, their kind will multiply; they will become known to the Greek people as *Atzinganoi* – *Untouchables* - and to the Italians as *Singari*.

They will be called other names too, many of them insulting and offensive. To themselves, they are the *Doum*.

The villagers of Pelion mostly leave them alone and the Doum, for their part, keep themselves to themselves, living in tents and taking what the land and sea freely give them. There is as yet no animosity between the two peoples and when brought together by accident or for occasional trade and barter, their relations are polite and respectful.

The Doum have no great skill at either agriculture or fishing but they have their own animals, which, along with coarse bread made from crushed wild seeds, provide the bulk of their diet. They have a talent for carving wood, and for working and stitching leather, which they make into saddles and bridles for their own ponies and for barter with their neighbours.

The shore along which Kolba and Tessera walk has a broad expanse of golden sand that sweeps round the bay and out of sight beyond the rocks. The light is poor but there is enough of it for them to see that the beach is not empty. A ship has come to grief in the storm. From headland to headland, the sand is littered with debris: broken chests whose contents have spilled out, splinters of driftwood, pieces of torn sailcloth and foodstuffs spoiled by the sea. Kolba and Tessera pick their way among these offerings, prising open the whole chests with broad-bladed knives, checking for items that might be of use in their camp or that can be sold to the Greeks for extra provisions.

Kolba, who is forty-five years old, has seen several shipwrecks. Only once has she known there to be survivors. The rocks take most of them, tearing their flesh and clothing into pieces so that what remains is no longer recognisable as having once belonged to a human being.

Occasionally, the sea throws up a human corpse and then there is an opportunity to gather weapons or jewellery; not that the Doum have much need of the former, being unskilled in the crafts of war, but they love rings, necklaces and other trinkets. And it is no crime to take such things when their former owners no longer have any use for them.

Today, neither Kolba nor her daughter sees any bodies, living or dead. They haul two complete boxes up the beach towards the cart and then look around for other items of interest. Near the shoreline is what appears to be a bundle of clothing tied to a wooden pallet. Beside it, something glistens in the last shaft of setting sun. Full of curiosity, Tessera runs down to the sea. The object that shines is a single gold coin. She bends to pick it up and as she does so hears a sound like the wail of an animal in pain. She prods the bundle with her finger. To her astonishment it moves.

With beating heart, Tessera pulls aside some folds of cloth and finds herself looking into the face of an infant of no more than a few months old. Its cheeks are blue with cold, its lips dry and encrusted with salt, but there is no doubt it is alive.

Tessera is seventeen. She has recently given birth to a child herself but it died before drawing breath. Now she wants to pick up this other. She wants to suckle it and warm it against her own body. She finds she cannot. The infant is fastened somehow to what she realises is a fully grown woman.

Her cry brings Kolba running.

'Are they alive?'

'It's a girl,' Tessera says. 'She is alive but weak. The mother, I do not know.'

Kolba kneels beside the bodies and touches the woman's neck.

'Her heart beats slowly,' she says after a moment. 'But she is badly hurt. Hold the baby while I cut her free.'

She takes her knife and severs the strap of the leather sling that binds the infant's body to the mother's chest and neck. Then she steps back. Tessera sweeps the infant into her arms. She has removed her shawl, worn against the cool of the evening, and she winds it round the tiny bundle before pulling down the front of her dress and coaxing the baby to feed at her still swollen breast.

The act of cutting the sling has loosened the strange woman's robe and as Kolba tries to move her it falls away. Underneath, she wears a belt unlike any that Tessera has ever seen. It is such, the girl thinks, as a prince might wear. It is composed of two layers of leather. The one that lies next to the body and fastens round it is thick and strong. From it, on the woman's left side, hangs a scabbard designed to hold a sword. The sword is in its sheath. It too is of royal design, Tessera thinks. The hilt is a coiled metal serpent, the pommel a large ruby grasped in the snake's jaws.

The outer leather is lighter and more flexible and is stitched to the inner on the right side to form two pouches or purses. One of these is open and Tessera sees that it is filled with coins, just like the one lying in the sand.

The slight movement of the body causes two more to spill out. The girl gasps in amazement. She picks up the gold pieces and weighs them in her hand.

'I have never seen such wealth, Mother' she says. 'Our family will be rich.'

'We are honest people, Tessera,' Kolba says. 'You know it is not ours to take.' She takes the coins from her daughter's hand and replaces all three in their leather pouch. 'As long as this woman lives, the gold belongs to her. Should she die, it will go to the child, and we must keep it safe for her. The sword too, though it is strange that a mother should carry such a weapon.

'Run back to the camp and send your father to me. I will need fresh water, a pony and a larger cart.' Kolba parts the shawl and for a few moments watches the infant. Its eyes are closed as it sucks vigorously at the foster breast. Already the blue tinge is fading from its face.

'The baby is hungry, Mother,' Tessera says. 'Is that not a good sign?'

'The gods are indeed smiling on us today,' says Kolba. 'Take good care of this tiny miracle, Daughter. I will watch over the mother so that, if she lives, they can be reunited.'

Saxony, more than forty years later

GRETL

The Woman with the Sword

i

I was seven years old when the Black Death came to Brunswick.

We heard of it in March, the day of my accident, the day I tried to sneak a look through the window of my grandfather's laboratory. This was a little chamber, jutting out into his herb garden, where he would sometimes shut himself away for days at a time. I had often wondered what was inside.

The window was at man-height from the ground and easily reached from the garden if I climbed onto a buttress. I could already scamper up a tree as well as any boy, so a wall presented no challenge at all. The stones were rough and I had no difficulty gaining a foothold. I reached up with one hand and gripped the gnarled ivy. It was even easier than I had expected. Using both stones and plant as leverage, I pulled myself up until I could rest one foot on the projection.

From there it was a short stretch to the ledge under the window. I supported my weight with one hand on a horizontal limb of the ivy, stepped across and grasped the sill. I was just tall enough to peer over into the room.

Opa sat at a table on the left side. In front of him were a book bound in black leather and some rolled-up paper. On a second table to the right were laid freshly cut herbs, plant roots, a pestle and mortar, and some other pieces of apparatus. Above, and fixed to the wall, were shelves stacked with rows of phials, stone jars and glass containers of colourful berries.

I had asked about the room only for Opa to say it was a grown-up and dangerous place and that he would show it to me when I was ready. Never had I imagined it to be such a treasure house.

Eager to see more, I raised myself on tiptoe and pushed my face closer to the glass. I did not want to be caught spying but it was an opportunity too good to miss, a chance to see him at work and to learn the secrets he hid from us.

Opa opened the book. He picked up a quill, dipped it into an inkpot and poised it over the paper. A sudden thought seemed to distract him. He unrolled one of the scrolls and spread it out on the table. It was covered all over with drawings, the like of which I had never seen before. They were pictures of people, but with all of their fronts cut away to expose their hearts and stomachs and some other organs I did not recognise. The different parts within the outlines were coloured with blue, red and yellow dyes.

My face was now very close to the casement and my heart was beating furiously. I edged along farther to get a better view.

My grandfather looked up suddenly. Either I made a sound or my head cast a shadow into the room. I ducked out of sight. Anyway, I had seen enough and it was time to retreat.

I was careless. In my haste, I missed my footing and took a step into nothingness. My fingers lost their hold on the sill. I grabbed for the ivy but could not reach it and fell with a scream that might be heard in Hannover.

My knee hit the corner of the buttress, sending a tearing pain through my body, and I heard the ripping of cotton as my dress snagged on one of the rougher limbs of the ivy. I must have hit my head too, or fainted with shock because, when I came to my senses, I was lying in a bed of thyme, bleeding from a gash in my calf. I had never seen so much blood. It oozed out of the wound like red wine from a cracked flagon and trickled down my leg, over the straps of my sandals and between my bare toes. My petticoats were ruined beyond repair.

As my head cleared, I saw Opa standing over me. At his side knelt my mother, looking very worried. The tears welled up in my eyes as she cradled me in her arms. There was a buzzing in my ears too.

'We must do something about that cut,' said Opa and grinned

wickedly. 'Otherwise, she will live, I think. My treatment will be the best lesson.'

He took me from my mother, picked me up and carried me indoors, paying no attention that my blood was dripping on the floor. I was still dazed by the fall but remember wondering how long it would be before my veins were emptied and, if I died, whether Opa would forgive me for spying on him. There was no time for more idle thoughts. Before I knew it, I was inside the room I had for so long wanted to see. My enthusiasm for its secrets had waned.

They sat me in a chair. Opa lifted my injured leg so that it rested on the tabletop. He fetched a needle and thread from a box on one of the shelves and without saying another word began to stitch the ragged edges of my cut. It hurt even more than the cut itself. I clamped my lips together to hold back a yell.

'Well, Gretl,' said Opa, when he finished stitching, 'I think you've seen enough of my work for one day.' He stood back to admire his repair, then covered it with a cloth soaked in foul-smelling paste. 'Now, off to bed with you!'

It was only late afternoon but I was too embarrassed and hurt to argue. Limping badly, I followed my mother upstairs to my bedroom.

Despite the throbbing in my leg, I must have slept three or four hours. I awoke to the sound of loud voices. It was dark. I slipped out of bed, hobbled to the doorway and peeped out. The passage was empty. My leg burned fiercely and every step was agony.

A tallow lamp flickered in my mother's parlour as I passed. I could hear the sound of her breathing and see her back framed in the glow from the candle. She might have been working with her needle at a seam. I slipped past hurriedly, hoping she would not look round and catch me.

The voices drifted up from below the stairhead. I crawled along to the gallery, ducked under a table and looked down. It was a favourite hiding place of mine, where I often crept after supper to spy on the adults. My grandfather knew I was there, of course. Opa knew nearly everything about my escapades, though he never told.

There were three strangers in the hall and one was holding the floor.

A pale, blond northerner, he had drunk too much and was very red in the face. Behind him, the logs crackled in the hearth. I wished I could go down to warm myself. Though it was nearly spring, the evenings were still cool and, aside from the burning in my leg, I shivered in my shift.

That evening would have begun like others, with good food and wine. When we entertained, we did it well and guests often became merry. My father and Uncle Roland were doing their best to be gracious as always, whether feeling hospitable or not. Opa was there too, sitting quietly in his favourite chair with both hands resting over the gold talisman he wore at his throat. His *Fylfot*, he called it. He always showed eagerness for the company of men from different provinces, and for his sake such travellers were tolerated. Those from the south would sometimes bring him letters, whilst to those headed towards Italy he would give packages to carry.

Women had no interest in trade or travel, or so it was supposed, and children were forbidden to stay in the hall past their perceived bedtime - especially girls. So the men were alone. But not all children obey their parents, which is just as well, for if they did, not only would the world be a sombre place indeed but many things would never be known that ought to be known.

'Our business didn't take us to Venice or Genoa,' the red-faced speaker was saying, 'but news travels far and fast. They say hundreds are dying from an accursed sickness. The plague. Thousands!'

'Surely not,' said Roland.

'Thousands,' repeated the merchant, 'Agonising deaths, by all accounts. Their bodies turn black from breathing poisoned air.'

Secure in my hiding place, I gave a gasp, which I was sure all six men must have heard. My father and Roland both shook their heads doubtfully. Opa glanced up in my direction and calmly took a sip of his wine.

'I see you don't believe us,' said another of the men, and his red-faced colleague muttered assent. 'But it's true none the less. Black boils and pus!'

'Surely it can't be as bad as that,' said my father.

'Worse,' argued the fellow with the red face. 'We've not seen this plague for ourselves, but we met traders from the coast, and they all told the same stories.'

'At least they ought to be taken with a grain of salt,' said Opa. 'We all breathe the same air. If it were poisoned we would all sicken and die.'

'I agree with you, sir,' said the third man, who seemed to have drunk rather less wine than had his companions. 'We've seen plagues before, and the numbers of dead are always exaggerated.'

'Maybe so,' acknowledged the second man, 'but I'll confine my business to the Guild until it's all over. Venice and Genoa are no places for an honest German merchant. They say the first to contract the disease were seamen, and that the worst cases are found in these ports.'

'I'll be a deal happier when I get home to Lübeck,' said the one who had spoken first. 'You can be sure my windows will be securely barred, and the doors double bolted at night. I'll take no chances on poisoned air!'

The talk deteriorated into arguments about guilds and barter, which I did not understand, until the three strangers announced they were ready for bed. I hoped my father and the others would follow soon, as I had spotted the remains of a pie on the table and was hungry. As soon as they were all gone, I would creep down to the hall and finish it off.

At last, my father and Roland retired, leaving Opa in his chair by the dying fire. I thought he was asleep and was wondering whether I dare risk venturing out when his eyes opened. He looked up. It was as if he could see through my table.

'You can come out now, Gretl,' he called. 'We are quite alone.'

I scrambled out, looked along the gallery to make sure he was right and hopped down the main stair, my hand holding firmly to the rail. My calf was throbbing and very painful. I thought my grandfather was going to scold me but he smiled and beckoned me towards the table, where he sat me down and watched while I devoured the rest of the pie. He then poured a little wine, diluted it with water and handed me the goblet.

'So, you are curious about my scientific work?' he said. 'Your father did much the same at your age, only he was more fortunate. He landed on his rump.'

I wanted to laugh but feared further reprimand. Instead, I supped the wine and immediately felt warm inside.

'Still,' Opa went on, 'six years is a good time to begin learning.'

'I'm nearly seven,' I objected.

'Seven then,' said my grandfather. 'Would you like to learn about physic and astrology, Gretl?'

I nodded.

'In that case, we'll begin tomorrow,' said Opa. He winked and held out his hand. 'But you must promise to do as you're told and not touch anything unless I tell you to. Solemn promise?'

I gulped down the rest of the wine, laid aside the goblet and grasped the fingers of his outstretched hand.

'Solemn promise,' I said.

ii

In the morning, the merchants' tale was the single topic of discussion.

The three men had left at dawn, cold sober and eager to reach Lübeck before the poisoned air caught up with them.

Family breakfast was the one time when we were always together, adults and children alike. Afterwards, we children usually played while the grown-ups discussed plans for the day. That day, I stayed at the table and listened. What I had heard from the gallery had given me a nightmare but I was curious about the mysterious sickness.

'I don't believe any of it,' Aunt Matti said. 'It must have been the wine talking.' She sniffed in her usual superior way.

'Don't dismiss it too lightly,' said Opa. 'Travellers' tales always have a foundation.' He scanned the adult faces round the table. 'Say nothing, any of you, in case the rumour spreads to the village and causes panic. I saw pestilence once in Italy. If something similar has struck there now, it is serious. There is no cure.'

I slid from my chair and put my arms round him as far as they would go. His tone rather frightened me. He patted my head. My mother tried to distract me with a game of *I Spy*, but I continued listening.

'These fellows who talked into the night and merrily consumed our food and wine ...' my father was saying, '... they blamed seamen. Perhaps it was the pox. Or else they handled poisoned cargo. Surely the sea air can't be to blame?'

'I remember the sea breezes well, Lou,' Opa said. 'It's true sailors suffer pains in the belly, loose bowels and bleeding gums. Sickness and even death are common enough between landfalls. But the causes are usually rotting food and foul water. Exposure to the ocean air relieves the worst symptoms of life below deck. And the crew's health always improves when the vessel makes port.'

'We may yet find that air is to blame,' my father persisted, quite excitedly, 'though not the air we breathe in.'

'How so?'

'Let me explain, Father. You always tell us that our health depends on the condition of our blood and on the kind of life we lead ...'

'True enough.'

'... and that there is seldom sickness in our house because we wash regularly, wear fresh clothes, eat good food, and bury our waste. In the towns, it's different. People live close together. Their rubbish and excrement clog the drains, so they sicken readily. Even when treated with proper medicine, they take longer to recover than the farmer or landowner.'

He became more animated as he pursued his argument. Matti sniffed again but said nothing. Opa nodded patiently. My mother seemed interested. She broke off our game to listen.

'We suppose, do we not,' said my father, 'that sickness comes of drinking polluted water, eating tainted food or touching a part of someone already suffering from a disease. The physician restores the blood to a healthy condition and in doing so purges bad humours from the body. But how do these leave? In the sweat, the urine, the excrement - the very substances you say are responsible for the sickness itself.'

'Not everyone agrees with my theories,' Opa said. 'Many side with Galen that only the letting of the blood itself can effect a cure. Still, I fancy you have not yet come to the point.'

'I'm almost there,' said my father. 'One natural function, unlike the movement of the bowels, is exercised many thousands of times a day. Why should the expelling of breath not be another way - maybe the most important way - of driving out bad humours? And being driven out of one mouth, are they not available to be drawn in by another?'

Matti tutted. I suppose the idea of bowels and bad breath made her uncomfortable.

'It's supported by observation,' my father went on. 'In the country, the peasant and his wife develop a cough. No one else is affected. Not so for the tradesman in his town house. There, sickness is spread quickly to the journeyman, apprentices, and domestics.'

'And how does this relate to the rumours?'

'Simple! Sailors live in small cabins or cramped decks. Whatever this plague is, it starts there. It spreads onshore in the inns and whorehouses where the men take their relaxation, before the bad humours can properly escape.'

My grandfather seemed to warm to the argument. He stroked his beard with one hand while fingering his fylfot with the other. Then he tapped his fingers on the tabletop. 'You may be right,' was all he said.

My mother hugged me tight. She had grown rather pale.

'God forbid that such a plague should reach Saxony,' she said, and there was an Amen or two from the others. I wondered what a whorehouse was.

'It'll not come here,' said Matti and tutted again.

My mother frowned. 'But if it does, Lou, what then?'

'Then we shall find the cure!' said my father.

I think he believed it. However, he was a bad prophet though, as it turned out, he was partly right. Both as to the cause and to the outcome.

iii

Opa kept his promise and that afternoon I was allowed into his laboratory for the first time. It was the beginning of my interest in the sciences.

During the week that followed, for one hour every day, he taught me all he could about his medicines and salves. I learned the names of the substances in his bottles and jars, and how to distinguish between those that were harmless and those that were poison. This proved more difficult than I expected. Many plants and berries, and the extracts from them, while beneficial in small doses, are deadly if taken in larger quantities. Nevertheless, by the end of that first week, I was able to recognise the contents of one complete shelf of containers from their appearance alone.

Opa tested me first. After I had guessed the substance and recited its uses, he would uncover the label and show me whether I was correct. I made only one mistake. Then he mixed up the bottles and invited my mother to observe my progress. She had been worried that it was too soon for me to learn these things, but her doubts were soon lifted. With the second test, I made no mistakes at all.

By the end of April, I had memorised another shelf. I knew the proper way to harvest herbs, how to cut and dry them and how to grind them into a powder. I had learned how to make perfumed waters with rose petals and lavender, much to my mother's delight. She hugged me and promised a treat.

There was no more talk or rumours of plague for a whole month so, in the second week of May, my grandfather took me to Hannover. That was a promise he had made hastily some weeks earlier, before the visit by the Lübeck merchants. It was to be my birthday treat, but my seventh birthday had come and gone. As it happened, my parents had begged him to reconsider, or at least to postpone the visit, and he had agreed. However, now that they perceived no real danger to me, they relented.

'I must visit the apothecary,' Opa said. 'And now that you are my little apprentice, it'll be an important part of your training.'

We took his grey stallion, with me mounted in front of the saddle on the beast's neck. Opa managed the reins with one hand whilst holding me firmly with the other. I loved the feel of the horse's mane after it had been groomed and never tired of running my fingers through it. My leg had healed and I could ride without discomfort. The worst had been when Opa cut and removed his stitches. It hurt so much that I screamed.

The sun was just peeping over the horizon when we left home. We reached Hannover by mid morning. I had not been there before and did not know what to expect.

'A hundred years ago, the city belonged to the sons of Henry the Lion,' Opa said as we rode along the highway towards the southernmost gate. 'And they gave it to the people by charter.'

I knew a little history of course and had heard of Henry Welf, Duke of Saxony, who was called the Lion. He was an ancestor of my grandmother.

'Why?' I wanted to know.

'Why what?'

'Why did Henry's sons give Hannover to the people?'

'It's called politics, Gretl.'

'What's politics?'

'Politics is about how countries and states are ruled,' said Opa. 'It's a matter for study like any other. Like mathematics or physic.'

He launched into an explanation, most of which went over my head. I had lost interest anyway, because I was gazing about me at the other travellers making their way into the city. There were not many on the road that day since there was neither fair nor market, but it amused me to study people's dress and to count the number of wagons and carts as we cantered past.

We entered through a tall arch and passed along the high street. I noticed a change. We were enclosed by houses and there was a stench like that of bad fish after it has lain on the midden for a week. My ears rang with the rattling and squeaking of cart wheels, the voices of tradesmen calling out from their shops and the yelping of dogs. We had dogs on the estate, but they were noble animals with sharp ears and sleek coats, unlike the mean curs of Hannover, whose fur was matted and dirty, whose ears lay flat against their skulls and whose green slit eyes gleamed with cunning and malice.

'It smells, Opa,' I said, screwing up my nose, 'and my head hurts from the noise.'

'You'll get used to it,' he laughed.

I did not think I would ever get used to it and covered my ears with my hands. Never in my life had I seen so many people and I was terrified by their proximity. The houses were tall and crooked. They seemed to reach over the whole street in an effort to embrace those on the other side. No promise however solemn, no treat however delightful, would entice me across the threshold of any of those buildings.

We turned into another road, even narrower than the high street and uncobbled. At the corner sat a beggar, a bag of bones and rags. He had only a stump for a right leg. Opa dropped a coin in his bowl as we passed. The smell was still with us but the houses were squatter, less mean in appearance and more sparsely built. Apart from the beggar's howling, the babble of sound was less menacing here and instead of holding my hands against my head, I clung tightly to the stallion's mane. Opa soothed me with the occasional stroking of my hair.

The apothecary's shop lay about half way down the lane. A wooden board hung on a spike above the door to mark the place, but it was so old and weathered that the sign was broken and cracked and might easily have been the emblem of any of a dozen tradesmen. Next door on one side was a candlemaker, on the other a locksmith.

The inside of the shop was dingy. The air was heavy with the scents of roots and dried flowers that lay around in open containers. Like Opa's laboratory, there were shelves with jars of fruits and berries, and bottles containing coloured liquids.

The apothecary was a little man with moist eyes and a flattened nose. He made a great fuss of me with his welcomes, his bowings and his scrapings, until Opa distracted him with a cough. I might have been the first child ever to enter his shop, and royalty at that, so politely did he behave, though I fancied it was all for Opa's benefit rather than for mine.

While they disappeared into a back room to transact their business, I amused myself by identifying the substances I knew and trying to guess the others. Remembering my earlier promise and, in any case, fearing I would be poisoned, I did not open any of the bottles, though I risked wiping the outside of a few with my finger and spittle to get a better view of the contents.

I was glad to be out of the shop. The vapours were making my eyes smart. The apothecary came with us to the door. He shook Opa's hand, bowed ceremoniously to me at least three times and gave me a stick of liquorice wood to chew.

Opa hoisted me into the saddle and, with him leading the halter, we turned along the lane towards the river. There was no wall in this quarter of the town and I could see again, in the distance, the welcoming countryside.

We had already crossed the Leine, at a point where the waters are shallower and more timid, and now we recrossed it over a narrow bridge. We reached the western bank. The houses here occupied only the left side of the lane and had thinned out.

When we had drawn clear of the last one, my grandfather remounted, slapped the stallion's rump and urged him into a gallop. The wind rushed past our ears. I smelt the freshness of ripening crops and newly mown grass. I had known these things all my life and loved them. My headache cleared and I breathed freely again. Even the reek of the maturing dung heaps seemed fragrant after the cloying stench of the city.

'How would you like to meet a princess, Gretl?' Opa had to shout to make himself heard.

I did not think he had such power but I nodded vigorously. Of course, this had been his plan all along, I supposed. Opa would honour his promise without exposing me for long to danger in the narrower lanes and disease-ridden hovels. Princess or no princess, I was only too glad to be leaving the clamour of Hannover behind.

We were riding through open fields. Ahead, the late morning sun shone on the river, twisting and wriggling across the land like a silver snake. I could see no castle or palace where royalty might reside. The only sign of human presence at all was a squat tower that peeped up above the topmost branches of a birch wood.

Opa spurred us forward. As we drew closer, I saw the tower was a castle of sorts, though unlike anything I had imagined from his stories. It was turreted but with parts of the turret broken off. There were window holes and embrasures, but no moat. The rise on which it stood was scarcely a mound and was completely hidden by trees. The whole building was less than half the size of our manor house.

We turned east and riverward, skirting the trees. The passage between mound and riverbank was narrow at this point and the ground ahead rose to a ridge. Opa slowed to a walking pace and I could see now that the tower was derelict. A stony path led through the grove towards it and into a courtyard under a collapsed gateway. On this side, the building was covered in green slime. Some of the stones around the windows and embrasures had crumbled or had fallen out altogether. Creeping plants grew over what remained of the arch, up the walls and in and out of the gaps.

It seemed altogether sinister yet for some reason I found it difficult to tear my eyes away. I could not hide my disappointment. No beggar would live there, I thought, certainly not a princess. The place would have no defence against a mob of children, far less a rival army. I glanced up questioningly at my grandfather.

'We're not there yet,' he said. 'Patience!'

He urged our mount to the top of the ridge where I gasped with astonishment. On the other side lay a wide meadow. Spread across it was an encampment of tents and wagons. Near the river's edge, a dozen or so dark-skinned men, naked to the waist, were working with picks and spades. A group of children stood nearby, watching. The youngest were naked while the older ones wore simple homespun tunics dyed with bright colours. Their arms and legs were bare.

At the other end of the camp, a fire had been made and round it sat a group of women, chattering. Two of them stirred cooking pots from which rose a delicious aroma of spices and herbs. A few more children played *Catch Me* round the wagons. Sheep, pigs, fowl and ponies roamed freely in the long grass of the meadow.

Opa made his way unchallenged along an avenue of tents towards one that was bigger than the rest and seemed to be made of a different fabric. It was near white in colour and painted on the outside with ochre-red and black pictures of strange animals and birds. The children saw us and ran towards us with great whoops and yells. They crowded round leaving scarcely any room for us to pass through.

Opa dismounted and lifted me down. He called out a few words I did not understand and, without waiting for an invitation, lifted the tent's entrance flap.

The most amazing sight met my eyes. The tent had a proper floor and was furnished like the room of a mansion. The painted decoration continued on the inside. There was a bed covered with a red blanket, a table, a stool and any number of brightly coloured cushions. In the centre was a fireplace. A fire had been lit and its smoke drifted upwards through a funnel opening in the roof. Seated beside it was the most unusual woman I had ever seen in my life.

She seemed very, very old. Her hair was silver. She had a brown, weather-beaten complexion with deep furrows on the brow. Yet her eyes were bright and she carried herself erect rather than being hunched over like the village widows. Her figure was that of a youth, plain breasted with straight hips. She was as thin as a willow branch and might, I thought, be blown and bent just as easily. Her hair too gave her a manly look. It was cut very short, as only a tradesman would have it, and grew in spikes on her crown and round her ears.

Adorning her withered wrists were bangles of various thickness and pattern with the look of gold though in such quantity I fancied they must be of some other metal. Her tunic and shirt were colourful, of different shades of red and green woven together in intricate patterns. Below, she wore a skirt of deep blue. Most astonishing of all, she carried a short sword, sheathed at her side like that of a knight or gentleman. Never in my life had I seen a woman with a sword.

She rose and advanced to meet us. She embraced my grandfather fondly while he, responding, kissed her on the cheek. I was too stunned to say anything, not merely by the manner of their greeting but by the woman's peculiar appearance.

I was not by nature shy but it took me some time to find my voice. Meantime, Opa said something in a tongue I did not understand, though I recognised my name.

'Welcome, Gretl,' said the woman in our language.' She knelt and touched her lips to my brow. Her kiss was gentle but I was embarrassed and drew away from her.

Opa patted my head.

'This is Princess Ennia,' he said. 'She is honorary chief of the Singari.'

I responded with my best curtsey but I was gaping at the sword. The hilt was of a yellow metal fashioned in the shape of a coiled serpent. Its wide-open jaws were fastened round a red jewel that sparkled in the light from the fire.

'You like it, Gretl?' Princess Ennia's mouth creased in a smile. ' 'Tis yours! Perhaps it will bring you good fortune. Many a time, I owe my life to it.' She drew the weapon from its sheath and grasping it by the blade extended the hilt towards me. I took hold of the serpent but the sword was too heavy for me and I would have dropped it had not Opa come to my rescue.

'Perhaps when you are older and have learned to use and respect it,' he said. 'May I keep it safe for you?'

'It's a very fine present,' I said to Ennia, not knowing how else to acknowledge the gift. 'Thank you.'

'And I have another for you, Gretl, but that is to be a surprise when you come again.'

'Do you always live here?' I asked her.

'Not always,' said Ennia. 'I live in many places. The Singari are travellers. They live with nature in the fields and forests. Their home is wherever there is fresh water and good grazing.'

'Are you really a princess?'

'After a fashion! My mother was a princess, certainly, and my father noble. But that was long ago. Now, to be chief is enough. 'Tis a title given to the oldest and fiercest of the band. Some say the wisest too, though ...' She chuckled softly. '... I fear I am no wiser than the rest.'

She reminded me of a character in one of Opa's stories and I liked her because of it. She was an outlandish creature to be sure, but kind and motherly. There was no sign of the fierceness of which she boasted. Indeed, in spite of the sword, I could not conceive of her having desire or strength to harm anyone.

I looked around the tent in awe, admiring the splendid furnishings and studying more closely the animal paintings. There were two lions, a green serpent and a black winged eagle, but my attention was captured by two creatures that might have been inhabitants of dreams. One had golden skin decorated with broad black stripes. Its jaws were wide open, displaying terrifying teeth that could have ripped open in a second any man or horse foolish enough to come within range.

By contrast, the other made me laugh. It was like a misshapen cow, with long legs and a goat's beard. Most astonishing of all, its body grew a grotesque hump as if a sorcerer had magically transported a mountain to the middle of its back.

My grandfather and Ennia were talking but I could understand nothing of what they said. I knew Latin but this language was quite different. Their speech was nonetheless punctuated with the occasional word that I seemed to recognise. Thrice I caught a word like *morte*, which meant death, and twice I heard another that sounded like *pestis*. What I had overheard from under the table in the gallery came back to me. I frowned. Ennia saw my look and broke off in mid sentence.

'The little one too should hear and know,' she said and I knew immediately what she meant and what they had been discussing. ' 'Twas true what they told you. It sweeps across the land like a storm.'

'So you will not travel south this year?' Opa said.

'We will winter here,' said Ennia. 'If the men can make part of the tower habitable, we will take shelter there if needs be. In autumn, we will work in the landgrave's fields and hope. This pestilence is not like a sword thrust - quick and clean - but ugly and brutal.' She reached behind her back and I saw to my horror that she had another weapon hidden there, a dagger the length of my arm, and narrow as a spit. In the space of a second, it was out from her belt and in her hand. With the energy of a youth she lunged, as I thought, at my grandfather. I screamed.

Opa did not flinch. While they were talking, he had begun to wrap up the sword in a cloth that had lain on a nearby table. Now, as Princess Ennia's blade came, as it seemed to me, straight for his heart, he gripped the serpent hilt and, in a single movement too fast for my eye to catch, parried the dagger and deflected it from its path.

Ennia sighed deeply and lowered her weapon. Then she laughed, not the cackle of a hag, but a gentle restrained laugh as if time had been turned back a hundred years and she was by magic a maiden again.

'Your eye is sharp as ever, my champion,' she said, and Opa laughed too. 'And despite your great age, your arm has lost little of its skill.'

I had not recovered from my shock and was breathing very fast indeed. My mouth was agape at the deadly game I had witnessed.

'Should a woman not be able to defend her life and honour just as a man would do?' Ennia said. 'Do not fear, Gretl. I would not have struck him for the world. We have been friends too long! 'Tis a game we have often played. Perhaps when we meet again I will teach you a trick or two with the stiletto.' She slipped the dagger back into her belt. 'Now,' she said, taking my arm, 'come and dine with us.'

She led us out of the tent and back along the avenue. The children had been waiting outside and they followed, jostling for position and jabbering continuously in their alien language. One or two girls dared to feel the material of my dress and were rewarded by Princess Ennia with a cuff on the side of the head.

By now, the men too had gathered by the cooking pots and we sat round the fire to break bread and partake of the most delicious stew I had ever tasted. When the pots were empty, one of the Singari took a wooden bowl, filled it with plant leaves and set them alight with a burning twig. The lighted mixture gave off pungent smoke and he inhaled it before passing the bowl to his neighbour. In this way, the smoking bowl found its way round the older men in the company, and a few of the women too. Most of the children had run off to play.

I was fascinated by the smoking ritual and would have lingered, but Opa shook his head.

'It's not for you,' he said when I showed an inclination to sniff the odours. 'Say your thanks, Gretl. It's time to go.'

I would never have argued and dropped my best curtsey as my mother had taught. Ennia kissed my cheek.

'We shall see one another soon,' she said as Opa lifted me into the saddle and mounted behind me. 'At midsummer. You will not forget, Gretl!'

Out of sight and hearing of the camp, I pestered Opa with questions. Who were the Singari? Who was Ennia? What was my other present to be? Why had she called him *her champion*? Did she really mean to teach me to use a sword? I hoped she would. My cousin Freddy always laughed when I said I wanted to fight him and I longed to teach him a lesson. Of course, we would never be allowed to use anything but toy swords but that did not matter; it would be enough to show him that girls were as good as boys.

I suspect that Opa had a very good idea of what was in my head for he said that, indeed, Ennia would teach me swordplay if I were willing to learn. There was no one better! But my mother would have to agree first. About the Singari he would say only that they were a race out of India.

I asked about the smoking bowls.

'Why do they do that, Opa?' I asked. 'Are they sick?'

'Sick indeed, but not as you know it, Gretl. The vapours dull the aches and pains of old age and bring them pleasant dreams and visions.'

'Is that not a wonderful thing?'

'I think not,' he answered gravely. 'And you would be unwise to copy it. Those who practise the habit lose their wits. They forget about pain and sickness. But when they wake from their dreams they are in greater pain than before, and need more of the smoke to make their lives bearable.'

He was evasive about the plague, though I could tell from his look that he was worried. In my childish way, I was too, for Ennia's parting words to him were imprinted on my memory. She had whispered them and I fancied I was not supposed to hear.

'I pray it may not travel so far,' she had said. 'Still, it may come, and you should prepare as best you are able!'

'Who is Ennia really, Opa?' I asked for the twentieth time as we reached the border of our land. He had not given me a proper answer. 'Is she really a princess?'

'To the world, perhaps not, Gretl,' he said. 'But she is a very dear friend. That is all you need to know for now.'

My curiosity knew no bounds but I had to be satisfied. When Opa made up his mind to be silent, I could never cajole him into small talk. And I pondered long and hard about the smoking bowls, and about what it would be like to be honorary chief of Singari and a mistress of swordplay. But there was something else on my mind and its memory made me feel chilled. The pleasure of the afternoon had driven it from my head like a fading dream.

The old tower. It must surely have been my imagination but for a twinkling as we passed it for the first time, I could have sworn I saw a man staring down at me from one of the broken window openings.

A man in a black cloak whose face was half hidden by a black hood.

iv

I was born in spring of the year 1341. My parents called me Margaretha. The name was settled without argument. It was my mother's. She had been Greta Queck before her marriage but as my father said, *two Gretas would never do*. So I usually answered to Gretl.

Our family name was von Hasenbach. My paternal grandmother, who died before I was born, was Lady Matthilde of Brunswick. She and her brother, the father of Uncle Roland, were grandchildren of Helena of Brunswick, and second cousins to Duke Albert the Second. The previous duke had become their guardians when their own parents died.

A portrait of my grandmother, painted in her youth, hung in the hall. Her hair, the colour of pale gold, was braided and fastened by a plain band, and she was wearing a blue gown that matched her eyes. Ludwig, my father, had her look. He was her only child. The painting was how I always tried to imagine her, before grief had dulled her eye and brought her to an early grave.

I know now that she grew old before her time, and would have been no more than forty when she died. They said that on the death of her brother part of her spirit died too and her zest for life was quenched. But there was more to it - there was more to all of it, as I would learn to my cost.

Oma Matthilde's final resting-place was the prettiest spot in the neighbourhood, where Opa had built an underground burial-chamber to serve many generations of the family. Beyond the bend in the River Leine, where the little church stood, the ground rose steeply into a coppice in the shape of a horseshoe. From this hill, we had a splendid view of the manor house and farms, of the Leine Valley, and of the forests in the distance. Trees were felled to aid the excavation and, when the work was finished, the archway cut into the hillside was closed with a finely-wrought iron gate.

My grandfather was no Saxon. My parents and my uncles and aunts never discussed the matter, but servants and villagers talked. Some said Opa was a Greek, others a Spaniard. A few had even decided he was a mixture of the two, with drops of other blood thrown in. The truth was that he came from a noble Italian family. He had lived much of his life in

Venice but he had travelled too in the Orient. That much I knew, though very little else. His name had once been Assano, which was now abbreviated to the simpler *Sano*. The family called him that.

What had brought Opa to Saxony was another matter of dispute in the locality. One thing everyone agreed upon was that he had performed a singular service for Duke Albert, or for the Duke of Saxony, or for the Emperor himself. And not even the family knew the truth of that! As a result, he was rewarded with the hand of my grandmother in marriage, the title of landgrave, and the estate. Opa had been warrior, merchant and diplomat in his youth. He had little enthusiasm for farming and his life's work now was the study and practice of the sciences. Especially physic and the art of healing.

Our manor was known as Bachhagen, which was also the name of the nearby village. Once, it had been Bachhausen, but it underwent a series of changes after which it took the name by which we knew it.

Ours was a large household then. There was no shortage of children to share my childhood. I had seven cousins on the estate - I should say rather second-cousins - including two sets of twins. None was much older than I was. There were also Leo and Karl, my mother's younger brothers, youths of twelve and fourteen, who lived only a few hours away in the town of Hameln. Then there was Uncle Thomas. He too had children but we saw little of him as the family lived some distance away in Brunswick City.

Opa had given over management of the estate and all the farms that lay within its boundaries to my father and his cousin Roland, whom I called *Uncle*, and to whose heirs the land might revert in any case, depending on whether my father had any sons. Roland had married a relative of the Grübenhagens, one of the ducal families, and had given her two sons and two daughters. The youngest, twin boy and girl named Frederic and Hanna, were a mere fifteen months my senior.

Matti, Roland's sister, wed Otto of Wolfenbüttel, who had died in the Emperor's service and left her in the care of her brother's home. She also produced twins, Sigmund and Lieselle, who were only a year or two older than me.

Though my mother taught me to read and write, and to speak Latin,

Opa saw to my education in most other respects. Though wary of priests, he permitted one to come to the house to teach me the Holy Scriptures, for my mother's sake. He always took a great interest in my welfare, perhaps because my hair was black and my complexion dark like his own, rather than resembling that of either of my parents. Though past his sixty-fifth year, he had the patience to teach me the names of plants and trees, of birds and insects, and of the constellations. He was a great favourite of Freddy and Hanna too, and we three would often climb onto his knee to listen to his tales of kings and queens, of princes and princesses.

Most were myth, I suppose; for every one I remember, I have forgotten ten. It was the way he told them that was so enthralling, as if he were part of the tale himself, loving, laughing and suffering like his own heroes. I was to learn later that all of his stories held a grain of truth, and that they were his way of telling his own history. He had indeed suffered but, like so many of my other guesses, I was wrong as to the cause.

There was no portrait of Opa to remind me of him, and I needed none. He was old before I knew him, but I pictured him easily as a man of middle age, tall and handsome, his jet-black hair and beard merely tinged with grey. His nose, though prominent, was not large enough to detract from his handsome appearance. He had a grave expression, so that, even when he smiled, his deep brown eyes seemed to be touched with sadness and an understanding of the world.

He had his moods and, even in those early years, I learned to recognise them. At other times, he was gaiety itself and not above playing childish games, such as *Catch Me* and *Hide and Seek*. He would be war-charger to my knight-in-armour and many an afternoon would run round the hall with me perched on his shoulders. Then there was the highly polished stair rail from the topmost storey of the house where he used to sit me and, keeping a firm hold of my petticoats, allow me to slide to the bottom.

There was no ostentation in his dress or appearance save the gold cross he always wore on a chain round his neck. Opa's fylfot was like no other cross I ever saw. It had the span of a man's hand and its arms bent to the right forming four incomplete squares. In its centre was a raised disc, engraved with the image of the sun. Sometimes, when he took me on his knee, I would breathe heavily upon it and polish it with the hem of my dress until the gold sparkled. I felt no curiosity about it then. It was as much a part of my grandfather as the thick eyebrows that remained black long after the rest of his hair had turned silver, and which he permitted me to damp with my spittle and smooth down until they were flat against his forehead.

For the rest of May and into June that year, I worked with Opa in his laboratory. I mastered the names of the substances on his shelves and he permitted me, under supervision, to mix some medicines. He took me on three visits and on one of these allowed me to prepare and dispense a draught of liquorice juice against a cough. He tested me repeatedly on what I had learned, first with only himself in the room and then in either my mother's or my father's presence. It seems I was a good learner.

Opa also taught me the rudiments of mathematics and how to read star charts. I learned there were special stars called planets that, like the Moon, crossed the sky with respect to the others and would be in different constellations at different seasons. My grandfather even had a special glass for looking at them on clear nights, so that they appeared larger than they really were. I never tired of examining it and looking through it.

The weeks passed quickly and pleasantly for me. My cousins, being older, had recently outgrown many of our games and sometimes left me on my own. It was thus sweet revenge for me to boast that I had put away childish things and had grown-up work to do.

The warm summer days were approaching. I had not forgotten Princess Ennia and looked forward to seeing her again, and discovering what my other present was to be. Moreover, if she could truly teach me how to use a sword, there would be something else to boast about to my elder cousins.

After summer would be harvest. Uncle Tom was coming to Bachhagen to help with the first two weeks of it and would bring his two children with him. Lisbeth was only six and Wilf four so I expected long hours of play with me as their leader. I prayed that my uncle would stay longer.

I had heard no more talk of plague. Perhaps it has passed us by, I thought. Opa had not forgotten, as I soon discovered, but he kept all his gloomy thoughts from me.

I noticed that my mother seemed to be growing. Though the bewitching smile was the same, her chin had become rounder, her cheeks fuller and pinker than before. When I nuzzled close to her, her breasts too seemed different, and I could no longer clasp her round the waist and feel my fingers touch in the hollow of her back.

At first, I worried she was ill, but as no one else had remarked on it or, indeed, had seemed to notice the change in her, my fears subsided. However, as the days passed, I became more and more puzzled by her condition until, unable to contain myself, I asked for an explanation.

'Shhh,' she whispered, and kissed me gaily on the nose. 'I'm making a little brother or sister for you, but no one must know of it yet.'

Perhaps because of my mother's pregnancy, she had less time for me and I was accompanying Opa more and more. And, on Midsummer Day, he took me with him to Bachhagen village.

The village in 1348 was a scattering of houses on the western border of our estate and close to the River Leine. The villagers numbered no more than sixty, including the children, and most had built their own dwellings from wood and thatch. Very little stone was used as importing it and making mortar cost money they could ill afford. However, a few had managed to utilise dry stones found in the neighbourhood for the construction of outer walls that faced the prevailing winds.

Bachhagen, though small, was not without its skilled tradesmen. There was a carpenter, who had made some of the furniture for the manor house as well as tables and stools for his neighbours.

The miller worked at the manor mill and, in return for his labour, received a small wage and a few sacks of grain that he made into flour, baked and sold round the village. He seemed to do well out of the arrangement, for he had a new tunic and shoes every year. Experimental husbandry, my father called it. I had no idea what the words meant but it sounded very grand.

There was no inn. However, the village boasted a tiny tavern whose tenant brewed ale for consumption by the locals and the few travellers who came that way.

Two houses only were exceptional, being entirely of stone to the height of the eaves and having solid roofs. The smaller was occupied by an old man called Jacob who kept himself to himself and did not seek the company of his neighbours. Even the priest left him alone. Jacob had some skill as a healer, though without Opa's learning, and tended to minor ailments in the community. Bunches of dried herbs were always hung around the doorway and window frame of his cottage. He had a strange gait that was more of a run than a walk and consisted of short, jerky strides. The village children made fun of him. They called Jew after him and threw stones because, as they said, the Jews had killed the Christ. I had heard this mentioned too by our servants but when I repeated it, Opa reprimanded me severely. A good man should not be blamed for the evil deeds of his countrymen, he told me. No more should a people bear the guilt of evil men in their midst. Besides, he added, the accusation was wrong as the men who had crucified Jesus were Romans.

We were on foot that June day. Opa believed we should not flaunt our wealth before those who were not so fortunate, as he put it. I expected to see Singari tents pitched in the lower pasture by the river, the only place where they could have camped. There were none. My spirits fell. Ennia had forgotten her promise and there would be no present after all.

Instead, we made our way across the village to the largest house of all, which belonged to the blacksmith. His name was Jan; at least people called him that. He was about fifty years old and had first appeared in the village when my father was a child. Jan and I were the best of friends and he always had time to talk to me when he came to the manor house. I had been inside his forge two or three times to watch him work. He was neither Christian nor Jew but something else entirely, though no one knew exactly what or even where he had come from. Like the miller, he made a living from the estate, and from the occasional traveller who passed through Bachhagen. They said he was a swordsmith too but, as there was little demand for weapons in the district, his skills were neglected.

The blacksmith's house had two storeys, the lower having a gate leading into the forge, the upper being separate living quarters. The gossip was that it had once belonged to a member of our family who had quarrelled with the then occupant of the manor, but no one knew what the quarrel was about or even whether the story was true. I thought the upper room empty.

Beside the gate, on the house wall, was a bell that visitors used to ring when they required Jan's services. I never grew tired of ringing it.

'May I ring today, Opa?' I asked.

'We are expected,' he said mysteriously, but nodded towards the bell in any case.

Instead of waiting for the sound to die and for Jan to appear, he strode on through the gate. I had never known him do anything of the kind before. I hesitated then ran after him. Jan was in the yard in front of the forge, shoeing a roan pony. Another, a small chestnut, already saddled and bridled, was tethered nearby. Jan smiled and gestured to the open staircase leading to the upper floor. Opa held out his hand to me and began to climb. When he reached the top, he knocked twice then pushed open a low door into the chamber beyond.

Princess Ennia sat on a bench by a table. She was dressed as before in her colourful tunic, shirt and skirt. Beside her lay two wooden swords, one on either side. There was no sign of her dagger.

When the greetings were over, she handed me one of the swords and showed me how to hold it properly. Unlike the metal one, it was no heavier than one of my dolls and I quickly mastered the feel of it. Then Ennia took up the second toy blade, wrapped it in a piece of homespun to avoid injuring me and invited me to strike her. I hesitated. She was as old as Opa, for sure, and seemed so frail.

'You will not hurt me,' she chuckled, 'but if you do, my vanity will be to blame, not your sword arm.'

I raised the sword and made a half-hearted swing at her. Ennia laid hold of my weapon in a weather-beaten hand and pulled it from my grip.

'You must do better, Gretl,' she said, returning the wooden sword to me. The amusement had died from her face and she looked rather stern. 'Try again.'

I raised the sword for a second time and aimed it at her arm, putting a little more effort into the swing. Ennia stepped back calmly and, as my blade cut through empty air, hit me sharply on the leg with her padded weapon. The blow did not hurt but I was angry at being deceived and swung at her again, wildly. Lithe as a kitten, Ennia bent to the side, away from my blow, and struck the sword from my grasp. I lost my balance and would have fallen had she not caught me in her arms.

'Anger has no place in swordplay,' she admonished. 'That was my first lesson and 'twill be yours too.'

As she said this, the stern look melted and she smiled. I was ashamed of my short temper and embarrassed that she still held me.

'I'm sorry,' I whimpered. 'I'm really sorry.'

'There is no need, child,' said Ennia. 'Now, shall we try again?'

Despite the humiliation, I was eager to continue. I picked up the sword and held it stubbornly in a guard position as Ennia had shown me. Now it was her turn to strike and mine to try to avoid the blow. I was nimble on my feet and was pleased when, by the end of the afternoon I had managed to dodge her thrusts twice. However, not once had I managed to touch her, which was perhaps just as well for, though of wood, my little sword had a sharp point.

When we had finished the game, my legs were numb from the times she had struck me. We sat down wearily on the bench.

'That will do for today, I think,' said Opa, beckoning to me. 'Your mother will be anxious. I persuaded her it would be safe but we have been here a good two hours.'

'Do not forget your present, Gretl,' said Ennia with a chuckle. 'She is in the yard. Ali-Hassan will give her to you!'

I looked up at her in utter bafflement. Ennia returned my look and for a second or two even she seemed confused. Then she responded to my gaze with the same young and gentle laugh I had heard in the camp at Hannover.

'Ali-Hassan is his proper name,' she said. 'He is Jan, the blacksmith. He came to us many years ago but did not love the Singari way of life. Your Opa helped him settle in his trade. *Jan* is a term of affection in my language.'

In truth, I had noticed that, once or twice, Ennia had used that word when addressing me. But in a wave of happiness and excitement that almost overcame me, I realised something else; that the present she was speaking of could only be the chestnut pony. I had always wanted to ride but the estate horses were too large for me. Now Ennia was giving me a pony of my very own and I had done nothing to deserve it. The tears formed in the corners of my eyes.

'But you have already given me a present, Ennia,' I murmured. 'And I haven't given you anything.'

'You have given me much more than you know, Gretl,' she said. She brushed my tears away and pressed her lips to my forehead. 'One day you will understand. Now promise you will look after Princess, because that is her name!'

'I do promise,' I cried and threw my arms around her neck. 'Oh thank you, Ennia. Thank you so much!'

She hugged me. I kissed her cheek. It seemed the most natural thing in the world. Until then, no one had ever hugged me except my mother. Only when she released me did I see there were tears in Ennia's eyes.

The Great Mortality

i

July, August and September were always busy months and that year they were more hectic than ever.

All summer, my father and Roland were preoccupied with affairs on the farm. The crops had come under threat from unusually large numbers of rats that descended on us and tried to devour the unharvested produce.

'I've never seen so many of the creatures,' I heard Roland say more than once. 'Thank God for the vigilance of the servants and for our army of cats! Without them, the kitchens would be overrun.'

My father agreed.

'It's one step forward and two backwards,' said my uncle. 'When we drive them from the fields, they only return more determined. When we kill them, others take their place. I swear, Lou, they're more resourceful and daring than ever before, and that they've grown larger and more ferocious than the rats of bygone years.'

'More aggressive, yes. But I've noticed smaller ones too. They're darker in colour and have tails longer than their bodies.'

'There speaks the man of science!' said Roland. 'You are your father's son and no mistake.'

'I'm sorry,' my father said. 'You need help and not a lecture. We'd better look to the harvest.'

Roland clenched his jaw. 'If we don't keep the rats at bay there'll be no harvest,' he said.

'We'll set traps for them, and drive them off,' said my father. 'Holes in barns have to be repaired, and new barriers erected in the grain stores. Greta will help too. '

He set about these tasks eagerly. Much of the work proved futile, for the rat is a cunning animal that can find its way through most obstacles. Before September was over, more repairs were needed and the barriers had to be reinforced.

Ludwig laboured through the daylight hours, often with my mother at his side. He would have rather worked with Opa, for his passion for science was no less than that of his father and his skill almost equal. Indeed, it was common for neighbours to seek his advice about their health. However, such were his estate responsibilities during those months that he had no time for anything else.

By the onset of autumn, we were to see the first cases of the scourge that would leave its mark on every town and village in the Empire. But the Mortality came upon us stealthily. Through July to September, my grandfather had tended most of the sickness on the estate - which was no more than usual - and had made the occasional visit to neighbouring towns.

'Rumours of plague are rife,' I heard him say one breakfast, as harvest time approached. Four months had passed since I had met Princess Ennia. 'The city streets are more crowded than ever, and the inns bustle with strangers. Yet I've seen nothing of the symptoms that were described to us.'

'More travellers than usual are passing through the valley,' said Ludwig. 'Servants are accosted daily by pedlars and clerics, soldiers and footpads, all making for the towns. I don't understand it. There are no festivals.'

'People see security in city walls,' Opa said. 'They take comfort in wooden doors and iron gates. In Hannover and Hildesheim, the churches fill to overflowing and the priests will admit no more. Migrants from the countryside are encamped in the streets with jugglers and musicians. I fear the lot of the poor, already bad, will become much worse as the population grows.'

'But no signs of this Black Death?'

'None,' said my grandfather. 'Yet I'm worried. The newcomers to the town wallow in filth and, in consequence, suffer disorders of the bowel and stomach from eating bad food. They seem to live in fear of one another and of any stranger who approaches. The poor shun the company of all but their immediate families or friends. Tradesmen shut themselves indoors and only venture out of necessity. Truly, it's well nigh impossible to make a proper study of anything. I've seen no plague, but who knows what lurks behind shuttered windows, in crowded churches, and in dark alleyways? If there's little work for me to do, it's not because of the absence of sickness, but because the population suffers in silence.'

Even we children were hearing stories. The servants and the villagers talked freely of boils the size of apples that turned purple within three days; of black warts that grew in the private parts and oozed black pus so that the sufferer died in less than a day from the loss of blood. There were folk who bled instead from the nose or ears, when the blood could not be staunched by any means. Anyone who touched them, or their clothing, or came near to them would be similarly afflicted. No one had seen any of these things themselves; it was always a sister, or a brother, or a cousin who had heard it from a son, or a father, or a mother.

There were reports of armies of phantoms, hovering over the countryside like black smoke and dispensing death to anything that moved. So many priests had died in France, they said, that there were none to dispense the last rites. Physicians were afraid to approach the sick, and spent their days in taverns and brothels, drinking and whoring, until they too, and all with whom they fraternised, fell victim to the pestilence. The worst reports came from the cities of Italy, where the dead, it was told, could be counted in tens of thousands. The plague had even reached faraway England.

Aunt Matti was sniffing and tutting more than ever, and when she did offer her opinion, it was only to say that she didn't believe any of it. I'm not sure anyone did. Yet many of the tales were true in part, as it turned out, though Saxony had still seen no plague.

It might have passed us by - who can tell? Opa would have protected us if he could but none of Ennia's warnings prepared us for what followed. I was to learn later that Singari have the gift of prediction and that many of their women were feared as witches. Did she know, I wondered, and did she hold back her knowledge?

Magic lives in men's heads and in their imaginations. It sucks their brains. It eats away their sanity and replaces sweet reason with foolish fantasy. Its fingers are long and crooked so that, sometimes, even the strong-willed are infected by its poison.

Nor are we women immune from its power. They say we are closer to nature than men are, and thus better able to resist, but I cannot testify to that. What we call magic, the magic whose twin allies are ignorance and fear, is an idea only, not an unnatural embodiment of all that is evil. And women are affected by ideas just as men are.

My great-grandmother would have said the true magic resides in all of us, that the real miracle is life itself: the heart that pumps the blood through our bodies; the breath that gives us speech; the fingers that pluck the lute; the mind that can grasp the knowledge of these things and use it for good.

I wish I had known her. I wish I had known something of my true heritage during those dark days of the Great Mortality. I wish that I had had the comfort of her words then, and later, at times when life seemed so cruel. But she is long dead. All I have to remind me of her is a legend, and the gold ornament that in those days hung about my grandfather's neck.

The *su-asti*. The fylfot was still bright in that autumn of 1348. I had yet to see its dark side.

October came. I was spending more and more time with my grandfather and less and less with my parents. Ludwig was busy building defences against the rats while my mother spent long hours resting.

All the while, I continued my lessons in swordplay with Ennia. She taught me how to thrust, parry and feint, and which parts of an opponent I should aim to strike in order to wound rather than kill. I was excited by the prospect of showing off my new skills to Sigmund or defying Freddy when he teased me and so paid close attention to everything she told me.

I managed to strike her once or twice, I fancy only because she let me. But I always kept my balance, my grip on the sword and my temper during her lessons. I must have made progress because Opa, usually seated by a window in the forge, or on one of Ennia's multi-coloured cushions in her tent, always nodded approvingly when we had finished. My parents worried about my going to the camp at Hannover though they did not forbid it. Opa now avoided the city altogether. Instead, we came to the old tower by a different route through the woods and fields. I had not seen the man at the window again.

One afternoon, we were heading homeward when we met a group of peasants. They were trundling makeshift carts piled high with their belongings. I was on Princess while my grandfather rode his favourite stallion.

The travellers were all strangers, and we would have ridden by with a *Good Evening* if one of them had not accosted us.

'Is it far to the town?' he asked.

'Hannover is an hour's ride at walking pace,' Opa said. 'You can just reach it before nightfall. You must be new to the neighbourhood since you don't know that.'

'Th'art right, sir,' said the peasant, biting deeply into an apple he had taken from his pack. He was friendly enough though his clothing was worn and patched, and his accent uncouth. 'We've come from south of Fulda Abbey to escape the Great Mortality. We would've taken refuge with the holy brothers, but the church be full to o'erflowing.'

He spat out a pip or two. His companions leaned on their carts or squatted in the grass. Their faces were lean and tired.

'Great Mortality?' said Opa. It was the first time we had heard the expression.

'Aye, sir, the plague. It strikes everywhere 'n leaves death behind. The monasteries be full of people prayin' for deliv'rance from God's judgement.'

He tossed his apple core onto the path. Two rats emerged from beneath the foremost cart, sniffed the promising meal and began to squabble for possession of it.

'We have heard of this plague,' Opa said, 'but we've seen no cases here.'

'Tha should thank Christ th'ave not seen it,' grunted the peasant, beginning to munch a second apple. 'Its black boils be enough to turn the stomach of the strongest man.'

I began to feel sick. The man had come rather close to us and I could smell his sweat. As if sensing it, Opa leant over and stroked my hair. The nausea passed.

'Tell me more,' my grandfather said. 'I'm a physician. I need to understand sickness if I'm to treat it.'

The countryman gave a bitter laugh. 'Tha can't treat the plague! God's curse can't be removed with a few medicines an' charms. An' we had better be moving if we're to reach the city by dusk.'

'Hannover is no place for anyone used to village life,' said Opa. He raised his voice so that all could hear. 'You run a greater risk of sickness there than you would here in the open. My family lives not far away. We're behind with our harvesting and could use extra labour. Free food and shelter could be yours until the grain is stored. The children can play safely in our fields. There's no plague there.'

I could tell the peasants were tempted. They had walked a long way and their provisions would soon run out. Those with children were talking among themselves. A few at the end of the procession began to turn their carts around. The apple-eating spokesman hesitated, swayed by the prospect of a safe haven and the protection of a noble house. I did not like him, his filthy ragged tunic or his coarse talk of black boils, and I did not much savour the idea of his urchins playing in our meadow. I looked up at my grandfather imploringly.

I was spared any inconvenience. Very likely the whole company would have followed us but for a event that changed its mood from one of expectation to another of rank terror.

From a point in the column just behind the leading carts came a moan, then a shriek. A youth tottered on the path and collapsed like a rag doll in a ditch. A woman, presumably she who had uttered the scream, abandoned her possessions and rushed to his aid. The man with her took a few steps towards them but kept his distance. The rest of the group scattered. With cries of *Plague*, they took to their heels, pushing their carts hither and thither, clutching their bundles to their chests.

The spokesman took one look at the prostrate form, grasped the handles of his cart, and would have run too if my grandfather had not stopped him.

'Surely you don't intend to leave him here? He is ill!'

'She that bore 'im can attend to him,' growled the peasant with a glance at the woman. 'Aye, we'll leave him. He be doomed to die here anyway. Thee, my lord, if th'as any sense, will leave too. Thank thee for the kind offer, but we 'ad better make for the town.'

'You don't know for sure he has the plague ...,' cried Opa, but he was too late. The whole group of migrants, save the sick boy and his parents, was on its way to Hannover, trailed by half-a-dozen rats that attached themselves to the column.

'Wait here, Gretl.' Opa gave me his reins to hold and dismounted. The stallion was always well behaved and I did not worry it would wrench the leather away and bolt.

'You don't fear the plague?' he asked the woman, who was bent over her son's body.

'Aye, I fears it, master,' said she. 'My husband too. But we're his parents and, if it be truly plague, who else'll look after him in his last hours?'

'Come,' said Opa, 'it may not be so bad. Let me look at him.' He knelt by the lad's side, put a hand on his forehead, and inspected the half-closed eyes and parched tongue.

The boy stirred. He was not much older than my cousin Sigmund. He had tousled brown hair, thick eyebrows, and the beginnings of a moustache and beard.

'Can you speak?' my grandfather asked gently, supporting the head and shoulders in the crook of his arm.

The youth coughed. 'Aye, sir, though my throat be parched. My whole body be on fire too. An' my eyes can scarce bear the light.'

'This sickness came on suddenly?'

'This morning.' The boy took a deep breath and clutched his chest as his body was racked with more coughing. 'My head ached. I thought naught o' it 'til I began shivering. Not wi' cold, for I was sweating in the heat of the afternoon. Then, this faintness o'ertook me.'

Opa came back and fetched a flask from his saddlebag. He gave it into the boy's trembling hands. 'Drink some of this,' he said. 'I cannot do much for you here, but there are medicines at my disposal if we can get you to the manor house. Come, Gretl, be brave,' he said and took the stallion's reins from me.

'Now help the lad onto my horse,' he told the parents. 'I and my granddaughter will lead and, if you walk briskly, we can just reach Bachhagen before it grows dark.'

It is strange how a child remembers certain days above all others, and that day was one I will remember for the rest of my life. When we arrived home, my parents had already supped and were playing chess. I took a cup of milk from the kitchen and sat at their feet.

I often watched my mother and father at their contests and, though I understood none of the play, I admired the delicate carving of the chess pieces. Their names, Castles, Knights, Kings and Queens, reminded me of Opa's tales and, in the silence that followed each move, I invented simple stories of my own in which my characters leaped about the board like real people instead of being tiny dolls of wood.

After he had made a move, Ludwig would frown mysteriously, rest his chin on one elbow, and allow his other hand to stray beneath the table until it rested on my mother's lap. She would wrinkle her nose in the manner that indicated pleasure. Then her hand would fall on his and they would move closer together until, by the time either called Shah Mat, their legs would be entangled in what I imagined was a most uncomfortable manner. I presumed this to be part of the game, and learned only at about the age of ten that it had quite a different purpose.

That evening, the contest had scarcely begun. Opa laid the sick youth in an anteroom and collected fever remedies and other preparations from the laboratory. The plague had been the subject of so much discussion that the possibility of a sufferer in our midst caused apprehension among the servants. Those that were nearby quickly dispersed and no other would come near.

The chess was abandoned..

The youth was by this time moaning and retching pitiably. Ludwig applied wet cloths to cool his burning face and brow. Opa removed the lad's shirt in order to bathe his chest and arms. Thus occupied, he remarked on the swellings in the boy's armpits.

'I see them, Father,' said Ludwig. 'If this is a case of the plague, there's no sign of the blackness we have been led to expect.'

'That may come later,' Opa suggested. He tried to raise the boy's head and force some liquid past his lips. 'The illness has lasted only a day and has by no means run its course. We should try to cool the fever. In the morning we'll see.'

The next day brought no improvement. The youth's fever continued unabated. His parents took turns to apply the wet cloths and Opa gave him hourly drinks of herbal tea. My father was sent off to supervise other work about the estate, a charge that he accepted with reluctance, being more concerned to study the progress of the unfortunate boy's illness. However, Opa persuaded him that, should his theory be correct and the exhaled breath be the means whereby the infection was transmitted, my mother and I would be at risk if he remained for long exposed to it.

At the end of the second day, the blackening of the skin, the terrifying mark of what we came to know as the Great Mortality, showed itself in the existing swellings and in new ones in the boy's groin. He tossed and turned on the makeshift bed, moaning and talking to himself in his delirious state until evening, when he fell into an exhausted sleep. He lay, his body soaked in sweat, his arms and legs motionless, his breath coming in gasps that gradually became weaker until he stopped breathing altogether. The plague had claimed its first victim in our house.

Within the week, the boy's mother followed him to the grave. His father, and all those members of our household who had come near the disease, were unaffected.

'You could still be right, Lou,' said Opa. He had hardly slept for four nights. His face was pale and haggard. 'The peasant woman was closer to her son than anyone else, and was the most likely to absorb the bad humours.'

'I now have doubts,' said my father, running his fingers through his hair. 'Neither of us is a stranger to death, but the violence with which this plague progresses, and the futility of our remedies against it, fill me with dread. You spent many hours with the lad. Is it conceivable you could have escaped if exhalations of air were the chief cause of transfer?'

'Perhaps we've been wrong all the time,' said Opa after a moment's silence, during which he stroked the arms of his fylfot pensively. 'Could the clerics be right? Have these people committed dreadful sins, and is the plague their punishment?'

'You don't believe that, Father! Those of us who have an advantage in life are no less sinners than those unfortunates who died in our care. It's not the condition of man's soul that drives this plague but something less spiritual.'

'My mind tells me you're right,' sighed Opa. He sat down and buried his face in his hands.

'I know I am,' said Ludwig. 'Whatever the priests say! And you know it too. Some ailments baffle us. That's not to say their causes are supernatural. Like the common cough and certain other fevers, this plague passes from man to man. Even the bishops are not immune! We know that from the stories. If the sickness were the result of sin, surely the clerics would escape its worst ravages?'

'Perhaps.' Opa raised his head wearily. 'But it was I who brought the boy and his mother to Bachhagen. I gave them hope, Lou, and they died. Perhaps the fault is mine.'

'It's no sin to give hope. Better they died in hope than with none. You're tired and should rest.'

'Later! I cannot rest while my mind is filled with such anger ...'

'Anger, Father?'

'Anger. Guilt. Despair at having failed with these first cases. I was so sure of myself. I was so sure I could save them. We must find the cause of this plague, Lou. And a cure. Before it's too late.'

'You'll find one. We'll do it together. If that means travelling south to find the plague's origins, so be it.'

'I have a premonition,' Opa said uneasily. 'Call it magic if you wish, but heed it. There will be no need to travel. Before long, many of our friends and neighbours will be struck down. Our services will be needed more than ever. If I'm not mistaken, it'll mean death for anyone who remains for long in the city. A black death! As winter approaches again, the plague will get worse, and the world we know will be threatened as it has never been threatened before. Neither by war, famine, nor flood.'

ii

My grandfather's prophecy came true. Though the manor house remained free of further infection as if by some magic power, there were within a week three or four more cases of plague on surrounding farms. Opa did his best to treat them but could discover no common factor that might point to the cause he was seeking. One patient survived.

Seven days later, there were a dozen more victims. Few of those lived beyond the fourth day. As the first leaves fell from the trees, there were more cases of illness in our part of the province than Opa and my father together could hope to attend. Still our house remained free of further symptoms.

News from Hannover, Hildesheim and Brunswick was infrequent, but it chilled our blood. The Great Mortality had struck the cities with unbelievable ferocity. It struck the well-born and poor alike. They died in their hundreds: merchants, journeymen, monks, priests; innkeepers, their wives, their serving wenches; thieves, whores, and all manner of deviates, their bodies swollen and blackened, piling in the streets to be collected twice or more daily when the city gates were opened and the gruesome death-carts trundled out to deposit their lading in communal graves. It was said that those who dug the shallow pits to receive the corpses were themselves afflicted as they worked, and often fell, stiff and silent, into the trenches they had prepared for others.

Too young then to understand these things, I was nevertheless affected by the talk around me, and my dreams were haunted by ogres and dwarves with black faces and loathsome, distorted bodies.

The tales from Hameln were no more comforting, and my mother began to fear for her family there.

'I should go to them,' she said. 'Bachhagen can spare me for a few days.'

'Please reconsider, my love,' my father said. 'Don't expose yourself needlessly to the dangers of the town.'

'Something frightful may have happened,' said my mother. 'I can't bear to listen to these terrible tales of plague without knowing they are well.'

'Don't go yet,' begged Ludwig. 'We seem to enjoy some protection while we live in this house. I hate to think your parents and brothers might be in danger, but it's better for the present that you stay here with me.'

'I'll go alone, with one of the stable hands as an escort,' my mother persisted. 'Gretl can stay here with you.'

'It's Gretl you must think of. She needs you. When she wakes in the night and cries out, it's your face she wants to see.'

'I know, Lou,' said my mother. She kissed me on the nose. 'It'll break my heart to leave you, my darling, but my mother and father need me too.'

'Perhaps you worry needlessly,' Ludwig said. 'Conditions in Hameln may be better than elsewhere, and your parents always enjoy the best of health.'

'If only I knew they were well,' said my mother.

'In that case, let us reassure each other by proxy. We'll send a servant. Your parents will love you no less. Gretl will still have her mother, and I my wife. If I seem selfish, it's because I love you. Please stay for both our sakes.'

My mother relented. 'But you must let me go at the first sign of sickness in my family,' she insisted.

Ludwig promised and, for the time being, she stayed at home while the plague raged all around.

Already my mother's pregnancy could not be hidden from other women and so it did not remain a secret long. Despite the gloom that surrounded us, my father began smiling more often than usual. I surprised him at all moments of the day embracing her, stroking the swelling in her gown and even, once, fondling her body beneath it.

'It kicked me,' he said.

My mother laughed. 'Then you know what I suffer day and night, Lou. Come, Gretl, you can feel it too.'

I hesitated, but my mother took my hand and placed it on her belly. Nothing happened at first. Then, as I was about to draw away, something inside her moved and I felt a distinct nudge against my palm. It happened again and I looked up in wonder.

'It's a boy for sure,' said my mother. 'You did not begin until much later, my darling!'

So began the last few weeks of that fateful year. Opa took me riding or walking so that my parents could be alone together. In any case, there was little else for me to do. Lieselle was growing up, the adults told me, and Hanna was in a black mood. Sigmund and Freddy were helping with the last of the harvest and Uncle Tom had arrived without his family.

I was now used to Princess, and she to me. Ali-Hassan had broken her in before giving her to me and she was as biddable as could be. Perched proudly on her back with or without a saddle, I forgot about plague and imagined only what my play would be like with my very own brother or sister to share it.

Still, I puzzled over my mother's condition and the mystery of life. If the infant was growing inside as she had told me, how had it come to be there in the first place, and however was it to get out?

Thanks to everyone's labours, the harvest was better than expected, but the celebrations that usually accompanied it were undertaken with little enthusiasm. Surrounded by so much death, it was difficult to shake off the gloom and foreboding that beset our lives, and marred what otherwise would have been a happy occasion.

Though both my father and grandfather reasoned against it, there was a prevailing belief that God's Judgement had fallen on the land, and that only by praising Him, and living in fear of Him, would the curse be lifted. The priests continued to pray, and the people continued to fall sick and die.

iii

The rats invaded our property in their hundreds, breeding with fecundity, living on the roofs of barns and among the chimneys of the house itself, attacking the fruits of our labours at every opportunity. They hid in hayricks, made their nests in cracks in walls and among the rafters of any building we left empty, or had not the foresight to seal against their onslaught.

Ludwig was disposed to study the creatures and their habits, to my mother's disgust.

'Let them come no closer to me than the end of a long pole,' she said with a shudder. 'They are loathsome animals, Lou, and treat God's gifts to us with contempt.'

'You're wrong to ascribe feelings to them, dearest,' said my father. 'Like all wild creatures, they have two natural instincts only, the pursuit of food and the search for a place to rear their young.'

'Death and corruption follow in their wake,' my mother insisted. 'Listen to your father. He no longer goes to Hannover, where the rats are out of control. There, the Great Mortality lays low pitilessly, and without respite. The rats are omens of disaster. Promise to have nothing more to do with them!'

'I'll do nothing that upsets you, dearest Greta,' said my father and kissed her. 'If it makes you happy, I promise.'

October was almost over. The grain had been stored, the apples from our orchards gathered and packed, the grapes harvested for winemaking. Uncle Tom returned home to be with his wife Martha and the children. There had been no case of the black plague in the manor house since the peasant boy and his mother died of the disease.

'Let us thank God it passes us by,' said my mother, 'but let us pray too for all those souls who are afflicted.'

Our good fortune was not to last.

One afternoon, I had clambered onto a window-seat in our apartments to catch a first glimpse of my father on his return home from the estate. From one side of the mullion I could look out over our pond. This was fed by a stream that flowed past the outbuildings, through a culvert and over a little waterfall. The pond was surrounded by a stone wall, built by a previous generation of labourers on the orders of the lord of the day, as a precaution against accidental drowning. Its water worked the mill wheel, whence it fell by stages into a lower field, and onwards to discharge itself in the Leine. The other side of the window gave me an uninterrupted view across the fields to the forest.

'Here he is!' I called excitedly, as my father came into sight, striding out from behind a deep ridge in the meadow, round the pond and between the barns towards the house. Uncle Roland was with him, and Sigmund. 'Shall I play the game, and hide?'

There had been good news from Hameln, and my mother was in wonderfully happy mood. Twice already that week, she had let me feel the baby kick inside her. The nudges were growing stronger.

'We'll hide together today,' she said, laughing at my eagerness, 'but be patient, Gretl. He's not at the front door yet. Wait until he climbs the stairs. It's dark in the closet, and I'm a timid creature!'

This particular window projected outwards supported by wooden buttresses. To left and right of it were two doors, one hiding a closet with a commode, the other a blocked-up winding stair that had once led to the roof. The space behind this second door, and the two or three steps that remained, were used for storage - blankets, surplus clothing, and some items of value my mother had brought from Hameln as part of her dowry. It was in this second closet that I would sometimes hide in order to surprise my father on his homecoming.

'Now ... now!' I urged. 'Let's hide now, or Father'll see us.'

My mother took me by the hand. 'Very well,' she agreed, almost as excited as I, though fully aware that Ludwig knew of our game and never tired of it. 'But don't laugh as you did last time, or he'll hear you as soon as he enters the ante-room.'

We pushed the door sufficiently ajar for us to slip through one at a time. A chink in the outer wall let in just enough light for us to see each other's faces. We held our breath, waiting for the sound that would signal Ludwig's entrance, a board that let out a crack when he stepped on it. It was then his custom to call out Where are you? whereupon I would rush out into his arms to be swept up high in the air.

That day, it was not the sound of his footfall that we heard, but a soft scratching and rustling. It came from the blocked-up stairwell at the back of the closet, above our heads. I looked up and, just below the wooden beam that protruded from stone and plaster, I saw something move. I started back and gripped my mother's hand.

'Look!' I cried. 'Up there!'

She followed my gaze. The light from the aperture in the wall fell on a spot from which a trickle of crumbled plaster oozed, and at the tiny hole thus produced appeared a whiskery snout and a pair of beady eyes. Before we could move, a lump of plaster gave way, and a huge rat slithered down amongst the dust and stones, to be followed by another, and yet another. My mother gave a cry of alarm and, clutching me tightly, burst out of the closet straight into Ludwig's arms.

'What new game is this, Greta?' he laughed, being so intent on embracing us that he did not see our terror or the cause of it. He had stepped across the offending floorboard in an effort to surprise us, and was himself surprised more than ever before.

'Rats,' cried my mother, clutching his tunic. 'The rats have burrowed through from the old staircase into our closet!'

She slammed the door shut but was not quick enough to prevent two of the creatures squeezing through into the sitting room. They scurried to and fro across the floor, under chairs, behind chests, along the window seat, then out into the bedroom. From our side of the door we heard the noise of more falling plaster and stones, the patter of feet, and the squeaking and squealing of the frightened animals as more and more of them fell through the hole their tunneling had created. They slid through, and being unable to climb out again, milled around in panic, scarce an arm's length from where we stood.

'What will we do, Lou?' said my mother. 'There must be a hundred of them! They are trapped in there. If we open the door they'll be all over the house; if we don't let them out ...'

'Take Gretl to my father's apartment,' Ludwig said. He had managed to chase the two rats out into the corridor above the main staircase, where a servant despatched them with a heavy stick. 'Find Roland. Call the stewards and stable lads. We have no choice but to deal with the rats in here. We can't allow them to overrun the house.'

'You mean to kill them?' said my mother with a shudder.

'Kill them and re-seal the old stairs from above as well as below.'

'Surely it only needs the hole to be widened and they can climb back the way they came? If you can reach the blockage from the other side ...'

Ludwig shook his head. 'There must be several nests up there. If we don't destroy the rats they will go on breeding and break through again. Besides, Greta, the hole must be quite large now to let in so many. If they had been able to leave, they would have done so.'

I was whisked away to my grandfather's rooms while Uncle Roland and a few servants assembled with my father in the hall. The window was open and I could hear the shouting below me.

'Begin from the roof, and re-seal the old staircase from there.' That was my father's voice. 'We can reach it through the attic, and hoist up the equipment we need.'

'Hurry now!' That was Roland. 'Fetch ladders, ropes and buckets ... and we'll need building materials.'

'Large stones too.' My father again. 'That'll be better than wood and mortar. And pulleys! We'll need pulleys.'

'Pulleys!' Roland. The stairs creaked as he mounted them, followed by his army of labourers.

They worked hard and soon had effected a temporary blocking of the upper end of the passage. My father suggested finishing that task the following morning, in full daylight. Now was the time to tackle the problem from the other end. It would be gory work, but the sooner it was begun the better.'

Many times, I have imagined what it must have been like that day:

Released from their prison, the rats come out like a flood, thirty or more of them - sleek black bodies with pointed narrow snouts, long tails and sharp, naked ears. The men strike them down mercilessly. Those that scurry beneath the beds are chased and devoured by our cats, brought in to assist. Any that try to leave are clubbed to death by labourers guarding the entrance. I see the horror of that slaughter in my mind's eye, hear the thud of wood on defenceless heads and watch the blood soak into the boards.

When the work was done, my father and his helpers blocked up the lower end of the old stair, scrubbed the rooms clean by lamplight, and gave the contents of the closet to be washed. When he arrived at Opa's door to fetch us home, he looked pale and exhausted. Thrice he sneezed loudly.

'I'm sorry. It's the dust from our workings,' he said. 'Either that or I've caught a chill. I've been for a bathe in the river to wash away the unpleasantness of what we have just done.'

My mother was reluctant to return to our quarters until she was satisfied everything was again normal, and the threat from the rats removed. However, when she saw how clean and tidy the apartments were, she managed a smile.

'Gretl may hide in the closet again if she chooses,' said she as she packed me off to bed. 'I never will!'

The next afternoon but one, Ludwig was attacked by pains in his back and limbs. Late evening found him in a high fever. My mother bathed him frantically and, fearing the worst, sent to my grandfather for advice.

'The symptoms are similar,' Opa said, 'but we can't be certain unless the swellings develop. Stay with him, cool him with water, and I'll come back soon with some medicines.'

It was an hour before he returned. Meanwhile, Ludwig had tried to rise from his bed but had fallen back helplessly.

'I bring the worst possible news,' Opa said. 'There are two more cases among the stable hands, and the wife of one complains of a headache.'

My father became agitated and struggled to speak, but could scarcely manage a whisper. My mother bent over him and wiped his forehead with a cloth moistened with cool water from a basin at his bedside. She was perspiring almost as much as he and her face had turned from pink to red.

'Save your strength, my love,' she urged. 'Don't try to talk when your throat hurts so.'

My father muttered something between his teeth.

'He's delirious,' cried my mother, holding back her tears. 'He can think of nothing but dead rats. Am I to lose my husband so soon, and with another little one on the way?'

Opa opened one of the jars he had brought, poured a little of the contents into a beaker to which he added water, and forced my father to swallow it.

'This will ease the constrictions of the throat,' he said, 'but Lou must drink plenty water too. And I have a second medicine here, an ointment that should be rubbed on the aching joints. And here's a third to cool the fever when taken undiluted. Can I rely on you to follow my instructions?'

My mother nodded.

'Then I must also do what I can for the servants.'

My mother assured him she would follow instructions to the letter and so, having carefully described what she was to do, Opa left us alone.

All night my father tossed and turned in his bed, perspiring freely and groaning miserably. By morning, the expected swellings in his armpits and groin appeared, discolouring the flesh so that the skin around the infected parts was no longer fair but almost black. He cried out frequently, his throat having been loosened by the medicine, but we made no sense of his ravings. My mother attended to him dutifully until, midway through the next day, he sank into a half sleep, dripping with sweat and drained of all resistance.

Opa made two visits and each time the news he brought was grave.

'One of the grooms has died,' he told us on the first occasion. 'There was no blackness, though the other symptoms were identical. The second, like Lou, has developed black boils. And the woman too shows all the signs of becoming a victim.'

All the colour drained from my mother's face.

'I have even worse to tell you,' Opa went on. 'Little Lieselle, her mother and a maid who attends them have succumbed.'

He returned when Ludwig's fever had reached its crisis.

'There are several more cases among the hands,' said he, averting his gaze so that we would not see his despair. However, his bearing and tone of voice told all.

'Tell me,' said my mother in an whisper.

'Now it's Roland's turn.' Opa said. I very much wanted him to hug me and tell me that everything would be all right, but he kept his distance. He had not come near me or allowed me to touch him since the onset of my father's sickness. I began to understand that evil had come into our home. 'I wish I could spare you these tidings,' he said, 'but Roland, his wife, and his elder son, have all sickened. Our house is no longer a safe haven. It has become accursed.'

The crisis in my father's condition passed. The fever died down and he slept soundly while my mother and I sat by his bedside. She did not want me to stay for fear that the mysterious sickness would strike me down too, but I made such a fuss, screaming, clutching her robe and beating my fists against the furniture, that she and Opa relented. We still feared Ludwig might die, for the hideous boils did not immediately disappear, and his face kept its ghastly pallor.

At last, his eyes opened. It was early evening on the fifth day after the adventure with the rats. Already a lamp had been lit. Ludwig blinked and looked about him. My mother wept for joy and unashamedly embraced him and covered his face with kisses. I laughed and danced round the bed. My grandfather looked very grave, and I knew, despite my joy, that more dispiriting news was to come.

We knew that half of the household was already infected. Three of our family were dangerously near death, including one of the children. Six tenants on our land had already died, and some dozen others were suffering. However, dark thoughts were put aside while we thanked God for Ludwig's recovery.

'I never thought to see any of you again,' he said in a hoarse whisper. It was several minutes before he regained his power of speech.

'Nor I you,' said my mother, kissing him yet one more time. 'You thrashed about so wildly in your fever, and talked so much nonsense ...'

'What did I say?' asked my father weakly. 'I remember only having terrible dreams, of being sealed up behind a wall with dead rats for company.'

'It was mostly of rats that you spoke. The grisly work that you and the others did five or six days ago has preyed on your mind. You raved like a madman.'

My father's memory seemed suddenly to return. He shook his head and with great effort raised himself on one elbow, fixing Opa with a penetrating look. No words were spoken but some silent message passed between them. It may have been the way my grandfather continued to stroke his beard and finger the fylfot, or it could have been that a flicker of his eyelids betrayed the emotion his otherwise calm countenance hid.

'Alas, I'm not the only one to fall victim to this accursed plague,' Ludwig cried. 'I see it in your face! Tell me the worst. Roland?'

My grandfather nodded.

'The steward? The stable lads?'

Again, Opa simply nodded.

'And the others who were here that day?' My father counted off some more names on his fingers.

'Yes.'

'Matti? Sigmund?'

'He has escaped, but Matti herself, Lieselle, and two farm children have not.'

'But that's not possible,' exclaimed Ludwig, gripping Opa's arm. He tried to get out of bed but my mother held him back. 'No, it can't be so! The others I suspected, but not the women and children too.'

My mother gave a gasp and held me tightly.

'By what magic could you suspect that?' she breathed. 'How could you know it would be so?'

'It's no magic, and I did not know for sure,' said my father. His lips trembled. 'Only I believe I have the answer. I know the cause of the plague!'

An hour passed.

'It's so obvious that I can't believe the explanation escaped us,' said Ludwig. Having drunk half a goblet of wine, he sat back on two pillows, a little of his normal colouring restored to his cheeks. 'I should say rather, the precise cause is not obvious, but we should always look to the unusual to explain the unusual. Why we did not think of the rats I can't conceive.'

'The rats,' said Opa. 'Yes, that could be it.'

'I told you they were an evil omen ....' began my mother.

'And I should've listened to you, Greta. They are the cause. Of that I'm sure.'

'But how?' Opa objected. 'The creatures are forever with us. They are a nuisance, it's true, but surely if they were the cause of this terrible plague we would have seen signs of it before?'

'They have never invaded in such great numbers, Father. They're always cunning but in the past they shied away from human contact. Think again of the conditions in the towns. There, their numbers are greatest, and they live always in close proximity to the people. And have we not, this year, seen how they follow caravans, and groups of travellers?'

'I noticed the rats when Gretl and I met the peasants going to Hannover,' agreed Opa 'but I attached no importance to them.'

'You see,' said Ludwig, 'but for an accident we would never have thought them important. Had the rats not burrowed their way through the plaster and wood sealing the old staircase, I would not have sickened, nor would the others, and this tragedy would not have come upon our family. All through the summer we fought them. Kept them at bay with sticks. We were free of plague. The peasant boy and his mother brought it with them. The farmers who died earlier must have harboured rats in their cottages.'

My mother shuddered. 'But where does this sickness come from, Lou, and how is it the rats infect us humans? Do these loathsome animals capture the souls of those who depart this life in mortal sin? Are they Satan's instrument for the evil he wishes to bring into the world?'

'Transmigration of souls is an old idea, Greta,' said Opa. 'But it's a myth! I suspect Lou does not attribute the plague to supernatural influences. We have often discussed the matter and concluded otherwise.'

'You're right, Father. The causes of this plague are not supernatural.'

'How then do you answer your wife's question? Do you have a theory of your own?'

'I have indeed, though I can't prove it yet. It depends upon the fact that the rats themselves are sick.'

'The rats sick!' My mother forced herself to laugh. 'What is that for an idea? I fear you are not yet yourself, dearest.'

'Wait, Greta,' said Opa thoughtfully. 'It's not such a strange idea. We know there are diseases that afflict animals. The bite of a mad dog can be deadly to a man. A poison is injected into an arm or a leg by way of the animal's teeth. It is a horrible death, as much so as the black plague.'

My mother frowned.

'How are such things possible?'

'I don't have an explanation,' Opa said. 'But consider that even healthy creatures can inflict poisonous wounds, the gnat, the viper and the scorpion for example. In some countries, there are snakes, and even insects, whose bite can mean almost instant death. Yet, Lou, I saw no tooth-marks on any of the plague victims I treated, and no sign of a rat's bite on your body.'

'The bite may yet prove deadly, but as I wasn't bitten I suspect another cause,' said my father. 'Some weeks ago, I began to study the creatures' habits. Always at a distance, for I promised Greta I would not touch them. Normally shy, they've become aggressive. Nocturnal as a rule, they've become more evident in the day. Never have we seen them reproduce at such a rate. Many are rats of a different kind and they die in great numbers too. When we drove them from the fields, they left their dead behind, like a defeated army. Only they were not killed by our sticks. I concluded that the rats are diseased, and that their sickness has driven them to madness. But I did not connect this madness with the sickening of humans. Not until now.'

He eased himself into a more comfortable position on the bed and moistened his lips.

'Three questions have to be answered. First, whence comes this rat plague? Second, how do the rats transmit their disease to man? Third, is there any cure? I have answers to the first two.

'As to the source, it's rumoured the plague had its beginnings in the south, in Italy. Among sailors. We have heard the story too many times, from merchants and travellers alike, to doubt it. We know rats do travel in ships! I think great numbers of rats have arrived from abroad, perhaps from the Levant, bringing their pestilence with them.'

Finding that he had again shifted uncomfortably, he tried to heave the pillows round so that they better supported his back, but he lacked the strength. My mother hastened to assist. Ludwig reached for his goblet, took another sip of wine and continued with his explanation.

'The other day, we dealt with thirty or more rats in these very rooms. At least half that number lay dead on the old staircase, and the labourers removed the carcasses before closing the passage again. You'll recall the staircase was sealed originally by placing wooden beams across the gap and filling the spaces with stones and rubble. Then gypsum was applied as a plaster to complete the process.

'The hole dug by the rats was just underneath one of the beams and, by the time all the creatures had escaped, it had been enlarged. When I examined the exit so that we might repair it, I noticed that the rats had deposited an oily smear on the wood. This oil must be exuded by the rats' bodies like sweat. As they ran below the chairs, behind the chests, and round the other furniture, they deposited more of the substance.

'I paid particular attention to these tracks. Later, I encountered the rats themselves, and noted their greasy sleekness. I feel sure the oil is a poison responsible for our sickness. By touching the infected animals, we ourselves become infected.'

In his enthusiasm, my father had worked himself into an unsupported seating position. Now, he coughed and lay back on the pillow. Fearing he was tiring himself, my mother bade him rest awhile, but he was keen to continue.

'As to the cure,' he went on hoarsely, his voice noticeably weaker, 'we will find it. For now, all we can do is avoid infection by driving off or killing the rats as we did before. We must urge our neighbours to do the same. On no account should anyone allow their skin to come into contact with the rats' bodies, or with the smears of oil left behind on furniture and the timber of buildings.'

'I feel sure you're on the right track,' my grandfather said. 'But might I suggest a minor objection that leads me to think you have not arrived at the whole truth.' He stroked his beard and twisted the chain of the fylfot. 'Why did all the men not fall ill? And why are the women and children, who weren't there, laid low?'

My father shook his head slowly. 'I don't understand that. When you told me Lieselle and the others were struck down, I could hardly believe it. I should go to them and ...'

'You will not,' said Opa firmly. 'There's nothing you can do that I have not tried. You must rest again and recover your own health.'

My father's condition continued to improve and within a few days he was on his feet again. Thanks to my mother's care and attention, his appetite returned, the pallor left his face and his muscles became strong again. He took great pains to write down everything he had observed concerning the rats, their habits, diet, the construction of their nests, and his theories on the origins of the plague and its transmission to the human population. As soon as he was well again, he planned to visit Italy, for it was there he expected to find evidence to support his idea - that the plague-ridden rats had disembarked from foreign ships. In truth, it was to be many years before he undertook the journey, and then the circumstances were quite different.

My father was one of the few who suffered the plague and lived. Within days of his recovery, there were four more deaths in our household. Poor Lieselle did not live to see her tenth birthday. Roland's eldest child, Rolf, died when only three days short of his twelfth. Roland himself and his wife, despite Opa's prescriptions and all our prayers, did not long survive their son. Meantime their elder daughter took to her bed with plague symptoms. Her illness lasted less than two days and she died of violent coughing. My father puzzled over this case as no swellings had appeared, and the fever had not reached its expected peak. Although he clung to his theories, there were many factors he could not explain, and his failure to solve the mystery gave him lasting anguish.

All told, we lost six of our servants and more than half of our tenants. Ali-Hassan the blacksmith was one of the casualties. Matti, like Ludwig, recovered. Roland's share in the property passed to Freddy. He was much too young to take over his father's duties and so, according to the will, and with Opa's agreement, my father became the boy's guardian and sole master of Bachhagen.

We waited a month for news of Uncle Thomas, Martha, Lisbeth and Wilf, and when it came, our misery was complete. Though Tom survived, he lost the use of one leg and remained a cripple for the rest of his life. Lisbeth lived too. Martha and little Wilf were taken. I was devastated and cried for three days.

My mother's belly grew even larger, her face rosier and more rounded.

'It'll come at Shrovetide,' she announced, but her gaiety had gone. Ludwig embraced her in silence. There were no words to dispel the grief or fill the emptiness we all felt at the loss of our loved ones. The deliverance of our little family and the prospect of its enlargement should have been a cause for rejoicing. But how was it possible to thank God for allowing the lives of so many to be taken?

In the final days of December, a messenger arrived from Hameln with the news that Karl was sick. Although there was a death in almost every household, the Queck family had managed, until then, to cheat the plague and its terrible consequences.

'I must go, Lou,' said my mother. 'You persuaded me against it before, but now it's my duty to be with my kin, and to be nurse to my brother.'

Once again, my father would have hindered her.

'Think of the unborn child, Greta,' he said. 'Allow me to go instead. You need to ...'

She placed a hand over his mouth and silenced him.

'My time is still months away, my love,' she said, 'and there are still many who need you here. Remember your promise.'

Ludwig reluctantly gave her journey his blessing. As preparations for winter were in hand and servants in short supply, Opa agreed to accompany her, and to return when she was safely installed in her father's house. I clung to her and pleaded to be allowed to go too but my father forbade it.

'Don't forget what I've told you about the rats,' he said as she departed. 'If they can't be kept at bay, they must be killed. Impress upon your father that, though we have not yet learned the whole truth, we're sure the rats are the source of the Great Mortality. Avoid contact at all costs.'

'I'll not forget,' whispered my mother as she kissed him goodbye. 'Take good care of Gretl until I return.'

She took me in her arms and held me close for a while. Although the occasion was a sad one, she did her best to smile. As Opa helped her into the carriage, I wept again. We had never been parted before. I was still weeping when the carriage reached the gate, turned into the high road, and disappeared from view.

I never saw my mother again.

iv

What do children understand of disease and death? In a year when no family was a stranger to death, the loss of a parent, a brother or sister, even all three, was a sadness that most had to endure. To lose a mother when one is scarce eight years old - a mother who has herself not long grown out of childhood, who is the centre of a loving family, whose youth and beauty endear her to all, is a tragedy no child should have to bear.

When my mother departed for Hameln, I had not understood. When they told me she would never return, that I would never again see her bright smile or hear her voice, I was inconsolable and determined to die too, so that I could be with her in heaven, for thither they said she had gone.

A premonition drove my father to follow her to Hameln after three days. When he arrived, Karl was near to death, his poor little body blackened and swollen by the poisons that had already claimed so many. The town had suffered terribly, especially in the poor quarter. No one knew how many had died. Ludwig's advice in respect of the rats was followed closely. Grandfather Queck could not bring himself to believe in the oily smears, but he needed no bidding to deal firmly with the vermin that had invaded his stores.

My mother remained with Karl until he breathed his last. She was already infected, but managed to hide her discomfort until she was seized with a fit of coughing and sneezing. Within a few hours the fever had her in its grip, and she died in my father's arms. There had been no time for the black boils to develop, so he was spared seeing the body he loved so much disfigured by the plague's worst symptoms. He brought her home to Bachhagen and she was buried with her unborn child alongside Oma Matthilde in the hillside tomb overlooking the valley.

Ludwig tried to occupy himself with the management of the estate, but he was half-hearted in everything he did. That he missed my mother sorely was evident, and it seemed nothing would ever reconcile him to her loss. He blamed himself for allowing her to go to Hameln, and for being unable to prevent or cure her illness. His desolation was made all the worse when, before the winter was out, he saw his theories on the plague and its origins seemingly shattered.

Although many followed his advice that the rats be driven out and killed, the spread of the Great Mortality was not halted. The plague flared up anew. Many of the sufferers were young. Like my mother, they had no swellings and died of coughing. Some were spared even that and were cut down in the bloom of their childhood with no symptoms at all. It was as if Satan himself, the infernal protector of all things evil, was angered by the death of so many of his own creatures and took revenge.

My father would sit for hours in Opa's laboratory, engaged in no particular task at all, silent and morose, preferring his own company, and sometimes quick-tempered and ill-humoured with any of his friends who offered sympathy. When he *did* speak, it was mostly to mutter to himself.

'What shall I do? I cannot live without her,' he would cry, burying his face in his hands. 'Why was I spared, when I have failed both as a husband and as a father?'

I was the only one who dared approach him when he was in these moods. We were closer now than we had ever been. He would kiss me on the forehead, and I would cling to his neck while great tears rolled down his cheek onto my hair. I had never before seen a man cry.

Thus comforting one another, we lived through the darkest days until, suddenly, it was over. The people, those that were left, finished burying their dead. The priests rang the church bells and thanked God. Our family was left with its memories.

v

Ennia survived the plague. The Singari had remained in their camp by the old tower, near Hannover, and had lived through the worst days there. To north and south, as far as the wooded mound, the men had cut a deep ditch, allowing the river to flow round the camp and isolating their people from the outside world. The woods around the tower supported a variety of wild plants that they used for food when their supplies of grain ran out. As they had their own birds and animals to kill and eat, they were better off than their settled neighbours in and around the city.

They built fires on which they burned camphor, sulphur and herbs, giving off pungent smoke that drifted among the tents day and night. Though Opa expressed himself sceptical, it seemed the strategy worked for few of the Singari caught the plague and only four - men, women and children - died of it. They burned the corpses on funeral pyres and scattered the ashes around the camp.

Ennia gave up her life of travel. She came to Bachhagen to live in the blacksmith's house for, as I learned, my grandfather owned it and was able to dispose of it as he pleased. We found another smith to take over the work and he lodged in a separate house in the village.

The day Ennia came to the forge was the first time I had seen Opa smile in many long weeks. She greeted me with a kiss on the cheek and my grandfather with a long embrace. It seemed strange to me that two people should cling to one another in such a way unless they were husband and wife.

'Would that the pestilence had taken us,' Ennia said to Opa as we drank some wine together. She still held herself erect though she seemed more fragile than before. 'I would have been glad to die if it could have spared poor Greta and all those others. We have had our youth and it should have been their turn of life.'

'Did you know my mother, Ennia?' I asked. She had never mentioned my mother before and I had never even considered that they might have met. My father never spoke of Ennia, and Opa had never shown any inclination to tell me her history. And recently, so much tragedy had beset our lives that there had never been the right moment to ask him again.

'Of course,' Ennia answered. She clasped me round the shoulders while I cried into her bosom. 'Her father and grandfather too!'

She added something to Opa in the foreign tongue I had often heard them use. For a few minutes they conversed and I was excluded. Opa's eyes held their wise, grave expression while Ennia's seemed fierce and penetrating. I waited for them to finish and when they did, Opa took my hand.

'I think it's time to go home,' he said. 'But we have agreed you can come to visit Ennia once every week.'

I resumed my lessons in swordplay in earnest. At first, it was merely to keep me from melancholy but then I began to enjoy it again. Now I think it was as much for Ennia's benefit as for mine.

We still practised with the wooden blades. Freddy was envious, as I knew he would be, when I boasted how well my skill was improving. My father seemed uneasy that I visit the village so often alone but he did not object. Matti and Opa exchanged angry words out of my hearing one evening and she was cool towards me at supper. I asked Opa if I had done something wrong.

'I'm the guilty party, I think,' he answered. 'Your aunt believes your afternoons could be put to better use.'

'Why does she think that?'

'I wonder if you are old enough to understand, Gretl,' Opa said. 'You see, Ennia is not a Christian. Matti is afraid she will try to teach you heathen ways.'

I wondered briefly what it might be that Ennia would teach me but eventually forgot the whole episode.

Soon I felt less clumsy with the wooden sword. I began to understand Ennia's meaning when she said it must become an extension of myself. Still, she parried or deflected most of my strokes and I hardly managed to hit her at all while she, despite her fragility, could score against me almost without trying.

'You are too exposed, Gretl,' she would say. 'Turn away when you attack ... like this!' She would take me by the hips and turn me so I faced her with one leg positioned behind the other and only my right shoulder forward. 'Now, use your feet more. You are young and agile, so use your youth against me.'

We would try again and I was delighted when, eventually, I found I could evade her thrusts - albeit one or two in ten - and dodge her cuts. After just an hour, Ennia was now breathing heavily. I suppose that, as my skill grew, I was testing hers more and more. Or was it that she had a sickness of the lungs? There was no reason why I should think that; the idea just popped into my head. Had Ennia, like my father, suffered the black plague and, like Uncle Thomas, been weakened by it?

When the lessons ended, she would take my sword from me and lay it down beside hers. Then we would sit together on her bed. Ennia would smile, fold me in her arms, hug me and tell me how well I had done. I felt her bones pressing against my chest.

Other days, we would talk - about life and death, about growing up, and about men. Rather, Ennia talked and I listened. I did not understand it all but she was patient with me and answered my questions simply and mostly without evasion. Occasionally, however, she would just smile in a most mysterious way and tell me to think about it. Or just to wait for a year or two! And often, when I did think about it, I could see I needn't have asked the question after all.

'I don't want you to die, Ennia,' I said to her one day.

'We all have to die, Gretl.' Ennia sighed and kissed me gently on the forehead. 'And you are right. It will be my turn soon, but not yet awhile. Not until you are the most fearsome woman warrior in all Saxony!'

We sat without speaking, listening to hammering and the clang of metal on metal from the floor below. Then Ennia ruffled my hair. I saw in her face a faraway look that reminded me of Ludwig and how he mourned my mother.

'Tell me about you and Opa,' I said, with sudden inspiration. If he would not tell me her story, perhaps she might.

'What would you have me tell you – that he and I were children together?'

I stared, for the moment struck dumb.

'What is it, child? Don't you believe me?' Ennia gave one of her gentle, maiden-like laughs. 'Oh yes. I have known your grandfather for sixty years and more. If I were to tell you all our adventures, it would take until the end of time ...'

'But how ... ?' I stammered, thinking it could not be true, and that even six years was an impossibly long time. Sixty was an eternity.

' 'Twill do no harm to tell a little,' Ennia said. 'You see, we both grew up in Persia. In a castle.'

'In Persia? But surely Opa was born in Venice.'

'No,' she chuckled. 'Whyever did you think that? He was to become a grand Venetian gentleman, Gretl. But that was later. He was not born in Italy.'

A hundred questions surged around in my brain but I could not decide which ones to ask first. I was wondering how many other secrets my parents had hidden from me.

'Tell me, Ennia,' I said.

'Yes, we lived in a castle.' She chuckled again. 'The prince and the princess. Like you, we climbed trees and walls. We used to play tricks on the castle guards. Sometimes we stole food from under the cooks' noses.

'But your Opa always made sure we were never caught red-handed. He was the cleverest person I ever knew. He discovered secret passages under the castle, which meant we could go everywhere without being seen. We even found a way to the room where all the gold and silver was kept.' She chuckled again. 'Then there was the lake where we went fishing. Once, he fell out of the boat. I laughed so much!'

'And did you fall in too?'

'He nearly capsized the boat trying to pull me in after him. But he failed! These are among the happiest times of my life, Gretl.' She sighed and patted my arm. 'But Fate is not always kind. Its pathways have many twists and turns. And of course we grew older.'

I pressed her for more.

'The time came when we parted,' Ennia said, 'and it was long years before we saw one another again.'

'When you came to Saxony?'

'Yes, though there were many adventures in between. Of my travels; of my life with the Singari.'

'Please tell me, Ennia.'

'Some other day, perhaps.'

'Tell me about Persia then.'

'Persia.' She sighed. 'I can tell you this, Gretl. 'Tis not like this Saxony. Persia is so large that all of this Empire could be fitted into one tiny corner. In the south, there are deserts, all covered in salt; in the north and west, there are great mountain ranges. For most of the year the country is hot and dry. But in the mountains the winters can be icy cold. Then, in spring, the snows melt and the rains come in the country round the Great Sea. Once every hundred years, the earth trembles and great chasms open up to swallow trees. People too. Sometimes I think it is angry at what we human beings do to one another.'

'That is sad, ' I said. 'That the ground should tremble because of the things we do.'

Ennia smiled. 'But Persia is a beautiful country. I would give a lot to be able to go back. Perhaps one day we shall go together.'

I knew that could never be, that she was dreaming for us both, but I held my tongue.

'Yes,' she said. 'It would please your grandfather too, though he would never admit it.' Suddenly there was bitterness in her voice, something I had never heard before. 'We should not have been parted. The gods should not have permitted it when I loved him so!'

I leant forward wide-eyed. Young as I was, I knew what she meant, or thought I did. Outside the family, Opa's manner would often be stiff and formal. But in Ennia's company he was relaxed and familiar, as he was with me and with my parents. And her affection for him was there for all to see. Was that the real reason Matti objected to our association?

'I'm sorry, Gretl,' Ennia said. 'I should not have told you so much! Life is not like the stories.' She fixed me with one of her most penetrating glances, almost as if she could read my mind. 'Do not make the mistake I made, child. When you find love, do not wait. Grasp it with your whole heart and soul!'

I waited for her to go on but she would not. She just shook her head and made me swear I would tell no one what she had just confessed to me. I did not understand. How could I? In the stories, the prince fell in love with the princess and they lived happily ever after.

There is a kind of magic, the magic of childhood, that shields us from the realities of life. We see it in a mother's smile or in a father's strong arms and we hear it in the stories they sometimes spin for our amusement. We see it too in the wider world around without seeing the realities that lie beyond the outer skin of beauty. The tempting glisten of ice on a pond conceals the freezing water beneath; the golden flower of the kingcup hides the treacherous marsh wherein it grows.

The coming of the Mortality and the death of my mother had already shattered my innocence. The suspicion, and then the realisation that many of Opa's tales might be plain truth after all was to deal a fatal blow to my childish credulity. It was Ennia who lit the way for me.

'When you find love, Gretl, do not let it slip away,' she was fond of saying. Many years later, I would remember her advice, and take it. As it turned out, that brought an emptiness of its own, so that I wondered if indeed Fate, the Fate that had shaped Ennia's life, had decreed a lonely life for me. However, at the age of only eight, I had a poor understanding of what she meant and was eager only for her to continue with her tales. She told me about her life among the Singari, sometimes about Singari legends, and how the women could make horoscopes and tell fortunes. She also told the story of a Persian king called Temuchin, and of the Caliph of Baghdad, and of a queen named Sharazad who kept her husband entertained for many nights with stories of mystery, magic and love.

I visited and practised at the forge for many months. In truth, I became quite skilful with a blade and was more than a match for Freddy when he teased me. Ennia could be stern, even fierce, as a teacher but she was warm and kindly as a friend. She was much too old to be a substitute mother but I do believe she took my mother's place, when I needed it, in one important respect. Not only did she teach me the elements of swordplay but she helped me cross that final bridge between childhood and maidenhood. I could never have brought myself to confess my ignorance to Matti, but Ennia seemed to understand there were things I needed to know without my uttering a word. How she explained the mystery of love and life was simplicity itself and once I understood it I felt very grown up indeed.

I was right to believe her lungs had been wasted by the plague. Gradually, she became more and more frail until she was scarcely able to hold her weapon, whereas I could now wield the steel sword with the coiled snake hilt and the ruby: the sword she had given me as a present. She died at last and was buried on the open hillside overlooking the Bachhagen valley. Opa laid a stone at her grave. There were only five mourners. Besides Opa and me, the burial was attended by the new Singari chieftain, the young blacksmith and Jacob the Jew.

Ennia never talked about Opa again. She had made a promise, she said, and would not break it. I suppose I could have pressed her but I did not. Though barely nine years old, I think I sensed there was something sad and private between them that it would do no good to unearth. Perhaps I should be grateful that she left me then with my illusions, for what would it have changed if I had known the truth? And yet, how different my own life could have been had I been more inquisitive.

Brunswick

i

I grew quickly. By ten, I was the second tallest child in the household, outstripping all but my eldest cousin Sigmund, who was thirteen. Parts of my education, begun by my mother so patiently, were continued by my father's cousin Matti. Having herself lost one child to the black plague, she became the foster mother to four more - Freddy, Hanna, Lisbeth and me. I continued my study of mathematics and star lore with Opa and under his tutelage my interest in the sciences developed apace.

There was so much to learn, about not only plants and their uses but also how to judge between proper dosage and over-prescription. Many medicines are beneficial in small amounts but deadly in larger. A draught made from poppy seed might cure a man of his headache while the same quantity would kill a child.

My body began to change and I found pleasure in exploring the changes. I knew from my time with Ennia a little of what to expect and was ready for it. But not all. Strange, unfamiliar sensations, thoughts and emotions surged through me - pain, expectation and longing, though I did not understand at first what I longed for or what the longing meant.

When I was thirteen years old, I was presented with my cousins Hanna and Lisbeth at the Duke's palace in Brunswick. It was Matti's idea and she had a talent for getting her own way. We were called together to a family conference though that mattered little, as we were not allowed to have contrary opinions.

'They are almost fully grown,' reasoned Matti. 'It's time they learned some manners.'

'I have no understanding of maidens' needs,' said my father, 'but I do know Gretl is happy at home.'

'And so am I,' said Hanna.

I echoed her thoughts on the subject but they ignored us. Lisbeth was devious and stayed silent.

'You must think of her future, Lou,' Matti went on. 'Hanna's and Lisbeth's too. They will need husbands and this backwater is no place to find them.'

'I don't want a husband,' I snapped.

'You say that now, Margaretha,' said Freddy in a very adult way. Now that he was fourteen, he thought himself grown up and very wise, though his voice had still not properly deepened. Often in the middle of a sentence, he would give a little squeak as if he were ten again.

'If men are all like you, Cousin, I shall never want one,' I said.

'This is no life for a girl,' said Matti as if I hadn't been there. 'Look at her! She wears men's breeches and sits astride her pony like a boy. A few days ago, I found her fencing Frederic with a dagger. That's what comes of associating with Egyptians and all these other freedoms she's allowed. If she remains here, it'll spoil her chances of a good marriage.'

My father was unconvinced. He, like Opa, had come to rely on me to perform little tasks in the village and round the farms, while he himself attended to the management of the estates. In truth, Bachhagen had prospered under his sole guardianship, and had caught the jealous eye of a number of more powerful Brunswick landowners, who had previously regarded us as a small and therefore unimportant manor.

As for fencing, poor Freddy knew already he was no match for me in skill or agility. I suppose he must have thought I had a natural talent. For a year, I had practised with Sigmund, who had studied sword craft with a master. He and I had a pact, sealed in blood, never to tell anyone of our secret meetings. We had cut our wrists with a dagger, not deeply of course, but sufficient to allow my blood to flow into his when we clasped hands. Our scars had healed within a week.

'The Langenfurths have sent both their sons and their daughters to court,' said Matti, attempting to convince my father by different arguments. 'So have the Grübenhagens and the Waldhausens. It's expected, and we must take our place there if the family is to have any influence in the province.'

My father frowned. 'Plague on these times, that it's a sign of weakness to mind one's own business! The Mortality left not only misery and impoverishment behind, but jealousy and suspicion too. Why else do the landgraves parade their sons in armour, and their daughters in fine clothes to catch the eye of their neighbours? Why else do we engage ageing warriors as a deterrent to occupation of our property?

'Anyhow, we were speaking of Gretl's future, and she's still a child. Send Hanna by all means. She is older.'

'You see her as a father, Lou, moreover as a father who treats his daughter like a son! Margaretha is nearly ripe for childbearing. Hanna may be older, but she is more backward. And we cannot deny Lisbeth the same opportunity. All three should go. Do not forget that Sigmund is there to watch over them.'

My heart missed a beat at the mention of Sigmund's name and my cheeks burned so much that I was sure everyone could see the fire. I had last seen my eldest cousin in the bright, new tunic and cap of a squire and felt tight all over as I thought about him. Not even Hanna, who was closer to me than anyone else, knew of my secret admiration, or so I thought.

As the argument swayed to and fro, we glanced at one another. That she was backward was quite untrue. She was by far the most forward of us all though she loved the pretence of innocence. It had not been in innocence that we had lain together on the eve of Hanna's fourteenth birthday and had enjoyed the touch of one another's bodies.

'I will go if you go,' I whispered.

'And I will go if you go,' she echoed.

'I shall go in any case,' said Lisbeth. She was the youngest and more flighty than either of us. 'It'll be fun!'

'Fun!' I sneered. 'It'll be no fun to have to bow and curtsey all day long, to be squeezed into tight gowns and have our breasts popping up all over.'

But, in the end, Aunt Matti's arguments prevailed. Hanna, Lisbeth and I were sent to join the Duke's retinue.

ii

The sights and sounds of Brunswick were new and captured my interest at first. The knights and squires seemed so handsome, the ladies so clever, and their gowns so fine. There were banquets and entertainments. Tumblers, jugglers and musicians performed for our amusement. Actors played scenes from the Garden of Eden, Noah and his Ark and Christ's Miracles in the open air, sometimes from dawn to dusk, to crowds that included every rank from the high to the low.

I had no interest in the politics of the Dukedom, which provided a source of constant gossip and rumour. It seemed to me unimportant how Saxony was divided or how the Emperor of Germany was chosen. I knew that Magnus, the son of Duke Albert who had been my grandfather's friend, resented that his territory had been reduced to a subsidiary province, while the Duke of Saxony and his heirs had the rights of Prince Electors, but I did not care. The nobility of Wolfenbüttel and Lüneburg strutted about in stiff, formal clothes and vied with one another for position and for Magnus's ear.

I soon grew tired of it all. I became homesick and longed for the open fields, the river, the forest and the rough but kindly people who inhabited the small farms and tiny cottages. Hanna was homesick too but pretended not to be. Of the three of us, only Lisbeth found the fun she was seeking. She truly enjoyed court life and, after six months, was sent as companion to a sister of the Emperor. And for all I cared, she might remain there, marry and have twenty screaming infants.

'Would you return to Bachhagen without a husband?' teased Hanna. During our first year at court, we had been inseparable companions. 'This city abounds in handsome men, and we've only to find two that suit us.'

'I would go home gladly,' said I petulantly. 'Brunswick city life is tedious, and I have no thoughts of marriage, whatever the hopes of our family. The youths are awkward and the knights presumptuous.'

'I fancy you don't find them all so, Gretl,' said Hanna mischievously. 'You seem very fond of cousin Sigi's company.'

'Sigmund's conversation is in the Saxon tongue, and he is amusing,' I replied. 'I don't have to listen to the ladies of the court with their new speech and their tall tales of love and carnal delights. They are shallow creatures, and each vies with the others to relate the most daring conquest or the most devious seduction.'

'Is this the same Sigi who is tongue-tied in my presence?' Hanna went on. 'I've seen him look at you with sheep's-eyes, and wager his thoughts are not always on conversation when you cling so intimately to his arm.'

'We're like brother and sister!' I maintained stoutly, though unable to deny the burning in my cheeks.

'Have you done it yet?'

I gave her a frosty look and then burst out laughing. Since our first experiments, we had shared a bed more than once and knew more about one another than we had done a year previously. However, neither of us had made any secret of our desire for male companions.

'Wouldn't you like to know, Cousin Hanna?' I said. 'Maybe. Maybe not. In any event, Sigmund's intentions lie elsewhere. He's forever to be seen with Kati Langenfurth.'

'It's the Langenfurth who's the huntress, and our poor cousin the prey,' said Hanna. She twisted her mouth hither and thither to mimic the High Tongue that was so much the fashion. ' *'Woldest thou nat bedde me, Sirre Knight? Thou connst see my lippes hunger far thine, and my maidenly body pines far a toche of thy stronge armes!'* Only I'll vow she thinks not just of tongues, lips and arms, but of other firm parts. Be assured she'll entrap poor Sigi before long.'

My cheeks burned even more fiercely.

'I'll swear you're unjust to Kati,' I protested in a fluster, 'but if he's so foolish as to engage himself to a harpy, I wish them joy together.'

'Take note of how she pursues him, Gretl,' said my cousin, with a sideways glance at my discomposure. 'You'll be sorry you did not rescue him from her clutches.'

On Midsummer's Eve, a great fair took place at Brunswick. It was the custom at this yearly event for the ladies to parade in their finest clothes, on the arm of their husbands or admirers, drawing envious glances from the townswomen and lecherous looks from their menfolk. In our first year, being newcomers, Hanna and I were paired with two slightly built, smooth-faced lads of no wit who, on pretence of stumbling, would touch us about our persons in a most prurient manner.

Wiser now, after almost two years under the Duke's protection, we determined to enjoy the attractions of our second fair without partners. Hanna saw an opportunity to test her theories concerning our cousin and his supposed lover, but Sigmund was away from Brunswick on a mission, and her plan was frustrated. Resolved, however, to escape from the amorous attention of some other eager squires, we arranged a distraction and slipped away from the rest of the party.

We drew some glances from the older apprentices in the crowd but, ignoring their coarse invitations to dally, we passed on unhindered.

'We're too conspicuous in these clothes,' said I, taking off my cap and letting down my hair.

Hanna inspected the result, and then shook her head.

'You'll never pass for a peasant in that silk gown and those shoes, Gretl,' she said, 'but if you loosen your girdle, the dress will hang lower.'

I did as she suggested.

'That's much better,' she said, and began to alter her appearance as I had done. 'Now, if we rub earth on our shoes, they'll never be noticed, and we'll be taken for town girls.'

These operations completed, we joined the general throng.

Flags and pennants of all colours hung around the field. The escutcheons of the noble families of our province were prominent. All sorts of goods were on display. Wines and sweetmeats were on offer to please the pallet. Perspiring smiths beat swords from fine steel and hammered shoes on their anvils. Horses were traded and other animals bought and sold. There were jugglers, fire-eaters, and keepers of dogs and bears that danced and performed tricks for the amusement of bystanders.

In one corner, a group of musicians played merry tunes, to which all who had a mind danced, chattering and laughing all the while. Another corner had been set aside for a wrestling competition, and there the contestants, their upper torsos oiled and glistening in the sun, locked together in fierce combat.

We saw the occasional monk's tonsure moving among the crowd. The monks enjoyed the entertainment as much as anyone, though they would be quick to censure any behaviour they regarded as lewd. We also caught sight of two black-robed and -hooded individuals who, it appeared, disdained every activity - and the people themselves even more. We took them for churchmen though they were certainly not local priests. They had a most sinister mien.

'Let's watch the jousting,' I suggested, linking arms with Hanna and drawing her away from the wrestlers' perspiring bodies. 'It's more fun when the knights are dressed as fools, their lances are wooden, and their chargers are mules.'

'It is no serious sport when there's no blood,' said Hanna with unnatural relish. 'There's more excitement among the bowmen and falconers. I don't care for archery, but they wager high, and often come to blows when a chance breeze deflects an arrow.'

'The whole afternoon is before us,' I said. 'You'll have your archery and I my jousting. There's time enough for everything.'

We wandered long and happily among the tents and sideshows. At length, engaged in small talk, we crossed the boundary of the main field into a smaller clearing where the tents were fewer, the flags and escutcheons less colourful, and the crowds sparser. In this corner were no proud knights, no tall caps, and little sign of finery.

Here we again felt conspicuous, and would have quit the area but, looking around for the best route to take, were accosted by a strange woman with grey locks and a yellow complexion. She was dressed in black and sat on a stool underneath a canvas awning. Beside her, on a crude table, lay some parchment, a few horoscopes and star charts, and an oval mirror.

'A piece of silver, Li'l Princess,' she called in the Old Saxon dialect. 'A piece of silver, and I read you' future in glass.'

I hesitated. I had not seen Princess Ennia's band since the year before I left Bachhagen, when they had camped in our lower pasture at harvest time. They worked hard and were honest people. However, there were women, young and old, who pretended to be Gypsies, and to tell one's fortune, but whose motives were to distract attention while their husbands or sons stole one's purse.

On the other hand, I had seen Singari that very morning when a group of them passed as we came out of the city gate. Some of them had since erected primitive booths from which they peddled their fine saddles and other splendid leatherwear. The crone who addressed us might well be one of them.

She repeated her call. Hanna laughed and shook her head, but pushed me forward. Seeing no harm, I pressed a silver coin into the woman's hand and waited. She peered into my face. Then, picking up her mirror, she polished it on the sleeve of her blouse and bade me sit on the grass at her feet.

'What you' name, Li'l Princess?' she asked.

'I am called Gretl,' I answered, 'but pray do not call me princess. I am from...'

The Singar held up her hand to silence me.

'It not good I learn family name or parents. Magic work better when I know nothing. Krettel? That begin with letter 'K', no?'

'The first letter is a 'G',' I said, trying not to sound superior.

She held the mirror to her face, breathed upon it so that it clouded over, and wrote a large letter 'G' on it with her forefinger. She then laid the glass on her lap and took hold of both my hands, palms upward. Her fingers were bony and her nails broken.

'A long life be you's, Krettel,' she sang, tracing the lines on my palm and staring all the while into her mirror. 'You bear children - many children - and they be pow'ful in land.'

Again I waited. There was no magic in these predictions. The Gypsy would say only what she thought I would want to hear. She glanced up from her mirror and looked at me intently before returning to it.

'Those eyes entrap many a man,' she crooned. 'You indeed a dark child, and could almost be of Eastern race.'

I drew in my breath. 'My grandfather ...' I began.

'Hush,' she warned, releasing my hands and continuing to stare at the glass. 'You not speak or spell be broken.'

I sat patiently while she closed her eyes and rocked back and forth on her stool. I was curious to discover if anything was really to be seen in the mirror, but did not dare to interrupt. Several moments elapsed before she spoke again. When she did, her words made little sense.

'Guard you' 'heritance, Krettel,' she said, still mispronouncing my name, and repeated the phrase more than once. 'Guard carefully. It should not be locked 'way. And a journey! You must go on journey. Journey where day become night.'

'I don't understand,' I breathed, quaking a little. 'Of what inheritance do you speak? How can day become night?'

This time she did not silence me.

'I tell only what I see in glass,' said she. 'Cannot explain it you.'

'May I look?' I asked, seizing the opportunity to confront my own future, or to catch out the old woman in a lie.

'May look now, Li'l Princess,' she said, resuming the earlier mode of address, 'but you see only reflection. The mirror dark except to those who have gift.'

I half rose and leaned forward to take up her glass, but she restrained me.

'Look, but not touch,' she cautioned. 'Mirror has lasted many generations, and were it broken, could never be replaced with 'nother.'

I looked. To my surprise, the surface had clouded over again, though neither of us had breathed upon it. I truly expected to see nothing but my own image, and to prove her prophesying nothing more than make-believe.

The strangest feeling came over me. Like in a dream, I was moving in space and time. I had given no thought for years to the old tower at Hannover, or to the imagined figure at the window, but now I saw the tower clearly. There was a man at the window but, though he no longer wore a hood, he was too far away for me to see his features.

Then I was in another place, dim and dank. A set of worn steps led from it, upwards to I knew not where. Something brushed my legs, thousands of shadows crowding in on me and hindering my movement.

I came back from my dream, if dream it was. The mist in the gypsy glass was clearing. The outline of a face took shape. Now fully myself, I started back in alarm, for the face I saw was not my own but that of a stranger. He was as dark as I was or darker, clean-shaven, with piercing black eyes and a prominent nose. I might have thought him handsome, only he was completely bald, not thin on the crown with hair growing round the ears and on the back of the head like many men of middle age, but having no hair of any description. I had never seen such a head, or such eyes, yet it seemed to me the visage in the glass was one I ought to recognise.

The Singari woman had seen it too. With a cry, she snatched up the mirror and held it to her bosom. She stared at me and I began to be afraid.

'Who are you?' she croaked, and I saw she trembled as much as I. 'Who are you, child, and whence come this gift of you's? No daughter of Saxon townsman may look in magic glass and see what you see.'

I answered her question with another question.

'That man - the man in the reflection - what is his name? For I can see you know him.' I was terrified beyond all measure and wanted to run, but I remained rooted to the spot.

The woman shook her head vigorously.

'Who are you?' she repeated, grasping my upper arm tightly until it hurt.

'My name is Gretl, as I told you. Gretl von Hasenbach. My father is called Ludwig, my grandfather Sano...'

'This Sano you' gra'father...' she interrupted me, '...he same Sano who marry lady of Brunswick? Healer who always wear gold cross with emblem of sun - cross like this?'

She leaned across the table and selected one of the horoscopes. It was drawn in an Eastern script, and in the top left corner was a crude image of the talisman that always hung at Opa's throat.

'You know my grandfather?' I asked in astonishment. 'How can you know him?'

'Twice I see him. It many yea's ago when our people camp on banks of Leine river, near town of Hannover. He two children with him. Two boys, one like you...' She ran her hand over her face and touched her hair lightly. 'Brown skin. Other pink skin, pale hair.'

'Sano has only one child, Ludwig, my father,' I exclaimed. 'I know of no other.'

She peered into my face, not for the first time, shook her locks again, and released me quite suddenly.

'Not forget what I tell you, Marg'retha von Hasenbach,' she whispered. 'Take good care of you' 'heritance. And beware one who wear Fylfot of Moon, emblem of Angra Mainyu!'

I took to my heels. Hanna was nowhere to be seen, and I wondered what had caused her to run off and leave me alone with the Singari woman. For a while I lost my sense of direction, unable to remember which way I had come. From the left came sounds of music and merrymaking and, judging I was not far from the corner of the main field where the minstrels had played, I set off towards the noise. However, it proved to be a different group, lads with pipes and tambours who stopped playing when I approached and called out to me in a foreign tongue.

I ran on, along an avenue of rude tents, until I arrived at the fringe of a wood. Now I could see that a meadow of long grass separated me from the arena where Hanna and I had first slipped away from our escorts. I stopped for breath, and was about to cross the ground in front of the last tent but one, when I heard raised voices coming from within. The flag that fluttered on the pole above was one I did not recognise.

'I make 'quiries as you ask, Ex'lency,' said one. He spoke the Saxon tongue, but the accent was rough and foreign like that of the fortune-teller. 'Inf'mation not easy to come by.'

'It was a simple task that I set you,' countered a second voice. This was no Singar or peasant but someone used to giving commands. The accent was that of Brunswick. His tone was even, but there was no mistaking the displeasure in it. 'Would you have me go myself?'

'No, Ex'lency,' came the reply.

'Have you discovered anything at all? What of Duke Magnus? Is he for Church or Empire? Does he hold the province together?'

The reply to this question came from a third man. He too seemed cultured. 'The province holds together loosely since the Great Mortality,' he said. 'Families were weakened by plague. Farms are deserted. There are too few craftsmen and the landgraves quarrel amongst themselves.'

'That is as I would have wished it,' said the man of Brunswick almost to himself, 'but it is too soon. Another year or two will make no difference.'

'But the people are restless,' muttered the third speaker.

'It's not enough. The rock must be so unsteady that it requires only a tiny push to topple it over the cliff. When that happens I shall be prepared.' He paused, and it was still enough behind the canvas for me to hear their breathing. Then he went on. 'What of a certain family?'

No one answered.

'What! Will you fail me in this, the most important mission I give you?' said the man of Brunswick. His words reached my ears like an icy blast in winter. The other two were clearly in terror of him. The voice of the fellow who replied shook.

'They say many perished, my lord. Land is under guardianship.'

'Is that all? It is so with many estates! I must know more than that. You will visit again in the west, in the county of Bachhagen. Learn what you can of Assano von Hasenbach, or whatever he calls himself now - whether he lives or no - and bring me news before the month is out. I would have news too of a son, and whether he survived the Mortality. Ludwig is his name.'

Behind the canvas flap, I gave a gasp. For the second time that day, I had heard a stranger speak of my grandfather, and now my father's name too had been uttered in my presence. I had not understood all of what I had overheard but was sure a plot was afoot, and it involved my family. The men inside the tent had stopped talking. If they were indeed conspirators, I did not wish to be discovered. I prepared for flight across the meadow.

Before I could move, there were footsteps behind me and a brown hand took hold of my wrist, pushing me towards the tent entrance. My captor was a swarthy fellow whose appearance matched the coarser voice I had heard. He may have been a Singar or one of those men who pretended to that people for gain. His black oily hair was as long as a matron's, reaching almost to his waist, and tied at the neck with leather thongs so that it fell over his back like the tail of a pony. He was young, not more than eighteen years of age, and he wore a jacket with no sleeves that exposed a chest covered in black hair, like an ape. The flap was pulled back by a man dressed in a black robe and hood.

The Singar, if indeed he was one, thrust me to the ground at the feet of the man whom they had addressed as Excellency. I looked up, and saw bending over me the face that had so recently stared back at me from the seer's mirror, the face that was to haunt my dreams and my waking hours for years to come.

The man was scarcely taller than I was, and of slighter build than those he commanded. From his bearing and dress I took him to be a nobleman. His nose was more prominent than I had imagined from the vision. The shadow of shaven hair was evident on his smooth skull and chin. He was dressed in a black tunic with gold braiding on the cuffs. There was a sword in a sheath at his side and a poniard tucked into his belt.

'A pretty fish you have caught me today,' he laughed, showing a set of white, even teeth. 'A little spy, if I'm not mistaken.'

His mood was relaxed and the Singar grinned at the thought of having pleased him. The hooded monk clearly took me for the maid I pretended to be and glared at me contemptuously.

'Leave me! You too, Erhart!' The man of Brunswick threw a glance in his companions' direction, and they both withdrew. He helped me to my feet but his black eyes never left me for a moment.

'You are a tasty piece, and no common maid, to judge by the quality of that gown. Who are you, and what brings you to Akhtar's tent, so far from the music and dancing?'

Akhtar! It was no Saxon name. He spoke courteously, but there was coldness in his manner that made me wary. Moreover, he was planning mischief against our family and property. It would not do for him to learn my identity.

'I'm Lisa,' I said, selecting the first name that came into my head. 'My father is a townsman of Brunswick, and will be searching for me already. Please let me go back to him. I've done no harm, and was not spying on you.'

'Would you not keep me company a while longer?' he begged. 'Your father may gaze on your beauty for the rest of time if I can have it for but one evening.'

'Do not detain me, sir, I pray you,' I said.

I looked about me. The tent was of a good size and had been intended, I fancied, for the storage of equipment for one of the sideshows. There were boxes heaped in one corner, some poles and a coil of rope, but nothing I could conveniently use as a weapon against him. I measured the distance to the flap and prepared to run.

'It's my pleasure to detain you, pretty Lisa,' said Akhtar. His eyes were fixed on mine, and they seemed to grow wider and brighter. The voice was gentler than when I had first heard him speak, and it came to me as if from far away. I found that I was unable to move.

Akhtar ran the fingers of one hand through my hair. Like faces in a dream, his began to dissolve and change shape. The hook nose straightened, thick blond locks sprouted on the crown of his head, and the chin grew a beard.

All at once, I came to my senses. The feeling of repose and deep contentment that I was beginning to experience was changing to one of utter terror. He was an enchanter, and held me in a spell. The noble face I saw was an illusion, and the only reality was the shaven skull pressed horribly against my cheek. Still I could not move.

Akhtar bent over me, forcing my body backwards and down onto the well-trodden turf. He laid one hand on my neck as, with his mouth, he sought my lips, my ears, my eyes, and my throat, covering them with his vile kisses, and breathing his foul breath into my nostrils. With his other hand, he lifted the hem of my gown and began stroking my thigh.

I struggled to free myself from his hold, but he was stronger and pushed me to the ground. My mouth was free and I bit him hard on the face so that the blood ran from the wound and fell in drops on my shoulders and breasts. The pain seemed to fire his passion all the more, and he continued to explore my body with open lips. His cruel hands were pressing against my knees, trying to force them apart.

'No one has resisted me with such strength before,' he said, panting and laying his full weight on me, 'but your struggles will be in vain, my sweet Lisa, and my pleasure will be all the greater.'

Although I knew his purpose well enough, I had in my innocence no real inkling of what was to come. I opened my mouth to scream, but no sound came. I beat him about the head and tried to bite him again, but he laughed. No words can describe, nor do I wish to recall the feeling of disgust and loathing, mixed with helplessness and despair, that came upon me as, brushing aside my weak resistance, he thrust himself between my thighs and pierced my maidenhead.

Thus ravished, and in agony of body and mind, I fainted.

iii

When I came to myself, I was alone.

His passion spent, Akhtar had crept away, no doubt with some other dark plan in mind. Fearing myself to be a prisoner and the tent guarded by his Singar servant or the black-hooded man, I crawled forward towards the flap and peered out. Every part of me ached. My arms were bruised, my shoulders scratched, and my dress was smeared with blood and soil.

No one was in sight. The sounds of the fair had died down for it was now late afternoon, and many revellers would have returned to the city. I stumbled into the meadow and vomited in the long grass.

Ahead of me were the city walls, still a long way off, and behind was the scene of my dishonour. I could not face the ladies of Brunswick as I was. My home was far away to the west, perhaps three days on foot I thought, and I might face untold other dangers if I tried to walk such a distance alone. In any case, how would I begin to explain my condition to an honourable father?

A little to my right was a grove of trees. They would at least hide me until I could decide what to do. With sudden resolve, I reversed my footsteps and plunged into the wood.

With no thought of the hour, or of what I might meet there, I went on and on, stopping only to pull up a few nourishing roots and pick some berries I knew to be harmless and refreshing. They were not fully ripe and left a sour after-taste on my palate. At length I was overcome by tiredness and by my throbbing, aching head, and I sat down to rest against the trunk of a chestnut tree. My eyes closed and I slept.

I awoke in near darkness. Noisy insects buzzed around my face and small night creatures rushed past me in the bushes. Remembering it was Midsummer's Eve, I looked up, and saw that the sky through the branches of the trees was grey with a faint glow. A few stars were visible. Not far from where I sat were lights. There was the smell of cooking and the sound of laughter and conversation. I crept towards the light, and came upon a clearing where a group of peasants were roasting a pig on a spit.

The flames of their torches cast long shadows, revealing the poverty of the costumes and the kindly honesty of the faces. That these were village folk about to celebrate the turn of the year I was in no doubt. Newcomers were arriving all the while, some with more torches, others with flagons of wine.

An elderly matron spotted me standing by the trees and beckoned me to come forward.

'Do not stan' there, Daughter,' she called. 'The meat is ready, and if tha wishes to share it tha 'ad better be quick. These hungry fellows would 'ave it all, and leave us poor womenfolk to starve.'

I needed no second bidding for I was as hungry as a wolf. As I came into the light, she glanced with curiosity at my stained and soiled dress, my dainty shoes, and the marks on my arms, but to my relief she asked no questions. She took my hand and led me to the fire. I guessed she had lost her entire family in the plague and longed for company, even that of a stranger.

The villagers numbered about twenty. Strips of succulent meat were cut from the boar and passed, piping hot, round the company. There was plenty for all, and we washed it down with rough country wine. When all the food was consumed, some lads brought wooden pipes, squatted on the turf, and began to play. The sound recalled to me how my father sometimes used to play on the flute, and I was struck by a sudden loneliness and pangs of longing for my home and kin.

'The dancing will cheer you,' said the kindly woman, seeing my tears.

She took hold of my hand again, and we joined the ring of merrymakers that had formed around the embers of the fire. The music was lively but I was in no mood for dancing and followed the steps stiffly and uncomfortably. I was beginning to hurt again.

Then the dancing stopped and the tone of the music turned to one of melancholy. I recalled then some of the Singari melodies I had heard when I visited Ennia's camp at Hannover.

Someone banged a tambour, and out of the shadows emerged two figures, their heads and faces covered by black hoods, with slits cut for the eyes. They carried baskets of leaves and finely cut herbs that they strewed around the clearing, so that the summer air was filled with the scent of spices and firs. They were followed by two peasants dressed as clergy, who rang bells and scattered incense.

The dancing began anew and there was much sniffing and sneezing amongst the villagers as the fragrances were carried to their nostrils by the breeze. The drum was struck for a second time and the pipers abruptly stopped playing. A deathly silence fell on the company, broken only by the rustling of leaves in the wood, and the occasional gasp of anticipation from a child. The dancers threw themselves on the grass and lay still, save one who seemed to spring from the trees. This figure - I could not tell whether man or woman - wore a dark red cape and a grotesque mask that showed a ghostly white under the light from the torch flames.

The pipers played again, slowly - a dirge whose notes I thought familiar, while the masked figure danced alone, stepping high, leaping across the dying embers, the red cloak swirling, as it darted here and there amongst the prone watchers. It came to me that I was witnessing the Dance of Death, a gruesome enactment of the Great Mortality, in which the masked figure represented Death itself, and the mournful melody piped by the musicians was a shrill parody of the priests' chant, Dies Irae - the intonation for the dead at the Day of Judgement.

All at once, the dancer feigned a leap in the direction of a family group on the edge of the circle, but at the last moment moved swiftly and cunningly to the left. She seized an unsuspecting youth by both shoulders, wrapped him in the folds of the cape, and whisked him off to the centre, where the captive was perforce made to dance clumsily the steps rendered with agility by the Death player.

I had decided the dancer was a woman, so delicate was the figure, so nimble the steps, and so sinewy the movements of the body. I had seen entertainers at the court dance like that, most often men of slight build who could twist themselves into all manner of impossible shapes, but I could conceive of no smallholder or peasant having the skill for it. The whole process was repeated until, having performed some new leaps and turns, the figure of Death glanced in the direction of where I sat with a cup of wine. In truth, I had drunk rather a lot of the heavy liquid, which, although unpleasant to my taste at first, had provided me with what I most craved - relief from my bodily pain, and from the memory of my ordeal.

Nearer and nearer the dancer came. The pale mask flickered with a red and orange light from the fading fires. The cape billowed as the figure swerved cunningly from my neighbour and reached out to take hold of me. I saw the arms. They were a man's arms, muscular and covered with thick hair. In an instant all my shame and agony returned. I saw in front of me not the plaster and paint of a mummer's disguise, but the face of my violator. The billowing cloak became the walls and flap of the tent, the scene of my humiliation, and the hands reaching out to snatch me into the Dance of Death were in my mind's eye those of the man who had robbed me of my childhood. I uttered a scream of terror, the blood rushed to my head, and my senses again left me.

iv

I awoke on a bed of straw. It was just past daybreak, and there was enough light for me to see I was in a peasant cottage. The woman who had befriended me the evening before was bending over me. She handed me a cup. Thinking it was more wine I shook my head.

'Drink it, Daughter,' she said, ' 'Tis only water from the stream.'

'Thank you, good Mother,' I replied, using the same idiom she had employed, and drank. She regarded me strangely, as if uncertain whether to begin a conversation.

'I've washed some of the dirt from tha face an' hands,' she said at length. 'They were much in need of it. 'Tis a great pity 'bout the gown ...'

She hesitated, and ran her fingers along the silk hem.

'Some stains will never wash out,' she went on gravely, and with double meaning.

I hung my head and did not answer.

'Tha should be with thy mother, child, and not walking 'lone in this rough country.'

'My mother is dead of the plague. There is only my father and ...'

'Fathers is fools, an' blind too when their daughters turn to women. A child who wears such a dress as thee must have female kin t' care for her.'

'I cannot go home,' I muttered, and turned away. She would not see me weep. The effects of the wine had worn off and I felt more wretched than ever.

'Would that I'd such as thee to come home to me,' said she sadly. 'I'd two daughters once, aye, an' gran'daughters too, but the Mortality took 'em, 'long with an 'usband an' son.'

I had guessed her circumstances correctly, and my heart was filled with pity for her. She was old, much older than I had taken her to be in the torchlight.

'I'm truly sorry, mistress,' said I, facing her again and laying my hand lightly on her arm. 'You have been kind to me, and if it were possible to make your life easier, I would gladly do it. But those lost to us can never be brought back.'

'Th'art a wise child, as well as pretty an' of good family. It grieves me that tha should lie with a youth who's such an oaf.'

I saw that she had misunderstood my condition. She had seen the bruising on my arms and shoulders through the tears in the dress. She had seen the blood too, and had drawn her own conclusion.

'I was forced,' I managed to blurt out, and hung my head again.

'Then go home, child. If tha were inn'cent, there's no shame. Some of the village maidens will escort thee to the city gate. Brunswick is not so far, after all.'

'I would not go to Brunswick, good Mother,' I said, thinking of Hanna and hoping she had returned safely. 'My way lies in the direction of Hannover.'

'That's on the other side of the world, Daughter.'

My cap was long lost, but I remembered I still had my purse with a coin or two in it. Akhtar had not deprived me of that.

'I can ride,' I said. 'If there's a pony for hire in the village, I can pay well.'

The peasant woman seemed amused. A tolerant smile creased her pale countenance.

'In the whole village there's only one donkey,' she told me, 'an' he's so old he could not take thee to the next village, let 'lone half way to Hannover.'

'What am I to do?' I cried.

For answer she rose, went towards a dark corner of the hovel and returned a few moments later with a bundle of rags. She unravelled it and placed the items on the ground before me. There was a pair of coarse canvas breeches, a torn shirt and man's jacket, sandals and a cap.

'If th'art determined, then a youth will attract less attention on the road than a maid. I've kept these garments many a long year. Leave me the gown! It's ruined but I may be able to repair it to suit a village girl. Take thy money with thee. Pr'aps it may buy thee a ride, or a crust to eat.'

So it was arranged. Clad in peasant's garb, I was escorted to the high road. The shirt smelled musty and irritated my skin but I soon became used to it. I walked until the sun was high in the midsummer sky, when I was overtaken by a man and woman driving a wagon, who allowed me to share their provisions and offered me company as far as the town of Hildesheim. My throat was dry and my voice husky, so there was no need to pretend the tones of a youth.

The following day I fell in with some friars travelling west from the church of Saint Michael. We made slow progress, for they made it their business to accost every wayfarer and rider whom they came across, or who overtook us. My feet were bruised and sore, and I had the utmost difficulty maintaining even my companions' unhurried pace. However, I felt secure in their society, and they were too preoccupied to take me for anything other than I seemed. Even so, I was uneasy when one of them approached too closely lest he penetrate my disguise. Of men on horseback I was doubly wary, and would stand well back from the road when the friars hailed one and engaged in conversation.

When evening fell on the fourth day after leaving Brunswick, we begged hospitality at a small settlement that I was surprised to find I recognised, being close to the border of the Hasenbach estate. In the morning, I bade farewell to the friars, and, before noon, I stood on the hill overlooking the River Leine and that part of the valley in which our manor house stood.

I knew where I would go. I needed time to think how I would excuse my presence, explain my appearance, look my father in the eye and tell him that I was dishonoured. I was fairly sure I was not impregnated, but what if I were wrong and had conceived a child in my shame. Once alone again, the pain and humiliation returned and I berated myself for having been foolish enough to leave the protection of the court party. More than once I found myself wondering about the gift of which the Singari woman had spoken - for I saw Akhtar everywhere - and whether I was blessed, or cursed, by having any power to look into the future.

I skirted the boundary of the manor house, picking roots and berries to keep hunger at bay. I avoided the church and, my footsteps very weary now, climbed to the coppice where stood the entrance to my mother's tomb. All was quiet. I pushed open the gate, crossed myself hastily, entered the chamber, and fell to my knees at my dear mother's grave.

I do not know how long I remained there. My tears fell unhindered on the cold stone, and I prayed aloud to any god or saint who might be listening to come to my aid and tell me what to do. The air in the tomb was cold, and I shivered. The only sounds were those produced by my own breathing and by drops of water falling on the coffins from the dome of the roof. I sat on the damp floor, my back against the stone, my legs drawn up and my hands covering my face.

He entered the chamber so silently that my ears picked up not the slightest noise, until a footfall to my left dislodged a pebble from the rock, and I started up in terror. A gentle hand was laid on my shoulder, and a soft, well-loved voice spoke my name.

'Gretl?'

I looked up to see the grave, bearded face of my grandfather, and with a great sigh threw myself tearfully into his arms.

He did not speak, but held me while I related all that had occurred. When I pronounced the name of my violator, he drew in a sharp breath and such a look came over his face as made me recoil from him. It might have been anger; I had never seen him truly angry. Yet there was something else there too, in the taught jaw and furrowed brow. It reminded me, though I had been but a child then, of the time when the peasant boy and his mother died in our house.

By the time I had finished my tale he seemed himself again. He pressed his lips to my tear-stained cheek.

'What will I do, Opa?' I said. 'What will I do? I can't face the stares of the household, neither my cousins, nor Matti, nor even the servants. My father least of all. I've disgraced the family, and I hate myself for it. He put a spell on me and now I can see only his eyes in my head....'

Opa laid a finger against my mouth and silenced me.

'A spell, yet not a spell,' he said, half to himself. Then he looked me in the eye. His expression was grim. 'No one must know of this yet, Gretl. No one! I will choose the time.'

I clung to his neck, unconsoled.

'Forgive me, Opa,' I cried miserably. 'Forgive me!'

'There's nothing for me to forgive. You have been used abominably by a fiend in human flesh. It is I who should beg your forgiveness, for it is I who am to blame for your misfortune.'

'You? How can you be to blame for what I brought upon myself with my thoughtlessness?'

'I have a tale to tell you, Gretl - a true one. Its telling is long overdue. But first, if you trust me, there's a way I can restore you. If spell there was, I can reverse it.'

I watched him, half in awe, and half in expectation as he removed the fylfot from his neck. He held it up so that a shaft of sunlight through the bars of the gate caught the bright surface, and I could see clearly the emblem of the sun engraved in the metal.

'Keep your eyes on it, Gretl,' he said softly. 'Rest them on the sun's image, draw your breath deeply, and listen to me.'

I took a deep breath and tried to empty my mind of the horrors of the past few days. However, no matter how hard I fought the images, I could not entirely rid myself of them: the face in the mirror, the shaven head, and Akhtar's cold eyes. I blinked and my concentration was lost.

'Do not struggle against it,' said Opa, without raising his voice. 'Do not think of that man, or of your pain and humiliation. Remember instead a happy moment and pay attention only to the bent cross and the emblem on it.'

I tried again. With my eyes fixed on the fylfot, I thought of my mother and of the time she had told me of her pregnancy; I thought of my pony, Princess, and how I had first seen her saddled and bridled in the blacksmith's yard. Gradually, I felt my taught muscles relax.

'Listen to me, Gretl,' Opa said, his voice now no more than a whisper. 'Listen. The healing rays of the sun are touching you, warming you. They sweep away all thoughts of pain from your mind. Your discomfort is passing already. You will remember, but the memory will be free of guilt and shame. The sun's power mends the broken flesh. It restores peace and comfort to your mind. Sleep for a moment and, when you awake, you will feel only contentment.'

Though the light in the chamber was dim, the fylfot seemed to glow fiercely. As I stared at it, I felt weightless. All the burdens I had carried for four days, fear, humiliation and lost pride seemed to melt away before the magic of my grandfather's words. I floated on wings of light to the vault of the ceiling and back to earth again.

I awoke from the trance to meet Opa's wise and tolerant smile.

'Are you recovered?' He held the fylfot in the palm of his hand, the shaft of light no longer upon it. I felt wholly sound in limb and in mind.

'How did you find me?' I asked. 'How did you know I would be here? And what is this magic you have worked ...?'

'You know better than that, Gretl,' he answered. 'There is no magic, except that already in you. As to why I am here - why not? Why not, when it is my solace too? But I shall explain all in good time, Gretl. First, you should bathe, then a change of costume, I think. Finally, what do you say to a small loaf, some fresh cheese, and a cup of milk?'

I rode with him silently, seated astride his horse's rump with my arms wrapped around his waist. My father was not at home though, in any case, I felt no great need to unburden myself to anyone else. It was Opa who had found me. He had healed my anguish, and had restored my spirits. If it had been done by magic, that magic was wholly wonderful and good in my eyes. And if there was no magic, what of the strange and frightening vision in the mirror, and of the very last words spoken to me by the old Singari woman? Who or what was Angra Mainyu, and what could be meant by the Fylfot of the Moon?

The Legend

Jemshid, son of Tahmuras, ruled Persia for seven hundred years. He was a wise and just monarch, skilled in forging weapons, weaving fine cloths, and shaping ornaments from silver and gold. They say he discovered medicine and knew cures for all the sicknesses suffered by the people of his country.

His most valued possession was a seven-ringed cup, one ring for each of the planets, a gift of the gods, in which he was able to see the whole world, past, present and future.

King Jemshid had two daughters, whom he loved equally, and spoiled equally with lavish gifts. Their names were Shahrinaz and Arnawaz. Both were beautiful in their own way; but whereas Shahrinaz had fair skin and golden hair, Arnawaz had a complexion and hair as dark as a starless night.

When the girls were sixteen, Jemshid gave each of them the most wonderful present of all - a gold necklace made by his own hand. On each gold chain hung a talisman of well-being - one of the su-asti, crosses on which each of the four arms was bent at right angles.

To Shahrinaz he presented the cross with arms bent to the right. In its centre was engraved the emblem of the sun god, Ormazd. To her sister he presented the left-handed cross, which carried the engraving of a crescent moon, symbol of Ahriman, god of darkness. For Jemshid honoured both gods and was afraid of offending either.

As it happened, the adjacent country was ruled by a prince named Zohak, who had been tricked by a demon into murdering his father and stealing his throne. Zohak was determined to seize the throne of Persia too and, at the head of a huge army, crossed her borders. King Jemshid was a proud man, blinded by his love and by his daughters' charms. He took no account of their different characters. A seventh part of his magic cup was dark and he did not see the danger until it was too late.

Because Zohak was handsome, Arnawaz fell in love with him and came under his influence. She conspired with him to kill her father so that she could become queen herself.

Whereas Jemshid had been a just ruler, Zohak used magic to oppress the people, and they lived in fear of him. On his shoulder and that of his queen, where once they were kissed by the evil lord Ahriman, grew two black snakes that consumed human brains, and each day the pair offered two of their subjects as sacrifice to these monsters. As for Arnawaz, because she wore the emblem of the dark god round her neck, she held the real power in the kingdom and through her Zohak ruled for a thousand years.

Shahrinaz was determined to avenge her father. She was patient, and prayed to Ormazd to help her.

The sun god answered. 'Is light not always greater than darkness? When the sun rises, does not the moon flee? You already have the means to lift the shadow of your sister from the land. She is Ahriman's creature, and cannot bear the sunshine.

'Take the su-asti, the cross your father gave you, and go to the palace. Hold my image in front of your sister, so that the daylight is reflected upon it, and the power of the one she wears will be broken. Then you will see Arnawaz as she really is.'

Shahrinaz hesitated. 'And what of Zohak? Even if my sister is destroyed, he is still king.'

'His time will come,' answered Ormazd. 'I have already decided his fate and have chosen your son, Faridan, to be the instrument.'

'My son is just a child,' Shahrinaz protested.

'Have faith,' answered the god. 'He will grow. When Arnawaz is no more, give the su-asti to Faridan, so that he will be protected from evil, and will be able to accomplish the task I shall set for him.'

Shahrinaz did as she was asked. When she held up the su-asti of the sun, Arnawaz screamed in terror and her human form shrivelled up until all that remained was a black serpent.

Then Shahrinaz said to her, 'Because you were once my sister, I will spare your life, but from today you are banished from human company. Crawl away to the desert, and to the wild places of the earth where you belong.'

As the creature slunk away, the cross of the moon fell from its body and was lost forever in the sand.

When Faridan was sixteen, Shahrinaz placed the su-asti of the sun god around his neck.

'Now you are ready to fulfil your destiny,' she said. 'Go and break forever *the power of Zohak. Lift the shadow of fear from the people and restore justice to the land.*

'But remember! Because the su-asti was a present to me from my father Jemshid, and because I now give it to you, it should always be passed from father to daughter and from mother to son, down through the generations.

'And tell your children this: the su-asti of the sun god will protect them as long as they do not allow evil into their hearts. For, should that happen, it will be as if they wore the left-hand cross of Arnawaz.

'Goodness will be despised, and the creatures of the night will rule again in the world!'

ii

I sat with my grandfather on a bench in the herb garden. He had managed to distract Matti long enough so that she did not see me in tattered boys clothing. A servant had brought me some water and I had washed as best I could before donning one of my mother's old gowns. Ludwig had never been able to throw them away.

We had finished our meal. It was a warm, sunny afternoon. Bees and other insects buzzed around the tips of lavender and sage. From time to time, a dragonfly would hover above our heads before darting for the nearby pond.

For the second time that day, Opa took the fylfot and chain from his neck. He gave it to me. Its weight surprised me, and I nearly let it fall.

'Tell me about it, Opa,' I begged him. 'And is it truly possible to see into the future?'

'Many people in the East wear hooked crosses,' he said. 'They are supposed to bring good fortune if worn as mine is, with the hooks pointing to the right. A fylfot with hooks pointing in the opposite direction is the symbol of evil. Such an ornament is worn by those who follow the Dark Path - necromancers and their like.'

I turned the cross over in my hand. Its chain was fixed at two points, mid-way along opposing legs. When looked at from this position, the hooks bent to the left.

'They're but mirror images of one another,' I said, laughing. 'How can one side bring good luck and the other bad?'

91

'Be patient and I will tell you,' said Opa, and he looked so grave that I stopped laughing and bit my lip. 'Did you know I was born in Persia, Gretl?'

'Yes,' I said. 'Ennia told me. She said you were children together. You lived in a castle, and had lots of adventures. But then you had to part, she told me.'

'She told you nothing else of my history, or of hers?'

I shook my head.

Opa smiled. 'So she did not break her promise! I expected no less of her.'

'Who was she, Opa? Who was Ennia? I asked you once before and you would not answer me.'

'I will tell you soon, Gretl. Ennia will be in my story but you must let me tell it in my own way.' He took the fylfot from me, laid it on the stone beside him, and continued. 'This necklace, fylfot and chain, came to me from my mother. Her name was Nadia. She was descended from the kings and priests who ruled in Persia more than eight hundred years ago.'

He smoothed some earth with the sole of his boot, bent over, and traced a crescent moon with his finger as if to lend mystery to his tale.

'You see, Gretl, the old Persians had two gods – Ormazd, the god of light, and Ahriman or Angra Mainyu, the god of darkness. And at the beginning there were two fylfots.' Again, he bent forward and traced this time two more shapes in the flattened soil, one with arms right facing like his own, the other its mirror image. Then he told me of King Jemshid and his daughters, Shahrinaz and Arnawaz: how he had presented to each of them one of the su-asti; how Arnawaz had betrayed her father with Zohak; and how Ormazd had punished her for her wickedness.

When he reached the climax, he frowned. Slowly and deliberately, he drew his foot across the three symbols he had drawn and removed all trace of them. I realised I was holding my breath.

'It was said that the su-asti of Shahrinaz should never be allowed to fall into the hands of anyone with evil in his heart,' he finished. 'Were that to happen, it would become by the power of Angra Mainyu the lost fylfot of the moon. Virtue would be despised, sorcery honoured, and the creatures of the night released upon the world.'

'It's a splendid tale, Opa,' I said with a nervous laugh, breaking the spell his narrative had cast over me. 'A little awesome too! But it's only legend surely, like all the other stories you used to tell?'

'Of course,' he said. 'But there is truth in there somewhere. Just as there are truths in all the religions and faiths of the world. That is what my mother taught me and it is a principle that has guided my life. I was fortunate that she lived long enough to teach me so much, even when I had grown past the age when men become their own masters.'

At this, a lump came to my throat and my eyes grew misty. I sank my chin on my chest so that Opa would not see my tears. But he knew my distress and patted my hand.

'I wish I had known her ... Nadia, your mother,' I said.

'I do too, Gretl. She was a woman with great gifts.'

I raised my head and would have sworn that his eyes too were damp. The sadness I had often seen when he told his stories was there now, the memory of adventures shared and of friends and lovers long lost. I began to understand him at last, or so I thought.

'My mother had one gift above the others,' he said. 'Some would say a curse. It was the gift the old Singar spoke of to you - the ability to look, however imperfectly, into the future. Her visions came and went, and she did not always interpret them correctly. They could make her happy or sad. She was never able to explain how she came by the power, but it was real.

'Nadia had other gifts too. She had a skill with roots and herbs, which she taught to me, and the ability to heal pain, not with medicines, but by contact with the mind. While many ailments could be treated with medicines, she said, others arose because of the condition of the sick person's mind. The cure was therefore best accomplished by the patients themselves. If they could be made to believe in it, a cup of water could become an emetic, or an anodyne, or a restorative. It was an example of this skill that I used with you today. A thing of beauty or a happy memory can bring about a miracle.'

'Then the fylfot *does* have magic powers?'

'Some would say so,' Opa said. 'In truth, it is an aid only. The magic already resides in all of us. And now you have seen this Akhtar has

Nadia's skill. But he uses it for evil and needs no fylfot to aid his power. You, it seems, have the gift of visions, albeit in small measure. I cannot explain otherwise why you should see Akhtar in the Singari glass. Unless it was a trick.'

'But why, Opa, and how? I don't think it was a trick. The Gypsy woman reacted with terror to the vision, as I did.'

'You have the gift, then. I wonder if the other ability is in you too, Gretl, undeveloped until now. Your father knows nothing of these things. He sees only the good in the world.'

He took up the fylfot again and fingered the gold surface almost absent-mindedly. 'It's a clever artefact,' he said after a long silence, 'and worthy of the master smith who made it. The arms are hollow and I use them to hold my most potent medicines. The join is almost invisible to the eye.'

He twisted one of the fylfot's arms and it came apart at the elbow, exposing a tiny thread. It occurred to me that, were he to remove all four, he would be left with a remarkably Christian cross.

'Perhaps if I had taken greater care of it, no one would have suffered,' said Opa. He reconnected the pieces and replaced the chain around his neck. 'Perhaps the army of rats would not have swept across the land bringing with them plague and death. Perhaps you would have been spared this ordeal!

'I've made it my life's work to study the sciences, and I know there is natural order in the universe. Yet there is much my science cannot explain. Men invent legends to explain it: how the world came into being; how the stars turn in the sky; what is the meaning of a vision in a glass. I do not believe the legends, but because I can't explain matters in another way, I doubt, and in the doubt lies my guilt.

'Akhtar held the fylfot in his hands once and worked mischief with it.' Now there was anger in his tone. 'Oh yes, I know him, Gretl, though Akhtar was not always his name. I know him, and to think that ...'

His voice trailed away and I waited, knowing in my heart there was more pain and guilt to come.

'It's time to tell you everything,' he went on. 'Ennia and I once judged you too young to understand. And I made her promise to keep our secrets.

But she is gone and I now acknowledge I was wrong. Wrong to make her promise. Wrong to keep the truth from you.

'We had grown up together, as she told you. My birth name was Hassan. I was neither Sano nor von Hasenbach in those days, though I think you know that already. Both my mother and Ennia's were wives of the Khan - the ruler of Persia - though we had different fathers.'

'How was that possible?'

'It is not unusual in the East for a man to have several wives, nor was it unusual, at the time I speak of, for wives to be inherited.'

'That is unjust,' I said. 'Are women to be treated as possessions for men's pleasure?'

'I am of the same opinion,' said Opa. 'Still, I cannot speak for all men, even here in Saxony. In some parts of this land, women may be treated no better. In Persia today, the marriage laws are different, or so I have been told. In my youth, things were as they were.

'When I was eleven years old, the Khan died. Nadia married a Venetian nobleman and we went to live in Italy. I was adopted. We had left Persia hastily and during violent times and I did not know if Ennia was still alive. I did not know if I would ever see her again.

'I lived in Venice four years, Gretl, but I was determined to go back to Persia. I longed to see the mountains and the deserts again. It is not something I can explain, but I knew I had to go back.

'I wanted adventure, excitement and to make my name as a warrior. And truly, I was to see war. In three years, I was to see so much war and death that I was sickened by it. It is not only enemies who die, but friends too. There is no glory in killing, Gretl, even when there is a cause to fight. I learned that soon enough.'

He spoke more sadly and bitterly than I had ever heard him do before.

'We are told to love our enemies, Opa,' I said, 'but I do not think that is an easy thing to do.'

'And difficult to forgive them, as the churches would have us do,' he said. 'But not so difficult to stray from the subject!

'I returned to Persia and took up the sword. There was a cause to fight. My half-brother, Ghazan, who should have been Khan, was denied his birthright by an ambitious cousin. I joined the rebels. We fought the usurper and defeated him. After the war, I entered Ghazan's service. I went with him on a campaign against the people you call Saracens. Then I became an envoy. And a merchant. My grandfather - Nadia's father - had died and made me his heir, so I was rich in my own right. I had gold, property and a share in many business enterprises.

'I travelled and traded. My missions took me to Constantinople ... to Greece, Venice and Rome. I met princes, dukes and bishops and became known among the merchant guilds.' He paused and fixed me with an expression I hadn't seen since I was a child, at once mysterious and meaningful - the way he looked when coming to the end of one of his tales. Except, this time, he had scarcely begun.

'I married too, Gretl!'

'Married?'

'Why not? Yes, I had a wife. Her name was Doquz.'

I tried to copy the sound of the name. Opa laughed and repeated it. 'You see, the eastern languages are not so easy. But you will hear of Doquz again and again. Perhaps if I tell you that the name means *nine* in the language of the Mongol peoples, you will see why!'

I was baffled and it must have shown on my face. Opa laughed again.

'Have you forgotten your Greek?'

'Greek, Opa?' I was still baffled. 'I learned only Latin.'

'But that is not quite true. You used to recite the numbers to me. *Ena ... theo ... tria ...*'

He was right, but it had been so long ago that I had all but forgotten. I was eight or nine years old. Opa had taught me to count in the Italian language, and in Greek, and in English. *Counting is the language of business*, he had told me, *and they that know it cannot easily be swindled*. I began to recite now, at first hesitantly to myself. *Tessera ... pende ... eksi ...*

Then I reached *nine*. I must have been half-witted, I think, for even after I had blurted out the word, it was several moments before I realised what I had just said. Excitement flooded through my whole being. My heart beat fast and I leapt to my feet with a cry of delight.

'*Ennia* - nine in the Greek language is *ennia*! And Doch ... Doquz. They were one and the same?'

'Yes, Gretl.' Opa smiled his most enigmatic smile.

'But I don't understand. How could she be your wife?'

'Patience,' he said. 'Let me explain.

'Ennia's ... Doquz's life was not always easy after I left Persia the first time. Her mother remarried in accordance with the custom and it was expected of Doquz that she too make a political marriage. But Doquz had a mind of her own. She had studied history and the sciences and had learned swordcraft. And she could shoot an arrow too, straight and true, and strike down an enemy at two hundred paces.

'She escaped the marriage and joined the rebelllion. And it was in the rebel camp that we were reunited.

'How can I explain what she was like in those days? You knew her only as an old woman, Gretl, withered and grey. But she was smooth-skinned and beautiful then. A proper princess. She was wild and stubborn too and I loved her for it. I had always loved her as a sister though we were not related by blood. Now I loved her as a man loves a wife. When the rebellion was over and Ghazan was Khan, we stayed together. Sometimes, she would travel with me on my missions.'

I watched him moisten his lips and waited for him to go on, remembering what Ennia herself had once said to me about her love for him. They were the Prince and Princess after all, I thought, but if that were true how did it come about that he forsook her for another - my grandmother - and left her to wander the world in a Singari band? And if he and Ennia were truly married, what did that mean for my father and for me? It was a question I did not dare contemplate.

'One day,' Opa said at last, 'I received a letter from my mother. It would have been towards the end of the year 1302, I think. She and my stepfather were to have another child. Their third.

'Of course, such letters are rare and take many months to reach their destination, that is, when they reach it at all. Nadia's letter was almost a year old when I received it and, of course, the child had already been born. But its arrival was timely because I was about to go on my travels again.

'Doquz had never seen Venice and I wanted her to come with me. But she refused. She said Nadia had first claim on my love; it was she who had nourished and protected me for the first fifteen years of my life; my little sister and brother, Yasmina and Nico, would be missing me, and I should see the new baby. We should all have a few months together before she intruded on us. She would wait six months and then follow me to Italy. We knew a merchant who crossed the ocean regularly and she would take passage with him, as his daughter.

'I did not understand women, Gretl, and I did not understand love. I sailed for Venice alone.'

We had been in the garden for hours and I could tell that Opa was tiring. Already his voice sounded strained. The afternoon shadows had lengthened though the sun was still strong and the summer warmth had not abated. Several times he wiped the perspiration from his brow. I fetched a flagon of wine from the cellar, filled a second with fresh water from the well and, when we had drunk, asked him to continue with his story. I wanted the truth; I wanted an explanation.

'My business completed, I stayed with my family for almost a year. Doquz did not come. So I left Italy and travelled back as far as Constantinople. There I heard that one of the ships on which I relied for my trade had been lost in a storm in the Aegean Sea. That was a blow in itself but much worse was to come. I returned to Persia to learn that Doquz had left as promised, several months earlier.

'In vain I followed her trail. I went again to Constantinople, to Corinth, to Sicily and twice back to Persia. Wherever I went, the news was the same. Doquz and our merchant friend had indeed sailed for Italy. However, the ship she had taken was the very one that had been wrecked off the Greek mainland. I searched, enquired for her in the Greek cities. My heart told me she lived still but at length my reason convinced me she was drowned.

'By the end of the year 1306 I was sure the woman I loved was at the bottom of the ocean. There was nothing for me in Persia now. Ghazan was dead and I had quarreled with his successor - Karbanda, called by some Oljeitu. The splendid one! Half-brother and only half the man!

'But I was wealthy, Gretl; I had credit with a banker in Constantinople and with merchant houses in Venice, Genoa and Florence. I sold my property in Persia, exchanged a part share in my business for a share in another and returned to Venice. I found a new partner, a Saxon merchant named Andreas Queck. Your great-grandfather!'

A breeze had sprung up suddenly, taking the heat from the day. I thought of fetching our cloaks but decided it might distract Opa from his tale. Anyway, there were still hours of daylight left and I was in no mood to go indoors. I was still eager to hear the rest though, so far, nothing in the story seemed to have anything to do with the man called Akhtar.

As if to reassure me, Opa patted my hand. Again, he flashed me that mysterious but meaningful look.

'There is still a long way to go, Gretl,' he said. 'My heart was right, my reason wrong. By a miracle Doquz was saved. But it was too late for me. Listen and I will tell you what happened.'

With wildly beating heart, I curled up at his feet with my head against his knee. Then he told me the story.

About himself. About Doquz - who had become Ennia. And about Andreas and Hypatia and the whole history of our family.

About fifty years earlier ...

HASSAN

Hypatia

i

Where do I begin?

The memories of old age are not like the recollections of youth. The seasons and years do not follow one another in obstinate order. They are so many that one spring is indistinguishable from the next, and one winter is much like the one that went before.

Old men's memories are not like the pages or chapters of a book, to be read one after the other if we are to make sense of them. They spring uninvited like shadows out of mist. A face, a smile, a red sunset, a bitter frost, the sound of weeping – all of these recall from the past, though in no particular order, the joys, the sorrows, the triumphs and the disappointments of our lives.

To remember is to wrinkle the parchment of time, so that all we have done, all we have suffered, becomes confused with the might-have-been. Time is a closed circle wherein the errors we make bring compensations, which themselves cancel out the original error. On reflection, I would not wish to have lived my life any other way, despite its trials. For had I not lost Doquz ... had I not left Persia, I could not have found Matthilde. Had I not ...

There is no point in speculating farther. If our lives were to be ruled by Chance, or by Fate, as some philosophers claim, in either case we are helpless victims. But is it not truly we who shape our own lives and that of others around us by the choices we make?

It is by Chance that we are born; it is our Fate to die. That much is clear, yet everything between depends on how we exercise the powers that nature has given us: to be merciful or cruel; to love or hate; to build or destroy; to make one's home in one country as opposed to another.

It was not Chance or Fate that brought me to Brunswick, but my own choice. And though I did not think so at the time, it was neither Chance nor Fate that brought the Singari to Bachhagen in the spring of 1312, but the strength of human will.

I was thirty-two and had been married to Matthilde for three years. They had been busy years. My business ventures were successful. The estate was productive. The work of rebuilding and repairing parts of the manor house was all but finished. My understanding of the sciences and their practical application to the art of healing had brought me lasting satisfaction. I could not forget but, as time passed, the pain of my loss diminished.

That March day, I had no inkling my life was about to change again. I was happy. I was comfortable. I was wealthy too, and that may have contributed to the other two. Matthilde had miscarried twice but we consoled ourselves with the thought that she was still young, only twenty, and had many years ahead of her in which to bear children.

The travellers settled in the pasture by the river. Their features and dress reminded me of another place and another time. Once, I had encountered a similar group on the Silk Road. Called the Doum, they were fleeing repression in the country of their birth. That recollection made me think of other things too - things I had tried to put out of mind: the bazaars of Tabriz; the smell of date palms; the scent of jasmine in my Maragha garden. I could see again the Zagros Mountains in the morning sun, and how their peaks took on the rich, golden colour of honey.

The newcomers pitched tents, unloaded their belongings from wagons and built a cooking fire. A few ponies had been left to fend for themselves in the long grass. Loose pigs and sheep there were too but they showed little inclination to wander far from the encampment, being hindered by the activities of a scrawny dog that snapped at the hind legs or rump of any animal unwise enough to venture more than a few paces from its companions.

Some of the men-folk were occupied in mending saddles or carving wood. A few naked children were chasing chickens round the wagons. Four or five ancients, their heads covered by colourful kerchiefs to protect them from the sun, were huddled together over a bowl of burning Indian hemp. The young women were washing clothes in the river and laying them on the bank to dry. Their upper torsos, like those of the younger men, were bare. Two of their number had been bathing in the shallows. Water glistened on their pale brown skin and dripped from their long black hair. Wet petticoats hugged their legs. There was an earthy beauty, a primitive grace in the girls' form and I could not deny my instincts to follow them with my eyes.

The group's leader was about forty-five years of age, I guessed. Unlike the other men, he wore a red silk half-tunic. He was not as tall as I but he had powerful shoulders. The bulging muscles of his forearms were taut beneath his weathered skin. I asked him if he spoke the Saxon tongue.

'I speak it,' the man said. He was either amused by the question or indignant that I should doubt his ability. 'I am Baras.'

'And what do your people call themselves?'

'We are called many things, my lord. The old men say we were once the *Doum* and came from the East.'

'It is as I thought then. I once met people such as you in Persia. Legend says the Doum were a race out of India.'

'It is no legend,' Baras said. 'We are descendants of that race. Our band is the first to venture so far from the Great Sea. But nowadays we are called by other names. In Greece, we were the *Atzinganoi*. The Untouchable. In Italy we were the *Singari*.'

'Then Singari you will be, if it does not offend you. I have kin in Italy.'

'It does not offend me.'

'Do you need food?'

'Some grain to make bread. We can afford to pay or barter. Otherwise we have enough.'

'I offer it freely,' I said. ' But perhaps when we know one another better we may trade. Those saddles that your people mend are fine work.'

'None are finer, sir. And know that my men are for hire in other ways, if you need building and repair work about the farms.'

He seemed pleased at my compliment. Then his eyes brightened. His thick brows puckered in an expression of wonder.

'Surely that is a **su-asti** you wear,' he said. 'If the gods grant me a hundred summers, I doubt I'll ever see another to match it!

I held my fylfot up so he could inspect it. 'You know this symbol?'

'Only by hearsay,' said he. I fancied he shrank back a little. 'Some older folks fear it as a sign of the dark arts. But one who travels with us, a widow woman, says it is not so. I do not know the truth of it.'

My curiosity was aroused. I wondered what else he had heard. Fylfots - *gammadions* to the Greeks - were common in Byzantium but I had seen none as far west as Italy or as far north as Saxony. I suspected that Christians thought it a perversion of their Cross. That the Singari should be familiar with the symbol and its meanings was worthy of investigation. I asked if I might speak with the woman.

'Sadly, that is not possible, my lord,' Baras said. 'She travels with others. To the north of here. Our clan numbers fifty men and women all told and what you see is but half.'

I swallowed my disappointment.

Baras made a sign and some women brought pannikins of river water and a basket filled with scones of rye-bread. I took one, broke it in two and bit into one of the pieces. Then I accepted a cup of water and took a token sip. By the customs of the East, our friendship was sealed.

Some Singari children, with flutes and miniature drums, had gathered round and they began to entertain us with their shrill piping and unmelodious banging. Despite my ears being assailed by the awful sounds, I applauded with good grace. At length, Baras led me away and we sat together on a grassy mound to talk.

'Fortune smiles on an estate such as this and on those who serve it,' he said to me. 'What is the name of this district?'

I followed his gaze across the meadow to the manor house with its shapely turrets, stained windows and broad, grassy terrace leading down to the wall of the herb garden. It had not always been so grand. Both house and lands had been long neglected when I purchased them, and their improvement had cost me three years of hard labour.

'This is Bachhagen in the province of Brunswick,' I said. 'The people hereabouts call me von Hasenbach.'

The Singar was scrutinising my person. 'Yet you were not always of this people, my lord, or even of their faith, perhaps.'

'Why do you say that?'

'It is no more than a feeling. I apologise if I offend you.'

'No, you are right,' I admitted. 'It's a long story. But I have lived many years as a Christian among Christians. And the name von Hasenbach falls from Brunswick lips more readily than any I bore previously.'

'What are names but hooks on which to hang men's deeds?' laughed Baras. 'What would Alexander be but a conqueror, Socrates but a philosopher, Omar a poet?'

My eyes wandered across to the tent where the old men squatted, engaged in idle conversation and smoking their hasheesh. Beyond them, near the riverbank, the girls were picking blue and yellow flowers and working them into garlands to adorn their necks and arms. Some young fellows threw them lustful looks as they sat stitching leatherwork on a nearby flat cart. I wondered even more that this lifestyle should have provided Baras with an education in the classics.

The children had formed a procession round the tents and wagons. Those with tambours struck them enthusiastically with every second step while the fluters piped their tuneless accompaniment. One boy had promoted himself to the head of the line of would-be musicians and, with pipe pressed firmly between his lips, was striding ahead of the others like a standard bearer leading his column into battle. His dignified march contrasted sharply with the halting gait of the smaller children, who shuffled along or waddled behind, their naked buttocks swaying absurdly from side to side as they strove to keep pace. A few infants, panting and flushed, brought up the rear.

The game was full of fun and laughter, yet something about that innocent picture made me feel strangely uneasy, as if the curtain of time had risen and I was beholding a scene from a solemn, less happy future.

Gradually, the stragglers tired and gave up until only two older boys were left. They flopped in the grass and began wrestling for possession of each other's flutes. Their brows were damp with perspiration and their eyes glinted with the pleasure of childhood.

ii

I had been twenty-six when I left Persia for the last time. My heart lay at the bottom of the Aegean and I did not think I could ever be happy again. The things that had sustained me at other times: my mother's love; my stepfather's wisdom; the adoration of my half-siblings, held me prisoner in the past. I had to make a decision – to live the rest of my life in a cage, or to escape.

That I was able to break free was due more to Andreas than to my own efforts. Business had brought us together but, over the years, we had also become good friends. We did not pretend to one another.

We were at Constantinople when he first issued his invitation.

'You should settle down, Sano,' he said. 'It's time you found a woman, my friend.'

'You know I'm no monk, Andreas,' I said.

'I mean a wife, Sano. Trade and travel are all very well but you need a home. And children. If you cannot love, marry for respect. The best partnerships are founded on it. Find a woman who is a pleasure to look at and doesn't think you disagreeable. Wed her and give her six sons and daughters to coddle while you are about your business, or buy an estate and share the burden of child-rearing. You are rich as Dives and can well afford it. Today's nobility are not so proud they would refuse to sell you a piece of Lombardy or Saxony, or even Brunswick. Or there is always winegrowing.'

It was true enough. I was wealthy by my service to the Khan. I had inherited my grandfather's wealth too, most of it in Persian property and trade. However, the wine enterprise belonged to the Montecervinos, my stepfather's family and it had been a condition of my adoption that I give up any rights in it.

'The vineyards will go to my brother Nico,' I said. 'As for Brunswick and Saxony, are not all your petty princes forever at each other's throats? To be in the favour of one is to make an enemy of the others? And love and respect go together, Andreas. How can I respect a wife who is fonder of my gold than she is of me?'

'She is dead, Sano!'

'Yet I still hope, Andreas. I cannot help it.'

'Come to Brunswick with me,' said Andreas. 'I promise no matchmaking. Enjoy some Saxon hospitality.'

I planned to return to the Veneto and look after the vineyards while my stepfather played politics in the Council of Venice. Nico was still too young and inexperienced to manage alone. Meantime I had affairs of my own to settle. I told Andreas I would think about what he had said. It wasn't as if I had not considered marriage and children. Brunswick, rather than Venice, might distract me from my morbid thoughts. But if I was to be miserable, I might just as well be miserable in Saxony as anywhere else.

Andreas was eight years my senior and a man of simple ancestry. He was fourth in a line of Brunswick merchants and the eldest of four brothers. By far the most adventurous of his family, he was probably the most ingenious when it came to turning a venture into a profit. And at winning an argument! Saxony was a land of green meadows, lazy rivers and wild forests, he told me. A land of mellow summers and snowy winters, where the women were fair and the men hardy. I might surprise myself, as he put it.

iii

'They are a rough band of knaves,' Matthilde said when I returned to the house. She was frowning.

Matthilde was always beautiful to me, but when she frowned she seemed vulnerable. I wanted to reach out and clasp all her beauty to myself, to hold it and protect it from the anger of the world.

With Doquz it had been different. Our love had been the love of equals, at once an intense passion nurtured by war, and an enduring affection born in the innocence of childhood. Our relationship had been complicated, even by Persian standards, as I had often admitted to Andreas, though not so in the families of the Mongol Khans. My natural father had children by several wives. Ghazan was son of the first in seniority; Oljeitu, who had become Khan on his brother's death, was son of the second. Nadia, my mother, had been the third. And Doquz, half-sister to Oljeitu through their mother, was child of a different father.

Matthilde was the daughter of a feudal lord. Surrounded by a cluster of female attendants, she had passed her childhood in a cocoon, not quite free, and preparing only for the day when she would be wife and mother to yet another of her dynasty.

'I know the Singari are honest,' I said. 'And there was a wisdom about their leader that I found out of place in a man who lives such a life. He spoke to me of Alexander, and of Omar the poet, and divined that I was more than the usual Saxon farmer. His people will prove friendly and reliable neighbours, I'm quite sure.'

I engaged a few of the travellers in unskilled labour about the estate in exchange for supplies. My trust was not misplaced and Matthilde was gradually won over. The early prejudices of estate workers softened too. I impressed upon all my tenants that, despite appearances, the Singari were not to be feared as Saracens. I had often laughed at their talk; to the Saxon people, the word Saracen incorporated every race of humanity east of Athens.

April came and the Singari showed no signs of departing. Around the middle of the month, heavy clouds gathered in the west and the weather turned cool. It rained heavily for several days. The river rose and the camp was flooded. I offered Baras a fallow meadow on higher ground, which he was glad to accept. There was some grumbling among the farmers but no trouble. Indeed, despite their elders' worst fears, friendships were forged between the children of both groups.

The Singari showed every sign of contentment among their new neighbours and I began to believe they might abandon their wandering existence and settle permanently. There were several empty houses in Bachhagen village - including the forge - that had been allowed by the previous landgrave to fall derelict. It was thus a complete surprise when I awoke one morning at the beginning of May to find the camp gone.

'Perhaps it's for the best,' said Matthilde.

'Perhaps,' I said, ' - though I have a feeling we have not seen the last of the Singari.'

iv

Albert II of Brunswick was a frequent visitor at Bachhagen. Until the death of his brother William, he had kept court at Göttingen but had now acquired some agreeable property in Wolfenbüttel and in Brunswick Town itself. Even so, his lands covered less than half of the old duchy, divided by his father and uncle fifty years before, and even less of the former domains of Henry, Lion of Saxony. Grübenhagen was held by his younger brother Henry, while Lüneburg and Hannover had gone to his cousin Otto.

Bachhagen, a small manor lying in a disputed sector of the divided duchy, had been neglected since late Crusader times and was of no interest to either of the cousins. It was with considerable relief that they had relinquished their claim and had allowed it to pass into independent ownership. Thereby, both Brunswick and Lüneburg had benefitted financially from the proceeds of trade in England and the Low Countries.

Not only was Duke Albert fond of Matthilde but he owed me a debt he could never repay in full. My purchase of the land had solved a thorny political problem and had helped Albert himself out of an embarrassing financial crisis. And should Matthilde and I have sons, as he hoped we would, he would benefit further without the estate being lost to the family bloodline. Moreover, he owed to my growing skill in physic the life of his eldest child.

We had completed the sale and purchase but had remained on good terms because of our shared passion for horses. I had already paid more than one visit to the Brunswick stables and had arranged to return to look at a roan mare. Albert, usually of jovial disposition, had seemed distracted.

'I'm sorry that your expertise with the horse does not extend to humankind,' he said. 'My son Magnus is sick. Indeed, the physician says he may not recover.'

'If I can help, I should be glad to,' I told him. 'I have some slight knowledge of physic, taught me by my mother and by one of Persia's greatest scientists.'

The bedchamber was darkened but I could see straight away how pale the boy was. Red swathes bound his right arm and two bloodstained basins lay by the bedside. Already, I knew it to be an all too common scene. Blood-letting and prayer! Unable to understand the ailment, Albert's physicians were depriving his heir of the very thing he needed to survive. They were squeezing the life from the boy's body in an effort to purge his liver of its evil humours. The only evil in that room was ignorance.

I controlled my anger with difficulty and begged to be allowed to question the lad. After only a few moments it was clear the malady was a minor one and that failure to deal with it in the proper manner had led to its worsening.

'I fear that in another week your son will be dead,' I said. 'And his death will be on your conscience unless you act to prevent it.'

Albert stared at me dumbly. If I had startled him with my bluntness, it was no more than I intended.

'You wonder how I dare on so short an acquaintance,' I went on. 'I dare because it's true. He is weak from the loss of blood. Give the lad to me for a week and I promise you will see improvement.'

'You ask a lot of me that I should trust him to you alone,' said the Duke.

'What have you to lose if he is as ill as your physician tells you? But believe me when I swear he is not! I'm a foreigner in your land, Albert. I am in your power if I fail.'

Within a week under my care, the youth's face had lost its pallor and his limbs were stronger again. His appetite returned. Albert pressed me to accept some reward.

'Unless I'm much mistaken, you have no money to spare,' I said, 'whereas I already have plenty. I'm satisfied with your thanks. Now, if only I could find a wife, I would be more than content.'

I had spoken half in jest, never thinking he might take me seriously.

'That is something I have already pondered, Sano,' he said. 'It will be a lonely life in the Leine Valley without the comforts of a woman.'

'I am used to it.'

'Perhaps I can help after all,' said Albert. 'Of course, the matter would be largely in your own hands and in God's. However, unless I have mistaken my cousin Matthilde's meaning, she would be more than willing to accept your suit.'

The Duke of Brunswick in 1312 was a man of about forty years of age. He had a generous build that had earned him the nickname of Fat Bertie, though none would have dared utter it in his presence. I had grown fonder of him as the years passed. It always gave me pleasure to show off my improvements to the manor house and - though the Duke was no more farmer than I - to explain to him the innovations I had introduced in farming.

'Incredible,' he voiced on seeing the new windows and woodwork, 'and in such a short time. I almost regret our bargain, my friend. I should have employed you as architect and builder for my own benefit.'

'Your cousin, my wife, deserves no less,' I said, 'but the quality of work owes little to my skill.'

'I see planted fields everywhere,' Albert said. 'And trees where there was only rotted wood not so long ago.'

'That is due to my tenants' efforts. I am no farmer by inclination and confess I am taking risks with the land management. But I do know men. Give them hope and a goal and they will do the rest themselves.'

'And this plot nearest to the house,' said Albert, 'the one enclosed by a wall? I have never seen its like. These plants are unknown to me.'

'It is a herb garden, an idea from my mother, one she imported to Venice from Persia. There is allium, thyme, and some others. The broad-leafed shrub is bay; the bright green spreading plant that seems like a weed is pulegium. Its fragrance repels bothersome insects.'

'Their odours are indeed strong. Some would say repugnant. And their appearance is plain.'

'All have their uses. In cooking or in medicine,' I said. 'We gather leaves and flowers, dry them, and infuse them in water and wine. We harvest roots and seeds, grind and crush them, make pastes with honey and ointments with lard. I hope in time to introduce new plants and to learn more of their benefits.'

'Then this is the science about which you once lectured me.'

'I am drawn to it more and more,' I said. 'And to other mysteries of nature: the pattern of stars in the night sky; why we grow old; why the winds change and the clouds form. I paid too scant attention to my tutors when I was a child.'

'I have reason to be grateful for some of your physic,' the Duke said solemnly. 'However, it seems to me, Sano, we should not meddle too much in the business of God.'

'Surely it is God who invites our study of his world by giving us intelligence and free will,' I said.

Albert laughed. 'Be careful, my friend, lest you make enemies in the Church. You are popular enough hereabouts to attract attention and some might think such pronouncements heretical!'

'I popular?'

'It's a strange thing,' Albert said, 'though not at first worthy of my attention. It happened in March, before the equinox. Twice my stewards reported the presence of foreigners in the districts outlying the town. Gypsies, the people call them, for it seems they are of Egyptian blood. Nomads. Brown-skinned and ...'

I interrupted him. 'They've travelled through this valley too,' I said. 'Singari, they are called, descendants through many generations of an Indian people. They will cause no harm. Anyway, what has that to do with me?'

'Only that, as they travel, they make enquiries after an Italian lord. So I have been told.'

'And? Is there not more than one Italian in Saxony?'

'The reports were more specific. These Singari, as you term them, seek one called Montecervino ...'

'Impossible! Other than my kin in Venice, my friend Andreas and yourself, no one knows me by that name. The band who came by here made no mention of it. Yet I conversed at length with their leader.' Despite my denial, I felt my pulse quicken.

'I cannot testify as to who knows it and who does not, my friend.' The Duke shrugged. Then his eyes darted towards the fylfot. 'But that's not all. According to my steward, that heirloom of yours was described very accurately by one of these nomads.'

'That makes no sense at all,' I said. I remembered now what Baras had said, that there was a woman who knew the gammadion symbol, but that too had been more than a month ago. 'There has to be a simple explanation.'

'I'll leave you to ponder it, Sano,' Albert said, 'while I embrace my cousin.'

Throughout May and into June, there was no further news of the Singari. I made enquiries in Hannover and in the Weser valley, where Andreas, when not travelling on business, lived with his family. Some nomads had camped for a while on the west bank of the Leine near Hannover itself but had departed after a month. None had been seen as far west as Hameln.

'It's a mystery indeed,' Andreas said. 'But you had friends in Persia, did you not? Perhaps they have tired of Khan Oljeitu's hospitality and are seeking to renew their acquaintance with you.'

'None would choose such an indirect method,' I said grumpily.

Over the next few weeks, I was busy again and the episode was all but forgotten. I was determined to pursue my study of the sciences and had converted and extended a room in the manor house for that purpose. I had brought from Venice a few priceless books written in the Persian and Greek languages and now I wrote to my mother for her lists of plant preparations. I experimented with distillations and concoctions of various substances, and prepared new charts of my observations of the night skies.

Matthilde watched with curiosity but did not interfere. Occasionally, she would question me about this or that and readily accepted my explanation although it was clear she did not understand it.

A day or two before the midsummer solstice, I was called to arbitrate in a dispute between two Bachhagen villagers. The matter was settled and I set off homeward. It was already evening. I had tethered my horse at the edge of the village and had not covered half the distance to it when I heard the sound of light footsteps on the path behind me. Though rare, robbery in the valley was not unknown and my first thought was that I was being followed by someone intent on stealing my purse. I gripped the hilt of my sword and turned. If a footpad was foolish enough to attack me, it would be his last mistake. Even if two or three, I thought with relish, I would at the very least send them running for their lives.

There were no robbers. The only person I could see was a small girl of eight or nine years with dark complexion and raven-black hair, who seemed to be hurrying after me along the path. I shortened my stride and allowed her to catch up. To judge by her appearance, she was not a village child but reminded me of those I had seen a month before about the Singari encampment. She wore no shirt but merely a homespun waistcoat, dyed blue, in addition to her full, red and dirt-spattered skirt. Where she had come from was a puzzle as none of the Singari people had been seen near Bachhagen since Baras departed with his clan.

I stopped. The girl was not inclined to come too close and stood shyly and silently a few paces away. I asked if there was something I could do for her.

She took a step forward and shook her head violently from side to side. I tried another approach.

'Do you have a name?' I took a coin from my purse and held it out. The girl made no attempt to take the coin but continued shaking her dark curls. It occurred to me that perhaps she spoke only a Singari dialect, in which case conversation might prove difficult. However, after another moment's hesitation, she risked another step and, instead of taking the coin, grasped my fylfot in her little fist and raised it to her lips. Having kissed the gold in this way, she seized my hand and tried to pull me in the direction opposite to that in which we had both been heading.

Then she spoke for the first time and to my amazement, the language was Greek. I had not heard it since I left Constantinople.

'Come, please! This way.'

'You want to walk with me?' I said in the same tongue. 'It's just a short distance to my horse.'

'I have a pony,' the girl said proudly. She ventured a smile 'But he is at the camp. We walk now.'

I was intrigued but cautious and asked where she was taking me. She might still intend to deceive me and lead me into a trap. However, her smile reassured me. She was a pretty child and, but for the dirt on her clothes, was well turned out. 'Will you not tell me your name?'

'I am Hypatia, sir. Come now please. Only as far as yonder stone house.' She pointed back to the forlorn building that had once been the forge. It might have been the best house in the village had it not been allowed to fall into disrepair by the heirs of Brunswick. I had a mind to restore it and find a blacksmith to occupy it, but had not yet had time to devote to the project.

'No one lives there now, Hypatia,' I objected. As I pronounced it, the name struck a chord of memory, though I did not know why it should do so.

Hypatia ignored me. She shook her curls again and pulled me towards the forge. We passed through the broken gate and into the yard, which was littered with stone and timber debris from the neglected building. The sun was setting behind the upper floor of the house and the blacksmith's workshop below was in shadow.

I peered into the gloom. I remembered there was a furnace, an old blackened hearth, an upended anvil and some rusted tools, but I could see none of those. Instead, just where I thought the furnace should be, I glimpsed movement. At first I thought it was a trick of the gloaming but as my eyes focused better I saw the outline of a horse and beside it the figure of a woman. I could not see her face nor judge her age but from the mode of dress I took her to be a Singar.

'Mama!' Hypatia released my hand and ran happily towards the stranger. 'He has come, Mama, he has come!'

'And why would he not?' This reply too was in the Greek language and was spoken in a hushed tone, just loud enough for me to catch. Her accent was of a purity I had not heard for many years. The woman came into the failing daylight and I saw immediately that her clothes were indeed of the colour and style of the Singari people, a full skirt in warm blue and a loose wine shirt that disguised her femininity. Her head and part of her face were hidden in a silk shawl.

'What do you want with me, mistress?' I asked, taking a step or two towards her, whereupon the woman and her daughter retreated into the shadows.

'For myself, nothing; for my daughter, a great deal perhaps,' she breathed. This reply was uttered so quietly that I became impatient and not a little annoyed at the game she was playing.

'If it is money you want, mistress, I should warn you, I am no charity,' I said. 'Nevertheless, if you and your daughter come forward again, we will discuss your business, whatever it may be.'

'And I am no beggar,' the woman retorted, and she laughed, moving with the agility of a youth and almost catching me off guard.

The mid-year sun, having reached a point in its path where it was no longer obscured by the building, glinted on the blade of a short sword that, as it seemed to me, she thrust with menace at my breast. As I stepped aside and grasped her wrist in an iron grip, the shawl slipped from her head and I saw her properly for the first time. She had an oval face with prominent cheekbones and full, sensuous lips that pouted in vexation. Her ears were small and delicate, her eyes brown and her hair raven black like the child's.

The sword clattered on the stone of the yard. My senses swam. I released her wrist and stared through the mist that was already obscuring my vision. It was impossible. It could not be she, I told myself, and yet it plainly was, a little older to be sure, yet much as I remembered.

'Forgive me, I could not resist testing you,' she said, the pout turning to a smile that lit up her whole face. 'Have I changed so much, my Hassan?'

I found my voice, aware that it trembled.

'I searched for so long. The ship was lost, they told me. There were no survivors. And still I searched.'

'I know,' she said, clasping Hypatia to her skirts. Tears formed in her eyes. 'But 'twas so long before I learned it,' she added in the Persian language. 'And in the meanwhile, life was given back to me. Not my old one, to be sure, but life none the less.'

'How is it possible?' I said. My heart was beating fast and I was almost overcome with emotion. 'I see you, but I cannot believe!'

I held out my arms to her and she, releasing her child, fell into them, laid her head on my shoulder and pressed her body against mine.

'What are we going to do, my Hassan?' she said. 'What are we going to do, my brother; my lover; my dearest friend?'

'In truth, I do not know,' I said. I kissed her cheek and then, my lips wet with her tears, I whispered her name – the name that so often over the years I had spoken in my secret thoughts.

Doquz.

v

'It will be dark soon, Mama,' Hypatia said. She gazed wide-eyed at the ball of red that was sinking slowly behind a distant line of trees. The sparse clouds hovering above the horizon were tinged with pink.

'It's almost midsummer, Hypatia,' I told her. 'The light fades but it does not disappear, and you should know there will be a moon coming up soon in the east.'

'Still, she is right,' said Doquz. 'Our camp is an hour's ride upriver. I would not risk our mount stumbling in the gloom.'

'I will escort you to the manor house,' I said. 'Hypatia can eat supper and we can talk.'

Doquz laughed. 'You have not changed, Hassan. There is still an innocence about you that beggars belief in a man of thirty-two. I am my own mistress and we would not be missed, yet for us to be guests at your table would be improper, even if the idea is most appealing. You have a Christian wife.'

'I have told Matthilde some of our history.'

'Perhaps so. But you and I are creatures of another world, Hassan. In Tabriz the scene would be commonplace. Here, for one wife to be confronted by another would be a threat. I have seen this Matthilde of yours. She is beautiful. She is understanding and tolerant of a dead mistress. But she rides with her legs together and to right or left of the saddle and is thus also dignified and proud. A live Doquz would be quite another matter!'

'You have seen Matthilde? You have been to Bachhagen before?'

'Many times,' Doquz said. 'You know how easily I can pass as a man when dressed in manly clothes. I have watched and waited for the right opportunity; I have enquired after your family. Baras told you of me, I think – the widow woman who talks constantly of su-asti and other mysteries. He is a discreet man and I fear he may have deceived you somewhat.

'At first, we were not even sure it was you who was master here. I had to be certain. Believe me, Hassan, the years have taught me patience – though I never stopped loving you.'

'But you refuse my invitation?'

'I must!'

'Then you shall remain until morning here in the village. You cannot ride with the child in the half-light. The blacksmith's house is much in need of repair, but the weather is fine and there's no risk of flooding. There is some furniture upstairs and a bed, I think. I will leave you my cloak and the blanket from my horse.'

'Then we shall have luxury indeed,' laughed Doquz. 'Do you remember how we once slept ....? No, the memories will keep. If you will come tomorrow, I will tell you how, like the Lord of the Christians, I came back from the dead.'

'So be it,' I said. 'I'll sleep fitfully if at all until we meet again.'

'I too, my Hassan,' said she. 'And I beg you, do not tell your Matthilde of me. At least, not yet.'

It was indeed a long night. As I had forecast, I slept hardly at all. I said nothing to Matthilde, seeing the logic of Doquz's words but feeling a gnawing guilt that the deception was unworthy of me. At first, I lay in the dark of our bedroom, my wife's warmth beside me, reliving my meeting with Doquz at the forge and questioning my feelings for her. I loved her still - that I knew for certain - yet I loved Matthilde too, which made my feelings of guilt all the worse.

Restlessly, I pondered my last voyage from Asia Minor and the events of the months that followed, when it had seemed to me that, despite the face of cheerfulness I presented to Andreas, life had dealt me a blow from which I would never recover.

It was more than a year before I took up his invitation. As it turned out, Andreas was to be my guest before I became his. At Constantinople, we found a vessel whose master was willing to take us to Syracuse. The voyage was arranged within a week, just long enough for me to make arrangements. On the morning of our departure, I arrived late at the quayside, having spent three days and nights with my banker, drafting letters and contracts and saying goodbyes on the Anatolian side of the Hellespont.

'I had almost given you up,' said Andreas. He glanced quizzically at the package I was carrying.

'A promise is just that, Andreas,' I laughed. I was not going to satisfy his curiosity until we were under way. 'It is merely a few letters. Nothing that need disturb our plans.'

The sailors began fastening the cargo and untying the ropes. The helmsman took his place at the rudder and it was time to embark.

The vessel creaked as it pulled away from the quay. The expanse of water between ship and land widened and the human figures on the water's edge diminished in size. The usual nausea rose in my belly as the swell gripped the hull. It would soon pass. I sat on deck with my back against the timbers of the aft castle, trying to ignore the retreating coastline. As a distraction, I removed my sword from its scabbard and began polishing the blade with a rag.

The sky was a pale blue with scarcely a cloud. A light breeze lifted the sail. I hoped the weather would hold. If this was to be my last voyage, I would sooner have fair wind and calm sea.

Ten days out, a bout of sickness laid Andreas low and he took three more to recover. My own mood of joviality lasted until the ship drew near to the Pelaponnese. It was here, I supposed, that the vessel carrying Doquz had been struck by a violent storm and lost. Andreas left me to brood and I was grateful to him for not intruding in my private grief. When at last we turned towards Italy, my depression had passed and I thanked him for his unspoken sympathy.

'I'll try to be a better companion from now on,' I said. 'And it's time I explained these papers I am carrying. Truly, I plan never to see the Levant again.'

'Then you meant what you said, that this is your last voyage. Literally? You do not intend ever to return to Persia, or even to Constantinople?'

I shook my head; I had made up my mind. I opened the package and handed Andreas the contents.

'I have sold my villa in Maragha, and my grandfather's share of the business in Kerman to his old partner. That will give me credit with agents, trade houses, and bankers in Venice and Florence. The banks of Florence are the best in the world. My other ventures, including my arrangements with you, will be unaffected. But I think our partnership should change.'

Andreas read the documents without comment until he came to the last one. Though I was certain there was no disadvantage to him in what I proposed, I had steeled myself for a refusal or at least resistance. We were both stubborn in our way.

'It is the draft of a contract,' I said when I was sure he had digested the contents. 'You wish to keep your investments in Anatolia; I do not. I suggest an exchange – all my interests in the silk trade for a share of your business in the north – in wool and silver. We can each give a valuation and agree on the figures to enter in the ledgers. But if the proposal does not meet with your approval, I will tear up the letter and we can still be friends.'

For a while Andreas just stared. I hoped I had read his thoughts correctly. He had long coveted a greater share in Turkish silks. Moreover, it was he who had suggested I take a share in his business with the German cities. Originally I dismissed it as a foolish idea. Now, if it was in his mind to add an enticement to his invitation to Brunswick, that would be much in my interest.

'Andreas?'

'Perhaps I should read the document again, Sano,' he said and held out his hand. 'But it is an excellent idea in principle and I feel sure we can agree on the detail.'

'Then let us do so in Venice,' said I. 'My mother will make you most welcome, and you will enjoy the wine.'

We made good time through Italy, travelling from Messina to Naples, where we rested a single night. By the time we reached Rome, Andreas was saddle-sore. He did not have the Mongol love of horses whereas I, in this one respect at least, was a child of the Steppes. I had Persian blood, it was true, but I had grown up at the court of the Mongol Khan and had learnt the Mongol secrets. The rider and his animal must move as one creature as if their minds are linked through the ether. The true horseman controls and directs with his knees and the muscles of his thighs, even at full gallop, so that saddle and reins become a hindrance to his progress.

Andreas could ride well enough but he relied too heavily on leather and looked uncomfortably insecure in the saddle at anything above a walking pace. After a morning's ride, his lungs were bursting from exertion and the sweat ran freely from his brow, blurring his vision.

The heat in Rome was sweltering.

'Your idea of a leisurely ride is too much for me, Sano,' he said. 'If you intend to keep it up all the way to the Veneto, then leave me behind. Besides, I have never been to Rome and a Christian should always visit the city of St Peter.'

'I want to reach home before the celebration of my mother's marriage anniversary,' I said. 'It will be fifteen years this July. But we have a few days to spare. Let us rest and see the sights.'

Andreas was grateful for the break but after a week in Rome, I was impatient. We rode even more furiously to Florence, where we spent three days transacting our business with the banking houses.

From Florence, the original pace continued without respite towards Bologna and Ferrara, which we reached in the evening, after two more exhausting days in the saddle. I almost lost count of the number of times we exchanged horses. On recommendation of a banker's agent, we had left what little baggage we had brought to be transported by a trusted courier.

We crossed the Po at dawn and travelled a few leagues east into the rising sun. The chill of the morning was just lifting when I saw ahead the familiar shallow valley, bordered on its northern side by a broad band of vegetation. First, woodland then, stretching down the gentle slope almost as far as the water's edge were the vineyards of my stepfather's estate. Rising above the furrows were the turrets of the Montecervino villa.

It was five days past the summer solstice in the year 1306, and I had come home to Italy. True to my word, I never returned to Persia.

The night wore on as I tossed and turned with my memories. In no time at all, it seemed to me, the early birds broke into chirping chorus. As the cocks began to crow, I slipped out of bed, fearing I would disturb Matthilde by remaining longer. In the darkness of the shuttered room, I fumbled for my hose and footwear, pulled them on and tiptoed out to the stairs. There was just enough light to guide me to the main door.

Outside the morning was grey. A thin mist clung to the meadow and hugged the houses of the village in the distance. Doquz was there, her rest disturbed too perhaps, like mine, with memories of our past lives.

Hypatia. I had remembered. How like Doquz to call her daughter that, after a woman she much admired, the Alexandrine mathematician so cruelly done to death by a Christian mob.

'Learning is dangerous in a woman,' she had said once, and it had been of herself that she spoke. 'More dangerous than skill in arms.'

I had replied with the simple answer, that it was as easily hidden. Then Doquz had chided me, that it was a different kind of danger. 'For,' she said, 'without the freedom to teach, learning has little purpose. Unless exercised, knowledge will wither and die, the mind along with it. And I think 'tis death of the mind that I fear most, Hassan.'

It was strange how I recalled that particular conversation when so many others had been forgotten. Perhaps it was because it so well illustrated the traits of her character I loved so well; her fierce independence of spirit and indifference to bodily injury; the wisdom and wit that so often left her mistress of the field in an argument; the stubbornness with which she pursued her own course when reason failed to win it. As yet, I did not know her story but it was that independence and stubbornness, I reasoned, that must have enabled her to survive when another of different temperament would have been lost.

As I walked towards the village, I was as excited as a youth on the way to his first assignation. There were only ever a few villagers about at this early hour but I was sure, though it was only fancy, that the two I passed on my way stared longer and harder than was usual. As I drew near to the forge, my heart was thumping in my chest and my mouth was dry.

Doquz came out to meet me. She greeted me in the traditional Persian way.

'*Salaam-e-lekum.*'

I gave the usual response.

'I did not sleep, Hassan,' she said when we were inside.

'Nor I!'

She laughed and I joined in. 'Is that all we have to say to one another after so many years?' she said, for I believe we were both tongue-tied at that moment.

I looked round the bare room. There was less furniture in it than I remembered, merely a worn mattress and an oak chest that was missing its lid. Hypatia was curled up on the mattress fast asleep. It was too narrow to sleep two, even when one of them was a child, and I realised Doquz must have passed the night on the floor. My horse blanket and cloak were folded together beside the chest to make a pillow.

' 'Twill be best if I wake her,' Doquz said. 'This room has no air and we should talk, perhaps on a walk beside the river, if you do not fear the gossips. Hypatia should come too; I cannot leave her alone. She will not disturb our conversation.'

'The gossips may exercise their tongues a while,' I said. 'But they will do so in vain. I have said nothing to Matthilde of your miraculous deliverance but it is my plan to tell her everything as soon as I return to the house.'

'Would that I were a flea on your shoulder to witness such bravery!'

'I'll struggle to find the right words.'

'I know it, my Hassan. Forgive me if I appear to jest about such a serious matter.' She tousled Hypatia's hair. The child opened her eyes, blinked, yawned and sat up.

'It must be done,' I said.

' 'Twas the greatest mistake of my life, Hassan. I know that now.' Doquz said. 'I had not wanted to entrap you, to tie you in a marriage when you were not ready. But I had never known loneliness.'

She walked by my side with Hypatia hanging to her skirt tails. We had reached a stretch of river beyond the village where there were rapids. The path twisted and turned but it was safe enough. However, the villagers avoided it and it was unlikely our walk would be disturbed by inquisitive neighbours. For all my determination to confess all to Matthilde, I did not want her learning it by accident.

'You were scarcely gone when I decided to follow,' Doquz went on. 'I could not wait until spring though, in truth, the arranging took several months. The merchant helped me. A Greek of his acquaintance was bound for the West and I travelled as his daughter. We took ship at Constantinople.

'I had never been at sea and nothing had prepared me for the vastness and wildness of it. Then, two and a half weeks into the voyage, the vessel ran into a storm.

'Even in the thick of a battle, I had never known real fear, Hassan, but now I felt it in my heart and in my bones. To describe my terror now would be to relive it. Even if the voyage had been uneventful I do not think I would go to sea again.'

She shivered though the morning was mild. 'It will be enough to say that the sea rose over the bows. Terrible waves lashed against the aft castle where we had taken shelter. A bolt of lightning hit the main mast. The ship broke and we were cast into the ocean.

'As you know, Hassan, I can swim well enough, but who could swim in such a sea? You are carried only where the wind and waves desire.

'I managed to clamber onto a piece of decking where I lost my senses. By a benevolent Fate I was washed ashore on a peninsula of Greece. Some of my clothing had been torn from my back. I was cut and bruised and my left arm was broken. The Atzinganoi found me; the native Greeks call them untouchable, but there are no finer people in the world. Neither a kinder nor a more honest.

'I had my sword and a few gold coins in a pouch on my belt. They were by my side when I awoke. It was lucky I knew Greek, for the Atzinganoi language was beyond me. My rescuers were heading north and they put off their journey to care for my injuries. Weeks passed before I was well enough to travel. What choice did I have but to go with them? I was a woman. I had no friends or family and I did not know the country or its people. I had money, but what use is that when one is alone?

'I knew nothing of crop raising, Hassan. I could not make clothes or stitch leather. The only animals I knew were horses. The nomads would not take my gold so how was I to earn my keep?

'The answer came by accident. As we travelled, I found myself often in the company of the children. I would tell them stories of Persia and about the stars, and about books. The clan leader overheard and begged me teach these things to the adults as well. It seems I have an aptitude.

'Then, one day, I defended a Singar who was being molested by three would-be robbers. A stick against three daggers, Hassan! You would have laughed to see them run, chased by a lone woman. My companions had weapons but they did not know how to use them properly. From that day I taught swordplay and knife-craft to the men and youths, as well as

Mathematics, Geometry and Astrology to the children.

'So began my travels in the West. I took a husband from among the Atzinganoi, not because I wanted it but because my situation would have been impossible otherwise. The Atzinganoi – the Singari - are a moral people, more so than even the Christians – or the Muslims! I took a husband. His name was Kolbas and he was a good man. He died of pestilence in Greece before we reached the northern border.'

I glanced at Hypatia. The child was hanging on, wide-eyed, to her mother's every word, and I wondered she had not heard the story before. In the daylight, I could see she resembled Doquz in every particular save for the shape of her eyes. Doquz came from the Mongol nobility, though her father was of Persian ancestry, and she had the look of Temuchin's race. Hypatia had the same cheekbones, the same nose and chin, the same raven-black hair, but her eyes were rounded with long lashes. How unkind of Fate, I thought, to give to another man what should have been mine.

As I studied her daughter, wondering what Kolbas had been like, and feeling to my surprise no hatred of my dead rival, Doquz was watching me. For the second time since our reunion, there were tears in her eyes, a circumstance so unusual through all the years I had known her that I was moved to put an arm round her shoulder. She did not resist, but turned towards me and clasping her hands round my head, pressed her body against mine. Our faces touched. I felt the thrill of intimacy. We kissed and it was not I who broke away.

'Would that the years would melt away,' said Doquz, wiping her damp face with her sleeve. 'To touch you and to lie with you again is all I thought about through long summers and winters. Even through good times, I never ceased to long for the comfort of your arms, the warmth of your lips or the thrill of your body nestling within mine.

'But time is inflexible, Hassan. 'Tis enough to know that you feel the same longing. I cannot expect ... I cannot demand more of you than that.'

I wanted to say she was wrong - that if she asked, I would go with her. I would leave Matthilde. I would leave the life I had built for myself and make with Doquz another, however and wherever the world would allow. The inflexible time she spoke of had scarcely for a moment wiped out the memory or the passion. I wanted her and there was nothing else on earth that mattered.

At that moment, I believed it, yet I could not say it. Something stopped me. Whether it was the way she now stroked my cheek with her forefinger, or the tenderness with which she gazed at the child, I do not know. All I know is that when she spoke again, her intense expression had changed. I thought at first she pitied me and despised my decision to stay silent but then I realised her look was one of tolerant amusement. She pouted her full lips.

'My poor friend!'

'Why so?' I stammered.

'You did not ask why I married Kolbas,' said Doquz, ' - why I had to take a husband. You did not remember my promise.'

'Your promise?'

'When they said that Arghun was father to us both. When we were already lovers.'

'You said if the rumour was false, I could come back to you. If true, were not the ties of kinship, of brother and sister, the stronger? I haven't forgotten.'

'But that was not all. I also said I would let no other man touch me and would die thinking of what might have been. I have been true to that promise, Hassan.'

Perhaps lack of sleep had deprived me of reason and filled my head with sheep's wool. I did not understand and told her so. She had a daughter; she had had a husband. I had not thought to question her further.

Doquz did not laugh. 'There was something I did not tell you, Hassan. I was two months with child when you left me and did not know. It was fully eight months later when I fell into the sea. And there were two survivors of the shipwreck. Hypatia was born in Persia, my Hassan. She is your daughter. Yours. Can you not see it?'

vi

'I should visit my brother,' said Matthilde unexpectedly. 'But I shall go with an attendant. You have your work.'

125

My resolution had failed me. I had not told her that Doquz was alive; that I had met with her; that I had fathered a child with her.

In Persia, for a man to have two wives, - or three, or four - is commonplace. Whether he treats them well or ill, with respect or dishonour, with love or lust, it is a mark of his status. And if so minded, he might just as easily abuse one as dishonour three. Even among the Christians of Tabriz, and elsewhere in their Eastern Empire, men did not adhere to the doctrines of the Roman Church. Rivalries between women are not unknown. It would be against nature if a wife did not seek to protect and advance her own children in preference to those of another. Yet, for all the advantages the practice of Persia gives to the husband, there is little place for duplicity in his relationships. The Western habit is quite different. In Saxony as in Venice, men pay lip-service to the laws of the Bishop of Rome; they speak of sacred marriages, then find their pleasure in the arms of mistresses.

I had long sat on the boundary between the two worlds. Now, through a twist of Fate, I found myself in a dilemma that was impossible to resolve without hurt to one or other of the women I loved. Doquz had sought me out knowing I had a Christian wife but despite her protest that she made no demands, I could sense the bitter conflict in her mind. I could not let her go, even less could I abandon my daughter. Yet how could I in honesty treat her – she who had first claim on me – as a concubine?

On the other hand, how was I to explain to Matthilde, who had been unable to bear me children, that I had a daughter by another woman whom, under Christian custom, she could not possibly acknowledge as a legitimate wife?

These are just some of the arguments that raged in my brain throughout the hours following my discovery that I was a parent. My heart told me I must confess all; my head told me I could not. Matthilde's sudden decision to spend time with her brother gave me the respite I needed to resolve the matter, if resolution was possible, with the least harm. And to remember.

Andreas had remained in the Veneto for a month. There was no urgent business demanding his attention and he was able to enjoy our hospitality without worrying about his German affairs. He carefully perused the contract I had drawn up and found it very much to his liking. It gave him the interests in Persia he desired in exchange for a share in the profits of his business in Saxony, the Low Countries and England. We signed the papers.

I stayed with my mother through the following winter and into the spring of 1307. Nico was not yet fourteen but Giovanni – my stepfather - had had his fill of politics and was coming home for good. That would release me from my obligations as estate manager and steward. I knew nothing about the German guilds and how business there was conducted and would have to learn, even though I had no plans then to make my home away from the Veneto.

So I went to Saxony. Brunswick provided me with connections in the Hanseatic league and an opening to the northern trade. I spent several weeks with Andreas, travelling between the German cities and ports before joining him for relaxation in Brunswick Town.

It was my custom in Italy to ride out in early morning and enjoy the dawn. I had persuaded Andreas to join me on these rides while he was my guest and we resumed the habit in Brunswick. He had warned me that German horses did not compare to the beasts found in the Veneto, so I had taken three of my best animals north with me.

One winter morning, we met a group of riders, men and women, exercising their animals in some open woodland.

'There goes an unhappy man,' Andreas remarked as we reined in to allow the group to pass. 'Though you would not think it to see him in his splendid riding garb.'

'And a singularly unhappy horse,' I said wryly, having noticed the leading rider's heavy build and large waistline. 'But why do you think him unhappy?'

'Duke Albert carries the world on his shoulders, and a debt as large as the Empire itself, if the stories are to be believed.'

'Duke?' I asked.

'Albert of Wolfenbüttel, heir to Henry the Lion.'

'Duke or not, he is much too wide and heavy for such a small filly,' I said. 'However, I have to say that the young woman who rides with him but a head or two to the rear has a most pleasant figure. Who is she?'

'I don't know for sure. Some niece or cousin, I fancy.'

As his party drew level, the Duke glanced in my direction. He stopped.

'That is a fine stallion, sir,' he said. 'Will you allow me to make an offer for him?'

'He is not for sale.'

'Name your price.'

'No price would be high enough, my lord duke,' I said. 'This stallion is both companion and friend. I reared him and brought him from Italy with me.'

'So you already know me, sir,' said Albert. 'May I know your name?'

'Assano di Montecervino at your service,' I said. 'At least, at your service in any matter save one. I will not sell my stallion.'

The Duke laughed. 'I see that you know horses, my friend. So be it!'

Just then, the young woman I had noticed sidled up to him and whispered in his ear. Albert laughed again.

'My cousin asks what brings an Italian gentleman to this cold climate.'

'It is no secret, my lady,' I said, speaking directly to her. 'I am here to trade.'

Again the pair exchanged whispers. I waited.

'She also wishes to know if you have other horses,' the Duke said.

'At my family's estate in Italy there are large stables. But I have only three animals here in Saxony. This stallion, the one my friend Andreas rides, and a third that is stabled at our present address. If I decide to settle in this province, I may arrange the purchase of some more.'

'And is that your intention, sir?' the lady asked, addressing me directly for the first time.

'Madam?'

'To settle in Brunswick?'

'I have not decided.'

Again there was a whispered exchange between the cousins.

'Lady Matthilde wishes that I invite you to see my stables,' Albert said. 'There are some fine animals there, which she suggests you might be interested in buying.'

I thanked him and promised I would come. Little did I imagine then that a friendship would ensue. Nor did I think I would ever meet the Lady Matthilde again. The women of Saxony, so Andreas told me, did not interfere in the business of their menfolk.

When I did see Matthilde again, she was kneeling in the straw of the stable beside a sick pony. The farriers would have cut its throat to feed the household, but she had held them back saying she knew of a physician who might cure it.

She had raised her proud but tearful eyes to my face and my heart went out to her. I think my decision was made in that moment, though I did not realise it – to settle down in this green but cold land, to practise my science and to raise a family. If Matthilde was too far above me in the eyes of her noble kinsman – though I had once been a prince – there would be other women of beauty and intelligence who would find my situation attractive. I had decided against love but I needed comfort and companionship.

Matthilde rose and I found myself looking down at her slender figure. In height, she barely reached my shoulders. She had a delicate white neck and a determined chin, but a soft mouth. Her hair, unlike that of Italian or Persian women, was blonde; her eyes were the colour of the Persian sky. They had widened at the sight of my fylfot.

'It is a Persian su-asti,' I told her. 'A gammadion to the Greeks. Some say it confers magical powers on the wearer.'

'It's like no ornament I ever saw! So this is the source of your skill, for Albert tells me you have a cure for all equine maladies.'

'None of its uses is profane or sorcerous, madam,' I said. 'And, if you permit, I shall attempt to heal your pony without. The art of healing requires no spells or incantations, but only painstaking work and patience. The true physician needs no magic, only his herbs and ointments, a keen eye and a gentle hand.'

'And surely God's blessing, sir?'

I did not reply.

'You doubt it, sir?'

'Not at all, my lady. But let us not discuss theology on such short acquaintance.'

I never forgot our conversation. The pony recovered and my friendship with Duke Albert blossomed. Although I was attracted to Matthilde as to no other living woman, I did not suppose we could ever be more than acquaintances. Yet, in the end, she had chosen me over a dozen suitors of the Brunswick nobility.

Doquz and Hypatia remained at the forge for a second night. Next morning, soon after Matthilde's departure, I hurried through the meadow to the village. Once again, the three of us walked by the river. As we talked, I could not help studying the child - my child - more closely. Doquz saw me do it and her face puckered in the expression I knew to denote pleasure.

'Why did I not come to Venice?' she said. 'I see the question on your lips, Hassan, but you do not ask it.'

'Yes.'

'Yes? Is that all you have to say? How do you suppose I found you ... how I came to be here in the cold north?'

I had not considered the matter. Amid the thrill of our reunion, I had given no thought to the why or how of the Singari presence in Brunswick. It could not be accident. Yet Doquz had told me she was cast ashore in Greece, and Greece was a long way from the Veneto.

'How long we travelled I do not know, Hassan, but I felt the months drift into seasons, and the seasons into years. I had made a promise to Hypatia that we would live, that we would find you, and that she would know her father. The Singari had no plans, no destination in mind, so I filled their heads with stories of the country you had described to me so often: of the city that lived on water; of the green tree-covered valley and the sweet grapes; of the mountains to the north through which the descendant of the Trojans had once led his elephants.

'Still we travelled. We have since learned that others of the Doum made the journey from the East, not only to Greece but to the heel of Italy. But that is unimportant. Kolbas and his clan were pioneers - explorers.

'I do not regret our relationship and I am not ashamed of it. Kolbas taught me things I would not otherwise have known. In some ways, he was like Ahmed, my natural father. Though he had no education, he understood the land, the mountains and the clouds. He had not read the work of Aristotle, the poetry of Homer or the tales of Firdausi – indeed he could not read at all - but he had a sense of history and could tell tales of his own. The Singari could sing and dance, things that many Persians have forgotten in their pursuit of the religion of Mahommet.

' 'Tis no arrogance to say that I influenced him too. And through him I influenced his sons and daughters, and his extended family. He often told them that the gods had sent me to light the path to a new homeland. I do not know how the idea came to him. He often laughed when he voiced it, though never in derision. You alone, Hassan, know that I have never placed trust in any gods, but Kolbas's simple belief made me feel very important and proud.

'And so we came to Italy and the Montecervino lands. There my courage failed me. Giovanni granted us permission to camp in a pasture. I discovered at once that you were not there and decided not to reveal my identity. I told myself it was one thing if Nadia or Giovanni recognised me but quite another if I suddenly blurted out my tale. They might not believe me. They had last seen me as a child; I was now a woman of thirty. I could only presume that they, and you, thought me dead.

'Nadia came twice to the camp, the first time to enquire after our needs, the second to bring a herbal remedy for one of our number who was sick. She knew me at once ...'

She broke off her narrative with a squeal of pain as I seized her by the arm and squeezed my fingers into her flesh. My heart leapt in my chest. Was I to believe that Nadia had recognised her and had not sent me a message?

Doquz shook herself free of me and rubbed the arm, her left. She raised the sleeve of her dress and I saw the white scar. It ran from the middle of the forearm to the elbow and beyond. It was the scar that I had made, when I had once cut her in a contest of swords – one in which neither of us had gained the upper hand. She had cut me too - across the chest. It was superficial but the line of it could still be seen.

'Forgive me,' I said.

Doquz pouted in vexation. ' 'Tis no inconvenience. But you do not know your own strength, my Hassan. Nor do you know when to listen rather than interrupt!

'Yes, Nadia knew me,' she went on. 'I do not understand this extra sense that enables her to dream the future, but she recognised me as if we had parted only yesterday.

' 'I sensed it, Doquz,' she told me. 'I sensed it so strongly. My visions said you lived. Yet they have played me false before. How could I give Hassan false hopes and see them dashed when I discovered I was wrong.'

'Then she told me everything: about your life in the Veneto; about your plans to travel in Germany; about your new enterprise in Brunswick; about Matthilde and how you planned to wed her.'

'My mother should have sent word. How could she not do so? It might not have been too late.'

'Do you wish it had been so, Hassan? Do you regret your marriage?'

'I do not regret it, but ...'

'No buts! I could not disrupt your new life. Even if you still loved me – and I could not be sure – how could I interfere with your plans? A wife? Children? I made your mother swear she would not tell you. Giovanni too. I made them take an oath on their holy book.

'Nadia asked to see her grandchild. Hypatia was six years old, old enough to understand. If she was willing, I said, we would both pass the winter in the comfort of the house.'

Hypatia had not spoken directly to me since that first evening. However, at this cue, she piped up and there was no stopping her. She told me how she had lived in the great mansion. She had learned to ride in the company of Nico, Yasmina and little Nadia, my brother and two sisters. My mother spoiled her, it seems. Hypatia did not use the word but I have no doubt it was like that.

I had been slow to accept that the child was indeed mine but once the fact was planted in my brain, I rejoiced in it. I loved Hypatia with all my heart. Yet, unless I could find a way of reconciling my two lives, that love would remain forever a bitter one.

Many men of my station kept mistresses. I knew that well enough. Indeed, they often kept them with the full knowledge of their wives. My position was different. Although the laws of Saxony would not recognise her, Doquz was no less my wife in my own eyes than was Matthilde, whom I had married according to Christian custom. It would be no difficult task for me to set her up comfortably in a house, with servants, stables and a new life away from the Singari. But Doquz would never accept such a role and I could never ask her to.

As for Matthilde, there had been no real betrayal and I resolved to tell her everything as soon as she returned from Brunswick.

Doquz and Hypatia spent a third night on the floor of the room above the forge. They must have departed before dawn because when I arrived in the village at first light, they had already gone. I would not see them again for another year.

Though I knew Doquz intended to rejoin the Singari for the autumn and winter, I had not expected her to leave without a final goodbye. She planned to travel south with them to the River Danube and remain there until the mountain snows melted. Then she would take Hypatia for a second visit to the Po Valley. I suggested she leave the child with me until spring but she refused, saying that Hypatia was too young to be parted from her. When we saw one another again, it would be time enough for decisions about our daughter's future.

The one decision we did make was the one over which I had so long agonised. Doquz had once been my sister, she said, and would be my sister again. As a wife, she would remain in the land of the dead. If Matthilde could accept that there was nothing other than friendship and sibling love between us, that was how it would be in the eyes of the world.

Matthilde was absent for a week. When she returned, I related all that had occurred, that Doquz was still alive and that she had given birth to our daughter. The reaction was quite different to what I expected. I had feared to meet with jealousy, accusation, reproach and condemnation – perhaps all of these – when my story was told. Perhaps Matthilde's lip would quiver a little, then she would defy me with a proud stare. Perhaps she would go directly to her priest, confess all and ask for absolution for the sin of adultery. If the clergy were allowed to interfere in the matter, the life we had built for ourselves would be in tatters. She would be humiliated, and I interrogated or censured. Or so I reasoned. Instead of any of these responses, my honesty was rewarded with silent tears.

I do not know how long she wept, refusing the reassurance of words or the comfort of my arm, but when at last the tears stopped flowing, she raised sad blue eyes to meet my gaze.

'Poor child, to grow up without knowing her father,' she said calmly. 'What are we to do, Sano? '

I told her what Doquz had said, that her life now was with the Singari; that she would make no claims on me other than that I should be a father to Hypatia; and that we would discuss and decide the child's future in one year's time.

'Yet she is still your wife?'

Here was a more intractable problem, one that I had however already considered. If Matthilde believed her marriage invalid in the eyes of her Church, she would still confess all to the priest, unless I could convince her there was no sin.

'No,' I said. 'The marriage is dissolved.'

The truth was that there had never been a formal ceremony in Persia. Doquz and I had spoken words to each other, no more. Moreover, the years of separation gave either of us the right to repudiate the agreement. I had done so long ago, by acknowledging that Doquz was dead and by taking new vows before a bishop of the Christian Church. Doquz herself had done so by virtue of her Singari marriage to Kolbas. Now we had both given voice to our separation by a threefold utterance of the talaq, the Muslim divorce ritual.

I said as much. I said it with as much sincerity as I could muster. Further, if Matthilde wished it, we would go to the bishop and renew our vows that very day. It was a small deception only and where was the harm?

And so my double existence began. Many men would have envied me. I had wealth and enjoyed the respect of my tenants. I had two women whom I loved and who loved me in return. I had a beautiful daughter, to whom I would settle what property I could and arrange for her a noble marriage. There were my business interests in Saxony, the Low Countries,

England and the near Levant. In the Veneto was my mother, a brother and two sisters whom I adored and a stepfather who was very dear to me.

So I was content. My only regret was that Matthilde had still not been able to give us children. In the spring of 1313, she told me she had again conceived, but that pregnancy too ended in tragedy when the infant, a boy, was born dead.

The Singari returned to the Leine Valley the following June and set up their camp in our pasture. Doquz and Hypatia were with them. I had not been idle during the year. In the hope that I might persuade Doquz to forsake her life of travelling, I rebuilt parts of the forge and equipped it anew. I strengthened the staircase to the dwelling above and renovated and furnished the latter to be fit for a lady of quality.

My efforts were in vain. Though Doquz was willing to give up the nomad life, she thought it improper that she should reside in Bachhagen village. And under no circumstances would she accept my invitation to visit the manor house. So it was that, with Andreas's help, I purchased a house for her in Hameln.

v

Doquz came to Hameln in the autumn of 1314 and took the name Ennia, the one she had used among the Singari. We were true to our resolve to be again the brother and sister we had been so many years before. Andreas made it known that she was the widow of a business acquaintance of us both. It was a harmless deception that satisfied the gossips, though whether they believed it or not was another matter. Whatever opinions they held in private, it came as no surprise when the frequency of my visits to Hameln increased. Yet Matthilde never had any reason to reproach me as an unfaithful husband. Not at first.

Hypatia was already ten and, as the years passed and we came to know one other as father and daughter, she became the most loving child a man could have. Matthilde, as yet unable to give birth herself, was to her as a second mother. If there was any jealousy in my wife's heart she hid it, and I never once doubted that she loved Hypatia as her own. I could not expect there to ever be a bond of friendship between her and Doquz. Nevertheless, I hoped. But though Matthilde many times extended the offer of hospitality, it was always refused.

'You must see 'tis impossible,' Doquz said. 'Though I wish her no harm, Matthilde is my enemy. How can I accept food and shelter at any house where she is mistress? Hypatia may come and go freely between the two; 'tis her right. And Matthilde may come with you to Hameln. I will treat her as an honoured guest for your sake, but more I cannot give.'

At the spring equinox of 1318, Hypatia celebrated her fourteenth birthday. On the threshold of womanhood, she was already very beautiful and had attracted the attention of several youths among the sons of the merchant families of Hameln. Whereas she resembled her mother in height, in the colour and texture of her hair and in the shape of her face, her eyes and her figure were Nadia's. Not all Saxony's inhabitants were fair. As in Persia and Italy, that country gave birth to all shades of complexion and there may have been as many maidens with brown eyes as there were with blue. However, Hypatia's heritage marked her out as different to any other, and as a coveted prize for the man who would win her hand.

Doquz and I did our best to guard her virtue against predatory attention without denying her the company of others of her age or imposing on her unsavoury customs of the society in which we had grown up. Marriages, contracted by the respective parents during their children's minority, and enforced for political or economic advantage, were not unknown in Saxony, yet Brunswick laws were for the most part interpreted liberally.

We made no attempt to guide our daughter in matters of religion. However, living under Christian law as we did, where in all solemn undertakings Saxons were guided by the clergy, it was inevitable that Hypatia would be drawn towards the Christian faith. Indeed it would have been impossible for her to own to any other.

In no way did I feel betrayed by her allegiance. Persian scholars had long since developed the doctrine of *taqiyya*, which allowed followers of one faith to maintain a pretence while living under another and, with almost fifteen years of experience, I had learned how to deal with the priests without provoking them or giving them reason to question my beliefs. Not that there was any real need for pretence. Even if I had remained loyal to the religion of my mother's people, after many years studying the teachings of Jesus, I could see little that conflicted with the wisdom of Mahommet. If there was indeed a God or a Paradise, which I doubted, it would be the same God and the same paradise for all peoples of the world.

On the other hand, Doquz, raised by a Christian mother but even more certain than I in her denial of the divine, saw the priests' influence as unwelcome intrusion in her daughter's life. It required all my vigilance to foresee and prevent confrontation.

For four years, all had been well. However, Hypatia's coming of age did not pass without a crisis looming in our lives.

'It's so unfair, Papa,' she said to me. 'To have you as an uncle is splendid, but what I would give to be able to shout to the world that you are my father!'

'As would I. But you understand the problem?'

'Of course, Papa. At least, Mama explained once and I think I understood, though not entirely. I would never tell.'

'Not even the priest?'

Hypatia frowned. 'Of course not. I am what I am, and there is no shame or guilt to confess.' She wrinkled her forehead in a manner that reminded me so much of Doquz. 'Why does Mama never visit your house in the country?' she went on. 'And why is she unhappy?'

'Did your mother tell you she was unhappy?'

'Of course not, Papa, but I know she is. You have your stewards, your farms, and your labourers to work them. You have your astrology, your physic, your berries and roots, and potions and ointments, and charts and diagrams. Mama has none of that. Oh, she has Uncle Andreas as a friend. And of course, there is me.

'But it is your company she craves, and when you stay away too long, or when I come back from a visit, I sometimes see her crying. She hides her face and lies to me, but I know.'

I questioned her some more and it came to me how blind I must have been. My own happiness had a price, and that price was the happiness of those dearest to me. However, in trying to lighten my own conscience, I was to make matters worse. I became blind in another direction – that of my daughter's wellbeing. My visits to Hameln became more frequent and, one evening in the summer of 1318, against everything we had agreed, Doquz and I lay together in the bed that had become the prison of her sensuality. And she was as weak as I, and not entirely blameless, for I did not force myself on her, but went merely to reassure her as a brother might do.

It seemed like a small betrayal. But the first consequence was the rekindling of the passion we had enjoyed together in the country of our birth. By autumn, the betrayal had become a regular affair.

The second consequence was that, in our preoccupation with our own pleasure, we failed to see what we ought to have seen, that our daughter was being drawn into a web of corruption. For two years, Hypatia had visited a priest at the abbey church of St Boniface for instruction in her faith. But as she grew in beauty and grace, Father Walther's eye was turned from teaching to something more sinister. Frustrated by his calling, he sought comfort in the arms of a maiden who, trusting by nature and inexperienced in the ways of men, was no match for his lustful intentions. Before the turn of the new year of 1319, he had ravished her and left her pregnant with his child.

By the time we learned the truth it was too late for, though we pressed Hypatia to reveal it, she refused to divulge the name of her violator. I think she feared she would not be believed or, at least, even if we her parents believed her, no one else would.

The blow that Fate had dealt us was in no way softened by what should have been a much happier spring. By coincidence, Matthilde had also fallen pregnant.

In the end, it was Doquz who discovered the priest's infamy by default.

Hypatia's devotion to the Christian religion was plain to see. She had been a regular attendee at Mass and was committed to her studies. When for her own sake we kept her to the house, we offered to send for Father Walther so that he might continue to instruct her. The invitation was much against Doquz's instincts, and mine, yet we could not deny our daughter spiritual comfort if that was what she desired. It occurred to me too that since Hypatia would not tell us the name of her ravisher, the good priest

– as I at any rate thought him – might succeed where we had failed and persuade her to confess her secret to us.

The gesture was met with a blunt refusal. Hypatia would not hear of Father Walther coming to the house but insisted that we send for a senior monk, a man of some sixty years of age. Her excuse when she calmed down was that she could not permit the younger man to see her in her present condition. And when, despite our having fallen in with her wishes, Father Walther himself arrived uninvited to ask after her well-being, Hypatia became agitated and uttered a high-pitched wail, until Doquz sent him away.

Meanwhile, Matthilde's time was also drawing near. Determined this time that she should have every chance to carry her child for a full nine months, I persuaded her to take to her bed. Just as in Hameln, the probability of a birth drew the attention of the clergy, though in rather a different way. Concerned about his cousin's welfare, Duke Albert persuaded his bishop to attend and pray for her. This bishop was a learned and worldly man and, though doubting the efficacy of his prayers, I welcomed him to our house.

The sudden disappearance of a young priest from the church of St Boniface's in Hameln was the subject of local gossip for a month or more. Father Walther had set out on a mission to give last rites to a parishioner but had not returned. He was never seen in the town again and the discovery of a body some distance down-river was never connected to the mystery. The River Weser claimed many victims and the body was so badly damaged by water and rocks that identification was impossible. It was to be seven years before I learned the truth of how Hypatia's violator had paid the ultimate price for his crime.

vi

During her four years at Hameln, Doquz had grown her hair. She had kept it fastened so I had not noticed. She cut it. A tunic, breeches and cap of a youth were easily obtained. The weapons, two short swords and a dagger, she always kept out of sight in the house.

Hypatia's sudden aversion to Father Walther had aroused her

suspicion. She learned his habits by following him unnoticed from the abbey church of St Boniface to the houses of his parishioners and back again. She had sat in the shadows of the church while he listened to confession. Many of the penitents were young women. She had dogged his footsteps as he walked for exercise by the riverbank and across the Weser bridge. Not once did he suspect he was being watched.

Some weeks later, Doquz slipped out of the house one early evening. She was armed. She had donned her disguise and wrapped a cloak round her shoulders because the weather was cool. As it was only an hour until dusk, the streets of Hameln were quiet. She made her way to the abbey and stood in the shadows in one corner of the square. Her anger had not diminished.

She did not have long to wait. Father Walther emerged from the church door in the company of another priest. They conversed briefly before the latter crossed the square and turned down a lane of shops and artisan houses. Father Walther glanced towards Doquz's corner but apparently seeing nothing to rouse his suspicion, set off in the opposite direction. He went towards the market where he spent above the quarter hour in a nearby house. Then turning westwards again, he made his way back to the Fish Gate, where he stopped at a second house. When he emerged, the sun had set and the moon had come up, though obscured by cloud.

The priest crossed the river. Doquz hastened after him, quickening her pace so that she did not lose sight of him beyond the apex of the bridge. He must have heard the soft footfall or else she kicked a stone against the parapet because he turned round.

'What do you want?' he demanded of the shadows. 'I know you are following me. I have no money, if that is your purpose.'

Doquz realised that he took her for a footpad. It did not matter. She stepped into the middle of the road.

'What do you want?' demanded Father Walther again. He had not quite reached level ground on the Weser's western side. Behind him, in the narrow ways between tall crooked houses was all darkness.

'Your confession,' said Doquz.

'I have no need of a confessor,' said the priest. He threw back his hood and fumbled beneath his cassock. 'I am armed and can defend myself.'

'So much the better,' said Doquz coldly. She had not expected a man of the cloth to be carrying a weapon, but it suited her purpose better if he did. 'It will be no murder when I cut your throat.'

'How have I offended you, my son, that you should wish my death?' said Father Walther.

'You do not know?'

'I am a brother in Christ. A man of peace. I call no man enemy.'

'Perhaps it is not a man who calls you to account,' said Doquz. She removed the youth's cap and tossed it aside, then threw back her cloak to expose her baldric and its two swords. The dagger was concealed behind her back.

'Are you a demon that you taunt me and talk in riddles?' the priest said, a touch of agitation creeping into his voice. It was clear he did not recognise her as a woman on account of her short hair and youth's build. He took a few steps backward, watching her warily.

'No demon but flesh and blood like you, if it is indeed red blood that flows through your veins,' said she. 'Shall we test it, or will you confess?'

'What would you have me confess? We are all sinners, I no less than any common man.'

'There are seven, I am told,' said Doquz. 'But one will suffice. Porneia, if you know the Greek. Fornicatio in the Latin tongue.'

'I do not know what you mean,' said the priest.

'You know very well 'tis lust in both languages.'

'I was a man before I was a priest,' said Father Walther nervously, 'and a man is easily tempted, especially when a woman is willing.'

'And if she is not? If she is a wife ... or a daughter, and lies with you under protest?'

'I have done penance for my transgressions,' the priest said. 'God will forgive me.'

Just then, the moon came out from a cloud and threw its silvery light on the bridge. Doquz had paid little attention to Father Walther previously, seeing only the cassock and hood, thinking of him not as a man but as a symbol of the faith he claimed to serve. She had imagined him from his voice to be a youth, no more than twenty. That would have been an excuse, she thought – a boy pressed into his calling by a father eager to buy a place in a non-existent paradise. Now, however, she saw a rugged, mature face, clean-shaven but with long flowing locks. His eyes were almost lost in the shadow of his prominent brows but she judged them dark and expressionless. He was older than she had once supposed him to be, hidden as he usually was by the robes of his profession.

In an instant, her doubts vanished. This was no youth, confused about life and love. Father Walther was a man who had lived in and knew the world. Hypatia was not his only victim. There could be no excuse for what he had done.

'Your God may do what he pleases,' she said. 'Now that I have seen your face, I will not forgive. I have known men like you, driven by lust or liquor, or both, to prey on children. Their God is the flesh that hangs between their legs!'

'That is blasphemy! A man would not risk the fires of Hell. You are a demon, posing as a man. Begone, back to ....'

He did not finish the sentence. In exposing the features of her adversary, the emergent moonlight had also fallen on Doquz's face. Whether the priest suddenly recognised it, or knew her by instinct of his guilt, she did not know. He retreated again. His jaw fell and his gaze shifted to her swords.

'What do you want of me, Mistress Ennia, if it is indeed you?'

'Do not doubt it,' said Doquz. 'And, since you know me, you know why I pursue you.'

'I know the face, but it is a phantasm. Demon or hellhag, you have taken possession of her body. You cannot expect me to fight you.'

'Perhaps you would rather ravish me, as you did my daughter?' said Doquz scornfully. 'As you did other maidens perchance! You will find me a tougher proposition, I can assure you. And yet you will fight me, or I will cut you down where you stand.' She drew both her swords and cast one on the ground at the priest's feet. If his cassock indeed hid a weapon, let him use it; if not, let him defend himself with hers. Trial by combat, the age-old ritual, and she knew herself to be both master and mistress of it.

The priest ceased fumbling in the folds of his cassock. Both hands came into view and he held them high in front of him, making a cross with his forearms. There was no sword, not even a poniard. *'Effugare, Diabole!'* he cried in a loud voice. *'Appropinquabit enim judicium Dei!'*

'You cannot rid yourself of me so easily,' laughed Doquz. His superstitious posture irritated her. She made a sudden mock lunge, not intending injury, and severed the cord of his robe. Father Walther, taken by surprise, uncrossed his arms, clutched at his garment and hitched it up.

'*A tooth for a tooth* is your creed,' Doquz went on. 'What, I wonder, is the punishment for beast carnality? At least some other child will be spared Hypatia's agony.'

'Hypatia,' echoed the priest. His face now showed real fear but whether for his life or his manhood Doquz could not decide. 'Yes, I confess and have repented,' he said. 'I did not plan it. Her innocence led me on.'

'Coward! 'Twas her innocence that should have protected her. Pick up the sword.'

'I will not. I am a priest of the Holy Church.' He backed away from the weapon on the ground, moving to his left, towards a low section of the parapet. Below, in the gloom, the Weser gurgled. The river was high.

Near the water's edge, some stones were dislodged and the path fell away in a steep bank. Father Walther's sandal caught the trailing hem of his cassock and before he could correct his balance, he slipped. As he fell backwards, the moonlight again illuminated his face and Doquz saw for an instant the terror of death in his eyes as he tumbled into the darkness. There followed the resounding crack of his head striking an invisible obstacle, then silence but for the rumbling of the water. She looked over but could see nothing.

vii

My son was born on the fourth day of March. I was not present at the birth but I took him from the midwife and laid him in his crib with a sense of relief and satisfaction. Matthilde was very weak but in her selfless way she insisted that I go to Hypatia, who was due within the week.

'You must go, Sano,' she said. 'I will be all right and you will be able to spoil the baby as much as you like when you return. The midwife reassures me this faintness is only temporary. Besides, the good bishop is still here to give me spiritual comfort.'

I kissed both her and the child and left for Hameln.

It was always going to be a difficult birth. Like her mother, Hypatia was narrow in the hips and at the age of only fifteen, though fertile, was not fully developed in other ways. Shortly after her waters broke, her screams began. Since the disappearance of Father Walther, she had been calm but now she began to curse God and cry that the infant in her womb was an abomination. She would not allow it to be born. The screaming continued fitfully for two days during which she frequently writhed with pain, the sweat running from her body like a flood.

Two midwives came but neither would remain and listen to Hypatia's ranting and blasphemies. We did not invite the Church. I had never witnessed a birth and despite my study of physic did not as yet have the knowledge or skill to bring a child into the world, especially one whose mother refused to have any part in the process.

Doquz was almost as frantic as our daughter and I, assailed by those dreadful screams, scarcely less so.

'You must do something, Hassan. The child must be wrongly placed and will kill her if it is not removed unnaturally.'

'We must wait,' I cried. 'If I were to cut her wrongly, she will die the sooner.'

Doquz bent over Hypatia's divan.

'I saw it done once in Persia,' she said. 'In the women's quarters at Tabriz. And if I had been in greater pain, Shirazi would have done it to me. He even marked me in anticipation. I remember.' She pushed Hypatia's shift up over her hips and ran her fingers under the swollen belly. 'Just here.'

'We must wait,' I repeated. My heart was pounding with anxiety. Propriety made me want to look away.

'There is no time,' said Doquz. 'Take your dagger and do it. I will hold your hand and we will do it together.'

'First bring some hot water. We must cleanse the blade,' I said, playing for time. The operation was known to me. However, it was a practice carried out, to my knowledge, only when the mother was already dead.

Doquz went to fulfil my instructions. When she returned, Hypatia's screams and curses became even louder. As it seemed to me, she was delirious with the pain. It was well into the second night.

'Do it, Papa,' she cried between laboured breaths. 'Cut this Devil's child from my body. I never want to see it! Do it now.'

I took the dagger and held it, hesitating, poised above Hypatia's abdomen. Her legs were apart and she was heaving and writhing on the divan like some mad woman. Her screams pierced my ears and my heart. Maddened by the curses, I longed to silence them and had she been other than my daughter I think I would have done so.

'No,' I said, my sanity returning. 'I will not.'

'Then I must,' said Doquz. She seized my arm and tried to wrest the knife away. I resisted but she was strong and knew a paralysing grip. The weapon clattered to the floor. I tried to kick it away but she uttered a wail to rival the screams of Hypatia and struck me with her elbow.

We had never argued or fought since the day on Mount Sahand when, deceived by her masculine costume, I had challenged her to a contest of sabres. I was unprepared for the violence of her assault. In a moment, she had seized the knife and held it poised, ready to cut into our daughter's flesh.

Hypatia's eyes were wide with terror. She stopped screaming and a single mournful cry escaped her lips.

'Mama!'

It saved her life.

In her fear and anguish, Doquz would have cut. Her reason sapped by panic, the woman I had first loved - had loved like life itself – would have destroyed the being we had created together. But that single word made her pause.

I gripped her wrist. She struggled with me for a moment. But all her resistance had gone and she collapsed against me. I took the dagger from her and laid it aside. Then I held her, weeping and helpless, in my arms. Only then, I think, did I remember the cause of our quarrel and, in that very second I realized something else. For the first time in more than two days, there was near silence in the room. I turned in apprehension towards the bed.

Hypatia's face was contorted with effort. With the pain of labour, most of her good colouring had already left her cheeks. Those same cheeks were now hollow. Her eyes were tight shut and her mouth set in a grimace. She had ceased heaving and writhing but every sinew of her limbs was straining to expel the hated burden from her loins. The baby was coming.

Doquz reached again for the dagger. Instinctively, I moved to stop her but she held me back with the palm of her left hand. She was laughing now and I saw she had recovered her wits. Reaching between Hypatia's open thighs, she began drawing from there a shapeless bundle of blood and flesh.

The quantity of blood took me by surprise. I had seen blood before – in truth, too much, even the blood of friends. I had killed and watched men die. I had done it too without pity or emotion. But this was my child – and her child - my own flesh. The thought disturbed me and I turned away.

When I could bring myself to look again, there on the table beside the bed was a squirming infant – a beautiful boy child that might have been the twin of the one I had left behind at Bachhagen only days earlier. Beside him lay the afterbirth. Doquz had cut and bound the cord that connected the two and was busy cleaning the blood from the newborn's skin.

Hypatia lay still on her bed, pale as death, her raven hair tangled and matted, her soft eyes wide and staring. A trickle of blood that formed a widening red stain on the linen was the only remaining sign of her labours.

viii

Hypatia was so still that I feared she might yet die. She showed no sign of awareness. We closed her staring eyes as we would have done with a corpse. Doquz reassured me.

' 'Tis often so,' she said. 'I lay senseless for a day after Hypatia came.'

We washed her hair and face as best we could. Doquz removed the soiled shift and with great difficulty replaced it with another. Together we changed the bed linen. Our daughter did not stir. After about an hour some colour seemed to return to her face. Her breathing became more relaxed and she opened her eyes.

Three times, Doquz tried to persuade Hypatia to take her infant to her breast; three times, she refused.

'It's useless,' I said. 'She does not want him.'

'Take the boy,' said Doquz. 'Find him a wet nurse. Leave Hypatia to me. Perhaps when he is no longer in her sight, she will change her mind.'

'Let us hope so, because he is a handsome fellow,' I said. I took the boy in his new wrappings to the next room and sat pensively, cradling him on my lap. He did not cry or complain. I sensed that all our best efforts would be wasted. Hypatia had thought her pregnancy a curse and would refuse to change her mind. I had seen her resolved and knew she would not yield to pressure. A child unwanted is a child neglected. My daughter would wish to be free to return to her former life.

While I was debating with myself what to do, a messenger arrived from Bachhagen with the dreadful news that Matthilde had relapsed and now had a high fever. I rushed home to be with her, taking Hypatia's infant with me.

The messenger had confused the facts. Matthilde was still weak and confined to her bed, but was recovering. The son I had long hoped for was sick beyond hope and died before I could again hold him in my arms. The bishop had remained at Bachhagen and he performed the Christian last rites over the body. It was what Matthilde wanted.

There was no plan of deceit. Several of the household had seen me with Hypatia's child without having any inkling of who he was. None had shown any curiosity. The Bishop himself had looked at the tiny face and said how alike the two brothers were. I wondered at this remark until I realised that, being excluded from the labour, he could not know for sure whether Matthilde had given birth to one boy or two. Seeing the second child, he had come to the natural conclusion.

Without thinking the matter through, I laid Hypatia's son beside my wife in her bed and watched while he sucked greedily from her breast.

ix

Hypatia was adamant she would not even see her infant. Doquz agreed that Matthilde and I should bring him up. He was certainly a handsome boy and, in the circumstances, it was a perfect solution. We called him Andreas in honour of my friend and partner. To the world at large, he was our son.

Doquz decided to take Hypatia to Italy, to the home of my mother who, although nearing sixty years of age, was in excellent health. My stepfather having died two years earlier, my half-brother Nico was now managing the Montecervino vineyards.

'Hypatia may later do as she pleases,' said Doquz as we parted company. 'But I think the Italian climate and the company of her cousins will do her good. Perhaps Nadia can find a suitable husband for her among the Venetian gentry. As for me, I shall not return to a life of leisure. Travelling is in my blood and I think the Singari will welcome me back as one of their own.'

I begged her reconsider but she had decided. Four years of idleness had softened her, she said, and she needed the open fields and the mountains once more.

'Do not imagine I will neglect you, Hassan,' she said. 'The summers in Saxony are pleasant. Perhaps I will be able to overlook my enmity with your wife and visit my grandson. After all, with Hypatia so stubborn, I owe Matthilde a debt!'

Often, it is said, the presence of one child in a family encourages the arrival of another.

So it was with us. By midsummer in 1322, Matthilde was again with child. I had learned much from my experience at Hameln and insisted on being with my wife throughout her labour and at the birth itself. My studies had, moreover, taught me how different women can be. Not only the mother's girth and shape determine the course of labour and birth but the condition of her mind.

My decision caused some muttering among our servants who, I suppose, fancied that some devilish work was afoot. The midwives I had engaged for the duration of Matthilde's confinement were suspicious of my motives and would have excluded me. But money is a powerful persuader and when there is sufficient of it, it overcomes the most strenuous argument.

Ludwig was born in the week of the winter solstice. The villagers said it was an good omen. The Church taught that Jesus Christ had been born in that very week, and that the celebrations attending the Yule festival should be accompanied by prayers and thanksgiving for His coming. These festivals were quite unknown in Persia but after nearly twenty years an exile I had begun to take them for granted. My only regret was that Hypatia was not there to share them with us.

Whatever the public opinion, that year was not to end without worrying developments. Andreas, now nearly four years old, became very jealous of his brother. Although Matthilde had never been in any doubt that he was Hypatia's child and not her own, such was her nature that she treated him in every way as if he had been born from her womb. He had become the son we had both lost. That being so, we had decided against telling him his origins, at least until he was old enough to understand.

Andreas had always been solitary, with a tendency toward mischief. As a three- year-old, his favourite prank was to hide in a closet, under a bed, or in a dark corner, and when no one expected it, to utter such a shriek as could almost awaken the dead, terrifying the maids and freezing the blood of any visitor who had not been warned of his perverse habit. And the household encouraged him in his waywardness. As Bachhagen's only child, he was pampered and cosseted by kinsfolk and servants alike.

Once, having escaped the watchful eye of a steward, he had slipped unseen into my laboratory. Free from adult eyes, he began to experiment with the contents of the jars according to his own preferences of colour, texture and smell. Alerted by the sound of shattering glass, I found him standing on the table, amidst fragments of broken pottery, glass beakers and phials, and eyeing longingly some containers full of attractive but deadly red berries.

Relieved that my carelessness had not led to tragedy, I thereafter kept the inner door securely locked when I was not working, and rearranged the poisonous substances on a higher shelf.

Now that there was a younger, more demanding infant to keep his mother's attention, Andreas began to sulk. When not allowed his own way, he flew into a temper at the slightest reprimand, and became more malicious in his pranks than ever before.

I had never seen such rage in a child. But the adventure in the laboratory had shown me Andreas's enquiring nature and I decided it was time I began instructing him properly in the sciences. I made every effort to kindle his interest in physic and astrology, and engaged a tutor to teach him reading, writing and the classics. Andreas was an able pupil in every way and gradually, with his mind fully occupied, his tantrums became less frequent.

However, as the months and years passed, I saw in my sons, the adopted and the natural, little of the usual signs of affection between boys of their ages. Thomas and Roland, Matthilde's nephews, had often fought like bitter enemies, but they never ended a day without embracing and vowing eternal friendship. Between Andreas and Ludwig there was no open hostility, yet neither was there the laughter that accompanied the play of their cousins. Ludwig smiled, but often his smiles were met by a stony stare.

'They are only children,' Matthilde would say. 'They will grow out of it.'

I wished I had her patience and optimism. Often, when the house was quiet, I would retire to my laboratory, light a lamp and sit alone on the bench. Sometimes I would take the fylfot and hold it between my fingers so that the flickering light glinted on its surface.

A moth would flutter against the casement. Occasionally, in summer, when the Singari were camped below, laughter and singing would drift across the herb garden. The sloping fields were warmed by the glow of their camp fire. These things should have cheered me as they had done once, but instead I felt empty. The shadow cast by the fylfot was grey and twisted.

I did not believe in omens but as I watched my children grow I was filled with apprehension for the future.

It was to be a special treat for the boys, the summer of 1326, when the

Singari came again to the Leine valley and camped near Hannover. Doquz was not with them. I had seen her the previous year but she had spent the past two winters in Italy to be with Hypatia who had elected to be with my mother until such time as she decided to marry. Those were her words and there was no doubt the decision would be hers. A beautiful woman of twenty summers who remains at once unwed and youthful has no shortage of suitors. Indeed, Hypatia had many.

Andreas and Ludwig were excited by the prospect of an outing. Ludwig was too young to understand much of what he saw, but he clapped his hands with delight at the colourful costumes, at the flames crackling on the cooking fires and the music of the Singars' instruments.

I begged Baras, who still led the clan, that if there were to be any smoking of weed, it would be done out of the sight of my sons and to this he agreed. He also agreed to send some families to camp at Bachhagen, for I expected a bumper harvest and would need extra labour.

Andreas was fascinated and totally absorbed by his visit to Hannover. After it was over, he pleaded with me to take him again. I could see no harm in his associating with the Singari, especially since his experience that day seemed to have taken him out of his moods. It was also, I reasoned, part of his heritage to spend time with a people who had played such an important part in the lives of both his true mother and of hers. Even Matthilde, who had doubts, could not deny him that. Thus it was that, when the Singari came a week or two later to our pasture, I gave Andreas leave to cross the meadow by himself to visit the camp.

He did so regularly throughout the summer. At first, his association with the nomads seemed wholly beneficial. Because he sulked less often, I was glad to encourage him in his new-found friendships, though I refused to let him have his own way and insisted he also pursue his studies.

However, as summer yielded to autumn, I began to have doubts. Andreas spent his time with the Singari youths rather than the children. Moreover, he shunned the company of Ludwig even more than he had done previously. And, whereas he had shown some leaning towards science, he was now developing an aversion to the physician's work. When I took him to visit a sickbed, he would stand back, his face unsmiling, his dark eyes expressionless, unless asked to assist. Only then would he come forward and perform simple tasks he had learned from me, without the slightest error but with apparent indifference.

I hid and tried to ignore my misgivings. There was no one with whom I could share my premonition that Fate had some mischief in store.

Duke Albert had died at harvest time in 1318 and was buried with ceremony in the cathedral of Brunswick. There was a dispute about which of his sons should inherit the largest share of his lands, settled eventually in favour of Magnus and two others. I knew Magnus but could not confide in him as I had done in his father.

Matthilde, tireless in her devotion to our children, was blind to their faults. Roland, her brother, with whom I had never been close, made as much of his nephews as of his own sons and daughter, and dismissed lightly even their most shameful misdemeanours.

Andreas became more sullen than ever. He rarely spoke except to answer a question and often, he deliberately avoided my eyes. And it disconcerted me how, from time to time, he would steal a look at the fylfot, half expectant, half fearful, as if the ornament had a life of its own. I had already begun to experiment with it in my treatments of sick farm workers and villagers. Andreas had watched me but at the age of only five I did not imagine that he understood.

I had supposed too that the matters of politics were beyond his understanding, but in that I was just as wrong. He approached me one day while I was working in the laboratory.

'What if Uncle Magnus were to die, Father?' he said. 'Who would inherit his lands and his castle?'

I was too surprised by the question to answer immediately.

Andreas repeated it, his eyes to the ground.

'Magnus is a young man,' I said. 'He will have children.'

Andreas raised his eyes and regarded me impassively. 'And if he has none, Father?' he asked. 'Will Uncle Roland become a duke?'

I realised that I had been mistaken and had underestimated his intelligence.

'I think not,' I replied. 'The Grübenhagens and Wolfenbüttels have much better claims than your uncle.'

Andreas digested this information.

'Does a duke not serve a king, Father,' he asked innocently after a pause, 'and does a king not, in turn, serve an emperor?'

'That is indeed the natural order.'

'Yet you are the son of a king, Father. Should it not be you who rules in Saxony?'

I was too taken aback to speak. Andreas's gaze flitted from my face to the fylfot and back again.

'Should it not?' he demanded. 'By the power of that magic cross you wear, you might do so if you wished.'

'Who has told you all this?' The agitation in his voice was so unnerving that I shivered with an unnatural chill.

'But it's true, is it not?' Andreas persisted. 'You were once a prince; I had it from the 'Gyptian chief. Master Baras, the Singar. He tells wonderful tales of princes and sorcerers in olden times. Are you a sorcerer, Father? Baras says he who wears the fylfot must be a mighty wizard, a master of all things.'

Now I was angry. It was true that I had used the fylfot to bring sleep and to relieve headache. And since my first experience, I had twice used it to relieve the pangs of childbirth. However, there was no excuse for Baras filling my son's head with thoughts of magic and sorcery.

'It is nonsense, Andreas!' I said. 'The art I practise works in harmony with nature. Healing is no magic but a result of long study and practice of the sciences.' I was trying to shrug off my unease but my heart was beating faster than usual. Some things were better not spoken to children.

I reprimanded Baras, but the damage was done.

The Singari remained in the pasture until the leaves began to fall from the trees. I employed them as I had intended, gathering the harvest and, when that was done, helping store the grain and weather-proofing the barns. At no time did I have cause to question their diligence. They were respectful in their manners, clean in their habits, and fond of singing and dancing in their leisure hours.

Some of their womenfolk claimed a talent for interpreting dreams and seeing the future in the lines of the hand. These practices were condemned by the priests, and Matthilde found them disturbing, but that did not prevent her personal maid and others of the manor house servants from visiting the Singari camp secretly to learn the name of their future lovers, or whether their children were to be boys or girls.

I was well aware of this intercourse and ignored it. Despite Baras having filled Andreas's head with superstition, I suspected the fortune-tellers of practising harmless deception.

In the last days of a damp October, the Leine began to rise and muddy pools of water formed in the lower pasture. The Singars packed their tents and belongings as quickly as they had unloaded them and quit Bachhagen without a word. I did not see Baras again.

The following year, I had business in Venice and decided to attend to it in person. It meant an absence from Bachhagen of a few months but, since beginning my life in Saxony, I had visited my mother only three times. I was forty-six years old, which meant she was past sixty and I felt that if I did not see her soon, I might never do so again.

There was always news of her and of my brother and two sisters. For nearly twenty years, I had trusted to the merchant guild to carry messages and gifts between us. However, my mother had never seen her grandchild nor, in Andreas's case, her great-grandchild, and it seemed to me that before she died, she ought to know both.

Matthilde parted with the boys reluctantly. It was a long and tedious journey for children, especially for Ludwig who, though big for his years, had not learned to ride and had to be carried on my horse. Andreas had his own pony, a present from Doquz on his seventh birthday. We had never told him of his relationship to her and he knew her only as an adopted aunt. She, being unwilling to accept hospitality at Bachhagen, had twice before arranged for us to meet at the Queck home in Hameln.

I promoted a steward to look after the estate while I was away. He had been in the family's service for ten years and we trusted him implicitly.

We were gone from Saxony from May until October. I had my wish and Nadia made a great deal of fuss over the children, for the first and last time.

'How could you father such a beautiful boy, Hassan?' she said of Ludwig. 'He is so pink and fair. We must protect him from the hot sun. As for Andreas, he might almost be ...' She stopped but I fancied I knew what she intended to say, that he looked every inch my son. However, despite his black hair and dark skin, I saw nothing of myself in Andreas and very little of Hypatia.

Hypatia refused to see the boy and I had to meet her in secret without Andreas's knowledge. She had engaged herself to a son of the Soranzo family, and planned marriage within weeks.

'If only you could be there, Papa,' she said. 'Mama is restless again. She plans to rejoin the Singari in the Veneto and travel north with them after the wedding.'

'Perhaps I could be there, if only you would see Andreas. It's true that Matthilde will be anxious if I stay away too long but another month or two will make no difference.'

She hesitated and I saw that at last she was torn.

'No,' she said at length. 'It is not possible.'

'It is possible!'

'What would I say to him, Papa? That I am his mother? That I abandoned him at birth? I know he did not ask to be born – to be conceived in sin and live inside me for nine months while I cursed him, the man who had seeded him, and God. Forgive me, Papa. You know I cannot do it.'

There was no more to be said. She parted from me in tears while my heart was heavy with sadness, wanting to comfort her but knowing that whatever I said she would not relent.

In the event, it was I who changed my mind. I did attend the wedding. Making my excuses, I left Andreas and Ludwig with my mother and joined Doquz at the side of the bride at the church of St Marcus. It was but a small sacrifice to see Hypatia's smile as she turned and left the altar with her new husband.

'If only you could stay longer, Hassan,' Doquz said to me afterwards. 'To see the children again makes me realise how we have grown apart.'

'If so, it is none of my doing.'

'No, 'tis all of mine.'

'Then come back with me. The house at Hameln can again be yours. We can be brother and sister again. Or friends. Or lovers if you wish.'

'Look at me, Hassan,' she said. 'My youth is gone, while that woman of yours grows younger every year. How old is she? Twenty-five ...'

I laughed. 'Matthilde is much older ...'

'Thirty then. Still young enough to conceive. Her breasts are proud; her thighs are firm and smooth. What man would not desire her? What man would not long to penetrate her and fill her with his seed? Against that, what can I offer?'

I had rarely heard her speak so. In truth, I knew she was as old, or older than I but I had never thought of her in that way. We had shared our childhood with its laughter and its discoveries; we had shared our youth, or a part of it, with its passion and its dangers; and, after a fashion, we had shared our maturity with its joys, sorrows, deceptions and disappointments. I had never ceased to love her, for all that Matthilde meant to me, and would always love her, as long as there was any life left in me. Now that our daughter was happy, why should she not return to Saxony with me? In a year or two we would tell Andreas the truth and enjoy together the remainder of his childhood.

All of these things I said to her as we watched the bridal carriage turn a corner from St Mark's Square and disappear from sight. I put my arm round her shoulders, drew her against me and kissed her forehead.

'Come to Brunswick, Doquz!'

She looked at me sadly and shook her head.

'Have you looked at him, Hassan?'

'Andreas?' I asked, puzzled.

'What do you see when you look at him?'

I thought I knew what she meant by the question though I did not understand its purpose.

'Sometimes he has the look of Hypatia,' I lied. 'He has your mouth and chin.'

'What a poor judge you are,' Doquz said.

'And Nadia?' she went on when I did not reply. 'Does Nadia see my mouth and chin when she looks at the boy? Does she see Hypatia when she looks in his eyes?'

'I cannot say. How can I?' I asked.

'Why are men so blind to the obvious?' said Doquz. ' She sees you. She sees you as a seven-year-old boy. Your raven curls. Your mouth. Your chin. Your nose. Your complexion ... what were the first words you ever spoke to me, Hassan?'

'How can I remember that?'

'You said: why are you crying, little girl? I remember, you see. And I remember how you looked too. Andreas might be your double at the same age but for one thing.' To my surprise and alarm her lips trembled as she spoke. 'His eyes! To be an occasional aunt I can bear. But 'tis because of his eyes that I cannot share his childhood.'

'I do not understand.'

'He has his father's eyes. How can I face Andreas every day knowing what I have done?'

She was right to call me blind for I was slow to grasp her meaning. As I watched Andreas grow I had thought often of Hypatia's ordeal, of her difficult labour and the rejection of her son. However, seldom had I reflected on the cause of it. Suddenly, with a force that jarred me to the bones, I remembered Father Walther, the mystery of his disappearance and the body in the Weser.

'Her violator deserved to die,' said Doquz.

'Yes. His God punished him.'

'His God!' Doquz smiled grimly, her full lips pushed together making lines in her face I had not formerly noticed. She pulled away from my embrace.

'You killed him?' I said. 'I wondered but was afraid to ask. Then, when the body was found, I saw that justice had been served. You pushed him into the river ...?'

' 'Twas not like that. I gave him the chance of life ... and repentance.'

'Repentance?'

'I could not murder him, even knowing what he had done. Besides, I had no evidence, only Hypatia's terror when he came to our door. Not once did she utter his name.'

'I suspected.'

'I could not allow you to do it, Hassan. You had wife and position. For me, there was only Hypatia. If the crime had been discovered ...'

'It should have been my task, Doquz. But, when he vanished without trace ...'

'I often thought to tell you, my Hassan, but there was never a moment.'

I took her face between my hands and held her so that our eyes met. Hers were soft and tearful.

'Then tell me now,' I said.

Andreas

i

I brought the boys back to their mother. The delight in Matthilde's face as she welcomed us and spoiled them with kisses made our long absence seem worthwhile. Lou laughed and hugged her while Andreas acknowledged her excitement with little more than the flicker of a smile. She showed no feelings when I told her of Doquz's refusal to return to Saxony, but her eyes lit up with pleasure when I spoke of Hypatia's marriage.

There was no news of importance to greet me on my return. Kunz, my steward, had managed the estate with economy and efficiency and there were few tasks requiring my attention. The harvest had been stored and we settled in for another winter.

Andreas Queck had departed on an expedition to the Levant and his eldest son was handling our business. I remembered this son as a boy of eleven or twelve. He had been apprenticed to a merchant house in Hamburg and I had not seen him since. Such family exchanges had begun in an effort to build greater trust between the cities. There had been talk in the Guild of a wider, more formal business enterprise, with outposts in England and the Baltic, though nothing had yet come of it.

My study and practice of physic had suffered during my six months absence and I set about making good the deficiencies. I determined that, come what may, I should succeed in re-igniting young Andreas's interest in the sciences. For a while, I believed the plan was working. Some of his early enthusiasm seemed to return. There were days when he hung on to my every word and questioned my theories and conclusions with a sharpness of intellect that belonged in a boy twice his age. I was deceived as to his motives.

The Singari came to Bachhagen the next spring. Doquz, despite the doubts she had expressed to me, was with them. I knew that, though not of their race and creed, she held a place of honour and respect among them such as was usually accorded only to an elected leader. Andreas spent many hours in the camp and I felt that, at last, she must have formed a bond with him.

They left again at the onset of autumn. Shortly afterwards, I fell ill. At first, my symptoms were not too severe and I expected that a preparation of herbs crushed in wine and water, drunk hot at bedtime, would carry me through the worst. It was ineffective. For three days and nights I was laid low with a fever. I had no appetite and wanted only water to quench my burning thirst. Bathed in sweat and with my throat tormented by coughing, I told Matthilde what prescriptions I needed and their method of preparation. Then I took to bed, trusting her to be both physician and nurse.

With the fever came the demons of nightmare. Though I had quelled my fears that Andreas's darker nature might prevail, they now returned, magnified several fold. Sometimes I was no longer in Brunswick. Again, I was Prince Hassan, captain in the army of the Khan of Persia. Bedposts, pillows and cabinets assumed new and terrifying shapes, gory spectres from my past rising up from the plains of sand and salt. In my delirium I was among my enemies again, hacking with a sword. As they fell, their faces would dissolve and reform with the features of people I loved. Most terrifying of all, when in the fantasy I turned from the horror to look in a glass, the reflection that returned my stare was not my own, but that of my adopted son.

By the fourth night, the worst was past. My appetite returned, the stricture of my throat eased, and I was able to drink some broth that Matthilde fed to me with a spoon. Then I fell into a tranquil sleep from which I awakened in early morning, weak but refreshed.

I eased myself into a sitting position and looked around me. The room seemed much as I remembered it. All the furniture was in its place. The hangings were as they had been the week before. An undershirt, tunic and hose were folded conveniently on a chest beside the bed, adjacent to them a basin of fresh water. Shafts of light played on the wall through the shutters. Yet, instinctively, I felt something was different.

I rose, removed my damp night-shirt and began to bathe. Only then did I realise what was wrong. The fylfot was no longer fastened round my neck.

'Matthilde!' I called. My voice sounded reedy and trembling. I rummaged through the bundle of clothing, throwing the garments carelessly right and left. The fylfot was not there.

Matthilde emerged from an anteroom.

'Where is my gold cross?' I demanded.

'Calm yourself,' said she. 'When you were tossing and turning in the fever, I was afraid it would choke you. I removed it and laid it beside your clothes and next to an empty goblet.'

'Then where is it now?' My head was pounding.

'Perhaps a servant moved it by mistake,' said Matthilde. 'I will enquire.'

'Let me dress and we'll do it together,' I said churlishly. 'I'll not rest until it's found.'

She nodded resignedly and sat on the bed to wait. Only then did a less than agreeable possibility occur to me.

'Where is Andreas?' I asked.

'I haven't seen him this morning,' said Matthilde. 'Surely he would not take your property.'

'He has shown an unnatural interest in the fylfot since the Singars filled his head with nonsense,' I said. 'I'm afraid he might work some mischief with it.'

'What harm can he do? He's a child.'

'He thinks it magic!'

'Then call the servants and have them look for him and your precious necklace,' said Matthilde shortly. 'Wake the whole household if you must! I have to see to Louey.'

When she had gone, I finished washing and dressed. The headache remained. When I reached the staircase, I saw there was no need to summon anyone. From the entrance hall came the sound of noisy conversation. A crowd of some dozen had gathered, among them my chief steward, a few house servants and some tenants in their working clothes.

I descended unsteadily, blinking in the sunlight that filtered into the hall through the decorated window above the main door. Kunz came towards me, his florid and usually jovial face grave.

'I am sorry to tell you there has been a tragedy on the estate, sir,' he said. 'Three children have fallen into the Leine and at least one is drowned. Swept away in the current.'

The crowd parted. On the floor lay two motionless forms that I saw with horror were the bodies of children. Panic rose in my chest and I rushed forward. Neither of the children was known to me. They were two peasant boys, five years old or younger. Their hair and torn tunics were saturated in water, their faces were deathly pale and their eyes closed. The smaller lay in an unnatural position, his head twisted to one side and I knew immediately he was beyond my help. The other was breathing faintly. I picked him up and carried him into the main hall.

'Bring the other,' I said to Kunz. 'I fear he is dead but we must care for the body until his parents claim him.'

I laid the older boy on a bench and bent over him, feeling for the beat of his heart.

The crowd had followed us in. A plump country girl, scarcely in her twentieth year, pushed her way through the others and tugged at my tunic.

'I'm 'is mother, my lord. Can tha save 'im?'

'I'll do what I can,' I said.

I examined the child's limbs, listened to his heart and lifted up one of the closed eyelids to peer closely at the pupil. A hush of expectation fell over the spectators.

'He is not hurt,' I said. 'It's merely a swoon. His lungs have already expelled the water.'

I went to the laboratory and fetched a jar of *sal ammoniac*, which I opened and held to the child's nose. He coughed, opened his eyes, and sat up. The mother uttered a scream of joy and threw her arms around him.

My knees felt weak. I was out of breath and perspiring from my small effort. A sea of indistinct faces swam before my eyes.

'How did this happen?' I demanded.

No one answered.

'Have there been rains? Is the river in flood and the pasture under water?'

'There 'as been no rain in a week, my lord,' one tenant volunteered.

'An' it was not in the pasture it happened.'

'They was seen a-playin' by th'old trees on the river bank,' said another. 'By the rocks.'

'I don't un'erstand,' said the boy's mother. ' 'E wouldn't go near that part of the river. We say it be dangerous.'

Panic gripped me again. 'Were others with you?' I asked the child.

He seemed confused by the question and clung to his mother's skirts. At length he shook his head. I sank into a nearby chair, trying to slow the thumping of my chest. My fears were irrational but the fylfot was missing and, in the midst of this tragedy, Andreas had disappeared.

'Shall I send for the priest, sir?'

Minutes must have passed. I became aware that Kunz was standing over me. He had dismissed the crowd and we were alone, save for the dead child.

'Priest?' My breathing was returning to normal and the throbbing in my temple was easing but my legs ached from thigh to calf. The fever had not fully left me.

'Yes, sir,' said the steward. 'He will know the family, I'm sure, and will be able to return this poor lad to his mother.'

'Forgive me. Yes, make the arrangements.'

Still weak, I climbed the staircase, clinging to the baluster and rail for support. Matthilde met me on the first floor. She was flushed and excited.

'I can't find Louey! No one has seen him!'

'He hasn't come this way or I would have noticed.' My one desire was to lie down again. 'And Andreas?'

'He hasn't appeared.'

'Could he be hiding in an attic?'

Just at that moment, Matthilde's lady's maid Frija, plump and pink-faced, her petticoats gathered in front of her, appeared at the stair head. Like Kunz, she had served the household for nearly ten years. She touched my arm.

'I didn't want to speak with all those people 'round,' said she. 'Master Andreas is not in the house.'

'Speak up, girl. You have seen him?'

'Yes, sir. He was with them children. Them as fell in the water.'

Cold fear again crept over me. What if, after all, Andreas had been with the others at the river?

'That's most unlike Andreas,' said Matthilde.

The maid coloured. 'I'm speaking the truth, ma'am. He was with them! Master Louey too!'

'I don't doubt your word, Frija. Where was this?'

'By the barns, ma'am, Where they keep the grain. Near the big oak tree.'

'Not at the river?'

'No, mistress. When the workers' littl'uns went to the river, there was no one else with them, I'll swear. '

'Thank you for telling us, Frija,' I said. Fighting down the tiredness in my legs, I turned away from the chamber door.

'Forgive me, sir,' said the maid. 'It's none of my affair. P'r'aps you gave it 'im. to Master Andreas that is.'

'Gave him what?'

'When I saw him earlier, he was wearing your necklace, sir. The gold cross. I noticed 'cos it seemed so large and heavy for a boy.'

I could feel the beads of perspiration on my forehead but, finding new strength I leapt down the stairs three at a time. I reached the main door and ran off across the courtyard towards the gate.

The barns were behind the house near the pond and the mill. The mill was on two levels, the upper housing machinery and grinding-stones, the lower being for storage of the grain. Two further barns were used to keep dry hay and straw for the horses, and winter feed for all the animals. Nearby, in the field, grew a single, very ancient oak tree.

I threw open the door of the dry grain store. It was empty save for a mill hand repairing the pulleys.

'Have my sons been here?' I demanded. I was ashamed of the aggression in my tone but it was no time for politeness.

The labourer looked up, startled, and shook his head.

Just then I heard the sound of childish laughter coming from a neighbouring barn. I bounded across the grass and burst into the bulging storeroom. In one corner, propped up on a bed of hay, was Andreas, an expression of malicious delight on his face. In one hand he was holding the fylfot and swinging it around on its chain above his head. The other hand was fondling shamelessly a little village girl who lay fast asleep at his side.

'What's the meaning of this?' I demanded. My face ran with sweat and my legs shook under me. 'And where is your brother?'

Andreas stopped what he was doing, threw the fylfot on the ground and cowered before me.

'I've done nothing,' he mumbled, his laughter changing to tears. His eyes flitted guiltily from the girl to a spot somewhere between the opposite corner of the barn and my left shoulder. 'It's the fault of the magic cross! I held it up and told him to go to sleep like the others, but he would not.'

I followed his eyes. Behind me, on a soft patch of earth near the door lay Lou, his face and clothing covered in filth, his eyes open and staring trance-like into the empty air, his mouth wide and emitting babbling noises like an imbecile. I picked him up and cradled him in my arms.

'Others? What others?'

'They don't matter,' Andreas said with a callousness that shocked me. 'They woke up and are long gone, except this one girl.'

'And where did they go, these others?'

' 'Cross the fields and down to the river. As I told them to!'

'You miscreant,' I cried, controlling my anger with difficulty and in the depths of wretchedness at my son's indifference. 'Your prank has cost the lives of two children, has rendered your brother senseless, and will surely break your mother's heart. Go to her immediately. Say nothing! I'll decide later what your punishment will be.'

Andreas fled. I laid Lou in the soft hay, knelt beside him and closed the staring eyes. I scooped up the fylfot and, carefully twisting one of its arms to the side, removed the seal of its cunningly designed container. Steadying my trembling hand, I brought the fylfot to his lips and allowed two drops of a clear liquid to fall on his tongue. It was a distillation of hops and rue, my own formula, and would soothe and heal any damage to his mind.

'Wake now, Louey,' I whispered. 'Wake and forget.'

I resealed the fylfot, replaced the chain round my neck and crossed to where the peasant girl lay in deep slumber. The jar of sal ammoniac I had used earlier was still in my purse. I opened it again and held it to the girl's nose. She coughed and opened her eyes.

'Don't be afraid,' I said. 'I'll not hurt you. You have merely fallen asleep in our barn. Be off home with you!'

I watched her go then, carrying Ludwig in my arms, I made my way back to the house.

Though the fever had abated by evening, I suffered another restless night. Now the phantoms were of a different kind, the disembodied souls of two children condemned to an early death. Whilst my reason told me I was not to blame, my heart told me otherwise - that by not curbing Andreas's obsessive tendencies, I was more guilty than he.

Was it possible to love and at the same time to discipline, I wondered? My memories of my own father were hazy, yet I knew love had never been part of our relationship. At the court of the Khan, I had been taught from an early age to hunt, fight and kill. And though I had studied philosophy with one of Persia's greatest minds and understood duty, punishment and revenge - how men behave towards men - I had learned nothing about how to be a parent.

Though I had discovered in Venice what it meant to be part of a proper family, perhaps it was already too late. Perhaps there was still too much of the warlike prince in me to ever be a proper father.

My soul-searching solved nothing. The question was, what was I to do? Though I could not ignore the incident, there seemed to be no sanctions I could effectively take. Andreas would suffer a beating in silence while the dark side of his nature grew. And if I did not punish him, he might commit the offence again. In either case, how would I explain my actions to Matthilde? I knew I could never bring myself to tell her what had occurred in the hay store, or to hint to her that the deaths of the village children had been anything other than an accident. I loved her too dearly to distress her with the truth. In the boys she had found happiness and fulfilment, and I could not threaten that with a careless word. Doquz, with whom I might have shared my dilemna, was travelling with the Singari. Whatever was to be Andreas's future, the decision was mine alone.

By morning I had resolved that the discipline of military life was the answer. I had begun my training when scarcely seven. Andreas was already a year older than that. And, earlier that summer, during a visit by Matthilde's brother Roland and his family, I had overheard them discussing a plan to send their son Thomas to Brunswick. Why not Andreas too? Under the Duke's charge, he would learn court manners and discipline and, later, how to bear arms and behave in a noble fashion.

'But he's so young,' Matthilde said tearfully when I told her. 'Let us wait another year.'

'I think now is the time,' I said. I had expected her opposition but was determined not to give in to sentiment. 'The company of boys his own age, and from the same station in life, is the very thing to cure Andreas of his wild tempers.'

'He has been so good lately. You admitted it.'

'By taking my fylfot he has broken a trust.'

'I see that,' Matthilde said, 'but it'll break my heart to see him leave the family home.'

I kissed her. 'It's for the best, Matthilde. And he will not be alone. Magnus has already agreed to engage Thomas, so Andreas will have a natural companion. Anyway, the province is at peace and he will have to fight only mock battles.'

When told of my decision, Andreas flew into a tantrum.

'I don't want to go!' he screamed, stamping his feet in an impotent rage. 'I *shall* not go to Brunswick. Not ever again!'

'It's settled,' I said. 'You will obey our wishes.'

Andreas glared back, his dark eyes burning with silent fury and defiance.

'If I had the magic cross, you would not make me,' he muttered through his teeth.

I returned his ferocious stare until he lowered his eyes.

'Then it is well you don't have it,' I said.

ii

We awaited every piece of news from Brunswick eagerly.

The arrangements had been completed within the week. Once Andreas's anger subsided, I took pains to point out the advantages of our plan and, as the days passed, he became more reconciled to his apprenticeship. Even Matthilde became excited at the opportunities opening out before him.

I convinced myself that we were doing our best and that he would benefit from his experience of court life. However, at idle moments, I was disturbed by dark thoughts. Twice, I had been reminded of the legend of Sharinaz and Arnawaz. Twice, I had glimpsed the power of Andreas's will. Soon, I feared, he would need no fylfot, and that merely a glance of his eyes and a certain tone of voice would be enough to command attention and bend the most stubborn mind to do his bidding.

Nevertheless, there was a great deal to please us during the early months of his apprenticeship. Magnus reported that he applied himself diligently to his duties and was no more mischievous than any of the other boys who shared quarters with him. Matthilde, despite her instinctive dislike of the military arts, was delighted. She felt vindicated in her belief that his sullen tempers had been no more than a phase and, now that he had outgrown them, he would prove a credit to the family.

Then, as the months ran into seasons, my own fears too subsided. My decision had been the right one. The iron discipline of the court and the duties of obedience and service it imposed had driven the childish moods and the obsession with magic from Andreas's head. And I would have been a poor father indeed if I could not forgive even his most heinous misdeeds. I put the episode of the fylfot out of mind.

It was not long before my doubts returned.

I have no cause to complain of Andreas, Magnus wrote at the end of a year, *though he does not find comradeship easily among those his own age. He runs with the older youths and shows a great desire to dominate by force of will rather than lead by strength of character.*

I did not share this confidence with Matthilde and buried my disquiet, just as I had buried the secret of Andreas's earlier mischief. There was so much of myself in the boy, I thought - the spirit, the innate curiosity about the world, perhaps even the quality of leadership. I convinced myself that with the dawn of manhood the good would shine through.

And so the seasons stretched to years. We were happy again. Long, mellow summers ripened our corn and dried up the streams; cold, crisp winters brought snow, sometimes lying so deeply that travelling became impossible. I had a great deal to occupy my mind.

Whilst I had long become accustomed to the northern climate, a world away from the arid, baking heat of Persia's salt deserts, her southern gulf or the chill, bitter winds of her far north-west, I had always been curious about the shifting positions of the sun. Here in Brunswick, at midsummer, it hardly set, and a pale light shone on the northern horizon from dusk to dawn; at the winter solstice, the days were short and grey. The moon too occupied a different place in relation to the stars, though her continuous waxing and waning marked the months with the same regularity as in the skies over Persia.

I recorded my observations faithfully and puzzled by lamplight over drawings I had made. So much could be explained, I decided, if we discarded the theories of the Ptolemy, and supposed that the earth not only turned about itself but moved in a fixed path around the sun. And, if it did those things, it must also shift from side to side like a spinning top when it is slowing down. I developed a theory of my own, using the principles of mathematics Shirazi had taught. The planets were further away than they appeared to be and were little earths turning on themselves and in circles, just as did ours, round the sun that gave life to all. Why indeed should there not be beings like ourselves living there, with their own sciences and their own gods, wondering about us as I wondered about them?

I observed and thought but kept my ideas to myself. The Christian clerics were zealous in their preaching that God had placed man at the centre of the universe, some even maintaining against all the laws of geometry that the earth was flat. I was enigma enough in the priests' eyes without bringing danger to my family by proclaiming a doctrine so contrary to the teaching of the bishops.

In the autumn of 1334, Matthilde became pregnant again, and my joy drove all thoughts of philosophy from my mind. In the heavens there was only beauty and in the seasons only charm. I had always hoped for another child but since Lou's birth Matthilde had seemed infertile. I had heard muttering that, because of her marriage to a foreigner, she was cursed. Scullions whispered it behind closed doors and sometimes stable lads crossed themselves as they swept the yard below her parlour window. However, at the prospect of another new life after so long, I doubted there was anyone in the household who did not share our delight.

'It is a little sister for Andreas and Louey,' Matthilde forecast. She gave no reason for her conviction other than the instincts of a woman who has already carried both male and female in her womb. 'You will see. A mother knows!'

'Neither of us can know that for sure,' I told her, yet I secretly shared her certainty that it would be a girl. I began to imagine the fylfot becoming lighter about my neck.

There was talk too among the servants of a Singari prophecy, by an old woman of the clan, that the next infant to be born at Bachhagen would be female, and this added weight to the speculation. Our mood was one of excitement.

All our hopes were dashed. At five months, Matthilde suffered violent pains in the belly. The child, whether male or female, died inside her and she bled heavily. And when it became clear she could never conceive again, the ominous muttering began again, of God's judgements, of curses, and of dark days ahead.

I tried to shrug it off. Fate was capricious in meting out joy and sorrow and we had our share of both. Yet still the irrational in my soul plagued me. The fylfot seemed to grow heavier again, the sun's image at its centre less bright, and I wondered at times if the gossip might be right, and the anguish I felt at the loss of the child was divine punishment for some sin in my earlier life.

None of these feelings I could confess even to Matthilde, and I was thankful I had never spoken to her of the legend. I consoled her as best I could and took comfort from managing the estate and from my work as a physician.

The gossip eventually died down and, after two good harvests, it ceased altogether.

Matthilde was determined Lou should not follow Andreas to Brunswick and so he began an apprenticeship with me. Alongside his studies in the classics, I taught him the elements of trade and business and endeavoured to interest him in the sciences. He was Andreas's equal in his capacity for learning, and I saw in him a real passion for the physician's work. Whereas Andreas had hung back, Lou pushed himself forward, and in a very short time was able not only to recognise the symptoms of a great many conditions but to treat them with little or no assistance. I congratulated myself on my foresight in keeping him at home.

'If you are selfish in that, I thank God for your selfishness,' said Matthilde.

'Thank neither God nor your husband too soon, I beg you,' I said. 'We command our children for only a few short years. I suspect that Lou, like all young men, will decide his own future, and may disappoint us both. Our task is to prepare him for whatever path he chooses. To read, write and count is not enough. A scholar should learn Italian, a physician Greek, whilst even a farmer should be able to handle a weapon.'

So Lou remained at home. To Matthilde, he was a loving child, honest in his friendships and pious in his Christian devotion. She entertained few ambitions for him, only that he make a good marriage and provide her with beautiful grandchildren. She closed her ears to insinuations by the local priests that, by giving him to the Church, she might gain an extra measure of God's favour and without my intervention resisted all attempts to have him tonsured.

I taught Lou all I knew of the Greek and Italian languages and when he had mastered those gave him a grounding in Arabic and Persian as well. We spent many leisure hours together exercising with sabre and poniard. It seemed I had lost little of my skill, even if at first my movements were slower and, on days following the exercise, I suffered painful stiffness in my joints. These handicaps were soon overcome. My heart beat fast and I experienced a delicious feeling of anticipation each time I grasped a sword hilt, as if I were greeting an old friend or embracing a lover. It was only with effort that I fought down my rekindling enthusiasm for the blade.

These were good years, marred only by the sadness of Matthilde's miscarriage. Brunswick found favour with the Prince of Saxony and the Emperor, and there were no family disputes to disturb the peace of the province. Our land was productive and we made profit from the growth in trade between Hannover and the cities of the north. Bachhagen flourished.

Lou's stature grew and with it his intellect and his understanding of natural science. I had a second key made to the laboratory and gave it to him on his twelfth birthday.

'All this will be yours one day,' I told him. 'Yours and Andreas's. The estate, the farms and my business ventures - you will share it all. But if you want to make your own way in the world, become a soldier or a churchman, I'll not stand in your way. But I think it is you who should continue my work in the sciences. Your brother's ambitions, I suspect, do not lie in physic or mathematics.'

Lou weighed the key in his hand. I watched his eyelids flicker. For several moments we were both silent. At length, he stopped playing with the key and laid it on the bench beside him.

'I suspect so too, Father,' he said. 'And you are right. My place is here - and that'll certainly please my mother!'

'It pleases me too,' said I. 'Let us hope that Andreas makes a fine officer, for I do not think he will ever make a physician or a farmer.'

Magnus's reports on Andreas's progress were favourable until well into the seventh year of his training. By all accounts, he was a star pupil.

I was eager to see for myself his transformation from wayward child to noble squire and proposed an extended family visit to Brunswick city. Matthilde welcomed the opportunity. Andreas's visits to Bachhagen had been few and she missed him.

The boy greeted us affectionately on our arrival and was a model of good behaviour throughout our stay. While Matthilde fussed over him, I sought the Duke's opinion in private.

Magnus led me to his audience room. I had been there many years earlier in his father's time and it seemed little changed. The side walls were hung with pennons and weapons, some of them of Saracen origin. Wild boars' heads, their savage tusks yellowed with age, their coarse hair covered in the dirt and dust of the centuries, were nailed to the oak panels in the spaces between. On the end wall furthest from the door, surmounted with the Brunswick coat of arms, was painted a chart depicting the Welf family lineage from Henry the Lion. The only recent acquisition that I noticed was the stuffed body of a leopard whose gaping jaws had lost in death all the magnificent savagery they had once displayed in life.

Magnus's greeting was warm and friendly. His figure had filled out in the years since his accession, and he tended to stoutness like his father. He could add nothing to his written reports, at least nothing deserving of censure. He even made light of his former misgivings.

'Andreas is an excellent squire,' he said. 'You should be proud of him! He performs with ease all the tasks set him, and shows exceptional skill in riding and great agility in wrestling. From time to time, he has even amused the court with a little magic.'

'Magic?' I felt a prickling in my neck.

'It's nothing,' said Magnus. 'Mere high spirits, but clever too. No one has been able to say how he did it.'

'Did what?'

'We had an envoy - I forget from where - who liked the sound of his own voice. He had drunk too much and was boring everyone with his chatter. Even so, no one was ill-mannered enough to silence him. 'Master Andreas,' says one of my officers. 'Come over!''

'Andreas left his place and joined us at the table. The envoy was out of earshot but I could hear the officer's whispers.

"Can you not shut this fellow up?' says he to Andreas. 'Show him your trick with the dagger and put us all out of our misery.' Then he hands Andreas his weapon.'

'Trick with a dagger?' I echoed. 'Andreas has learned no such mischief from me.'

'Mischief indeed,' said the Duke and laughed. 'I would have done, Sano, but I was frankly slow in my speech and unsteady on my feet.

'Before I can say a word, Andreas steps up boldly to the envoy and fixes him with those black eyes of his.

"Watch closely,' says he, holding up the dagger. He mumbles something in a low voice. Then he goes on loudly to the benefit of everyone in the hall. 'I think you must be tired after your journey and would rather sleep now. My blade shall be the means. Watch again!'

'The envoy stops talking and stares at the dagger. Andreas moves closer. He holds the weapon by the blade and kisses the hilt. A hush falls over the room. Even the most inebriated stop their chattering. Everyone in the hall seems to be fixed to his chair.

' 'Do your eyes feel heavy?' Andreas says.

' 'Indeed they do,' says the envoy and yawns.

' 'Sleep then,' says your son, moving so close to him that their faces are nearly touching. 'I'll count. When I reach ten, your eyes will close. Before I reach twenty, you will be in the land of nod.'

'To everyone's great merriment, the fellow's eyes closed. He rested his head on his arm and on the count of fifteen or sixteen fell fast asleep, snoring loudly.

'Andreas has since performed the trick twice for our entertainment. There seems no harm in it, though I confess I now have the habit of avoiding his eyes when we meet.'

I met the Duke's laughter with a serious face. Never could I wipe from my memory the scene in the barn at Bachhagen: Lou, dirty and babbling; the sleeping peasant girl; and Andreas swinging the fylfot carelessly round his head.

'I beg you not to encourage him, Magnus,' I said. 'These tricks are not a game! Who knows to what danger they could lead?'

The amusement in the Duke's face died. 'Danger, Sano? You are jesting, surely.'

'I do not jest about the Dark Path,' I said. 'As you once owed me your life, I urge you to forbid Andreas a repetition of his trick. Promise me!'

Despite the Duke's promise, I remained apprehensive. From time to time, I was disturbed by frightening visions - that Andreas's power would grow and with it his influence, and that those whom he had been engaged to serve would become his servants instead. Yet, if that was what the future held, there seemed little I could do to prevent it. Fate was indiscriminate in her choice of victims. On returning to Bachhagen, I filled my mind with pleasant thoughts of grandchildren and applied my energies to other matters.

I continued to nurture Lou in the sciences, and sparing no expense in procuring manuscripts that would assist his study. With great difficulty and no small cost, I obtained copies of the works of Aristotle, the sayings of Hippocrates and the writings of Galen. I set aside a small area in a locked cellar for Lou's benefit and encouraged him to undertake there the study of pigs, rabbits and other small animals that had died of natural causes. This work had to remain a secret between us, and I went to great pains to keep it so. Matthilde would have been distressed and the clergy would have certainly branded it sorcery.

For months I drove the boy hard, paying scant attention to the changes in him. All of a sudden, I realised he was no longer a child. One day, through a chance encounter at the doorway to the laboratory, I found to my surprise that, tall though I was, Lou was nearly my equal, and had to stoop to enter the room.

I would have remarked on it, only Lou seemed preoccupied with his thoughts. He sat at the bench and began playing carelessly with the pages of the leather-bound book that lay on the table. Feeling the seeds of guilt at having put science above personal welfare, I put an arm round his shoulders.

'To open one's heart to a friend is worth a thousand elixirs,' I said. 'So the Persian poet wrote. To open it to one's father should have equal value. If you have a problem, you can come to me. We all experience new feelings, new urges, on growing to manhood.....'

'It's not that, Father,' said Lou, looking up with a knowing smile. 'Touching *that*, there's no mystery!'

'Well then?'

'What is the Dark Path, Father.'

'Where did you hear that expression?'

'Twice you have used it in my hearing, once in this very room, again when you were talking to Mother about Andreas. You thought I was asleep. It's long ago now and I had forgotten until a few days ago. The lamp went out when I was on the cellar steps and suddenly I remembered. The Dark Path! But I did not know what you meant.'

The question was such a simple one that I wondered why it filled me with dread. I reached to one of the topmost shelves and took down a jar containing some berries that were dried and shrivelled like black stones. 'What are these here, in this jar?'

'The fruits of the 'fair lady', Father - the deadly nightshade.'

'Indeed. And their uses?'

'In small doses, it can relieve spasms of the muscles.'

'And if the dose were larger?'

'Death!'

'And this?' I took down another jar.

'Poppy seeds, Father,' said Lou. He was responding to the questions as if they were a test, pleased that he was able to identify the substances. 'From them we distil a liquid that causes sleep, or relieves pain.'

'And if we over-prescribe?'

'The sleeper will never awake!'

'So, there you have it,' I said, replacing the jars in their places. 'All power comes from knowledge. Science is neutral. It is how science is used that matters. By the physician or by the sorcerer. The True and the Dark Paths. The Right and the Left.'

'Is it so simple?'

'Let us try something else.' I took up some tinder and a flint, and lit a candle. 'Now, Lou, oblige me by putting your hand in the flame.'

He laughed. His voice alternated between the shrill timbre of a boy and the croaking tones of a growing youth.

'What kind of a fool do you take me for?'

'No fool,' I said. 'But watch!'

I stretched out my own hand, placed it in the centre of the flame, and withdrew it again, smiling at the look of bafflement on Lou's face.

'Where the flame is broadest,' I said, 'there is less heat and, as you can see, my hand is unharmed. Were I to have placed it higher, the tip of the flame would have burnt my skin. It's like understanding the properties of berries. These paths are but different sides of the same coin, the one leading to health and life, the other to injury or death.'

'I understand,' Lou said. 'It's like Good and Evil. God against the Devil. Still, I'm confused. Are we ungodly because we treat sickness even on the Sabbath? Are we evil if we fight and kill an enemy in the name of justice?'

I snuffed out the candle. Shirazi had once lectured me on good and evil, but it had been a meaningless lesson to a ten-year-old child. Only long years after had I learned it. The horrors of war had brought me wisdom. Dying men with gaping bellies, severed arms and broken skulls, beating the earth in their agonies, their souls half gone, had been my apprenticeship. Blood, sinew, bone, putrefying organs had been the diet of my mind. I had become immune to suffering, but it was eventually from these sacrifices, once human but now reduced to clay, that I had learned. Was there ever honour and justice in war, I wondered, or was there only futility and the sickening physic of death?

I picked up the fylfot and weighed it in my hand, remembering the legend.

'The nature of good and evil has long preoccupied philosophers,' I said. 'My answer is this. Good and evil are no more separable than day and night, than summer and winter. Our lives are a continuous struggle between the two sides of our selves that merge together like dusk and dawn or like autumn and spring.

'Most men are neither wholly good nor wholly wicked. Their characters are shaped by random events and experiences under whose influence pride vies with arrogance, honour with shame, love with lechery, temperate living with gluttony and intoxication. Each individual makes his own choices.'

By his answers, Lou had shown me he would make the right ones. Andreas, through the supposed magic he had practised for the amusement of the court, had shown that he was hovering at a crossroads, the meeting place of the two paths I labeled True and Dark. However, his predilection had been discovered in time and with proper guidance he too might be steered towards good works.

What I did not know then was that, whilst his accomplishments were real enough, the face Andreas presented to all around him was a lie. His life at Brunswick was a facade. Throughout the years of his apprenticeship, he had managed to hide his true character while hatching in his disturbed mind schemes of domination and disorder that would be the ruin of his family.

Not only was there good and evil in the world. There was madness.

iii

At the age of fourteen, Andreas was a handsome youth, with my features and colouring, they said. By eighteen, he had become a striking young man. His hair had thickened and he had grown a beard. Young women in particular were vulnerable to his charms, and he used these to full advantage with the lower classes. If he was less successful in gaining the favours of daughters of the court, it was not through unwillingness on their part but due to the vigilance of their guardians.

Other squires were, willingly or not, accomplices in many of his misdeeds. He led and encouraged them, in a series of wild escapades, drinking, wenching and creating mischief in the town. Much of this activity was put down to youthful spirits, overlooked, and hence not mentioned in the Duke's despatches to Bachhagen. It often happened that the blame fell on my nephew Thomas, a year or two Andreas's senior and thus deemed responsible for his conduct.

It was only when this conduct put at risk the security of Brunswick, and touched on its honour abroad, that it could no longer be lightly treated.

Perhaps the affair was something I could not have foreseen. Magnus chose to keep it private, and I was to learn of it only two years later from Tom's lips. Yet I would never cease to blame myself that Andreas's mischief was able to go so far.

Towards the end of their apprenticeship, Tom, Andreas and two of their friends were chosen as escort for an envoy to Thuringia. There, Tom fell in love with the maid-in-waiting attending a princess of that province. They were settling in their quarters for a third night in the city of Erfurt when the banter between the young men took a new turn.

'I confess I didn't notice the maiden, Tom,' one youth said indifferently. 'My eyes were on the princess herself. But if your Martha's a goddess, she'll have no part of a scrawny mortal like you.'

'I fancy she had an eye for me,' Andreas announced. 'She has some fine attributes on view, and I'll wager the ones she hides are even finer.'

'I'll swear she looked at me too, Tom,' laughed the fourth squire, winking broadly.

Andreas slapped him heartily on the shoulder. 'By the pox, Erhart,' said he, 'this wench has had a taste of every knight at court! Still, a maid is a maid, and what will that matter to Tom when he gets between her plump thighs.'

Tom had listened with disapprobation. He saw no virtue in prudery but at times he found his cousin's lewdness difficult to swallow. In any case, his affection for the girl Martha was genuine.

'You go too far with your sick humour,' he protested. 'Martha is no whore! She's the sweetest and most chaste creature on earth, and, if I can't wed her, I'll die here of love-sickness.'

'Love!' sneered Andreas. 'That's not something to die for! I admit we were teasing you, but if you're truly set on the wench, why don't we take her back to Brunswick with us? In truth, we might have a wench a-piece. Doubtless the princess has other beauties around her.'

'That'll be a capital matter if we're caught,' said Erhart, drawing his hand across his throat in a gesture that left none of them in any doubt as to his meaning.

'Not unless Ulrich persists in his desire for the princess,' said Andreas. 'We're not in one of these eastern kingdoms that my father talks of so often. The Thuringian court is no harem. Four handmaids will not be missed. Let's select our prizes and, if we manage carefully, we can snatch them and none the wiser.'

'They don't slit a fellow's throat for looking,' said Ulrich. 'Still, I might be persuaded to settle for a plump lady's maid. The princess has too little flesh on her bones for my liking.'

'I'll not be party to a kidnap nor disgrace the good name of my family,' Tom said. 'If I can't win Martha fairly, I'll do without.'

'You're a real man in truth, Cousin!' said Andreas. 'A moment ago, you were dying of love. Now you'll venture nothing to gratify it.' He lay back indolently on his mattress with his hands clasped behind his head.

There was a gleam in his eye as his gaze flitted from one squire to another. His voice became silky. 'Listen to me. I have a plan. If the wenches aren't game, we shan't hold them against their will. But you can rely on me for a prescription that will guarantee their compliance. My apprenticeship to my father wasn't wholly wasted, and I offer you the benefits of his learning.'

'A love potion!' cried Erhart.

'A simple infusion of herbs that'll hasten the effects of the wine,' said Andreas. 'I'll give you three each a phial. Rely on me to distract the guards and bring the horses ready for our escape.

'And another thing. The girls should not learn our true names. We must all select a pseudonym in case our scheme goes wrong. I have already chosen mine. It will be *Akhtar*, which means *star* in the Persian language. Tom, you will be *Titus*, which is *honour* in Greek. Erhart can be *Esau*, biblical brother of Jacob. Ulrich – let me see! The letter U is less common so I think we need to modify ...'

'What about *Ulysses*, hero of Troy?' suggested Ulrich in the spirit of the game.

'You are mad, all of you,' said Tom. 'As for honour, there is none in what you are proposing. I'll not join you.'

However, in spite of himself, Tom found his objections melting. He could not account for his change of heart. There were times when in Andreas's company that he felt his will was not his own. His cousin's dark eyes and silky voice seemed to cast a spell over the room so that the most hideous scheme became a piece of harmless fun.

In the course of a day or two, the friends' choice fell on Martha and three other maidens. The four were pressed into an assignation. Tom, Erhart and Ulrich stole into the women's quarters under cover of darkness while Andreas waited at the stable gate.

As it happened, the four girls were as eager for adventure as the youths and allowed themselves to be bundled into the wagon that Andreas had procured with seduction in mind. To this vehicle he had harnessed his own horse, whilst the mounts of his fellow conspirators stood nearby. The party left Erfurt, travelling towards the River Werra and the north-western border of the province. Andreas himself drove the wagon and the others rode escort.

'Hey, Akhtar,' called Erhart after half-an-hour. 'Rein in like a good fellow. We've come far enough for now! There are two full flagons of wine in that cart, and four maids willing to share them with us under the moon.'

'Hey, Master Akhtar, if that is indeed your name!' giggled one of the damsels, reaching forward and trying to seize the reins. The cart lurched as Andreas brought it to a halt, and she fell back inelegantly on her rump.

'By the Rood, Lottie, you've drunk quite enough wine for one night,' another girl chided.

Lottie sat up and straightened her petticoats.

'By the Rood, Trudie, you're right,' said she, giggling again. 'All this bumping and swaying is a great inconvenience. But now Master Akhtar has stopped, I can relieve myself. After that, by the Rood, he can have his way with me if he chooses.'

'I feel strangely lustful myself,' laughed Trudie. She unfastened her girdle and loosened the braid in her hair. 'And there are three more fellows to satisfy me if they have a mind. Martha has already settled on Titus Tom, but that still leaves two. Elsa is fast asleep in yon corner and has no need of either.'

Andreas glared at Tom, who understood the meaning of the look but had said nothing to betray the true identity of his companions.

Martha had drunk rather less than her friends. Hearing her name, she turned on them angrily.

'Your babbling tongues grow longer by the minute and will lead you into trouble,' said she. 'If you're wise, you'll both keep your mouths shut and your knees together. That fellow who calls himself Akhtar has the Devil's eyebrows, and will not be content with a game of kiss-in-the-ring. Behave like harlots and you can expect to be treated like harlots.'

Tom, Erhart and Ulrich tethered their horses and clambered aboard the wagon. From the driver's perch, Andreas surveyed the scene with relish.

'This is a fine state of affairs,' said Ulrich, his gaze falling on the sleeping Elsa. 'We promised ourselves a maid a-piece, and here is my choice gone off to the land of nod.'

'Wake her, or take her as she sleeps, I don't care,' muttered Andreas sourly, 'but don't take all night.' He looked around for Lottie, but she had taken the opportunity to slip out of sight and relieve herself behind the wheels of the cart.

Ulrich touched Elsa's face and sprang back in alarm.

'She's cold!'

'There's a chill in the air, and her stomach is not used to liquor,' said Martha. She knelt at Elsa's side and shook the limp shoulders gently without drawing forth any response.

'She's no longer breathing,' cried the girl's would-be lover, staring at the still form in horror, and then at Andreas in accusation. 'You've made the love potion too strong, you fool. It has killed her.'

'What does he mean, Tom?' demanded Martha. 'Have you poisoned us?'

The full implications of their actions were beginning to dawn on Tom, but he replied as steadily as he could.

'It was only a herbal infusion to make you think well of us,' he said, 'but, on my oath, I gave you none of it. I dashed Andreas's phial against the cobbles as we rode through the town.'

'So it's Andreas!' snapped Martha, striking Tom hard on the cheek with her open hand. 'Your sweet talk was all lies. You planned to seduce me and nothing more.'

Lottie chose that moment to reappear from beneath the wagon. Her complexion was a deathly hue in the moonlight and beads of perspiration ran down her forehead.

'I feel really unwell,' she said, and vanished again from their view. The sounds of moaning and retching reached them through the slats.

'So do I,' groaned Trudie. A spasm of pain crossed her face and she thrust the ardent Erhart aside, though not quickly enough. She retched, and emptied a mouthful of vomit over her suitor's tunic and hose.

'It's you who are bungling fools!' screamed Andreas. 'The prescribed dose was a drop or two. You've given them too much!'

'It's not our fault,' rejoined Ulrich. 'You gave us each a whole phial of the mixture. You said nothing about using it sparingly.'

'You mistook my meaning,' retorted Andreas, his temper cooling as quickly as it had been kindled, 'yet your mistake has afforded me some amusement. My prescription is harmless, even in larger doses. Elsa isn't dead. Look, she's already waking up. And the other two will recover soon enough.'

Elsa had indeed wakened. Uncertain of her whereabouts, she set up such a caterwauling as to arouse a whole city. Before the friends could silence her, some inquisitive villagers from the outlying dwellings of a nearby settlement appeared with lamps.

'Is this your idea of harmless fun, cousin Andreas?' said Tom. Martha's slap had brought him to his senses and he realised how Andreas's sweet talking had fooled him. 'It's to my regret and shame that I didn't put a stop to it before it began. Before long we'll have the Thuringian militia on our heels.'

'I suggest we don't argue,' said Erhart soberly. 'Let's release the maidens, and ride for Brunswick with all speed.'

'You're behaving like common ruffians,' Tom said. 'These are gently-bred girls, landgraves' daughters and the like. It's our fault they're in this state. Upon my life, I'll see to it they are escorted back to Erfurt. You may do as you please, and go to the Devil!'

He took the reins of the wagon, and with the four girls mounted behind, headed back the way they had come.

Andreas, Erhart and Ulrich made off in the other direction.

Lottie and Trudie had shaken off the worst effects of Andreas's potion and the two sat silently, huddled together for warmth. Elsa would not sit down. Despite Martha's attempts to pacify her, she continued screaming until, exhausted by the effort, she slumped against the side of the wagon, weeping pitiably.

Tom whipped the horse through the city streets, hoping all the while that Andreas's assessment had been correct and that the girls had not been missed. Three or four hours only had passed since the adventure began and he still had plenty of time to return them to their beds before dawn. He had learned his lesson and prayed only that the four would keep silent about the affair.

The women's quarters were shrouded in darkness. A single lamp burned in a castle watch-tower nearby but there was no sign of a guard. Tom slowed the wagon so that the noise of the wheels would not wake the other residents. He began to breathe more easily. Lottie and Trudie were by now asleep. Martha, wide awake still, sat silently in the opposite corner with hunched up knees.

Just as he brought the wagon to rest fifty paces from the entrance, Elsa began to scream again.

'Help!' she cried before Martha had a chance to silence her. She began beating Tom about the shoulders and when that had little effect she clawed at his face and eyes with her fingernails. 'Help! Kidnap!'

A light showed in a first floor window, then another. Sleepy, inquisitive faces appeared in doorways. Before long, the wagon was surrounded. Tom looked round in vain for a gap in the crowd, but the arrival of a small troop of men-at-arms from the postern finally put paid to his chances of escape. He was seized and dragged, helpless, from the wagon perch. His head struck the rim of one of the wheels and his senses left him.

He looked up as the morning light crept through the tiny, barred window of a dungeon. He had not slept, but had spent what remained of the night hunched on the damp floor. His gaolers had not chained him, but neither had they allowed him food or water.

His head throbbed, and his cheek stung where Martha had slapped and Elsa had scratched him. He touched his face and drew a finger along the weal the latter's nails had raised across the bone. He felt his nose and traced the trickle of blood that had congealed on his upper lip.

His career and life were at an end, Tom thought. He had lost the woman he loved and now he was to be branded a kidnapper, fated to die miserably in a Thuringian prison. As a child he had occasionally been victim of Andreas's mischief, taking blame when there was none and suffering punishment when none was merited. Throughout their apprenticeship together he had watched his cousin's influence grow. More than once he had stood back while others were disciplined for offences they had not committed, while Andreas laughingly boasted to this damsel or that of the success of his scheme.

It seemed now that his cousin had descended into madness. His deception, to make the girls senseless and then ravish them had been intended from the start. Even the name with which he was baptised was no longer good enough. But Tom knew he could not stand up to Andreas. His influence was too strong. Even some of the older knights were deceived as to his true nature.

Tom knew that the code demanded his silence but even if it had not, he would be powerless to redeem his situation. He had only to imagine Andreas's dark glare for his arms to grow weak and his tongue to dry in his mouth. He could not have admitted his fear any more than he could explain it, but he would rather have stood against a hundred enemies than face his cousin's anger.

He rose and began to pace the cell. In the corner opposite to the one in which he had sat was a sink-hole that stank of excrement. Tom turned away from it and retched in disgust. Then, feeling neither hunger, thirst nor the need to relieve himself, he returned to his former position.

Even now, he could not believe Erhart and Ulrich would leave him to face Thuringian justice alone. They would return and own their share in the prank. Surely even Andreas would not leave him to die in a foreign gaol. Yet, as the thought occurred, he knew it to be a false hope. Only Martha and the other three maidens knew of his predicament, and they were scarcely likely to show mercy.

The morning wore on and he was imagining for himself the worst possible fate when there was the rattle of a key in the lock, the sound of a bolt being withdrawn, and the dungeon door creaked open.

'You're free to go,' a voice grunted.

Thomas scarcely heard. He raised his head wearily, looked past the surly guard to the sunlit opening behind him, and blinked in astonishment. In the doorway behind stood Martha carrying a jug of water. She came into the cell and squatted beside him while he quenched his thirst. Then, with the remainder of the water, she cleaned the blood from his face.

'I'm grateful for your kindness,' said Tom, failing to comprehend her presence but finding he could move his tongue again. 'But you should not be here in this cesspit.'

Martha touched him lightly on the cheek.

'Then we should leave together,' she said sweetly. 'I've told them the truth, that you were not to blame. Truly, you are free!'

'It doesn't matter now,' said Tom. 'I'm condemned in any case. When the Duke of Brunswick hears of this, my commission will be revoked. I will have my life, but there'll be no honour in it.'

'You have only yourself to blame,' said Martha more harshly, yet with a touch of sympathy. 'Three guards were found asleep at their posts. Lottie's father is swearing vengeance, and the Prince has despatched an envoy to Brunswick demanding recompense for our indignities. Still, you may be treated leniently. My father has influence here, and you were the least guilty!'

A week passed and all four perpetrators of the seduction were back in Brunswick. Tom and Andreas were summoned into the ducal presence. Magnus's anger was apparent in the cutting iciness of his voice.

'So you are the chief villain in this conspiracy, Master Andreas?'

Andreas was silent.

'Answer me, sir,' demanded the Duke.

'I no longer answer to that name,' Andreas said carelessly. 'From now on, I will be called Akhtar.'

Tom's eyes had been fixed on the floor throughout the hearing and he did not dare raise them now, but he fancied he could feel the heat in his cousin's glare of defiance. He almost wished he was again in the Thuringian dungeon. He had not spoken to Andreas since his return but had endured two days of mental torture while he awaited the inevitable summons.

His suffering had been made all the worse by Andreas's habit of exaggerating his own exploits to the point of pure invention. A quite fictitious version of events was being whispered round the court and, though it did not implicate him by name, Tom felt that all eyes were on him, judging him or laughing at his misfortunes. He had lain awake at night, planning what he might say in his own defence but now, faced with the Duke's displeasure, he found himself tongue-tied.

He knew now for certain that Andreas was quite mad. His

pseudonym, like his potion, was an obsession. None but a madman would defy his lord in this manner. Andreas, on the contrary, seemed to care little about the hearing or the possible consequences of his actions.

The Duke's tone became even more icy.

'Andreas or Akhtar, you will answer me, or I'll have you whipped here in this chamber until your blood stains the floor.'

Andreas looked Magnus in the eye defiantly.

'Which of my comrades has betrayed me?' he demanded.

'Are you going to deny it?' said Magnus. 'Is your honour so tainted that you allow others to suffer for your misdoings.'

'Which?' repeated Andreas. 'If it was you, Tom, you'll be eternally sorry.'

Tom risked a look. The Duke had risen from his chair, tight-lipped, no taller yet an imposing figure against Andreas's slighter build. Behind him in the portrait gallery, the grim faces of his ancestors, Otto of Bavaria, Ludwig the Bold, even the Lion of Saxony himself, seemed to echo his fury and disappointment.

'Silence!' thundered the Duke. 'Your other accomplices have chosen not to show their shameful faces at court, and will be dealt with according to their offence. Your cousin has uttered not a word against you.'

Andreas gave a bitter laugh.

'Then I am condemned on the word of a Thuringian maid,' he said in a low voice.

'On hers, and on that of others who testify to your boasting.' the Duke replied. 'You are condemned by your own arrogance, Master Akhtar, if that is what you wish to be called. Leave my presence and my service! You are dismissed.'

Andreas turned very pale but his eyes still burned with defiance.

'It was no more than sport,' he muttered. 'The maids were not harmed.'

'By Christ's blood, sir, is there no honour left?' said Duke Magnus. 'And five thousand guldens is no small sum to pacify an angry neighbour. Go! You can thank God that for your parents' sake I do not deal more harshly with you.'

Tom at last found the courage to speak up.

'My Lord Duke ... '

'Hold your tongue, Master Thomas. You will bear witness to my judgement and keep quiet about the whole affair. Both Matthilde and your own father should be spared unnecessary agony.

'And do not think you are to escape further punishment. The girl Martha and her father have spoken well on your behalf, but seduction always has a price. By my oath, you will engage yourself to the maid before the month is out. And marry her too, if I have to drag you to the altar myself!'

iv

I knew nothing of the Thuringian affair at the beginning of 1339. Nor did I know of the other incidents which would have shown me Andreas's preference for deceit and dominance. I had not received word from Magnus for more than half a year. There were rumours from the court that a young officer named Ulrich of Ehra had taken his own life following an indiscretion. However, I was not fond of gossip and did not connect the story with the boy on whom I had once pinned such hopes.

When the Duke wrote later, tersely, that Master Andreas and Brunswick have agreed to part company, I should have been even more enquiring but at the time I had other things on my mind.

The years following Matthilde's miscarriage had brought a change in our domestic circumstances.

In 1335, her elder brother, Roland, died. A widower since the birth of his daughter, he had inherited a small estate that bordered on ours and separated us from the domains of Duke Magnus's nearer relatives. Roland's marriage had produced five children, of whom only three survived childhood - a daughter, Matti, and two sons, Thomas and Roland. Tom was the second child to bear this name, the first having died at the age of only ten. His younger brother Henry had died in a hunting accident.

Since the miscarriage, Matthilde had been in poor health and the loss of her brother was a severe blow. Though younger by ten years or more, she was as close to him as any sister can be.

At the time of their father's death, Matti was fourteen. Roland was fifteen while Tom was a year older than Andreas and thus seventeen. Tom might have taken over the management of his father's land but he was of an independent mind and had ideas quite removed from farming. Thus it was that I accepted the task of guardian of the two younger children and of their inheritance. There being no disputes between our two families, our interests were merged until such time as Roland, according to his father's will, should become more responsible.

The house occupied by the elder Roland and his family was small, scarcely enough to accommodate his sons should they both decide to marry and have children of their own, whilst the manor at Bachhagen was spacious enough for four families.

I employed a second steward and installed him in the smaller property. Both young Roland and Matti came to live with us. The arrangement suited. We had extra company and additional labour in times of need. Moreover, the overseeing of two estates with trustworthy employees was no more difficult than caring for one.

Only one problem remained which, had the future taken a different turn, might have proved intractable. Over the years I had given only occasional thought to how Bachhagen would be divided on my death. Although my marriage to Matthilde had produce only one legitimate child, for all the world knew we had two sons. Hypatia was already well provided for by her husband and by her considerable dowry, and it had always been my intention to divide my remaining wealth equally between Ludwig and Andreas. Matthilde, who had loved the latter as if he were her own, raised no objection.

But I had begun to see problems with this plan. Should either of my sons marry and have children while the other did not, how would this change matters? Things being unequal, could I in all conscience allow a greater portion of my legacy fall to my great-grandchildren than to my grandchildren?

I had never solved the problem to my own satisfaction and it was continually being put out of mind as the children grew. Even a man approaching the end of his sixth decade does not care to contemplate death and, since the memorable fever I had suffered years before, I had been in excellent health. I had thus put off the decision to make a fresh will.

In March 1339, I was to be given a harsh reminder of how fragile and transient life can be.

Ludwig

i

The manor house of Bachhagen stands on a knoll to protect it from flooding. The slope down to the river is gentle but in every other direction is undulating countryside. From the nearest point of the high road the track is steep in places and unsuited to an elderly traveller on foot.

One afternoon, a stranger came to our door and presented himself to the steward. He was out of breath and made himself comfortable in a chair until he realised Matthilde was watching him from the stairs.

'I beg your pardon for the liberty, your ladyship,' he wheezed, 'but I've been running most of the way. My name is Jonas Graube and I'm here on behalf of my employer to ask if he may come up.'

'An employer who makes his man run when he might ride!' Matthilde said, half in jest.

'Don't judge him harshly, my lady,' the fellow said. 'It was my choice to come on foot. I did not think it would be so far.'

'Then I shall not judge,' said Matthilde, indicating that he should resume his chair. 'But tell me, sir,' she went on with more than a little curiosity, 'who might your employer be?'

'I beg your pardon,' replied the stranger. 'He is Master Queck of Hameln. He waits on your pleasure at the gate - with our horses.'

'Andreas Queck is always welcome,' said Matthilde. 'Your master does not need permission to visit.'

The man mopped his brow with his sleeve and inhaled twice deeply.

'You mistake me, my lady. My employer is Johann Queck, his son.'

Matthilde realised then that all was not well at Hameln; Andreas never stood on ceremony and always visited without a servant. Moreover, though she was familiar with the Hameln household, the visitor was quite unknown to her. However, she asked no questions and bade him take refreshment while she sent someone to fetch his employer.

Lou was away from home, visiting our shipping interests at Lübeck.

When estate business permitted, I encouraged him to travel between the cities, to learn how people there lived, and discover for himself how their trade and commerce was conducted. Such outings, I told him, were essential in developing a young man's character and understanding of the world. He had been once to Venice to visit his grandmother, already in her seventy-seventh year, and had come to know Hypatia, but had travelled no farther. I had kept that side of my life from him until then and it was a pleasant shock to him that he had a sister.

I had given young Roland a role in managing the farm properties on both Bachhagen and his late father's land and he had responded well to the challenge. He had married and started a family. Matti too had married and was already well into her first pregnancy.

During Lou's absences, I attended the sick, busied myself with Matthilde in the garden, or closeted myself with my writing, star-charts and diagrams of human organs. Though I had reached the age of sixty, I suffered none of the ailments that caused many men twenty years my junior to retire from their profession and adopt a sedentary life. I felt my mind was as enquiring as ever and my body just as active. In this latter respect I fear I was sadly mistaken but it was a pleasant delusion to carry into old age.

Occasionally, memories of my early life would distract me. An incident, a face, a chance remark would recall to mind the arid plains of Persia, friends of my youth, or my many adventures in the rambling passages and secret corners of my father's castle. Though I no longer had time for regrets, there were days when I imagined ways my life might have been different, had I chosen another path, and I often wondered, given back the years, what decisions I would change. I had seen Doquz rarely in the past five years. She travelled with the Singari one year in three, the rest of her time being spent in Venice with Hypatia. But there was always an exchange of messages and gifts.

That March day, I was working in the laboratory when I heard strangers' voices. As my work was sometimes lonely, I enjoyed new company and conversation.

I had met Johann Queck only twice, twenty or more years ago, and did not recognise him. He was about forty years old now, a small man scarcely Matthilde's height, with a round face and figure, blond hair, pale blue eyes and a beard in which there was already a strand or two of grey. Indeed, there was nothing at all of Andreas about him and I saw in him very little of his mother, who had died young.

I had no reason to expect bad news but I saw by Matthilde's expression that I was about to be given some.

'Delaying my task will not make it easier,' said the merchant when we had sat down to a glass of wine. 'My father is dead. He died in his sleep a week ago.'

I closed my eyes to prevent the tears forming. Andreas Queck was probably the best friend I ever had. He had been a party to secrets I had confided in no one else, among other things, the truth about Doquz and Hypatia, and about the grandson I had named after him.

'He was nearly seventy, you know,' the merchant said, 'though he scarcely seemed so old. I'm sorry I could not come sooner but I had to handle other business before I broke the news to you. And that brings me to the second reason for my visit. I am in need of a physician.'

'Forgive me, Master Queck,' said Matthilde, 'but I must say that you seem to be in the best of health.'

Johann's countenance reddened in embarrassment and he coughed self-consciously.

'I will leave you together,' said Matthilde. 'You and your man must spend the night with us, Master Queck.'

When Matthilde had gone, the merchant became quickly at ease and lost any inhibitions against speaking frankly.

'My health is good in general,' he said, 'but, lately, travelling has had an ill effect on my digestion. In short, I am plagued constantly ... ' He lowered his voice and looked round to make sure no one else was in earshot. '..... by wind!'

'Wind?' I suppressed a smile. It was not a complaint I had ever been asked to treat.

'Just that. My gut grumbles continuously, I belch like an animal and, if that weren't enough, I annoy my wife and acquaintances with loud farting.'

'These are common enough symptoms among men of business, in my experience,' I said as seriously as I could. 'May I venture to suggest their cause lies in your mode of existence. I have known merchants all my life and most were afflicted as you describe, to a greater or lesser degree. The remedy is in your own hands, if you'll excuse my bluntness.'

'How so?'

'We who live on the land are fortunate,' I said. 'Estate owners have riches and property enough to sustain a bad harvest. The farmers and peasants have few possessions to worry about, and provided they pay their dues, or give service, they can be assured of our protection. But like your father I have travelled and traded too and understand the pressures. A merchant depends on the next ship, the successful conclusion of a bargain, the prompt payment of a debt, or the understanding of a creditor. His prosperity is hard won and he must strive hard to keep it. He travels, he eats bad food and devours it quickly. He frets, he lies awake at night, and his body responds by producing these gases that cause discomfort and embarrassment. At least, that's my opinion.'

'What you say is true, I fear,' said Johann. 'I worry constantly about my business – more than my father ever did, and many a night I stay awake with my ledgers. But, as to my food, that's no worse than the next man's.'

'I did not mean to give offence,,' I said, 'only to draw a distinction between meat prepared in one's own kitchens, eaten at leisure, and what might be purchased at an inn, which is generally inferior.'

'Your meaning is clear and I'm not in the least offended,' said my visitor. 'But you spoke of a remedy?'

'I can recommend an infusion of seeds from the plant the Persians call karwiya. If made according to my prescription, it will relieve the wind and soothe the stomach. Allow me to give you a supply of the flowers.

'And, apart from this medicine, there are two pieces of advice I can give,' I went on, studying our guest's face anew. He had a strong, honest jaw and a fine set of teeth but had allowed his brow to become furrowed with anxiety. 'Spend more time in chewing your meat; it'll digest more easily. And find a diversion!'

'A diversion?'

'A musical instrument, perhaps? I myself find comfort occasionally in a flute.'

'I've no talent for music making, though my daughter has a pleasant singing voice.'

'Perhaps hunting, or hawking. You have horses.'

'Indeed I do, but I've had no training or practice in these sports.'

'To another I might recommend a young mistress,' I said, 'but I see you are a man content in his home and family. I would not dare offer such a remedy to you.'

'You are right. We are happy. My wife Anna has given me three children, our daughter Greta, who is fifteen, and two small sons. I venture to say that Greta is a pretty maid, well endowed with the qualities men find so appealing. We have high hopes of finding a good match for her before long.' He coughed. 'But forgive me, I'm boring you. I will take your medicine and try to change my habits.'

Johann was happy to accept our offer of hospitality for the night and during the course of the evening his manners and conversation reinforced my good opinion of him. I had known he was married and had a child or two – Andreas had mentioned it - but I had supposed them infants. Time plays tricks on the old.

We discussed the trade in tin, wood, silk and other commodities until it was late. I listened as my guest talked of his new interest in glass and of his travels. He had taken up half his father's interests and shared the rest with a younger brother.

'I was in Venice twelve months ago,' he told me as we dined, 'and in Persia – Tabriz - a year before that. That is a hazardous place for Christians in these times...'

I scarcely heard what he said. It was thirty-five years since I had seen Tabriz, the city where I was born. My thoughts drifted to near-forgotten days. I could see the sun creep above the crest of Mount Sahand. Just beyond the castle wall rose the dome of the mosque, and the plain tower from which the muezzin intoned his solemn call to prayer. Two boys were playing with wooden swords on the dry, dusty ground and one of them, I knew, had not lived past his thirty-seventh year.

The merchant must have guessed my thoughts were elsewhere. 'I fear I'm stirring painful memories,' he said. 'Let us converse on another topic.'

I assured him his talk did not disturb me. On the contrary. It was merely that the mention of Tabriz reminded me of things I had long put out of mind.

'Just memories,' I said. 'Tell me, do descendants of Genghis Khan still rule in Persia? When I last heard, Abu Sa'id, the son of Oljeitu, had succeeded to the throne.'

'Abu Sa'id is dead and Suleiman is Khan, or at least he was when I left the country.'

'Dead!' Suddenly, I felt very old and sad. Oljeitu and I were the same age. We had not been friends beyond our boyhood; indeed, we had become rivals, if not enemies, yet when the news had reached me of his early death, it had been a hard blow to take. Now it seemed that his son had followed him to the grave. I listened politely throughout supper as Johann spoke of his travels in Asia Minor, and of his family. Still, my thoughts returned continually to my half brother Oljeitu, to our quarrel, and how that quarrel had been one factor that caused me to leave Persia forever.

As he took his leave the following morning, Johann insisted on my paying him a return visit. He had sold property in the north and intended to move into his father's house at Hameln. I was to bring Lou with me.

'Let us wait two months,' I suggested. 'That will give you an opportunity to test my advice and my medicine.'

The time was agreed and one afternoon in May, Lou and I rode to Hameln by the forest track. I have to say I suspected our friend had motives other than mere hospitality behind his invitation, and that the charms of his daughter might have played a part, but I said nothing to my son.

The Queck family was settled in one of the finest houses in the town, a tall stout building of stone and handsome beams, with a high, sharply-sloping roof and many windows. From high in the gable wall, they looked out over the roofs of lesser dwellings to the River Weser and the dense woodland beyond, while the chief rooms had a view of the town square and the St Boniface tower.

Their front door opened onto a broad cobbled street in the heart of the town's merchant quarter. Nearby was the bakery, a wine-cellar, a candlemaker and a tailor. To the left, the road narrowed and divided into two lanes, so dim that even a resident could easily miss his footing in the middle of the day; to the right, it led to the town gate and a stone bridge that was well able to take a carriage. Across the square was another road leading to the river, and here were houses belonging to some other of the wealthier citizens.

The house was one I had known for many years and had visited often. However, it seemed different, now that Andreas was no longer there to welcome me. The welcome was no less for that. Johann himself met us in the stable yard.

'Well,' I asked him, 'did I give you sound advice or not?'

He beamed and shook me warmly by the hand, then, turning to Lou he did the same.

'You were right in every particular,' he said, leading us indoors. 'My digestion has improved beyond all expectation, and I'm in much better humour as a result. Now I hope you'll allow me to reward you with some small token of my thanks. Let me to show you some very fine items of silver and some jewels. Choose some trinket for your charming lady or for yourself, as you prefer. And you, Master Ludwig, what say you? I have a splendid dagger of Toledo steel that I acquired in Spain. I'll make you a present of it.!'

He carried on in this cordial but embarrassing manner while conducting us on a tour of the dwelling. The rooms were the same as always, yet different. Andreas had been a collector in his way but Johann had rearranged the treasures as well as bringing some of his own to his inheritance. All kinds of ornament were hung on the walls or laid out in cabinets. Plates and goblets of silver, fine wood carvings and poniards in jewel-encrusted sheaths were displayed side by side with tin artefacts and gold coins from Spain and England. As a result of our host's pleading, Lou finally agreed to accept the Toledo dagger as a gift.

'That blade is worth half the herbs and ointments in our laboratory,' I said, 'whereas a physician's reward is to see his patient restored to health. Even if you had not been the son of my dearest friend, I would have taken no payment.'

Johann yielded reluctantly. He led us to the parlour where his wife was waiting to be presented. Mistress Anna Queck was a rosy woman, not unlike her husband in height and build. Two small boys peered out saucily from behind her aprons.

'You are welcome, sir,' she said, dropping a curtsy. 'I heard nothing but good of you from my late good-father and now my husband is a new man since he took your advice.

And you, young master,' she went on, addressing Lou, 'are also someone of whom good is spoken in these parts. Allow me to present to you my daughter, Greta.'

At this, the inner door of the parlour opened and into the room came one of most delightful girls I had ever seen. Lou's cheeks turned a very obvious shade of red and though his mouth opened, his tongue seemed frozen to his palate.

Greta blushed too and I saw at once that if it had been Master Queck's intention to match-make, he had succeeded beyond all his expectations.

It was several minutes before Lou found his voice and then to assure the maiden he was her most obedient servant. She on her part assured him very coyly that she had no need of a servant at present but would be very glad if he would be her friend. Then she turned to me.

'My grandfather told me once you had lived among the Saracens,' she said and now there was no trace of the coyness. 'Tell me, sir, are you Christian or Infidel?'

'Hush, Greta!' The merchant laid a hand on his daughter's arm. 'Where are your manners?'

I waved his objection aside.

'It is a proper question and deserves an answer,' I said. Never had I been challenged with such charm and innocence. The girl already had a lovely face and figure that might bewitch any man, and she could scarcely be in her sixteenth year. Had I been younger, it would have been my heart that was lost and not that of my son.

'It is my most ardent wish, Greta,' I said, 'that one day men will abandon war and live in peace with one another, whatever their faith. If that does not satisfy you, then I will admit I was brought up to follow the teachings of Mahommet. But I have lived among Christians for a long time. I have adopted their customs and ways. And I say to you, there is good in all, just as there is evil.'

Greta smiled. 'And you, sir?' she asked Ludwig.

'As to that, there is no doubt,' he replied. 'I was baptised by the Holy Church and am a Christian like my mother and all her kin.'

'How strange,' said Greta, lowering his eyes from what I thought from Lou was an extremely insolent stare. 'By all accounts, you practise your father's healing trade but ignore his race and faith.'

'Hush, Greta,' Johann admonished for the second time. 'What has your grandfather been telling you?'

She paid him no attention but again addressed me. 'And, sir, it is also strange that you, who once belonged to a people we are taught to regard as our enemy, should willingly treat my father and other Christians as Our Lord would have wished. For Jesus himself went about curing the sick. 'Tis a wonder to find a Saracen who does the same, and for no reward.'

I bowed to her in admiration. Her pale blue eyes were lit up and the corners of her mouth wrinkled pertly when she smiled. She was so very like Andreas, I thought. And she had spoken so inoffensively that I did not think to correct her error - that I was no Saracen but had once fought against them – that my father had once sought an alliance with the Christians. To what end was the bitterness between the races, I wondered in that moment? To what end the killing? Would men's faith forever remain a barrier between them?

'I do not presume to compare myself with Jesus Christ,' I said. 'He was a good and holy man, and was able to aid the sick with miracles, whereas I rely only on tried and tested medicines.'

'Yet there are those who would call your cures miraculous, your remedies magical,' said Johann.

'All healing may seem as magic to those who do not understand the principles involved,' I admitted. 'Some so-called physicians seek to hide the secrets of their craft behind incantations and charms, and as a result may more truly be called magicians. You have already seen I have no need of spells. And there's little of my trade that cannot be learned by the simplest soul.'

'You acknowledge then the miracles of Christ?' asked Greta.

'I cannot deny them,' I said. 'Would that there were cures for leprosy, or for lameness, but there are none. I can only suppose the hand of the Creator raised the cripple from his bed and made the leper clean again, as recounted in the Holy Book. Perhaps, one day, I might show you something of the physician's skill, if you have a mind to it.'

'Perhaps,' said Greta sweetly. 'I am only sorry I shall not have the opportunity to convert you. You are more than three-quarters-way to being a Christian already.'

The consequences of that day were inevitable.

Throughout the summer of 1339, Lou was a constant visitor to the Queck home. He gave to his host and hostess the respect due to them but had little time for their polite conversation, having eyes only for the smile of the girl he had set out to win, and ears for nothing but the sound of her voice. He knew he loved her and, though still some way from his eighteenth birthday with little experience of women, he was certain he could be happy with no one else. I saw it all in his face.

He and Greta talked, I supposed. They gazed amorously at one another and occasionally their hands touched, but they were rarely alone together, and never for long enough to permit more intimate expressions of affection. Mistress Anna Queck continued to guard her daughter's virtue in the manner of the times and according to the customs of her class, and Lou was ever conscious of her watchful eye.

Their betrothal was a matter of great rejoicing yet Johann and I felt it was too early to celebrate a marriage. Let six months pass, we decided; Lou would be seventeen and Greta sixteen, and both families would give their blessing.

For me, the months passed quickly though I fear that for Lou they were the longest of his life. There were new and for the most part welcome changes to our household. We continued to run the two family estates as one. Roland, two years Ludwig's senior, had already one son and one daughter and his wife was expecting a third. Matti had given birth to the twins Sigmund and Lieselle though, sadly, she had lost her husband in the Eastern wars.

We had seen little of Andreas at Bachhagen since he left Brunswick and the Duke's service. Of course, we knew as yet nothing of the escapade that had led to his dismissal and accepted his homecoming as the result of a mutual understanding.

'I'm sorry to be a disappointment to you, Mother,' was his only apology, 'but I cannot endure the monotony of this soldier's life.'

'You are home,' said Matthilde, embracing him, and she was not disposed to enquire further.

I was less inclined to accept the plain facts but Magnus could not be drawn further. Tom too remained tight-lipped when questioned. I sensed that he knew something of the affair, and my suspicions were aroused even further when his new bride, Martha, refused to visit Bachhagen while Andreas was in residence.

For several months, Andreas had continued to enjoy the benefits of the estate whilst contributing nothing and absenting himself from the house on one pretext or another. He rose before dawn, went off as soon as it was light, and returned usually at nightfall, except on those winter nights when he did not return at all. Sometimes he stayed away for days at a time, always leaving with no servant to accompany him, and arriving home by himself. He was never seen to have any companions or friends, and would reply curtly to enquiries after his health, or questions as to his recent whereabouts. At last, he embarked on what in his words were his travels. I worried that he had somehow learned of his true parentage and was intent on finding Hypatia but that was far from the truth. We did not see him for two years and when he returned he only reverted to his old habits.

Though I was to learn the details only much later, it seemed that he took Lou's news with a bad grace.

'I hope you know what to do with her,' Andreas had laughed in an offhand way.

'Be assured I do,' Lou said. 'I pray you'll be as fortunate as I in finding a maiden who is both beautiful and of a ready wit.'

'A pox on maidenly wit!' said Andreas coarsely. 'Give me only a damsel who is ready to pleasure me when I've a mind. If she's fair, so much the better; if ugly, she can cover her head with a sack while I enter her.'

'My happiness is too great to be dented by your ribald humour,' said Lou stiffly. 'You can't provoke me on the eve of my wedding. Indeed, I had hoped it would be an occasion for reconciliation between us. I know we have little in common, but nothing will please me more than if you were to attend my marriage feast.'

'You have found your heart's desire very easily, little brother,' Andreas replied. 'I almost envy you. The road I plan will be hard but will bring at its end great rewards.'

'I'll never understand you, Andreas! What greater reward could a man have than the love of a wife? What could he desire more heartily than the health and happiness of his fellow creatures, the laughter of his children, or the company of his friends?'

'I don't value these things as you do, Louey,' said Andreas. 'You think too much of others. A man has only one duty, and that is to himself. He should listen to only one voice, the voice of his passion; he should acknowledge only one law, the law of the same nature that fashioned him. I've no patience with this social order under which we live. It's a conspiracy by weak men to keep the strong in check. A strong man might be raised to a dukedom, or even higher, if he had a mind. And why should he settle for one wife when he might have a harem like the Persian princes?'

'Where's your passion, brother? Your ambition? Or are you just like our father in that you have none? Content to be forever a servant of the poor and sick, he would condemn his sons to the same fate. And when he could unlock for us the secrets of the universe, he continues to play the farmer and merchant.'

'You're talking nonsense, Andreas,' cried Lou. 'What secrets?'

'Those he hides from us! The Dark Path, as he calls it. True magic! The knowledge that might capture a throne!'

'What absurdities are these?' said Lou. 'The Dark Path is a perversion. Those that follow it are rewarded with misery and the judgement of God. As for the Dukedom, you're mad if you believe the succession can ever be set aside in your favour.'

'Mad I may be, or not. But even Princes may die!'

Lou recoiled in horror.

'Now you're speaking of treason or of sorcery,' he said. 'And you dare to link Bachhagen and our father's name with such devilment!'

'It was merely a jest, brother,' declared Andreas with a laugh. 'You're such a serious fellow, and I can't resist teasing you. Who knows? Perhaps I'll accept your invitation after all.'

With the death of my friend and the coming marriage, the matter of my will began again to trouble me. I had a new plan. Andreas had never shown an interest in managing the estate and he clearly had no attachment to a military life. But he had a head for facts and figures as well as mastery of three or four languages. I decided that after my death he would become the sole owner of all my business interests outside of Bachhagen, which, with silver mines, glass and ships and my share in the English trade, were worth every bit as much as the land and the farms. Lou and his heirs should have the latter.

I felt it would be unfair to discuss the matter unless both lads were present and I looked forward to meeting them before Lou's wedding plans were finalised. However, mid way through the period of the engagement, Andreas disappeared again, much to Lou's disappointment and to mine, and the opportunity was lost.

Doquz had meantime returned to Saxony. She had a single companion, a strongly-built man of middle age and Persian appearance.

'His name is Ali-Hassan,' she told me. 'We knew his father.'

I was so startled by this announcement that I could only stare. His resemblance to the man I had once known was astonishing, yet I had not noticed it until Doquz had uttered the name. Ali had been our comrade-in-arms in the rebellion against the usurper. He owed me his life as I owed him mine, and it was a great joy for me to welcome his son.

Ali-Hassan had crossed the ocean in search of me, at his dying father's request, and had arrived in Venice some three years previously. He had some skill as a smith and expressed his desire to settle down in our neighbourhood. I gave him the forge for his own use. Doquz decided to spend the winter at her house in Hameln.

The marriage was arranged for the winter solstice and on midwinter's eve the festivities began. A Yule log was lit in the Queck family parlour. Branches of holly and of fir were hung in their hall. Two tables were laid with the finest meats, the largest loaves, and the tastiest cheeses. The autumn harvest of apples was taken from the store and piled high in baskets; flask upon flask of the best wine from the cellar was set beside the food.

Falls of snow throughout Advent had made the way from Bachhagen treacherous but this did not deter our household from making the journey by horse and by carriage. We could not allow the weather to dampen our spirits. And there were few in Hameln who did not join in the mood of rejoicing.

What should I relate of the wedding itself: that Lou was obliged to perform the dawn song under his bride's window; that Greta was radiant in a gown of silk from Turkey; that the pair rode to the church in a dray pulled across the snow by two apprentices?

Tradesmen and their wives, in snow-flecked furs, stood by their doors and waved cheerily as the cavalcade passed. In the square, groups of artisans and labourers, with cloaks or skins wrapped tightly round their shoulders, applauded as they stamped their feet against the cold. Hameln urchins, faces red with exertion from their snow fights and breath white in the midwinter air, raised a cheer as bells began to peal.

Much else could be said that is expected of any wedding celebration. Johann Queck provided hospitality for those guests who had travelled a distance and took no offence when a few overindulged in food and wine. Several town worthies, having found a quiet corner in one of the public rooms, took advantage of his good nature and curled up for a snooze, preferring the warmth of festal logs and the proximity to limitless supplies of sweetmeats over the prospect of even the shortest walk across snow-covered cobbles.

The feasting lasted until Christmas Eve. By afternoon, only the new in-laws and a hard core of guests remained. The days had passed without Andreas putting in an appearance, and Lou began to believe his invitation had been spurned. Daylight was beginning to fade when a snow- and mud-bespattered horseman dismounted in the stable yard.

Johann conducted Andreas to the warmth of the Yuletide fire.

'You are most welcome,' said he. 'There's plenty food, and I still have a flagon or two of the best wine. Join us in a toast to your brother and his new bride.'

'I'll be glad to,' Andreas replied civilly.

As he spoke, I saw his eyes flash. Though still unsuccessful in my attempt to discover the reason for his departure from court, I knew youthful passion well enough. I now suspected that a woman was at the bottom of the affair, an opinion reinforced by the behaviour of Martha, who left the room as soon as Andreas entered it.

Greta came forward to be presented. She extended her hand. Andreas took it. However, he held it much too long, and his lingering look was such that no man should permit himself when addressing his brother's wife.

I watched them all at supper. Though Martha had returned for the meal, she and Tom sat at a table on the far side of the room, separated from the bridal party. Clearly no trivial quarrel between the cousins had prompted this behaviour and I determined to get to the bottom of it. Perhaps I could succeed with cunning where direct questioning had failed. A flagon of wine was a sure way of loosening a tied tongue.

Andreas's presence was a boost to Lou's already elated spirits. He took it as a sign that any tensions between them were in the past. He cared only that the family was together to share his joy, and dismissed his brother's previous crude utterances as mere banter.

But as the newly-weds exchanged fond glances and whispered nothings, oblivious to everything but one another's attention, I remarked that Andreas's gaze fell frequently upon Greta. Though the impropriety was unlikely to have been noted by the other guests, least of all by Lou, I saw again a glint of lust in his look.

At other times, I caught him eyeing the couple with cold appraisal. Once, while Lou was refilling empty goblets and the others applying themselves to the business of eating, I saw Greta's glance flit from my face to Andreas's profile and back again as if puzzled by what she saw.

I noticed a lack of gaiety in her manner and cool apprehension gripped my heart.

ii

The days remained mild until the middle of January. Twice the snow came and went, followed by heavy rain that left the rutted lanes like muddy water courses and made travel, even by the highway, hazardous on horseback and out of the question by carriage. Towards the end of Lou's and Greta's honeymonth, the weather became colder, the ruts and puddles froze over and ice was seen in the river shallows. When snow fell again it did so thickly, and the estate was gripped by a frost such as I had not seen in all my sixty years.

Andreas did not return to Bachhagen after the wedding and weeks passed without there being any news of him.

In the autumn of 1340, Greta announced that she was pregnant. Lou could not believe his good fortune. She took his hand and held the palm against her belly, then she looked at me with a warm smile that might have melted ice on the pond.

Shortly after the equinox began a series of puzzling incidents. First there were the thefts from farms on our estate and those adjoining. Several animals, chickens, sheep and pigs went missing. This was unusual as food was plentiful. We investigated but the perpetrators were never discovered. Then, three village girls went missing only to return a week later. Though their mothers beat them, they would not or could not say where they had been.

Lou was absorbed in estate work, but he had the habit of riding out on a pretext to acquaint neighbours and friends of the coming happy event. On one outing he met a shepherd trudging across a meadow with a black and white hound at his heels. This was a man he had previously treated for winter sores. The fellow wore a sleeveless shirt and his arms were red and blotched from the elbow to the wrist. His hands were almost raw with open pustules.

'Your symptoms appear to be worse,' Lou said. 'Has my ointment been ineffective?'

'I used the med'cines ev'ry day. Truly, Master Ludwig,' replied the shepherd. 'All seemed well at first but now the sores 'ave returned painful as ever.'

'Didn't I tell you the problem is caused by exposure to the weather,' Lou said. 'Handling the animals without protection for the chapped skin is the reason the wounds re-open. Use the ointment again, and cover your arms when you work. I feel sure that'll do the trick.'

'Your pardon, sir,' said the other, 'but mayn't be the cure lacks magic words to give potency?'

'I don't deal in magic words,' said Lou, more amused than angry. 'Cover your arms and my ointment will suffice. Where did you hear this nonsense?'

This question threw the shepherd into confusion. He fixed his eyes on the ground, tightened his grip on his staff so that his hand turned bright red and he began muttering to himself.

Lou shook his head and with another warning to heed his advice rode on. He gave no further thought to the matter until three or four days later, when he was waylaid by a woman whose husband he had attended the week before. Preoccupied with thoughts of Greta and their plans for the coming child, he did not recognise her at first. However, he could never refuse help when it was needed and followed her to her home.

The sight of the tiny, well-kept cottage jogged his memory.

'Surely I was here recently,' he said, looking at the woman's face more closely. 'If I'm not mistaken, you have a daughter who undertook to nurse her father and give him his medicines.'

'She has done that, to no avail, sir. My man be no better.'

'We'll have to see about that,' said Lou. He entered the single room. It was poorly furnished but clean. The sick man half sat, half lay in his bed, his head supported by a plump girl who was bathing the sweat from his forehead with a coarse flannel. On a nearby rickety table were the remains of a meal, a few beakers, some wilting herbs, and a little heap of crushed seeds.

The child raised her rosy face.

'I done what tha say'st,' she sang, with a glance at the table. 'Three times a day. Three times a day till 't goes 'way. An' I said the charm ev'ry night, jus' as 'e told me!'

Lou stared at her in astonishment. 'Charm? What charm?'

The girl began reciting without any sense of understanding.

'I 'jure you, elves an' demons, depart by th' names of th' sev'n sleepers ...' She paused to take a deep breath. 'An' by th' moon 'n' stars, *nema sutirips, soya, soya, soya, enimon ni!*'

Lou's astonishment was turning to alarm. Never had he heard such gibberish, and there was something disturbing about the child's vacant look as she spoke the words.

'How came your daughter by this rhyme?' he asked the mother. 'By the saints, she did not learn it from me.'

The woman shook her head.

'I don't know, sir. She said she 'ad it from the physician, but she's only twelve years old, an' is easily confused.'

Lou attempted to question the girl but she was making no sense. Like the shepherd before her, she hung her head in confusion and seemed more in a trance than conscious of her surroundings. Then she brightened up. She laid down the wet flannel, flashed him a vacant smile and ambled towards the door, singing softly to herself.

Lou picked up a bunch of herbs from the table and held them to his nose. Scarcely any of their fragrance remained.

'It's no surprise to me that your husband is weaker,' he told the woman, holding out the withered herbs to her in the palm of his hand. 'These must be freshly picked or they'll have no effect. I advise you not to rely on the child but take care of your husband yourself.'

Over the next week or two, both Lou and I had several such experiences. Either the sick person had misunderstood instructions, had drunk quite the wrong medicine, or had misused an ointment. A few had memorised charms or worthless rhymes, and would recite them almost with pride, much as the country girl had done. A madness had infected the people of the Leine valley, one we were powerless to treat.

'I don't know what to make of it,' Lou said. 'It's as if they're trying to make a mockery of our work.'

'It will pass,' said Greta confidently, wrinkling her nose. 'Be patient and you will see.'

Instead of improving, things went from bad to worse. There were fewer calls on our advice and, more than once, Lou at any rate was refused entry to houses where formerly he had been welcome. A few acquaintances even tried to avoid him on the road. If a meeting became inevitable, they would cross themselves fervently and pass on their way without speaking.

My delight at the prospect of a grandchild had driven all dark thoughts from my mind. I had tolerated the whims and superstitions of Brunswick country folk for too many years to be upset by their odd behaviour.

'Perhaps we are being shadowed by an itinerant healer,' I suggested. 'We are being blamed for his mistakes.'

'The friars have never been any trouble,' said Lou. 'And if one utters an adjuration or two, it's harmless nonsense. It doesn't interfere with our treatments.'

'I suspect our rival is no cleric. There are would-be physicians, neither skilled nor godly, who will sell charms, talismans and exorcisms to the weak and uneducated for a few coins or for favours. We must find this charlatan, Lou, and put a stop to his activities.'

We spent a week to no avail. No strangers had been seen. Some rascal was working against us, yet he seemed to be invisible. My happy mood was changing to one of annoyance. I sensed that our rival's interference had gone beyond simple mischief. Few cases of sorcery had come before the municipal court in my memory but that did not mean necromancy as an art was dead.

One evening, the chill of foreboding that had so often plagued me descended on me once again. I retired to the laboratory with some old manuscripts. After an hour or two's study, I believed I had found what I was looking for.

'What words can you remember of the charms and recitations?' I asked Lou when he had joined me.

'I couldn't recite them exactly,' he said, 'but they had this in common: they began by addressing demons, elves or angels. As for the rest, in every case it was either the most unspeakable nonsense, or no language I ever heard.'

'Perhaps neither is the case.' I pushed away my manuscripts and drew towards us on the table paper and writing materials. 'Many a Christian monk in the old days would begin his cure with a prayer or a blessing. He might even address the illness itself, and command it to leave the patient's body.'

'I have nothing against prayer and blessing, Father,' said Lou, 'but you have taught me disease is the result of natural poisons in the blood, rather than demons in the brain.'

'Indeed, but when faced with a stubborn illness, and when all your remedies fail you, the answer may be to deal with the sickness in a man's mind. You know how I have used the fylfot. My mother taught me that, and she was wise in so many things.

'But a sorcerer relies on a similar principle. If a victim believes he's possessed, he will not be cured until he believes the evil spirit has left his body. He might sicken and die for no other reason than his conviction that an amulet containing the blood of a field mouse is the cause of the malady. And, as an aid to magic, the necromancer might read a benediction in reverse, or incompletely. Can you recall anything that fits that category?'

'One word comes to mind, for it was repeated several times,' Lou said, 'and by more than one of the unfortunates I visited. It was *soya* or *soy-ha*.'

'Repeated three times?'

'I believe so, Father. How do you know that?'

I took the paper and wrote across it in large letters -

HAGIOS HAGIOS HAGIOS

'Now, Lou,' I said, 'give me your opinion of that. What do these words signify?'

'It's Greek. It means *Holy, Holy, Holy* in that language.'

'And if I reverse the letters...?'

'SOIGAH - *Soya!*'

'We are making progress. Now let's try something else.' I pulled over the paper again and this time wrote some other words, in letters the same size as the others:

NEMA SUTCNAS SUTIRIPS TE ILIF TE SIRTAP ENIMON NI

'Now,' I challenged, and watched Lou's features wrinkle in a frown as he tried to read the words aloud.

'These are the words a madman would use ...'

'Indeed. But ...?'

'But the sound is familiar!'

'And again, if the letters are reversed?'

Lou took my pen and, starting at the end of the line, began to rewrite the sentence backwards:

IN NOMINE PATRIS ET FILI ...

He stopped and stared at the paper.

'It's nothing but the common benediction,' he cried, rising from his chair.

'And proof,' said I, 'that we are not accidental victims of a fool's mistakes! Either we have a common rascal pretending to the skills of a necromancer, or the beginnings of some real villainy.'

We left home the next day at sun-up. I was eager to find other evidence of necromancy for, as distasteful as such evidence might be, we could not hope to catch the criminal without it. It was my intention first to pay a few visits on the estate, to families with cause to be grateful for our protection, and for our science.

At three farms we were greeted with the usual civility, at two of these with a beaker of country wine. Nothing out of the ordinary had occurred. At another, the tenant had heard of disturbances in Bachhagen village but knew no details.

In mid afternoon, we came by a tiny homestead on the borders of our land. Here, in a field, the farmer had kept a cow, a pig or two, and had raised a vegetable crop. As we neared the place, we saw it was deserted save for a mangy dog that slunk in and out of the buildings. We dismounted and led our horses towards the dwelling. In the vicinity of a broken-down wooden structure, once an outhouse for storage and a protection for the animals in winter, our nostrils were assailed by the odour of decay.

'The property has been abandoned,' said Lou indifferently. He held his hand to his nose.

'It was occupied a month ago,' I said. I removed two rotted planks from the wall of the outhouse. Inside was the carcass of a sheep, disembowelled and smothered in flies.

The cottage door was badly in need of repair. I pushed it gently and it swung ajar on one hinge. Lou, his interest already kindled, left his animal and followed me. The farmer lay on his back. Two broken flagons sat on the earthen floor beside him, besieged by an army of ants intent on recovering what little sweetness remained of the liquor, which had already seeped into the ground. The meagre furnishings were covered in dust. On the table were the remains of a meal of stale rye bread and mould-ridden cheese. The smell of urine and vomit pervaded the air.

I prodded the body with the toe of my boot and the man emitted a groan.

'Drunk,' I said in disgust. 'Help me drag him outside before we are both overcome by this stench!'

We hauled the fellow into the open where half the contents of a pitcher of water from a nearby stream, emptied on his person, sufficed to wake him from his lethargy. He spluttered and opened his eyes. Seeing Lou bent over him, he seized him wildly by the hair, wrenched him to the ground and began snarling over him like an animal.

Lou prized open the man's fingers but succeeded in freeing himself only with my help. Together we propped him up against the cottage wall. The rest of the water, poured over his head, restored his speech.

'I knows thee!' he cried, peering at me through swollen eyelids. 'Aye, I knows thee, Master von Hasenbach. An' a young un!' He rolled his bloodshot eyes. His head flopped to one side and he would have slid once more to the ground if I had not gripped him by the shirt.

'I can't help you unless you come to your senses,' I said. 'Where's your wife? If I'm not mistaken, you have a wife.'

'A wife!' repeated the farmer. He gave a demented laugh then began sobbing like a child. The tears seemed to restore some of his sanity. 'There be some things thee can't treat with tha physic, Master,' he mumbled. 'Aye, a 'ad a wife, but they took 'er. Mounted an' took 'er!'

'Took her - who took her?' I demanded.

'Incubus!' He roused himself and took hold of my wrists. 'Sheep's entrails 'roused 'er. There were two of 'em, a sossrer an' 'is 'sistant.'

'A sorcerer?'

212

'Aye, Master, an' they killed and gutted the sheep ...'

He was beginning to slip back into delirium so I shook him hard to rouse him again. 'Who was he? Did you know him?'

'Know him, aye ... Incubus!' the fellow repeated. He gripped my tunic to pull me closer and whisper in my ear. I caught the stink of his drunken breath before he lapsed into unconsciousness. I allowed the body to slump over onto one side.

'He'll come to himself in time,' I said to Lou. 'We've seen and heard more than enough here.'

We continued our ride in silence. Lou took my mood for meditation and did not intrude on it. However, my mind was in turmoil, suspecting - indeed knowing the answer to the puzzle, the one piece of information that made terrible sense of the chaos of the past weeks. For, in his half-crazed stupor, the drunken farmer had given it to me. One word, a name, and I had heard it plainly. I had heard it, knew it, and its echo made me sick and wretched to the heart.

But the day was not over. Our return journey took us into Bachhagen village. We rode along the village street, past the forge to the end nearest the river. Here, standing apart from lesser dwellings, was the cottage of Jacob of Munich. Jacob had lived there for thirty years or more. In his youth he had been a healer in his home city but had been banished on account of his religion. He had suffered a beating too that had left him crippled in the legs and able to walk only by shuffling along on his toes. It was true the local children made fun of his unusual gait and tormented him with name-calling but in the years I had known him he had always been popular among the grown-ups.

Our welcome was anything but friendly. About twenty angry peasants armed with sticks and tools were gathered round the cottage. A lone woman wielding only a broom stood between the mob and the object of its fury. Lou spurred forward into the midst of the besiegers. They fell back but did not disperse. One turned from the door of the cottage and aimed a blow at Lou's horse but happily failed to connect with it. The animal, perceiving the danger, snorted and swung its hind quarters away.

Angry crowds are no respecters of rank. But, though unpredictable and not disposed to listen to reason, they are impressed by the threat of cold steel. The man with the stick raised it again, but lowered it as Lou drew his sword.

I dismounted by the side of Jacob's solitary defender, took the broom from her and disarmed the nearest man. Some of the besiegers recognised me and lowered their sticks. Others were too enraged to know who I was or to care.

Lou saved the day. He seized one of the villagers by the hair and collar and hauled him off the ground. I had never seen him so angry.

'Silence,' he roared. 'Stop this madness or I swear I'll spill blood.'

His actions had the desired effect. The villagers quietened. It gave me the chance I needed.

'What is the meaning of this?' I demanded, stepping out among them but with a wary eye on those I took to be the leaders. 'Whatever your grievances are, they will not be settled by a savage attack on a helpless old man.'

'Tha were our frien' once, Master von Hasenbach,' replied one of the villagers, pushing himself to the front and standing before me with hands on hips. 'Now th'ave let loose a devil on us.'

'Aided by the grey-beard wizard tha protect,' added someone else.

'Devils ... wizards,' said I. 'What nonsense! What has Jacob done that has you baying for his blood?'

'It's no more than 'e deserves,' said a woman. 'He let the fiend among us.'

'Fiend indeed!' Lou snapped. 'The only fiends I see here are men armed with cudgels and women with sharp tongues.'

He lowered his victim to the ground. The fellow rubbed his scalp and slunk off to lose himself in the crowd.

Tempers were cooling and no one now seemed eager to speak.

'Well?' said I. 'Do you have a spokesman or not? We know there has been mischief afoot in the district, but why do you lay the blame at my door and at Jacob's?'

There was some muttering from the ring of villagers until at length someone threw a bloodstained bag at my feet. I prodded it with the toe of my boot and it fell open, spilling its contents on the grass. There were some pieces of mangled animal flesh, a few stained feathers and the disembodied head and feet of a cock. Our horses snorted.

The man who had first spoken stepped forward again and, giving Lou and his weapon a wide berth, sidled up to me.

'Aye, sir, it's mischief all right. Black villainy!' he said.

'And this?' I asked, indicating the bag and its bloody contents.

'Sorcery! It's his way. To rouse their desire.'

' 'Tis true,' said another man. 'My wife's with child an' I be not the father. He came to 'er in 'er sleep. An' two maids he's left in the same condition.'

'One was my sister,' said a teenage girl. 'Thirteen she were, an' she threw 'erself from a rock with shame. Drowned herself in the river.'

'An' 'e pretends to heal an' then poisons us with 'is med'cines.'

'A mere look from 'is eyes is enough.'

'This demon who takes the shape of a man!'

There was no stopping them now. One after another, they came forward with their tales. Most were so garbled I could make nothing of them but notwithstanding I began to feel cold and sick.

'But who is he, and why do you blame me?' I said quietly, glancing round the ring of faces.

'Does 'e not practise magic in thy name?'

'In my name?'

'Aye, an' it was Jacob who welcomed 'im to the village. Bade us put our faith in 'im - in 'is evil herbs an' am'lets. In 'is black sorcery.'

Again I glanced round the circle. 'But who is he?'

'You do not know?' said another man. 'Yet he calls himself by Ludwig von Hasenbach!'

Ludwig had meantime remained in the saddle, saying nothing. Now, hearing his name pronounced with such venom, his anger was awakened anew and he leapt from his horse's back to stand face to face with the last speaker.

'How dare you,' he cried. 'How dare you accuse me of sorcery! Retract or you'll answer to my blade!'

Jacob's former supporter sprang to the man's defence. She left the shelter of the cottage wall and tugged at Lou's tunic.

'Please, sir. 'E don't mean it. He knows it weren't thee or tha father. But that was the name the demon used. Hasenbach.'

There were still some mutterings from the mob but they were now half-hearted. A gaunt man with the marks of smallpox on his face went up to Lou and seemed to study his person.

'That's true,' said he after a silence. 'This is Master Ludwig. 'E cured my cousin of a fever. Last autumn it were. 'An I saw the demon. 'E was dark-haired. But I heard him too. Has'nbach was the name 'e gave.'

The shouts began again, though less vehement than before.

'Then why did Jacob protect the devil if 'e knew 'im to be an impostor?'

'Aye, Jacob is still to blame.'

'Aye, Jacob,' they chorused.

'Believe me, my friends, we shall find this impostor,' I said. 'And believe me, he'll get no mercy from the municipal court. And if Jacob has helped him he will pay. But you are surely mistaken. Go back to your homes now. There will be no more witchery and devilment, I guarantee.'

There was more muttering but gradually the crowd gave way. Relieved, I turned my back on them and entered the cottage. Lou followed. The occupant creased wrinkled features into what passed for a smile of thanks. He beckoned us to make ourselves comfortable.

Inside, the room was swept and tidy. The smell of peppermint hung in the air. Freshly-cut bunches of pulegium lay on the floor on both sides of the door, and had been tied to nails at various points in the single room. As Lou crossed the threshold, he looked about him in astonishment.

Jacob missed nothing.

'It drives away the fleas,' he grinned. He bent down slowly, picked up a bunch of sweet-smelling herb and sniffed it. 'What say you to that, young sir?'

'I knew that,' said Lou. 'And the horseflies do not like it either. Boiled in wine with a little honey, we use this herb to cure toothache.'

'And I knew *that*, young man,' said the ancient. 'But it has other uses! With eggs it makes a tasty meal, and a drink made with the leaves is most refreshing.'

Lou regarded our host with new respect.

'Yes, I was once a healer too, young sir,' went on Jacob. 'Then, one day, your learned father cured me of a sickness that all my own knowledge and skill could not relieve. And now you have saved me again, Master Sano, and I am even more in your debt. Yet it might have been better if I had died at the hands of the mob rather than cause you grief because of what I know.'

'I told them you were no sorcerer,' I said, 'and nothing will shake my belief in that. Lou and I know already there is a villain who would discredit us, and it seems you too have been the victim of his trickery. What more harm can be done by speaking out?'

'It's a long time since you visited,' Jacob said. 'In that time I've grown weaker. My eyesight is no longer adequate for a physician. My old joints creak and my bones ache. When a young man passed through the village, a young man claiming your skills and your name, I was glad to give over the care of the people to him. I had heard you have a son, though we had not met.'

'So it's true he claimed the name von Hasenbach?'

'Aye. I allowed him to treat some simple ailments,' the sage said. 'He cured them with ease. But the symptoms returned and, on his second visit, the healer I had recommended to the people attempted to strengthen his medicine by the recitation of charms. Then he brought a companion to assist him with his hocus-pocus. I knew something was wrong but I dared not challenge him.

'On his next visit, he sacrificed a sick calf, sprinkled its blood in the spaces between the houses, and ripped out its organs to use as amulets. He hung foxes' tails on the doors of comely maidens to make them think pleasurably of him. It is foolish nonsense, I know, but the people still believe ... Then, at night, he crept into their beds. But no one saw him come or go, and the maids themselves have no memory of their ravishing. Only the outcome was clear. One girl, as you heard, has taken her own life. Since before the snows came, he has had the village in his clutches.

'I have seen many strange things in my life,' the ancient went on with a shake of his head. The large vein in his temple throbbed. 'I'm no simpleton like some folk here. Though most feats of magic are brought about by trickery, there are others no science can explain. I would have objected and put a stop to this miscreant had I been able. I may be old and weak, but I have not lost my wits. I should have found a way to rally the men of the village but I could do nothing. This necromancer, if that is what he is, has a power I have known no mortal man possess. With a mere look, he is able to sap my will and make me a helpless onlooker. When he fixes his eyes on me I feel pain. My movements, always slow, become slower. What little strength I possess leaves me.'

'Just a look, Jacob, you say?' I was doubtful. 'He wore no talisman? No gammadion?'

'None. I swear it.' Jacob's bony fingers took a firm grip of my arm and he peered closely into my face. The next words were almost inaudible. 'So alike, yet so different. I saw what he did not mean me to see.'

'What did you see?' My voice quivered. I dreaded the Jew's next words.

'Master Ludwig has his mother's looks.' The sage reminisced. 'I saw Lady Matthilde once, when she was young and beautiful ...'

I could bear it no longer.

'What did you see?' I cried in frustration. I grasped him by the shoulders and shook him so violently that his words were choked off. Just as suddenly, I regained control of myself and begged his forgiveness.

'It's two and thirty years since you first came to my aid, Sano von Hasenbach. I have every reason to remember that visit, and how you looked then. You were a stranger in the land as I myself once was. After you had taken the Lady Matthilde to wife you came again. And again. Once you had a child with you. He was to be your 'prentice, you said.'

'Andreas?'

'I know not, but a handsome boy, curly-headed with dark skin and black eyes. He will be fully grown now. The curls will have gone and I'll warrant the once smooth complexion now wears a beard.'

'You are right. My son Andreas is now a grown man.'

'But that is not the name! Would that I could have spared you, but I cannot. Akhtar is the name he calls himself by. And he is a devil indeed. The eyes that once looked on with curiosity as you mixed your herbs now burn with hate and envy. They burn into the very soul. I do not know how or why he has become so, but the child is the antithesis of the father.

Antithesis in character though image in looks. The child may once have been Andreas, but now to the people of Bachhagen he is Akhtar. Akhtar von Hasenbach!'

iii

We travelled homeward. Lou's face was pale and wore a mask of disbelief. I was slumped in the saddle with my chin on my breast, deep in thought. I had no words of wisdom or comfort to offer, and could only guess what was going on in my son's young mind. Lou was never inclined to believe the worst of anyone, so how was he to come to terms with the realisation that his brother – the man he believed to be his brother - had set out not only to discredit the family, but also to perpetrate the basest acts of degradation in our name?

Though I would rather have denied it, I had not for a moment doubted the word of the old Jew. I knew it was Andreas who had committed these unspeakable crimes, who, under the pretext of healing, had brought misery by the aggravation of symptoms and who, by subtle falsehood, had tried to sully his brother's good name and reputation, and mine. Because I had drawn Tom out at the wedding and made him under the influence of wine tell the story of Andreas's disgrace, I knew the name Akhtar. The name the drunken farmer had whispered in my ear a moment before losing his senses. But even had I not, the effect would have been the same. I had always recognised Andreas's dark and brooding nature, because it was the part of my own that I had conquered thirty and more years ago. Yet the extent of the boy's perversion, and the ease with which he seemed to practise it, filled me with recrimination. In the face of such evil-doing I felt helpless. Worse, I had been unable to anticipate and prevent it and was thus as guilty as the doer.

Either he was sick or he was mad, and I did not know which!

If we had needed further evidence of Andreas's plotting, we were to be provided with an abundance of it. Relieved of their fear, the villagers talked. Others did too. It took us several days to assemble all the evidence. On the estate, among the freeholders, and in the village, people told us their tales. At one cottage, I was in time to prevent a mischievous prescription, intended as an embrocation, from being drunk as medicine for a bad throat. Here, the false physician had deliberately called himself Ludwig. At another, using that name, he had given a potion to a sick woman, causing her violent spasms and vomiting. At yet another, a father had been forced to violate his own child while Andreas and a companion watched. Over the entire district, we found six girls who believed they were carrying Andreas's or his accomplice's seed.

That day, we knew none of that, but we knew enough. I had never ridden with less joy in my heart. In Lou's face, instead of the joy of the coming birth, I could see only horror and confusion.

'It is Andreas. I know it's Andreas. But why?' he repeated over and over again. 'What is this name he uses? Akhtar! And where has he learned this sorcery? And who's this unknown accomplice of whom we've heard more than once?'

'I feel sure his name is Erhart,' said I, 'but it does not matter ...'

'The name means nothing,' said Lou. 'Greta warned me of Andreas. She said he hated me. There was envy in his eyes, she said.'

'Hated you? When was this?'

'On our wedding night. I laughed at her foolishness. Andreas was the model of politeness and good behaviour that evening. But since then, I've dreaded facing him, disbelieving yet not knowing how to behave.'

He went on more to himself than to me. 'Why should he hate me when I've done nothing to him? Greta said that Andreas's eyes betrayed his heart. How could she know he was plotting mischief?

'By his own admission he would raise his station, even contemplating treason and murder. But that was a jest. He could achieve nothing by attacking me. Why is he doing this to me? Why?'

'What did you say?' I swung my mount alongside, suddenly alert. I threw out the question sharply, like the thrust of a spear in the side. 'What did you say about treason?'

'Did I not tell you some weeks ago, Father?'

'Some brotherly banter, I thought. You said nothing about treason ... or murder!'

'I thought nothing of it a the time. Andreas would have me believe you possessed the power to raise yourself to the dukedom, and that he would aid you in such a plan. It was meant as a joke, he said. Now I almost think he was serious.'

'You cannot know how serious,' I said. 'Only now I begin to understand the ambition that drives him, and the ease with which he can fool others into aiding him. Your brother is mad. His dark side is already supreme.'

'He must be mad to do these vile things. But how do they serve ambition?'

'Do not underestimate it, Lou. Once I had a throne within my grasp. But Ormazd and Ahriman battled for my soul.'

'Ahriman, Father?'

'The gods of my Persian ancestors. Good and Evil. God and Satan in Christian philosophy. I had only to press home the point of my sword.'

'But you did not, Father?'

'I did not.'

'You never speak of your life in Persia, Father. Could you truly have been ruler there?'

'Yes!' I paused, afraid of my own thoughts. Yes, I had once known hate and ambition. 'But never in Saxony!'

After so many years, the memories were dreamlike, tales of fantasy from the Thousand and One Nights. Oljeitu, concerned only with his own glorification like the Sasanian kings of old, was bent on personal revenge. I had the support of three regiments had I wished to contest the succession. I did not, but he challenged me - insulted my mother to goad me into a contest. Yet it was I, Prince Hassan, who was now sixty years old, while my half-brother had not reached forty. I had loved him once but might have destroyed him had I not decided only a Creator had the right. It would have been so easy. Yet I had often thanked whatever gods were in the sky that his death was not on my conscience.

'But I resisted the Dark Path, Lou,' I said. 'I resisted it and forfeited my claim for ever. One day, perhaps, I will tell you. Now is not a good time.'

'But Andreas cannot advance your cause in Brunswick, or his, by blackening our name. Especially not mine. And we know he has claimed it more than once.'

'As to that, I fear he is driven by desire,' I said. 'It's simple! You have married a wife.'

'He doesn't envy me that. In fact he spoke quite rudely of Greta.'

'When was this?'

'The same day. The day I invited him to share in the festivities. And he spoke of magic ... and of setting aside the ducal succession.'

'Then it was no banter. And now he has met Greta. I watched him at the festal table and recognised the look he gave her. Tom told me that night of Andreas's appetites, and of the reason he left Brunswick. That same night I heard the name Akhtar for the first time. Tom is an honourable fellow, and wouldn't have spoken had I not pressed him when he was full of liquor. I wish I could have known sooner. I should have seen his madness coming.'

I shook my head. Life in Brunswick had been too easy, too sweet. My own actions – my turbulent youth – Doquz – Hypatia ... all had brought the tragedy about. Because of me, it was in Andreas's nature to prefer the Dark Path once he had learned of its existence, and I should have seen it.

'How could you, Father?'

'I should have protected Andreas more against the dark side of his inheritance,' I said. 'He has my blood! Now it's too late. He is enamoured of Greta and wants her for himself. These unspeakable things he has done are in part to bring you down and leave the way free for him to pursue her. Perhaps he doesn't even realise it. These charms, amulets and disgusting rituals with animals are mumbo-jumbo to terrify the simple folk. It is Andreas's real power, the authority he exercises with a mere glance, that you must fear. I have let this thing go too far.'

Lou touched me on the shoulder. 'You are not to blame, Father, whatever he has done.'

'I think a father is always to blame if his son follows the Dark Path. Now it's time to put a stop to these tricks. I have no choice.'

For the rest of the way I was again silent. Lou brooded. By the time we reached home, his earlier reason was gone and his anger again bubbled over. In the stable yard stood a bay stallion, unbridled, unsaddled and tethered awaiting the groom's attention.

'That's Andreas's horse,' he exclaimed, vaulting to the ground, his fists clenched in rage. 'The villain's here!'

He strode through the kitchen and lower apartments, giving no thought to his own animal's comfort, and met his mother on the stairs. She was still very pale from her condition but smiled in welcome.

'Andreas has come home ...' she began, but Lou cut her short.

'Where is he? Where is the devil who calls himself my brother?' he demanded, his voice rising uncontrollably so that Matthilde shrank back in terror of him.

'In the hall,' she stammered, 'with your...'

Lou did not wait for her to finish. With a yell, he dashed up the remaining steps, a dagger drawn, threw back the door on its hinges, and strode into the hall with murder in his heart. I came in his rear, breathless from the exertion.

The scene that met our eyes was one of innocent domesticity. Greta was sitting politely attentive while two of her new kinsmen arm-wrestled over a small table. Andreas stood at the chimney, watching this activity with some amusement, apparently oblivious, or indifferent, to the trouble he had caused. But Lou saw only an enemy who had set out to destroy his name and reputation, and who now waited for an opportunity to seduce his wife. He took Andreas by the throat with one hand and they both fell to the floor.

Their two cousins, believing this was only a game, did not try to interfere. However, the blade of Lou's dagger pierced Andreas's shoulder. Greta screamed. Uttering a howl of pain, Andreas broke free and struggled to his knees.

'Have you gone mad?' he gasped, holding his hand to the wound and fixing Ludwig with a cold stare.

'One of us is mad,' cried Lou, 'but it's certainly not I. We have uncovered your scheme. Don't deny it! And brother or no, I'll extract payment in your guts and blood.'

'It was but a game, a youthful prank,' sneered Andreas, backing away and trying to rise to his feet. 'No harm was intended by it. You've gone too far....'

'It's you who have gone too far. A prank you say! Is it a prank to leave sickness and misery in your wake? Are sorcery, rape and murder no more than youthful games?'

'May not a man take his pleasure wherever he can,' retorted Andreas. 'I've killed no one and, even if I had, what is one peasant more or less?'

The callousness of these words roused Lou's passion to a new height, and he lunged forward. Andreas side-stepped and grasped his right wrist with two hands, endeavouring to shake the dagger from his hold. Lou, much the heavier of the two, lost his balance and again the antagonists fell to the floor, wrestling furiously.

'One girl lies dead,' breathed Lou, struggling to regain a grip of his brother's throat but losing the dagger in the process, 'and you would dare to add my wife to those you have seduced and ruined. Peasants or not, they'll all be avenged.'

Engaged in this mortal contest, I fancy he found himself looking down into Andreas's face, the mouth twisted in fury, the eyes blazing. A strange, long-forgotten memory from infancy may have stirred within him. Once before he had seen Andreas's eyes flash like that. They were together in a barn, and his brother held a gold cross, the fylfot their father usually wore. Perhaps at the same time he recalled the words of the old Jew, Jacob of Munich:

... with a mere look he is able to sap my will and make me a helpless onlooker.

Did he, suddenly, know their meaning? Andreas was willing him to release his hold and, despite his superior strength, Lou was unable to maintain it. He could still see the face, but it was a long way off. He could hear his brother's voice, but the sound came to him as if across a huge chasm.

Although the spell was incomplete, it lasted long enough. Lou relaxed his grip and Andreas sprang to his feet. Seemingly little affected by the gash in his shoulder, he snatched the heavy curved sword that hung on the wall above the fire opening and swung it two-handed around his head.

'Mary preserve him!' screamed Greta again, and rushed upon her brother-in-law, clawing at his face with her fingernails.

The sword, aimed at Lou's unprotected head, swept down harmlessly, cleaving a wide gash in the wooden panelling.

Andreas thrust Greta aside and prepared to raise the weapon again.

Lou, no longer dazed, regained his feet, and now unarmed, seized a chair to use as a shield.

Had I moved an instant later, the great Persian scimitar would have smashed through the wood. But as Andreas swung it in the direction of his brother's head, I put myself between them and with my own short sword deflected the longer weapon from its target. It was a trick I had learnt as a boy and just as well. I no longer had the strength to meet the force of such a blow which would otherwise have broken my arm and driven the hilt from my grasp.

'Back!'

My order had the desired effect. Surprised, Andreas lowered his weapon. As a child, he had once faced my fury, but that experience must have seemed as nothing. I knew it. I knew it because the dark eyes that held my gaze were as images in a glass. We were more alike than I had ever imagined. As Andreas had often used his strange power to bend the mind of others, he now faced a will stronger than his own. His arms sagged and his eyes fell before my cold rage. Lou clasped Greta to his bosom and watched us in awe.

'Do you have any defence at all for the black deeds you have done?' I demanded. Andreas was silent.

Matthilde, now standing behind me, could never have heard me give way to such passion.

'What is it?' she asked, her voice and limbs trembling. 'What has Andreas done?'

I paid her no attention.

'I see you do not pretend to one,' I went on, addressing Andreas, but now afraid of my own anger. 'I have overlooked and forgiven your excesses in the past in the hope that manhood would bring about an improvement in your character. But this attack on your own family, this unashamed corruption of everything I ever taught, I can never forgive or forget.'

'What has Andreas done?' Matthilde repeated. She put out a hand to touch him but he shook her off.

'What does it matter?' said he. 'You are not my mother!'

Poor Matthilde was aghast. She stumbled. Lou, who had by now released Greta, caught her in his arms.

'If that is so, Andreas,' said I, 'you will know you no longer have any claim on this house. Go from it today! Leave Bachhagen! Make your home wherever you will, so long as it is far from Brunswick. Never let me look at you again or, by all the gods, prophets and saints who ever existed, I'll make you sorry. I will deliver you up to the law for the crime of necromancy and the practice of black magic.'

Andreas was struck dumb. Avoiding Matthilde's look of anguish, he stole from our company, down the staircase, and out through the main door into the courtyard. Only once did he turn, and that was to fix me with such a venomous glare that I shivered.

It is in a father's nature to forgive his children. Or his grandchildren. Had Andreas begged me in humility, fallen on his knees in remorse, promised atonement, I knew I would have relented for Matthilde's sake, if not my own. I thought of his true mother, my daughter Hypatia, and how she had rejected her child before she ever knew him. Was there enough of Nadia in her, I wondered, to have seen what the future held. Had she seen it then and did she, far away in Venice, know there was no way back?

I did not know how Andreas had discovered the truth, if indeed he had. I believe now that it was merely an outburst of his madness. There was to be no apology, no remorse, no atonement. Could I have acted differently? Could I have cured him? Could I have prevented what should have been prevented - the terrible consequences of my words?

But they were spoken and I could not take them back. Moments later, with a heavy heart, I watched the son I had not sired but chosen ride off at a gallop and disappear into the gathering dusk.

Fifteen years later ...

GRETL

Fleas

We sent word to Brunswick that, being homesick, I had returned to my family. The news was greeted with joy by Hanna, for my sudden departure had not passed unnoticed. While waiting for me at the Singari tents, she was carried off in a crowd of revellers who happened to pass. As soon as she could escape them, she returned but saw no sign of me. Frantic with worry, she reported my disappearance. A search was carried out, and enquiries made - which lasted two days and brought no result. At length, the Duke sent a rider to Bachhagen with the news but, having a second errand to perform, he did not arrive at the estate until after I had returned there.

I was tired. My body still ached and my thoughts were confused. Wonder, horror, disbelief, fear and revulsion were mixing inside my brain in equal proportions. All I knew for sure was that my childhood had been taken away and that I wanted it back. I wished for my mother's soft smile and gentle touch; I longed for Ennia's sympathetic wisdom; I craved my father's restraining hand as I took my very first steps, and Opa's firm grip as he hoisted me into the saddle of his stallion.

But it was far, far too late. I was a woman whose virtue was spotted, whose temple was despoiled.

I had listened to Opa's tale until well past midnight, stopping him only occasionally to ask questions or to bring him refreshment. He had explained much and yet there was much still unanswered. Uppermost in my mind was the disturbing realisation that we were in danger. Fifteen years after being banished from Brunswick, Akhtar - for I could not think of him as Andreas - had returned and was plotting to take revenge on his family for having sent him away.

'If you heard truly, Gretl,' Opa said, 'not only we, but the whole province is in danger. It's true there is jealousy among the ducal families, and if it were to be fired by ...'

'Surely the common folk will not rise against their rulers,' I interrupted.

'Not here perhaps,' he agreed, 'but in some districts the peasants have been oppressed, and are envious of the landgraves' wealth and power. It has been so since the time of the Mortality. If a bitter, vengeful man were to make use of that envy and persuade the common people to take up arms, he could divide the province against itself. Even Saxony or the Empire!'

'I don't understand these things, Opa. I've never seen hatred or envy in the eyes of the villagers, or of any of the people who work in our fields.'

'May you never see it, Gretl. However, the possibility of a plot cannot be ignored. We must tell the Duke.'

'Why would the Duke believe me?' I objected. 'These were only snatches of conversation I overheard. I hate Akhtar for what he did, but I would not want the whole world to know of my ordeal. Surely it would be necessary to tell all if I were to lay evidence of treason? Besides, he's your grandchild too, my true cousin, unlike Hanna and Freddy who are so dear to me. For your sake I could not betray him, even though I would drive a sword through his heart had I the chance.'

Opa's face was troubled, and I wondered with what effort he spoke his next words.

'For fifteen years I have had only one son. Let it remain so. Andreas will betray himself, along with his accomplices and any others with whom he conspires. The Duke need know only that there are those who threaten his position. I will name no names. Of your part in events I'll say nothing. For your absence from the court we'll find other reasons.'

I had a poor grasp of his philosophy. Only afterwards, having been the means whereby Akhtar was once again able to hold the fylfot, did I begin to understand, to doubt and, in doubting, to feel guilt myself.

But, for the present, our course of action was decided. In a second dispatch, sent to the Duke in a private letter, my grandfather acquainted him of the possible threat.

'I haven't mentioned your part in the affair, Gretl,' he told me, 'nor have I named Andreas, but Magnus is warned how easily the people could be duped into revolt by promises of greater wealth and prosperity.'

My grandmother had died within days of Akhtar's banishment. The shock of learning about his misdeeds, added to the sorrow of her brother's passing, was too much for her fragile health. Opa had made a new will dividing his property unequally between my father and his male cousins and nephews. Ludwig was to receive three-quarters to give to his heirs. If he had none, the estate would pass to the children of Thomas and Roland. Matti, should she marry again, was to receive a handsome dowry, as would Hanna.

I learned nothing more about Hypatia other than that her husband was rich and that she had given birth to four more children. The lands belonging to the Montecervino family were now in the hands of the third generation, a son of Opa's half brother Nico.

Jacob of Munich, having by some miracle survived the plague, died while I was at Brunswick. They said he had reached the age of ninety-six.

There was so much more I wished to know and for that I had to wait. None of it plays a proper part in my story so I will pass over it for now.

Opa was unable to offer an explanation of the Singari woman's words. And I could make sense of none of it. Apart from Matti, and Freddy to annoy me, no one ever called me Margaretha. As to the family surname, how the Gypsy could attach it to me was a complete mystery. The sinister journey from day into night that she had predicted for me was one I did not care to make, and I had inherited nothing unless it were my mother's love.

'Might it be that the mirror-gazer was able to guess your secret desire?' suggested Opa with a knowing smile. 'Such predictions are easy to make and difficult to deny. Children. Rank. Wealth. And if there is a young man of whom you are especially fond ...'

'There is none, Opa,' I said, blushing, thinking all the while of Sigmund's handsome face and manly body, 'and I have no secret desires unless ...'

'Unless, Gretl?'

'... unless it be to learn more from you about plant lore, and about the stars and planet, and perhaps ...' I hesitated, thinking he would call me a foolish girl. It was enough that women were not expected to be learned in such matters. My other dream, formed once while I was with Ennia at the blacksmith's forge, and recalled and given new stimulus that afternoon, was as out of reach as the stars themselves.

However, with a look, my grandfather was encouraging me to go on.

I swallowed hard. 'Well,' I said, 'I would think it the most wonderful thing to be able to travel and see the world as you have done.'

My grandfather did not laugh.

'Well, Gretl,' he said, 'as to the first, I will teach you what I can. You'll be a good pupil, I am certain. As for your other secret wish, who knows what the future holds?'

'You will not betray my secret, will you, Opa?'

'So long as you do not betray mine. Say nothing of what has passed between us today, nothing of the legend of the fylfot, not even to your father. By rights it should go to Hypatia but somehow I feel it belongs elsewhere. Lou cannot have it for it must not go from son to son. I shall bequeath it to you. Promise me you will guard it well when I am dead.'

Neither of us realised then the significance of these words. I promised, and he embraced me.

My excuses made, I lived at home, assisting Opa in his laboratory and my father in whatever way I could. Freddy was of an age to take a more active and responsible role in the estate, and Ludwig was freed to pursue his own interest in the sciences.

The following spring, some minor outbreaks of plague occurred in the neighbourhood, and he was able to test his theory that the disease was present only where rats bred in large numbers in close proximity to human dwellings.

'I was right!' he said. 'There's no doubt the rats are to blame for the black plague, but I fear my theories are incomplete. Killing the rats, and disposing carefully of their remains, seems to result in more cases rather than fewer.'

'But if the oil from the rats' fur is the cause, as you suggested, it may already be too late,' I said. 'Even with the rats dead, the deposits remain.'

'I've thought of that, Gretl. However, I would not expect the sickness to spread at such an alarming rate. And there's something even stranger about this disease. It strikes down the young and strong, rather than the old and weak. In particular, anyone who suffered during the Great Mortality, and survived, seems now to be immune.'

'That's contrary to nature,' I said. 'Having once been weakened by a disease, is not a person more likely to succumb to it again?'

'That's what I would expect,' agreed Ludwig. 'But many of the victims in Hannover are children, not even born when the Mortality struck. I have to admit we haven't discovered the whole truth. If only the townsfolk would look after their households, and provide better conditions for their servants ...'

His voice rose in pitch and I sensed he was about to launch into one of his tirades on cleanliness and the evils of town living. He often lectured me in this way when upset or frustrated by what he saw around him.

'But surely,' I said, 'even if they follow your advice, and keep rats from entering their kitchens and larders, it'll never be possible to drive them all from a town. We might as easily catch their fleas or trim their whiskers! As long as the poor and uneducated believe their misfortunes are caused by demons ...'

He did not let me finish, but sprang to his feet flushed and excited, knocking over the stool on which he had been sitting. His next act was to take me by the waist and hoist me into the air as if I were a child again.

'Father!' he roared at the top of his voice, setting me on my feet once more and galloping off through the lower apartments like a spooked stallion. When he got no answer from the laboratory, he charged up the main staircase three or four steps at a time, whooping loudly. 'Father, come down at once. Gretl has given me the answer!'

Hearing his cries, Freddy, Matti and some servants appeared in the hall and, thinking he had gone mad, followed him upstairs with a view to restraining him. Quite unaware of what I had said that was so important, I ran up after them. Ludwig was pacing up and down outside my grandfather's rooms, muttering to himself.

'That must be it. There can be no other explanation.'

I too began to think he had lost his wits.

'What's the matter, Father?' I cried. 'What have I said or done that has taken you so?'

'The fleas, Gretl, the fleas!'

'What fleas, father?'

'The rat fleas of course. The fleas you cannot catch, my dear, sweet Gretl. It's the fleas that cause people to sicken. It must be!'

'What can the fleas have to do with it?' I asked.

'It can only be that! The fleas feed on the rats' blood, and when the rats die, or we kill them, the fleas feed on our bodies as a substitute. They carry the plague poisons with them. It's clear to me now, and I have you to thank, my dearest Gretl, for making me see what should have been obvious all along.'

Opa had joined us in the corridor, his expression as grave as ever. He listened to our conversation without comment.

'It was but a chance remark,' I said, trying to make little of my part in his discovery.

'It was more, Gretl. It was God's inspiration. This explains so much, and I must write down my thoughts in case I forget.'

'Then we'll go to the laboratory,' Opa said. 'Our diary is there. You too, Gretl. And Lou can tell us both how this new theory explains matters when the other did not.'

'You'll remember I asked three questions,' Ludwig replied. He was beginning to calm down. 'Where did the black plague originate, how was it transmitted from the rats to man, and how is the disease to be treated? I have no reason to change my opinion on the first. To the second I answered that the sick rats deposited an oily substance from their fur, and that this contained the poison that infected us with the plague. You, Father, objected to this proposition.'

'I did indeed,' Opa agreed. 'But it was only because you could not explain why your wife and child escaped, whereas the family of Roland and the others did not.'

'Your objection is answered by my new theory,' said Ludwig. 'Our house is little troubled by fleas. We hang pulegium and other herbs. You will recollect that Jacob of Munich also did so. Our family views the custom as odd and laughs at us. But the herb is effective; more so than any other. That is the first point to note. The second is that I bathed.'

'Why is that important?' I asked. 'Did no one else do so?'

'They may have done, but not before returning to their wives and children. On the other hand, I swam straight away in the river and gave my soiled clothes to be washed. We all suffered flea bites. Several of the men remarked on it, I recall, but who considers a few pricks as more than a nuisance?'

'So the cause of the Great Mortality lay with the rat fleas, and not with the rats themselves?'

'Not quite,' said my father. 'The rats are still to blame. They are primary agents. Fleas are parasites. Without the rats to feed on, they would not exist. Let's not forget that the condition of the blood determines the health of the whole body, but apply it to this case. Here is a possible connection between the blood of a sick animal and the blood of man. Consider! The organs of the rat are poisoned with this plague. They die. The fleas look for another host and find human prey; they bite, and the poison is deposited in human flesh.'

We reached the laboratory. Opa turned the key in the lock and the three of us entered. I felt quite honoured at being treated to such a conference and hovered at the door while the men sat down at the bench.

'But so little blood - and such a small creature,' I said.

'Yet not impossible,' said Opa. He turned over a page or two of the book that lay open in front of them. He stopped at a paragraph that interested him, one written in my father's handwriting. 'What's this?'

'Don't laugh,' said Ludwig. 'Sometimes, as well as the results of careful experiments, I take moments to write down my own idle thoughts. These sentences are not the careful work of a scientist, but fantasies of the mind. Don't pay them too much attention.'

'Sound ideas may spring from idle thoughts,' mused Opa. He peered closely at the text, then read aloud. ' *'Why did I live while others around me were taken? Was it merely God's will, or am I possessed of greater strength to resist the pestilence. Others too have lived through it. It is as if our bodies were able to produce their own antidote. Could it be that all who have suffered are now immune, including myself?'*

'Perhaps these thoughts are not fantasy, Lou. It was said in Persia that the prince who would protect himself from the poisoner's hand should accustom his body to many poisons by swallowing them daily in small doses. My own father used to take precautions of this kind.'

'That principle can't be applied here.'

'Don't dismiss your ideas so lightly. Let me think about it. As for you, you have long delayed visiting Italy again. You could not go while Gretl was a motherless child. Don't delay any longer. Freddy can manage the estate with my help.

'Go to Venice, Lou. Visit your sister again, and your aunts and cousins. And there must be many others alive today who remember the plague. Perhaps some were sick and survived like you.

'Go to Genoa too, and to the university of Bologna. Go even to Constantinople. Track the plague to its origins. Discover whence came the black rats. Even if you do not find an antidote, it's a journey worth making. A young man should see something of the world.'

'You are right, Father,' said Ludwig, 'though I'll find it hard to leave Gretl behind.'

'It'll be hard for us too,' I smiled, 'but I think you must go. You've spoken many times of such an expedition. I'll stay with Opa and if we tire of one another's company I can always go back to Brunswick.'

My father made his preparations and within the week left to join a merchant caravan travelling south on the road to Fulda.

The days following his departure were not without anxiety. Rumours reached our ears of quarrels between neighbours. Boundaries were breached, armed men made sorties into lands held by rival princes, crops were fired, hostages taken, and manors ransacked. Where there had been tolerance there was ill-will; where an uneasy truce had existed there was now open hostility. For the first time in living memory, the descendants of the Lion of Saxony made bloody war on each other.

Our house and farms, however, remained secure. Half-hearted attempts were made on two occasions to annex some outlying meadows and small farms, but the invaders were beaten off with the help of our retired men-at-arms. On both occasions, the peasants and smallholders stood on our side and resisted the assault with cudgels and farm tools. These minor incursions beaten off, we were left in peace.

Real danger was to come from a totally unexpected quarter.

Sigmund

Not far from the Castle of Brunswick was a narrow street of timber buildings known as *Rittersweg*, for no better reason than it was - or rather its two taverns were - a haunt of the military. The first and meanest of these houses was frequented only by the lower ranks whereas the second boasted as customers the officers and their squires. This second inn had as its emblem a lion, in honour of Brunswick's founder, Duke Henry himself. Its wine was indifferent, but the company was pleasant and friendly.

In the autumn of 1356, having reached his eighteenth birthday, Sigmund received his commission. Being quartered in Brunswick, it was his habit to spend some leisure hours at the Lion with his fellow officers.

One evening, shortly after being given his command, he arrived at the inn to find two of his acquaintances, Harry and Will, already sprawled on their usual bench. Nearby, a stranger in priestly garb was performing sleight of hand for the amusement of a small crowd of townsmen who had gathered round his table. They applauded with enthusiasm as he produced a silver gulden from behind his ear.

'Heh there, Sigi,' called Will. He sat up and moved over to leave another space on the bench. 'Come and join us. We have here a veritable sorcerer with a feast of tricks for our pleasure.'

'By Christ's blood, that's the truth,' added his companion. 'It's a great pity the Duke doesn't allow these clerical magicians to perform in his great hall. They're really most entertaining. This fellow has been suspending coins in mid-air and making a loaf of bread dance to a tune from his pipe. Fill a goblet and sit with us, Sigi my good fellow!'

'I'll join you gladly,' Sigmund said. 'But I'll have no appetite for magic until I've satisfied my hunger with a crusty pie.'

He took his seat with the others and ordered the host to bring food and wine. From beneath a broad hat, the stranger seemed to be watching him with more than casual interest.

Sigmund returned the stare.

'Who is this priest?' he whispered to the innkeeper.

'I don't know,' replied that worthy, 'but he's been there four or five ev'nings now. I fancy he's no real priest, an' I was wary of him at first, but his tricks are harmless enough, an' his money's as good as the next man's.'

'Let's have the magic egg!' demanded one of the spectators.

'The magic egg!' echoed several others including Will and Harry. They banged the table with their fists and setting up a chorus of loud clucking. 'Show us the magic egg trick!'

'As you please, sirs,' said the stranger. He took an egg from the folds of his cleric's cape, leant across his table, and handed it to Will. 'First, my lord, you must satisfy yourself we begin with a regular egg. This one was fresh-laid this morning.'

'Is he telling the truth?' enquired two or three customers all at once.

Will turned the egg in his palm and gave it back to its owner, who tossed it carelessly from one hand to the other before placing it on the table.

'I'll swear there's no magic here,' answered that young knight, feigning disappointment. 'I can almost smell its freshness.'

'Watch!' cried the stranger so sharply that a hush fell on the company. He bent forward so that his lips just touched the egg. The broad hat hid his eyes but Sigmund noticed that the nose was prominent, the complexion dark, and the teeth very white.

To the amazement of the onlookers, the egg seemed to acquire a life of its own. As the magician straightened his back, it began to roll from left to right, and finally to raise itself wholly from the table and hang motionless before their eyes. Sigmund watched this performance soberly.

'You're easily fooled when your bellies are full of liquor, comrades,' said he good-humouredly. 'I'll wager that egg is hollow, and that he moves it with a single hair pulled from his mistress's head!'

'That can't be so,' said Harry. 'Will held it in his hand, and vouched for its completeness.'

'Another, I'll be bound,' laughed Sigmund. 'The priest exchanged it while you were distracted by his juggling. He's no more sorcerer than I.'

This was spoken in an undertone, but the would-be magician heard. He smiled slyly, and made to return the egg to a pocket in his cape. Will leapt up and snatched it from his grasp. As the knight's hand closed round it, the shell was broken, and a sticky, evil-smelling fluid oozed from between his fingers.

'He has exchanged it again,' said Sigmund gleefully, 'and you are doubly deceived!'

'By the Rood, I'll be the butt of no fool's trickery,' Will cried. He wiped his fingers on his breeches. 'Let's have a look at your face, magician, and see what else you keep hidden under that broad brim!'

He reached over and, with his clean hand, dislodged the stranger's hat. It fell to the floor to reveal a shaven head and dark, brooding eyes that flashed angrily.

'Have a care you don't provoke me, sirrah,' growled the magician.

'That has the sound of a challenge,' rejoined Will.

A number of civilians, sensing trouble, dispersed quietly and quit the premises. Others, anticipating a different sort of entertainment, remained but withdrew to a safe distance.

'Leave him be,' said Sigmund. He rose and put himself between the stranger and his comrade. 'You're twice his size, Will, and if you were made to look a fool, it's your own fault. You encouraged his nonsense.'

Will scowled, but he swallowed his pride and resumed his seat. Sigmund was aware that the magician was staring at him again.

'Do you have something to say to me?' he asked.

'I see you are not impressed by my magic, Sigmund of Wolfenbüttel,' said the stranger, 'though I'm grateful for your concern over my welfare.'

At the sound of his name, pronounced so unexpectedly, Sigmund peered closely at the magician's face. Although the shaven skull reminded him of a death's head, there was something about the profile that seemed familiar.

'How is it you know me, when I've never seen you in my life?' he asked.

'You have seen me, though you are unlikely to remember, for it was fifteen years ago,' said the stranger. He lowered his voice. 'Can we be overheard?'

'If you wish to speak privately to me, my friend, we can remove ourselves to a corner bench,' said Sigmund, bewildered by his new acquaintance's familiarity. He turned to Will and Harry. 'It seems the priest and I have some business together. Excuse us, and I'll rejoin you shortly.'

'Tell me, Sigmund,' went on the stranger, when they were out of earshot, 'was your father not the noble Sir Otto who until lately served His Imperial Majesty, Karl the Fourth? And is your mother not Matthilde of Bachhagen, the younger of two Matthildes, that is; and was your grandfather Roland not landgrave of a neighbouring estate? If I presume correctly, you are undoubtedly the great nephew of Sano di Montecervino who now calls himself von Hasenbach. The renowned astrologer and physician.'

'You are right in every particular,' acknowledged Sigmund, 'but how is it ...?'

'I have waited patiently every night for a week in the hope of exchanging words with you,' said the stranger, not allowing him to finish the sentence. 'My name is Akhtar. Once I was a von Hasenbach too, and we are related.'

'I accept the first name if you say so, but the second cannot be yours. My cousin Ludwig has no male kin. If it had been otherwise, my mother would have spoken of it.'

'Because a father forgets his son, and a son his brother, the blood relationship is not severed,' said Akhtar. 'I am Sano's son, and your mother's first cousin none-the-less. A youthful misdemeanour brought my father's wrath on my head, and drove me away when I was little more than your age. I bore resentment for many years, but the loneliness of my life made me reflect. I acknowledge I was in the wrong, and am now anxious to make amends.'

Something in the other's tone convinced Sigmund that this was the truth. He felt strangely at ease. Akhtar's nose had lost its prominence, and his eyes their cold intensity.

'If you seek your father's forgiveness, why do you come to me?'

'I would not be welcome at Bachhagen, I fear. But were I to have a friend there, a friend who would speak for me, I could grant his heart's desire. What would you have most in the world, Sigmund? A wench? The Duke's, or perhaps the Emperor's favour? Or would you choose to be the lord of Bachhagen itself? In return for your advocacy, I might be willing to help you to all three, and to perform such a service for the manor as would assure me of the family's gratitude.'

'In matters of love I've no need of a proxy,' said Sigmund, 'and the Duke's favour I already enjoy. As for Bachhagen, I'm content to leave well alone, so long as it is managed for the benefit of all its dependants. On the other hand, I might be persuaded to assist a truly repentant cousin in a reconciliation with his kin. What is this great service you can perform?'

Akhtar leant forward so that their faces were almost touching.

'Listen to me carefully, Sigmund,' said he. 'The manors of Brunswick are restless, and the landgraves wary of their neighbours. None is more ambitious than Walther of Langenfurth. He is wealthy, and has his own army.'

'He has fifteen men, experienced with sword and lance, whom he employs for the manor's defence. The Langenfurths have never been a threat to us!'

'That's an army compared to the defences of his neighbours. Times are changing, Sigmund. On Walther's eastern frontier is Grübenhagen territory, and the lands held by the Duke. To the west lies the manor of the Waldhausens. Bachhagen shares its borders with all three, and would be a rich prize to an aggressor intent on threatening the fragile stability of this province. Perhaps it is in need of firmer stewardship than your cousins can provide. Ponder these matters until the next time we meet.'

Having said this, Akhtar retrieved his hat, which had lain all the while in the dust, replaced it on his shaven head, wrapped his cloak around his person, and abruptly departed.

'I've been having the strangest conversation, and could almost believe that I dreamed it,' Sigmund confessed to his friends. 'I've discovered a cousin I never knew I had, and have received some disturbing news of my home.'

Duke Magnus had listened in silence to Sigmund's report.

'If this intelligence is confirmed, it is a serious threat,' he said at the end of it. 'I hope this unnamed informant of yours is deceived.'

'Or I in my informant,' Sigmund said. For his own private reasons, he had not spoken Akhtar's name to the Duke. Had he done so, the outcome might have been very different. 'The Langenfurths have always been friendly neighbours, as have the Waldhausens, and there have been no skirmishes so far west. A few farmers have perhaps argued over possession of a meadow or two, but that is all. I can't believe Walther is a troublemaker.'

'Yet you bring further evidence of the unrest among the population. Since your great-uncle wrote warning me of sedition, there has been ample support for his opinions. Have you heard from him?'

'I have no news of Bachhagen since my cousin Gretl returned there so hastily, sir.'

The Duke knit his brows.

'I would have long since been food for the worms if my father had not trusted my life to Sano von Hasenbach. He would not deceive me. However, I have my suspicions that he didn't tell all he knew, and that there was somehow a connection between his report and Margaretha's sudden departure from Brunswick. You and your command are bound for the eastern provinces, I know, but stay awhile. Although you have your father's name, I suspect your heart is in the country bordering the Leine. Learn more of this supposed revolt. Take a few men. Visit your mother, but travel by way of the Langenfurth and Waldhausen manors. You have my full trust. If you meet any opposition to your presence, deal with the situation as you see fit.'

Returning to his quarters after this interview with the Duke, Sigmund was astonished to find Akhtar awaiting him there. He could account for neither the sense of discomfort awakened in him on seeing his visitor, nor the feeling of cordiality that gradually replaced it as they conversed.

On this occasion, their talk turned to the subject of love and alliances made through marriage.

'Walther Langenfurth has nephews, but no sons,' said Akhtar casually. He fixed Sigmund with his usual penetrating stare, and continued to address him in his familiar manner. 'He also has two daughters, I believe - and one is of marriageable age.'

Sigmund laughed. The implication was clear.

'Would you make a match for me, Cousin Akhtar?' he said. 'For, if so, I tell you it will not be with Kati Langenfurth. She pursues me relentlessly, and though a handsome wench, she's empty-headed.'

'Some would see that as an advantage in a maiden.' Akhtar winked knowingly. 'But no, I merely state a fact.'

'Perhaps it's a fact that needs to be examined in detail,' said Sigmund, without quite knowing why the thought had occurred to him. 'Walther might gain a great deal by marrying Kati to the son of a neighbouring estate, and one of these nephews to another landgrave's daughter.'

'I'm glad you've considered that possibility, for it was one that occurred to me. Might your cousin Frederic be tempted by such an alliance? He too would benefit. Bachhagen has two blooming damsels of quality, or so I'm told - and Frederic himself may not find the Langenfurth girl so lacking in charm.'

'Freddy is not his own master,' frowned Sigmund. 'Uncle Lou's agreement would be needed to any match, and if I know him, he will not lightly give it, especially when his own daughter is involved.'

'I fancy you're right,' said Akhtar. 'My brother was always one to put happiness before ambition. However, he is abroad - and much as it is my desire to be reconciled with him, he may not return. In that unhappy event, how would the girls' future be settled?'

'The Duke himself becomes their guardian. However, Freddy will soon reach his majority, and he's not so witless as to sacrifice his sister or his cousin and the manor's independence in a dubious alliance. Were he to do so, he would answer to me!'

Sigmund felt a sudden unexplained surge of anger as he uttered these words. Under the spell of Akhtar's intense gaze, deceiving smile and soft voice, suspicion had begun to take root in his nature. New and unrecognised ambitions flooded his brain, and he was willing to attribute hitherto unimagined weaknesses to the companion of his boyhood. If Akhtar had noticed this change, he preferred not to remark on it. Instead, he immediately reverted to military matters.

'The Langenfurth men-at-arms are again patrolling their western and southern borders,' said he, 'and now the landgrave of Waldhausen is recruiting mercenaries. They have been seen on the left bank of the river.'

'How did you come by this intelligence?' demanded Sigmund. 'You can't have visited the valley of the Leine and returned since we last conversed.'

'Be easy, Sigmund,' said Akhtar calmly. 'I have my own spies in the west. They are Singari – Gypsies if you like - but reliable for all that, since they pass unnoticed about their business. But I would suggest you don't take their word, but check the reports for yourself.'

'Be sure I intend to do so,' said Sigmund. 'I have only to complete some business here in Brunswick, then I shall ride to Langenfurth. If any neighbour has designs on Bachhagen, I swear I'll put a stop to his plans.'

'I beg you do not act hastily, nor expose yourself to needless danger. There may be innocent explanations for these facts I lay before you, in which case I shall be as relieved as you. On the other hand, if some deep treachery is afoot, you may count on my assistance to thwart it. As you will have guessed, this priestly attire is a temporary disguise. You will find I am no stranger to the sword. Moreover, I have some experienced men at my disposal.'

'I trust neither of us will need recourse to weapons,' said Sigmund, holding out his hand. 'Ride west with me by all means. Whatever occurs, I have not forgotten my promise to be your advocate.'

As Akhtar clasped his extended hand, it seemed to Sigmund that the eyes were brighter than usual, and the smile more reassuring. Beset by new doubts and fears, he was nevertheless convinced that he had one true friend in the world.

Sigmund had not yet realised it, but he had already succumbed to Akhtar's influence. The suspicions that had been engendered in his breast made him irritable, and he was ready to attribute sinister intent to the most innocent words and actions. Try as he might, he could not dismiss these feelings, nor understand the reason for them. Much more terrifying was his unshakeable impression that this and his later conversations with Akhtar were part of a dream from which he could not awaken.

Akhtar was ever at pains to stress his desire for forgiveness and reconciliation and, though the nature of his offence was never mentioned, such was his skill that Sigmund became convinced the punishment meted out had been harsh beyond all measure.

Unworthy thoughts occupied most of his daylight hours and gnawed at his soul as he lay awake in the night. As the days passed, he became more and more distrusting of his family, and more and more confused as to his commission until, by the eve of his departure from Brunswick, he had lost touch with reality altogether.

Thus, less than a month after Ludwig's departure for Italy, Sigmund became an unwitting tool in Akhtar's scheme to wrest the Bachhagen estate from its lawful owner.

The Battle for the Manor House

i

It is easy to be wise with hindsight. Had I known of these events sooner, much hurt and injustice might have been averted; lives might have been saved. However, though I thought often of Sigmund in the silence of my bedroom, I had not seen him since before I left Brunswick.

Akhtar had chosen to misrepresent the facts but his intelligence concerning the actions of our neighbours was not false.

Walther Langenfurth did indeed aspire to an alliance with Bachhagen, though his were the natural hopes of a father eager to secure his daughters' happiness and the future of the family line. To begin with, his overtures were met on our side without enthusiasm.

'I'm in no hurry to wed,' Freddy confessed. 'If Kati Langenfurth can wait, I may decide to have her. If not, there's always her younger sister.'

I had not acquainted him of Hanna's opinions, or of what I then believed were Sigmund's intentions.

Walther accepted the rebuttal with good grace. His greater priority was to build a lasting peace with the Waldhausen family, with whom relations since the Great Mortality had been uneasy, and he bent his efforts to this project. At the conclusion of lengthy negotiations, a contract of marriage between the eldest of Walther's nephews and a daughter of Bruno Waldhausen was signed.

The two landgraves decided that, in celebration of their reconciliation and in honour of the bridal couple, a jousting tournament would be held, and that each estate would provide ten combatants for this spectacle. In this, Langenfurth had a small advantage, as their defensive force boasted several knights experienced with sword and lance. It was left to Bruno to engage some additional warriors, past the age of crusading but in need of income, to make up the required number. This done, groups of riders in full armour began exercising, and practising their skill, in the flat meadows near the Leine, and in the fallow pastures separating the manors.

The Langenfurth cavaliers, mistaking one wing of Sigmund's approaching troop for their sporting counterparts, mounted a charge with blunted lances, were met with pointed steel, and were easily put to flight. Confirmed in his delusion that he faced a dangerous enemy, Sigmund, with Akhtar at his side, besieged the Langenfurth manor, occupied it by force of arms and, with the rest of the company, rode unhindered across Bachhagen land. The deception was all the greater for, although this company wore the insignia of Brunswick, all but a handful were Akhtar's men. These were discredited knights of the province, and of Thuringia, who owed their allegiance only to their paymaster, Akhtar himself.

Matti had gone out to welcome Sigmund, but when she saw his companion, she drew back with a gasp. Akhtar was dressed as I had seen him in Brunswick, all in priestly black, but with a mail shirt protecting his chest. He sat astride a frisky black colt. I could not tell how the years since his banishment had changed him, but it was clear my aunt recognised him.

'Why is this wretch with you on a visit to your mother, Sigmund?' she demanded.

'He's a friend,' said Sigmund. '... a cousin who has been ill-used by our family. And this is no normal visit, Mother. I'm here to occupy the estate and secure it against attack by outsiders.'

Freddy had followed Matti into the courtyard and, at this, he turned deathly pale.

'You can't take possession of something that belongs to others,' he said, his lip tight with anger. 'While Lou is away, I'm acting master here. What do you mean by commanding armed men on my property, without my consent?'

'Would you fight me, Cousin Freddy?' taunted Sigmund. His voice seemed to belong to a stranger. 'If you wish to do so, I'll oblige you, but rest assured you'll be the worse off.'

Freddy's hesitated but Matti would not stay silent.

'What can you hope to gain by this violation?' She clasped Sigmund's knee as he sat in the saddle. 'If your father were alive he would be ashamed of you. It's clear Andreas has corrupted you ...'

'Please don't interfere, Mother,' went on Sigmund, quite out of keeping with his usual character. 'Bachhagen guards the province's western flank and must be made secure if its enemies are not to take advantage.'

'Enemies!' said Freddy bitterly. 'What enemies? At the moment I see only one - a cousin who betrays his kin and wants to turn his home into a battleground. And who is this dark knight riding with you? Your mother, it seems, has no cause to welcome him here.'

Akhtar's lips formed a smile but there was no humour in his eyes.

'Ask my cousin Matti who I am,' he said. His voice held only irony. 'I'll wager she'll spin you a pretty tale of the model son who was banished for daring to play harmless tricks on his brother.'

Freddy turned to his aunt.

'He is Andreas von Hasenbach,' she said. 'He bears the same relationship to me as you do to Sigmund. He is Sano's elder son.'

'A son who is anxious to see how his father has borne the years since we last met! It'll amuse me to wander through the old house again.'

So saying, Akhtar dismounted and swept across the courtyard to the main door.

I had seen and heard all this from an open casement. Eager to greet Sigmund, it had been my intention to call down to him from my room. Seeing Akhtar however, all my fear and loathing, and the memory of what he had done to me, came flooding back. My heart pounded. I pressed myself against the wall lest he should spot me. Though I had dressed that morning as a youth, which was often my custom, I was sure Akhtar's keen eye would recognise me, not as a daughter of the house, but as Lisa, the maid he had ravished.

Sigmund ordered the men to post themselves at all the exits, in the stables, by the pond, and at prominent positions near the high road.

'Assemble the household,' he told Freddy. 'I want to be sure everyone is accounted for.'

Neither the voice nor bearing belonged to the Sigmund I knew. Terrified, and understanding nothing, I had only a single thought, and that was to find a place to hide. Hearing footsteps in the corridor, I lay on the floor and crawled quickly under the bed. The door of the room swung open and one of the invaders stood on the threshold.

'This one's empty,' he called back to another, who was just emerging from the chamber normally occupied by my father. Together they went off to the second floor. I heard their heavy tread on the stairs.

I breathed again and waited. After a few minutes they returned, clearly satisfied that the upper rooms were unoccupied.

The members of the household were gathering in the hall below. Opa was there, his face pale and angry. Matti and Freddy were there too, marshalled by a sour-looking man-at-arms. There were two stewards, the grooms and their wives, my own maid and others who served the family, all muttering and grumbling as the invaders herded them into a group.

I had counted twenty armed men in the courtyard, including three of Akhtar's Singari followers, but there could have been more. Sigmund, Akhtar, and four others were visible from where I now lay on the landing, hardly breathing and as motionless as I could manage.

'Is everyone here?' asked Akhtar, carefully taking note of the faces present but avoiding my grandfather's furious gaze.

'I believe so,' nodded Sigmund, 'except I do not see Gretl.'

'She has returned to Brunswick,' Opa said quickly and I loved him for the lie.

Akhtar looked questioningly at Sigmund.

'I didn't know that until now,' said my cousin, and I fancied his face showed relief. 'Still, it's possible. Her place was reserved.'

'We can find no one else in the house,' said one of the Singari, 'but do not blame us, Master, if a wench has escaped.'

I expected an angry outburst from Akhtar but, to my surprise, he took the news calmly.

'So I'm to be deprived of the acquaintance of my brother Louey's child,' he said with a laugh. 'So be it. There'll be time enough later.'

He fixed his gaze on Opa..

'This time, Father, you'll not stop me. You can't banish me twice, and any foolish move will bring down my wrath on these people you love so well.'

He swung round and strode across the hall. Those who were in his path retreated.

'Bring me a goblet of the best red wine,' he ordered one of the servants then, turning to another, added 'and a white rose from the garden.'

The wine and the flower were brought. Akhtar drained the vessel without drawing breath.

'And another!'

He swallowed half of the second and, without lowering the goblet, took the rose in his other hand. Slowly and deliberately he breathed upon the flower. It began to darken, to take on a pink hue, and finally to turn a deep red to match the colour of the wine. There was a gasp from the onlookers.

'Don't be deceived,' Opa said. 'It's a cheap trick that any apprentice can perform.'

'Believe what you like, fine people,' sneered Akhtar, tossing the rose aside and putting the goblet again to his lips, 'but which of you is prepared to risk my breath of fire?'

His next movements were so quick that I was unable to tell whether trickery was involved, or sorcery. What I saw him do was to trace the shape of a circle with the heel of his boot, cast the dregs of the wine within it and, gathering his cloak to his body, blow in the direction of the spillage. From the floor rose up a bright yellow flame that flickered and grew until the tongues of fire were almost as tall as Akhtar himself. From where I lay I could feel the scorching heat. I closed my eyes and felt suddenly cool again. I opened them. The flames were still there, flickering still, but sinking towards the floor. So it was in part unreal, an illusion. The fire had existed, produced by some chemical substance hidden on Akhtar's person, but the intense heat had been a trick of my own mind. However it had been accomplished, the demonstration had produced such fear and consternation among the household that I was conscious only of a deep despair overcoming my soul. What hope was there of resistance if they believed Akhtar capable of controlling the elements?

'Now, Sigmund,' said my violator. 'I've a mind to look again at my brother's rooms. Accompany me, if you will. You others, watch the old man carefully. Do not harm him, but ensure he does not leave the house.

And beware, he may be capable of tricks the equal of mine.'

He turned towards the stairs and I retreated. Where would I go? The outer doors were guarded. I dare not appear in the hall now that I had been given out as absent, and I was sure the men-at-arms would continue to patrol the house. Then I remembered the closet - the closet in the room that had once been my parents', the one in which my mother and I had played our game of hide-and-seek. That room was empty now, Ludwig having moved to another part of the house to avoid painful memories, and I had not been inside it for eight years. The tiny sealed space was still there and a heavy key sat in the lock. Akhtar would remember the room and might wish to see it. He mustn't find me, but I could think of nowhere else to go.

Before he had reached the first landing I was at the door of my mother's old sitting-room. Fortunately, I did not forget the creaking floorboard. Stepping over it lightly, I ran to the closet, removed the key, secreted myself behind the door, and locked myself in.

Time passed, each moment seeming like an hour. I sat on the floor clutching my knees and staring up at the smooth plaster. My worst nightmare returned, and I imagined small holes in the unbroken wall, a rat's face at every one of them. I relived the worst moments of my life at the Brunswick fair, and vowed to kill myself rather than allow Akhtar to take pleasure of me again.

Still no one came. How long could I remain in hiding? Sooner or later I would have to eat and drink, to satisfy other bodily needs. I did not understand what was happening. I knew only that Akhtar was mad, and that he had turned Sigmund against his family. Could I escape, go to the Duke, plead for help, and return with swordsmen to retake the house? What would become of my darling cousin then, and could I risk condemning him because Akhtar had cast a corrupt spell over him? I did not know.

While I was arguing these matters with myself for the hundredth time, I heard voices. I peered through the keyhole. Akhtar and Sigmund were standing in the middle of the bare room.

'As you can see, Cousin Akhtar, there's nothing here now.'

'This is a room I remember from my childhood. There was a table and chair over there, and the beds were in the chamber next door. It was there too my mother had the cribs. If I'm not mistaken, there was a privy, and that heavy door to the left of the window concealed a stairway to the roof.'

I felt my limbs quiver with fright.

'It's only an empty closet,' said Sigmund indifferently. 'The stairway was blocked up many years ago. I suppose the key has been lost too, now that the rooms are unused.'

'Lou was given these apartments on his marriage,' said Akhtar, shifting his position and looking round at the unhung panels and empty alcoves. 'He was always the favourite son. I feel uneasy here. I know my brother has gone on a journey, but it's as if his spirit lives on, restless and unforgiving.'

He stared suddenly at the door that concealed me. I almost fainted for fear he had seen movement at the keyhole as I drew my eye away.

'I need to purge the room of his presence,' said Akhtar. 'What say you to a little innocent fun?'

Sigmund did not reply. Perhaps he was not wholly under Akhtar's influence and might still be saved.

I looked again. Akhtar drew his dagger, knelt on the floor, and cut some marks in the wood. What the writing was I could not tell, but it was evidently part of a dark ritual. His next movement was to open a pouch at his waist and take from it a handful of powder. He scattered it over the spot he had defaced. Then he trod the powder firmly into the boards using the sole of his boot while muttering to himself words that my ear could not distinguish. I shivered to think this might be no trick but some real sorcery learned during his years in exile.

'That will suffice,' he said after a moment or two's silence and, taking Sigmund's arm, he led him out. The familiar boards creaked, the sound of their feet died away, and I was left alone and in near darkness again.

I felt hungry and wondered if I dare leave the security of the closet. As I was familiar with every nook and cranny of the house, I could easily evade the strangers posted in the corridors and at various exits, but Akhtar must know the manor as well as I, and my terror of meeting him face to face was so great that I shivered again in my uncomfortable hiding-place. Moreover, I had no idea how Sigmund would react if we accidentally met. With his mind warped by lies, how could I tell whether he would behave as friend or foe?

The urge to discover what was taking place became so strong, and my hunger so fierce, that I had almost plucked up enough courage to venture out, when a slow footfall alerted me to a new presence in the room. There was a soft rap on the door, and Opa's well-loved voice called to me in a whisper.

'I know you must be in there, Gretl. Unlock the door and come out. We've no time to lose.'

I obediently inserted the key, pushed back the door, and fell into my grandfather's arms.

'Quickly, Gretl, you must go and bring help. Your cousin is quite out of his mind and believes he is surrounded by enemies. Only five of the troop are loyal to Brunswick and they have been sent to patrol the river bank. The rest, including the Singari, are in Andreas's pay and will listen only to his voice.'

'I must know what is going on, and what Akhtar has written on the floor.'

'I'll tell you what I know so you can tell our rescuers,' said Opa, 'but I've been able to learn very little. They've taken Langenfurth manor, and aim to capture all the Waldhausen land on the western side of the Leine. Once he controls all three manors, I believe Andreas will threaten Brunswick itself. Sigmund has been persuaded he has a right to Bachhagen and its wealth, worse, that Andreas has been ill-used, and is his dearest friend. He has in confusion taken advantage of the Duke's trust. I fear for the others in the house. Andreas is more powerful than I ever imagined he could be. He performs illusions to keep the servants in check. The years have not dampened his ambition or cured him of his madness, and his resentment has grown.'

'I saw his tricks, Opa,' I said, 'and Sigmund and Akhtar were here together. Akhtar worked some magic with his dagger - there on the floor. It was exorcism - or a curse!'

There was a dark patch on the floorboards in the centre of the room. Some of the lettering, into which Akhtar had ground his powder, was still visible. I made out a U, a D, and part of a G. The letters could easily have spelled the name Ludwig.

'He has put a curse on my father!' I exclaimed in quite a loud voice.

Opa silenced me with a glance.

'It's nothing, and there's no time,' he whispered. 'A watch is kept on my rooms and I'll be missed if I stay longer. The guard I deceived and sent to sleep will waken any moment. Your father will not be harmed, I promise, and I'll look for a chance to bring Sigmund to his senses. It'll be difficult, because Andreas never leaves his side. Go to your grandfather Queck at Hameln. It's closer than Brunswick, and there's a detachment of knights and foot-soldiers there. Let Johann decide what should be done. Take my Arab stallion. Do not hold his rein too tightly and he will carry you gently and speedily wherever you wish.'

He bent his head, removed the gold chain bearing the fylfot and hung it around my neck.

'It will bring you good luck,' he said. 'Show it to the stallion. Press the cross against his neck. He'll recognise it and be your obedient servant. And I have brought your weapon too.' He reached inside his tunic and withdrew my short sword with the serpent hilt and the ruby. 'Take it and use it if you must,' he said. 'I know you can. Now I must go back. Good luck, Gretl!'

I dared not go down the main stairs but crept along the corridor to where stone steps from the tower led directly to the kitchen. No one was guarding them. However, just as I reached the ground floor I heard voices. Two of the company sat at a table making free with provisions from our pantry. One looked up from his food and I froze in my tracks. My terror may have saved me. Clearly he took me for a servant.

'Bring me that other flagon of wine, lad,' he called gruffly.

Bowing as low as I could so that he would not see my face, and hiding the sword behind my back, I obliged him. He seized the flagon roughly, took a gulp of the liquid, and passed the vessel to his comrade. I edged away towards the door. Once in the open, I bent low and ran for cover behind the wall that encircled the pond. A solitary knight, wearing the insignia of Brunswick but doing them no justice, guarded the stables. I threw a pebble to distract him and while he looked in the wrong direction slipped past. I had not eaten since breakfast and my legs responded weakly. The fylfot weighed heavily on my shoulders and against my breast.

Opa's Arab stallion whinnied softly as I opened the gate of his stall. I held up the cross to him as Opa had instructed and pressed the metal against his jowl. He nuzzled my face. As quickly and quietly as I could, I unhooked his bridle and rein from their nail and passed them over his head. I slipped the sword through my belt. For a few moments I struggled to place the bit, then I heard the sound of the armed guard returning. There was no time for the saddle and I trusted I could manage without one. Never before had I mounted such a horse without stirrup and block. I grasped leather and mane together in one hand, put my left foot awkwardly on the spar of the gate, and heaved myself onto the Arab's back. He neighed loudly, kicked back the gate and trotted into the yard.

I no longer cared that the knight saw me, nor that he reached up to pull me down. My cap fell from my head. I touched the horse's flank, flicked the rein and with my hair blowing in all directions, took off like the wind in the direction of the forest.

ii

Opa's stallion was more than a match in speed and endurance for any other horse in the world. I took comfort from that. More than once, I felt myself slipping from his smooth back but he seemed to recognise my predicament and did not object when I dug my heels into his ribs and hauled on his mane to pull myself erect again.

I did not fear pursuit, only that I would bring help too late to save Bachhagen. Even if the guard had recognised me as a girl – and I do not think he did, so brief was his glimpse of me without my cap, he could not know who I was or where I was headed.

It was growing dark when I reached Hameln and the lamps were lit. The glow of candles from the casements warmed the route from the town gate. These signs of security comforted me and relieved my feelings of despair and apprehension. However, when I at last slipped from the stallion's back in the Queck stable yard, the muscles of my arms and legs aching from their recent effort, some of my worst fears returned. What if Opa had been wrong and there was no garrison in Hameln? How then could we hope to recover the manor house?

My grandparents did their best to reassure me. Having recovered from their surprise at seeing me arrive alone and in such a manner, they made me no less welcome than on any saint's day. I needed no persuasion to eat a slice of Anna Queck's best pie. After that, and with the grime of the road washed from my face and hands, I felt much better. However, all my grandparents' protective fussing did not detract me from the job I had to do.

'We cannot set out until morning,' said Johann when I had told my story, 'but I'll speak with the Duke's commander straight away. I think there is a large enough force here to retake the house, but I don't wish to see innocent blood spilled.'

He bustled out into the darkening streets and returned within a half hour with the captain of militia.

I repeated my tale.

'We'll have to rely on cunning and surprise if we're to recapture the manor without sacrificing lives,' the captain said.

'That should not be difficult if there are only twenty of them,' said my uncle Leo. 'They'll not be expecting a counter-assault. How many men do you have, Captain?'

'Sixteen only. That makes eighteen of us if you join the attack. Enough if we divide our force and catch them unawares.'

'Nineteen,' said my grandfather. 'I can't use a sword but I can wield a cudgel.'

Between them a stratagem was devised. We went to our beds but I scarcely slept. The next day dawned and found me impatient as well as anxious.

My grandfather bade me stay safely in Hameln to await news.

'I'll not hear of it,' I said. 'Unless the captain locks me in the cellar, nothing will prevent me from taking part in the expedition. No one knows the lie of the land better. I can show you furrows along which ten swordsmen might approach the house without being seen. I can fight too.'

Johann smiled at that but he saw sense in the rest and, to save time in argument, consented to my riding with the party. A saddle was found for the Arab stallion so that I might travel in better comfort. One of the men-at-arms gave me a mail tunic to wear in case I should be struck by accident in a skirmish. I fastened my hair inside another cap. They made me promise that, having shown them the hidden approaches, I would stay out of the fighting. It was a promise I had no intention of keeping. I was a von Hasenbach and if this was anyone's fight, it was mine.

Eight swordsmen hid themselves in a wagon belonging to my grandfather who, with Leo, drove boldly through the gates as if nothing were amiss.

I took the road with the captain and the rest of his troop. We came by stealth upon the five men who patrolled the river, a few more in the outer pastures and those who guarded the rear entrances. The troopers disarmed them - twelve in all, knocked them senseless and trussed them together with ropes and chains. Three of Akhtar's Singars realised what was afoot and would have given the alarm but the captain despatched them by the sword.

When we reached the gate and spurred our mounts into a charge, the rest of the relief disembarked from the wagon and stormed the house from the rear. On both sides of the manor attackers and defenders met and engaged.

Taken by surprise at the speed of the attack, I would have been left behind. However, my stallion seemed to know his duty. He bounded forward, almost throwing me off and, willing or not, I found myself in the thick of the fighting.

I had underestimated the strength of the enemy. Excluding the men we had disarmed, there must have been at least fifteen of Akhtar's followers. I watched in dismay as sword met shield, helmets were dislodged, and mace or gisarme struck at unprotected heads. Men fell heavily, their mail resounding against the stones, and their blood spurting on the beds of herbs and over the sweet Bachhagen grass. Through the open door I could hear the crash of weapons and the cries of the wounded as both factions strove for control of the hall and staircase.

I slid from the stallion's back. A man came towards me, his sword raised. He did not know me but I recognised him as one of the invaders. I dodged instinctively and swung upwards with my own weapon. It connected with the mail on his arm. He laughed at my feeble effort and lunged.

Luckily for me, the stallion seemed to understand we had an enemy in common and lashed out with his forelegs, catching the swordsman on the temple. He crumpled with blood pouring from his head.

The realisation came to me that this was no game, no exercise with wooden swords or blunted blades. It was real warfare and I might be killed. But there was no time to dwell on the thought, or to feel dizzy at the sight of spilled blood. Another man was coming towards me. I parried his stroke and wounded him in the leg. Then I ran across the forecourt with the intention of regaining the house. Akhtar was in the doorway, with the Persian sabre from the hall, fending off two fellows who were trying to force their way inside. Sigmund was there too, and three others. I shouted his name but he did not heed me. My cousin was engaged by one of the Hameln men and, no mean swordsman, was trading blow for blow. I rushed to his aid, my blood hot, but my way was blocked by one of Akhtar's followers. He swung at me. I ducked and pierced him in the groin.

Akhtar stood stock still on the threshold, his cold eyes gazing at the scene of carnage before him. Other than those eyes, his face showed no emotion at all. He had killed one of his attackers and fought off the other, who had now re-joined the melee. I do not think he saw me. If he did, he saw no threat in what he took for a youth with a short sword, and I suppose my disguise saved me. I could never have defended myself against that sabre.

But Sigmund was being pressed back against the stone by two opponents, one of whom was the man I had taken for our ally. It was an easy mistake to make. Most of the combatants wore similar colours and, in the confusion, it was difficult to distinguish between them. With sudden insight, I saw with sinking heart the true situation. Either my cousin had come to his senses or he was beginning to be free of Akhtar's influence.

Akhtar was urging the two men into the attack. Frustrated in his objectives, he had turned against his one-time ally and had ordered his death.

'Sigmund!' I shouted again.

I cannot say whether he heard me; I judged not. But in that instant I had to make a decision between my own safety and the life of the man I loved. Ignoring Akhtar's sabre, I threw myself at one of my cousin's attackers with a yell of rage, swinging wildly with my sword. The man half turned to meet the threat but my blade cut into his neck and he dropped at my feet.

Sigmund had been forced onto one knee by the superior strength of his second opponent, who thrust his shield to one side and, as I watched helpless, brought his sword down forcibly on my cousin's exposed left arm. At the same time, Sigmund raised the point of his own weapon and, piercing the other's guard, drove the steel into his belly.

As they both fell, I ran forward with a cry of despair and knelt at Sigmund's side. The mail had protected his arm to an extent, and the wound, though bleeding heavily, was not mortal. However, I saw to my horror that he had sustained another in his side. His tabard was scarlet with blood. He was pale and scarcely breathed, but managed to focus his eyes on my face.

'Gretl,' he whispered. 'How did you come to be here? And where am I?'

'At Bachhagen,' I said. 'You are home at Bachhagen.'

What he had done had been under a wicked influence, and I could not blame him for it.

Meantime, I realised how fortunate I had been. At the mercy of the sabre, I was saved by half-a-dozen of the Hameln troop. They had besieged Akhtar from all sides and were trying to despatch or disarm him. It was no easy task. He had learned the craft of swordplay well and swung the great Persian weapon over and round with strength and agility. However, seeing he had no hope of victory, he retreated, mounted the stone parapet separating the forecourt from the garden and, still grasping his weapon, addressed his attackers with icy calm.

'Stay back and allow me space,' he cried, unclasping his cloak and throwing it on the ground at their feet. 'May all the demons of Hell pursue you if you take one step forward!'

The cloak fluttered and seemed to rise into the air by itself. The soldiers stared as if at an apparition and lowered their swords. I looked again and saw only a black cape, its folds ruffled by a slight wind. Whatever illusion Akhtar had created, and was maintaining for the benefit of his opponents, I could not see it.

'Take him!' I cried, pointing my sword towards him. Sigmund had fainted from the loss of blood. 'It's only a trick. That is your real enemy. Take him before he escapes!'

The skirmish in the garden was over. The fighting stopped. Strong arms took Akhtar from behind and wrested the sabre from him. Leo emerged from the house accompanied by Freddy and some servants. Both were armed and looked as if they had been fighting too. They had blood on their clothing but seemed unhurt. Matti followed. She gave a cry when she saw Sigmund and rushed to his side, pushing me roughly away from him in her anguish. With the servants' help, she carried him indoors.

Akhtar, now a prisoner, stared at me long and hard but without recognition, though it was scarcely more than a year since our first meeting. However, my hair was loose again and he could have been in no doubt that I was a maid. His eyes fell on the fylfot.

'So I have been brought to heel by the daughter of Ludwig,' he said with mock humility.

I did not reply.

'You are Margaretha von Hasenbach, are you not?. Despite that tunic and those breeches? There's a resemblance too,' he went on, seemingly with no sense of the gravity of his position. 'You have my father's colour and your mother's nose. I do believe you might even be more beautiful than she, by all the fallen angels.'

My contempt for him knew no bounds.

'How dare you speak of my mother!' I said, 'and since I am Gretl, why should I deny it?'

'Indeed, why should you, Gretl? But you are a long way from Brunswick, and with my father's fylfot about your neck, I suspect you were never there in the first place, since it was about his yesterday.'

One of his captors pushed him roughly forward. Akhtar fixed the fellow with a contemptuous look; it was one of our own men-at-arms, a Hameln trooper. His voice hardened.

'You would regret that, peasant, if the odds were but halved. If six blades were not within an inch of my side, I might perform such an illusion as would turn your hair white and cause you to choke on your tongue.'

We took him to the hall where I was relieved to see both my grandfathers, grim-faced but well enough. Akhtar glared at them but remained silent.

'Have you nothing to say?' Opa demanded. His voice shook with emotion.

'Only that you are a fool, Father. You might have succeeded once where I have failed. A throne was once yours for the taking!

'Oh yes, I have been to your homeland in Persia. During my years of exile I visited many places - Spain, England and Egypt. But it was in Persia that I heard the story of a prince who, but for his cowardice, might have gained a kingdom.

'The proud and mighty General Hassan, favourite of the old Khan. Scourge of the Egyptian sultans! Yes, Father, only one weak half-brother stood in your way. Prince Oljeitu, the vain! Have you told your precious family how you fought him and, having stood over your disarmed opponent with sword raised, spared his life?'

'You heard nothing but a half truth, Andreas. Yet, had you learned from my experience, you might have earned my forgiveness one more time. I have nothing with which to reproach myself. Even a throne is not worth gaining at the expense of a brother's life, if he has prior right!'

'Fool!' said Akhtar again between his teeth. He turned to Leo, adding with menace, 'and you and your father are fools too for having meddled with me. You've made an enemy of Akhtar, and I shall be even with you.'

'You'll do no more harm,' said Opa. 'I warned you once, and you have chosen to ignore me. Now I have no choice. You will be taken to Brunswick to be tried for sorcery and treason.'

Akhtar's hands were shackled and he was set on a horse between two troopers. Four men-at-arms were commanded to follow behind.

'Do not fear his anger or his taunts,' said Opa, 'but don't look into his eyes. Guard him carefully, and remember that Andreas is at his most dangerous when his voice is softest.'

From the forecourt I watched them move off. Just as they reached the path, Akhtar looked back and saw me standing stiffly, alone and to one side. Still he showed no sign of recognising the maiden he had violated and humiliated.

'You and I might yet be friends, Gretl,' he called. 'There's something of the Tartar ... something of the Persian warrior princes in you.'

'After what you have done, there can never be any kind of affection between us,' I said dryly.

'So be it then,' he retorted, 'but do me one last favour and fetch my cloak from the dirt.'

I saw it merely as an act of Christian charity. Much as I hated him, I could not deny such a simple request and, picking up the black cloak, I caught up with the small procession and held the garment out to him. He took it in his shackled hands and laid it across the horse's withers, concealing from view the chain that bound the hands together. The procession moved off.

Akhtar's movements were so rapid as to deceive the eye. Somehow he had one hand free. The chain and loose manacle were swung in an arc above his head, striking one knight full on the temple and knocking him from the saddle. The second tried to draw his sword but was struck by a similar blow on the shoulder. As they closed, Akhtar seized the hilt of the sword and pulled it free of its scabbard. Being without full armour he had the advantage of greater agility, and struck the knight again with the iron before he could recover.

The men-at-arms were slow to react, so great was their surprise. Only one had advanced far enough to offer a challenge. Akhtar wheeled his mount. With a deft movement of the wrist he freed himself completely from the shackles and threw them against the challenger's breast-plate. The captured sword rose and fell, and a fountain of red sprang from the half-severed neck. The limp body crashed to the ground, rolled over once, and lay still.

Akhtar dropped the sword, urged his horse into a gallop, and made his escape over the fields.

The Betrothal

Duke Magnus offered a reward for Akhtar's recapture, adding the crime of murder to his offences, but, though word was put out and a search made, no trace of him was found.

We had recovered our home at the cost of eight lives, and I had seen such bloodshed as I never wished to see again. The soldiers from Sigmund's own troop were pardoned. Those recruited by Akhtar – the survivors – were tried by the law, found guilty but released on the understanding that they never set foot in Brunswick again. Walther Langenfurth and his family were released from a wet cellar under their manor house, and the planned celebrations took place to the delight of all. Bachhagen was given a small picket.

I gave the fylfot back to my grandfather. Whatever magic it possessed and had used to protect me on my mission, it had served its purpose. I found wearing it a burden, and supposed that I was not ready to accept it as my inheritance. Indeed, I prayed it would be long years until I felt it about my neck again, for Opa was as dear to me as anyone in the world, and I desired nothing more than that he should have a long life.

Despite his terrible wound, Sigmund survived. He lay prostrate for a week, attended daily by Opa, and watched over by his anxious mother. Twice, I had gone to see him but had left in tears. At the end of the week, he showed signs of recovery, begged Opa to tell him the whole story of what had occurred, then sent for Freddy to ask his pardon. He had little recollection of his own part in the affair, until the last few moments in the garden, when he knew only that he had been deceived. After ten days, I visited his sick bed to administer a prescription.

'I owe my life and my return to sanity to you, Gretl,' he said, taking the medicine and lying back on the pillow. 'It seems you had knowledge of this cousin that I did not. I used to laugh at the magicians and their tricks, but never again. Is Andreas truly a sorcerer?'

'He has strange power over people,' I admitted, ' - a gift that he uses for evil purposes. As to sorcery, I've heard there are those who can conjure up demons, but I don't believe in such things. There is only natural magic, be it good or evil. Demons exist only in our nightmares.'

Sigmund tried to laugh and a spasm of pain crossed his face.

'You are a true heir to Sano,' he said. 'He used to tell us that all things are capable of rational explanation, that the whole universe is governed by natural laws, if only we could discover them. Will you come again, Gretl?'

'I'll come again,' I said, feeling a flush of blood to my cheeks and a tingling in my breasts, 'but ...'

'But what?'

'Nothing,' I said, and rushed out, covering my face with my hands to hide my blushes.

I returned the next day. He had better colour, and we talked again. He told me how he had met Akhtar in the tavern, and how he had been deceived. Then I related to him what I knew of his assault on the two manors, and the consequences.

'I swear I remember scarcely anything of that,' he said weakly. 'Suddenly, I was in the middle of a battle and there was blood on my sleeve.'

I saw he was tired and would have left him, only he took my hand. That was not unusual, for we had grown up together as brother and sister, but I trembled. I wanted to fall into his arms, yet feared he wanted nothing but sisterly affection from me.

'You should always dress as a woman, Gretl,' he smiled, '... as you have done today ... as you did those days in Brunswick when we talked together. A cap and breeches are not becoming to one as lovely as you.'

I drew my hand away. This time, he had not spoken as a brother.

'Forgive me if I have offended you,' he stammered.

'I'm not offended,' I said and ran from the room in confusion.

For three more days I administered Sigmund's medicine. By then he was taking a few painful steps across the room. He had not touched me again, but each time we sat and talked I had a strange emptiness inside me, not unlike hunger but pleasant and more insistent. I warmed at the thought of what it might be like to have Sigmund's love.

On the morning of the fourth day, he was stronger and I thrilled to see how handsome he looked. We sat facing one another.

'I'm glad ...' He seemed at a loss for words.

'I am too ...' said I. '... glad you are nearly well again.'

'Yes, but not that, Gretl.' He leaned across to me and took both my hands inside his. 'I'm glad you have not abandoned me is what I meant to say. I feared you wouldn't return when I spoke to you as a woman and not as a sister. It's only that I do find you beautiful. I've often wanted to tell you but could never find the courage. A poor officer I will make!'

Before I could say anything, he knelt beside me and kissed my hands. His lips were gentle against my skin. I touched his cheek and he responded by drawing me towards him in an embrace.

The memory of my humiliation rose to haunt me. Though I found pleasure in his nearness, I was torn between my desire and my terror of enforced intimacy. Deep inside me too was the fear that Sigmund would not want one who had been sullied as I was. He would find out, and know I had already shared my body with the fiend who had almost brought him to disgrace and early death. I broke free and left him without a word.

About a week later, he came one evening to my apartment. He had never done so before, and I had never before seen him so agitated. There was a trembling in his lip and a flush in his cheek. I sat on the edge of my bed and my heart leapt with joy as he sat in a chair opposite. As we talked. I watched his eyes, his lips and the movement of his limbs and felt my desire for him grow. I held out my arms to him.

'Hold me, Sigmund,' I said. 'Just hold me.'

He hesitated and I wondered if I was being too forward or had wrongly judged his feelings for me. Then he rose and came over to the bed. He took my hands and lifted me up.

'Gretl ...'

There was a weakness in my knees and the blood seemed to surge faster and faster in my veins. I grasped his hand tightly and pulled it against my bodice. For what seemed an age, we just stood there, silent but for our breathing until, at length, he cupped his palm over my left breast.

'I love you, Sigmund,' I said.

Sigmund did not seem at all surprised by my confession. He bent over me and kissed me on the lips. As he pressed his body to mine, I felt his manhood through my clothing, and a new sensation of delight overcame me. I unfastened my bodice and pulled it down so he could touch me.

'I'm leaving soon to join my troop, Gretl,' he said. 'We're bound for Bohemia and the new settlements. When I return, I wish the honour of becoming your husband. Please let me know if ...'

'Shhh, my love,' I said, cutting off his proposal. 'You have my promise, but first you should know ...'

'I wish to know no more than I can see and touch,' said Sigmund, denying me any explanation. He reached out with his free hand and stroked my hair. 'I love you, Gretl. I have loved you for so long.'

In that moment, I wanted him above all else in the world. I did not protest or resist when he explored clumsily for the fastenings of my dress. Then he laid me on the bed and took me in his arms again. His lips were soft against my breasts, his hands gentle as he caressed me to fuel my desire.

And so I lay with Sigmund in my own bed and found love, knowing full well it was soon to be snatched away.

The next six days dwell in my memory as the most wondrous of my life. Until that moment, I had regretted the passing of my childhood. I had longed for the return of those innocent hours, watching my father at work or clinging to Opa's neck while he told his stories of prophecies and magic. The bodily pain of my ravishment at Brunswick had long vanished yet, for all my grandfather's tender affection, the hurt to my mind had remained. My continued preference for youth's clothing was a denial of my womanhood; in any other apparel, I was defenceless. There were times I could not look in my mirror or in the still water of the pond without dread of seeing not my reflection but the leering face and groping hands of my violator.

Suddenly, I was free. This new love had a magic of its own, one that no gold charm could augment or diminish. My glass was no longer a bane but a joy, an enchanted country to be explored for the means to please my lover.

During daylight hours, we rode together in every corner of the estate, galloping breathlessly through the long grass of the fallow, or trotting in silence along the winding forest paths. When we tired of riding, we strolled arm in arm in the pasture by the river, talking and laughing. Sometimes, we swam naked in the shallows out of sight of the house. We would allow our limbs to touch in the water. I would hold Sigmund tightly against me in anticipation of the delight of that moment when he would pitch us both into the soft grass of the bank and whisper his love in my ear. We had our own special spot that no one else ever visited or passed.

Most nights we spent in one another's arms, our bodies entwined, our hearts beating in unison, delighting in our love but dreading the moment of parting.

On the morning of the day of his departure, we climbed the hill to the coppice. Sigmund was wearing his mail and leading his charger. I walked at his side. I carried in my purse a tiny likeness of myself, painted on vellum and mounted in a gold frame. We sat together in a little hollow by a beech tree and there we gave each other our promises.

'I've never been so happy,' I said, trying to dispel my feelings of despair and emptiness at his going. I gave him the miniature.

'Nor I, Gretl.' He kissed the token and brushed away the tear that had fallen on my cheek. 'And when I come back we'll know it again.'

He put a ring on my finger and drew from beneath his tabard a tiny silver dagger in a jewelled sheath.

'You shall have these as pledges of my devotion,' he said. 'One is a symbol of our betrothal, while the other may have more practical uses. Take care. It's sharp, and may pierce an enemy's heart just as surely as your love has pierced mine.'

'I accept them gladly, though I have no need of tokens,' I said. A faintness came over me and I was now almost blinded by my tears. 'I want nothing more than for you to touch me one last time.'

He pulled me towards him and when we had finished our lovemaking, we lay exhausted and content on the grass.

'Now go, my love,' I said. 'Go, before my heart breaks!'

He released me, spoke my name once, then, without another word, mounted the charger and was gone.

Still tingling from his touch, I adjusted my clothing and walked down the hill to the manor house. I wondered if I would ever see him again.

The Black Plague Returns

i

Ludwig was gone many months. With both he and Sigmund absent, time passed slowly. I returned eventually to Brunswick, where Hanna too had become betrothed, but the visit was a short one. News reached me that Opa was dying.

I saw how he had aged. He was no longer tall and straight. Since the battle for the manor house, his brows had turned completely white. His once dark complexion was now grey and the furrows that lined it had become deeper. He had learned in a letter from Venice, delivered by one of his trading houses, of the death of Hypatia and that news hastened the end. Though the brightness of his eye was not extinguished, the sadness behind his look seemed more profound than before. His movements were slow and I knew, without him telling me, that he suffered agonising pains in his muscles and joints.

These things I could see, yet I could only imagine the agony of spirit he endured as a result of Akhtar's vengeful hatred. His greatest wish was that he should live long enough to see Ludwig again, and that one thought sustained him well past the autumn equinox. Still, his devotion to me was as great as ever. When the weather was fine, we sat together in the garden. I spoke to him of my love for Sigmund, and of my fears that he would never return. Opa would only smile and kiss me on the forehead. He never said so, but I felt sure he approved my choice.

It was almost winter when my father returned to Bachhagen. His journey had taken him through Italy, and thence on a vessel to Constantinople. He had visited all our kin in the Veneto and had seen his sister again before her last illness. He had made many discoveries in the Levant. He found evidence of the black plague in Asia Minor and learned that the Great Mortality had struck there two years or more before it came to Saxony. From the merchants he heard how hordes of rats had invaded their grain colonies, embarked on their ships with the cargo, and disembarked again in the ports of Venice and Genoa. He had consulted with physicians and itinerant healers, finding support for his theories, and deriving hope of a cure. In Persia, he had met with a Chinese mystic who knew of a new treatment against the smallpox. This consisted of infecting a person with a weakened form of the disease, in order to prevent a more serious attack.

All this and much more was the result of his expedition, but these things had to wait to be told. Opa had taken to his bed, weak and sick beyond hope of recovery. Wine mixed with water was his diet. He refused all else, sleeping through most of the day and, when awake, allowing no one but Ludwig and me to come near. In this condition he clung to life for five days. On the fifth evening he expressed the wish to speak to me alone. My father had already been to his bedside and had spent nearly an hour there.

For a moment Opa gazed at me fondly. He stretched out a feeble withered hand to grip mine tightly. I kissed the ashen forehead. I loved him dearly and there were no words to express my sorrow.

'I shall be sad to leave this life, Gretl,' he whispered.

I muttered some meaningless words, trying to comfort him. Opa struggled to find his breath.

'The fylfot!' he cried with renewed vigour. 'Andreas must not have it!'

'It's still about your neck, Opa.'

He drew my hand across his breast so that my fingers touched the cross.

'It's yours, Gretl. Remember your promise and guard it well.'

'I'll not forget, Opa.'

He sighed and closed his eyes. After a while he opened them and, still clutching my hand, addressed me again.

'I wish to bless you, Gretl,' he said weakly but clearly enough. 'You will be my advocate when men speak ill of my race.'

'Why should they do that, Opa, when you are a good man?'

'One day the world will change, perhaps. But we are bred to be suspicious of difference ...'

His voice faded away and I could see there was something else on his mind.

'Opa?'

He gripped my hand tighter than ever. 'My brother ... Andreas ... I did not wish to quarrel.'

I feared his mind was going at last but then remembered Akhtar's final words to him. Of the half-brother called Oljeitu, whom he had fought and defeated.

'I know, Opa,' I said. 'Save your energy.'

No,' he said and shook his head violently. 'Let me speak. They were only insults. He insulted my mother and for that I took up the sword.'

But spared him to rule, I thought. He had since told me the whole story.

'Oljeitu?'

'Yes. Are you still there, Gretl.'

'I am here, Opa.'

'You are a good child. May all the gods bless you and open up the pit to any who would wish you harm.'

I kissed his forehead again.

'Andreas,' he said so faintly that I could scarcely hear. I bent closer, my ear to his lips. 'Louey must...'

'What should I tell him, Opa?'

He looked up into my face and shook his head, but said no more.

'What should I tell him?' I repeated. The tears stung my eyes.

Opa did not answer. He drew one final breath. The white beard sank silently onto his motionless chest, his eyes dimmed, and the pressure on my fingers relaxed. I made the sign of the Cross and laid my head beside his, sobbing quietly. He would not have wanted a priest.

Opa was laid to rest on the fourth day before Christmas. A large crowd of country people gathered outside the house, for truly he had been loved and respected by all. I wore the fylfot as we sealed him in his coffin, but believing my promise would be best kept if it were protected by the sanctity of the grave, I stayed my father's hand. I had the memories to comfort me, and had no need of a talisman. How bitterly I was to regret my choice.

Whether magic or no, the gold cross of Shahrinaz was thus interred in the tomb of my grandfather - Prince Hassan of Persia. The old Singari woman's prophecies were forgotten, and my inheritance was locked away.

ii

The Great Mortality returned. It was as if it had never left but, like a being with an evil soul, had lain asleep in some underground cave, awaiting the right moment to waken and catch its victims unprepared. This time, the plague did not reach Saxony from the south, but erupted amongst us like a summer storm. The monastery hospices were quickly full. As before, people believed the plague to be God's punishment for their sins and that their only protection was to take refuge on holy ground. Thus not only the sick looked to the monks for aid, but the healthy too.

In the second spring following my grandfather's death, the rats began again to breed in great numbers.

'It has the same beginning,' said Ludwig. 'They no longer hide in the haylofts and stone crevices, but dare even to invade the manor house. They snatch at anything we throw away and steal scraps from the very dogs and cats.'

'There's no sign of illness among them,' I said. 'Perhaps there'll be no plague.'

My father shook his head.

'It'll come soon enough,' he said, and I shivered.

We beat the rats off with sticks and continued to take precautions against fleas by regular bathing and the hanging of various herbs in our apartments. By the autumn, we were finding dead animals among the stubble of the fields, in the barns and floating on the surface of the pond. News came from the towns of the first cases of the black boils. Many of the victims were young children.

Meanwhile, Ludwig had begun a study of fungi. Having learned on his expedition to Asia Minor that a physician there had been able to relieve plague symptoms with an extract from these unusual plants, he had brought some back with him. They were dried and dead of course and he searched the neighbourhood for other species that grew and reproduced themselves in similar fashion. He wrote continually, sometimes by lamplight well into the night.

When he caged two healthy rats and hid them in the cellar, my curiosity was aroused. I knew he had dissected animals, perhaps even rats. Why he should wish to do so again I could not imagine. And when by chance I saw him carry one of the dead creatures indoors, I was repelled. Ludwig did not take me into his confidence, and I stayed away from the place where he worked.

At length, overcome by my desire to discover what he was doing, I approached him in the laboratory, where he sat with the record of his work in front of him. He was in good humour..

'Why have you stayed away, Greta?' he asked me. He had taken to calling me by my mother's name, whether absent-mindedly or on purpose I could not tell. 'Have you forgotten me because you wear your betrothed's ring? You used always to take great interest in my work and in the substances I prepare here.'

'I think of Sigmund every day, Father,' I replied, 'but it's not that. I thought perhaps you had secrets you did not want to share ...'

'I have no secrets from you, Greta. If I was careful, it was because I did not wish others to see. The servants would gossip, and Matti would find my experiments distasteful. And the Church ...'

I looked around the laboratory. No rats were to be seen there. All the containers of dried herbs, ointments, tinctures and other natural ingredients were in place on the shelves. The bench was empty save for the book in which he wrote and two small bottles containing reddish fluid.

'What did you do with the rats, Father?' I asked casually, reaching out to take up one of the bottles. He pulled my hand away before I could touch it.

'Don't interfere with the bottles,' he said sharply. 'You life may depend on it! As for the rats, I kept them always in the cellar. And they are both dead.'

'Both, Father? I counted three, and I can vouch that one was dead already.'

'That has gone too. I've no further need of it. So much has happened, I don't know where to begin. Many of my ideas have been proved correct. I know for sure the rats are the primary source of the plague, that is, of the

Great Mortality; there are many kinds of plague in our midst. And I'm satisfied the fleas are one means by which it is transmitted.'

'There are other means then?'

'There is one that may be just as important. I learned so much from the Eastern physicians, Gretl. They are advanced in their science beyond anything I ever imagined. Here in Saxony, I'm alone in seeking the answer to disease in nature itself. There, many follow that path, and because they are not blinded by superstition and by talk of demons, they make progress.'

He went on talking at such a rate and with such enthusiasm that he was quickly out of breath.

'The Great Mortality spread in Asia Minor as it did here. Learned men took the rats and their fleas to be the main cause. Only they could not discover how the plague took hold. Driving the rats away was thought to be the best way of ridding towns of the sickness, yet, even with the rats gone, the people continued to die. The physicians suspected a secondary cause. Not normal exhalation of breath as I once did, but sneezing. It's often the first symptom we observe.

'So, you see, the fleas carry the disease from rat to man. Men and women pass it to each other, by transfer of the fleas for sure, but also in the spray of saliva expelled forcibly by their sneezing. The secondary procedure is just as deadly for not only the blood but the lungs are poisoned. It was this last infection that killed your mother ...'

His eyes misted over. I placed my hand on his, and begged him to go on. He looked at me gratefully and continued.

'The doctors in the Levant told me more,' he said. 'There is even a third kind of plague that invades the brain. Madness ensues. Death is swift and agonising. But they devised a means whereby the black plague could be prevented, or at least controlled. I told you how Chinese physicians were able to control the pox. It was a method practised in their country centuries ago. They cut the skin and inserted diseased flesh beside the patient's own. I'm not yet convinced of its efficacy against the black plague, being unable to test it, but the idea sprang from the observation, also made by me, that having once suffered the sickness and survived, a human being could not suffer a second time. Under Chinese guidance, a

Persian doctor treated himself with a prescription that I've attempted to duplicate. Having scratched his arm, he smeared a potion on the cut. He developed a mild fever, but that was all.'

He picked up the bottles carefully and held them up to the window so that the daylight illuminated their contents. The fluids were clearly of different texture and colour.

'The smaller contains a poison,' said Ludwig, ' ... an evil fluid made from the blood of a sick rat. As you can see, it is truly liquid. The second bottle contains the potion, an antidote, made according to the formula the Persian gave me. It has a brownish tint and flows sluggishly. I tested it on my own arm and it was harmless. But then, I have already suffered the plague.

'If I'm right, were a drop of the first to fall on a cut finger, the fever would be on you before the day was over. You would die in torment from a madness of the brain. Thus the scientists in Asia Minor described its effect to me. I have no proof of course but I have no doubts of its malignancy in respect of rats.'

I uttered a gasp. He did not need to tell me more, or what he had done with the live creatures he had kept in the cellar.

'Some would accuse you of sorcery, Father,' I said.

'Indeed, Gretl. The churchmen would condemn it, and me. All the more reason why no one else in the house must know. But I used no adjurations or spells and, if good comes of it, surely the experiment is justified. Consider! If we could go fearlessly among the people, helping the sick and treating this vile disease ...'

'Let me test the antidote,' I said. 'I haven't suffered the plague, so perhaps the potion may work on me, and I may become immune as you are.'

Ludwig shook his head.

'I could never allow that,' he said. 'We shall have to find another way to test the prescription.'

I argued with him to no avail. He would not submit the Persian physician's formula to further proof.

This conversation had taken place shortly before my twentieth birthday.

Not long afterwards, there were happenings that led to suspicion within the household, and almost to a quarrel with the Singari who, that year, had returned to our lower pasture. Despite my experience of the knaves who had served Akhtar, I had wonderful memories of these people from my childhood, and we moved amongst them as neighbours. They traded their artifacts and leatherwork for extra supplies and a few coins. They were always clean, bathing regularly in the river and burying their waste in the ground, and had always shown themselves to be honest.

On the Sabbath, my father and I, often accompanied by Matti and Freddy, would walk through the village or by the riverbank, or ride out into the woods. Sometimes, I lingered behind, gathering flowers along the paths I had trod with Sigmund, or stopping to caress a tree where we had stood to kiss and exchange soft nothings.

One afternoon, as we set out, I felt I was being watched by a pair of unseen eyes. Several times I had had such feelings and had dismissed them as mere fancy. When we returned towards evening, I discovered that my closets had been rifled, my wardrobes rearranged. Suspecting my maid of being careless with my things, I reprimanded her.

'I have touched nothing, Mistress Gretl,' she said, looking hurt.

'Someone has disturbed my dresses,' I said.

At that moment, Ludwig came past the door and overheard.

'My bed linen has been deranged,' he said, 'and my clothing is not laid out in its usual order.'

'How strange,' I said. 'It seems a practical joke has been played on us.'

'I'll make enquiries,' said Ludwig.

He did so and was met with denials from all sides. However, as no harm was done and nothing was missing, the matter was forgotten.

The second, more serious incident took place one day when Ludwig and I had ridden out to visit sick tenants. Plague had been suspected, but the ailments turned out to be minor ones. Returning to Bachhagen, we found our apartments again in disarray. With an angry cry, my father bounded down the stairs ahead of me. There was a great commotion below of raised voices, heavy footfalls and sobbing. When I reached the ground floor, a small crowd of family and servants had already gathered outside the laboratory. The key was in the lock and the door wide open.

'Is it not possible you left it open by accident?' Freddy was saying.

'I did not,' said Ludwig. 'This door is always kept locked when I'm not at work, and the key is hung in my bedroom. It's not a matter of trust, but a precaution against foolish curiosity. Some of my medicines are dangerous if taken in the wrong dose.'

'I can vouch for the door being closed at noon,' said Kunz, the steward. 'I know where the key is kept, but I've no interest in potions and the like, and would not take it.'

'No one would enter your room uninvited,' added Frija who, like Kunz, had continued to serve the household after Opa's death. Ludwig had spoken harshly to her and she was crying.

I stepped past these scenes of disharmony and entered the laboratory. Nothing seemed to have been disturbed. The book that Opa and my father had composed of their work in the sciences lay on the table in its usual place. The bottles and jars sat neatly in their proper order. I had expected chaos, but here was a to-do about nothing at all. Ludwig however was pacing the floor, his countenance flushed, his voice shrill.

'It's not there, Gretl. The bottle has gone!'

'The bottle, Father? You mean the antidote you worked so hard to produce?'

'It's not the antidote that is missing, Gretl. It's the other bottle - the one containing the poison!'

I crossed to the bench. In a shallow well in the wood, where I had seen it so recently, was the larger of the two bottles containing the brown fluid. Of the smaller bottle with its pinkish contents that had stood beside it there was no sign. The book lay slightly askew and, as I straightened it, I noticed that one of its pages was loose. Ludwig noticed it too. In two strides he was at my shoulder. He snatched the book from the table and opened it at the offending spot. The loose page fell to the floor and with it another. Both had been torn from the binding, along with several others. Some of Ludwig's notes on the Great Mortality, its symptoms, its causes and his search for a cure were gone. A thief had been at work and had in his possession perhaps the knowledge to destroy life a thousand-fold.

As I stared at the open book, the writing seemed to fade, and in my mind's eye I saw a vision of the old Singari woman who had prophesied to me at Brunswick. I felt suddenly cold and nauseous as a new understanding dawned. I knew who had violated our privacy, and why.

A search was made but nothing was found. The servants were pronounced innocent and Ludwig began to look around for other suspects. The finger was pointing at the Singari.

'I'll tear down their tents and search every inch of their carts,' he vowed, more agitated than I had ever seen him. 'And when I find the culprit, I'll slit his throat and hang his corpse from a tree.'

He could not have committed such an act of revenge, but that so much of his work should be lost enraged him, and he believed what he was saying.

'Wait, Father,' I said, running after him across the forecourt. 'Don't be too hasty. The Singari will consider an unsupported accusation an insult and fight for their honour.'

'I don't care. They'll not steal from me and escape justice.'

'Consider a moment, Father,' I said. 'Why would the Gypsies steal from us? Our dealings have always been honest. Moreover, why steal an unmarked bottle rather than any number of more valuable items in the house? If our apartments were searched it was for a reason, and not just to find the key of your laboratory. As for your writings, why would a Singar steal those? Did you ever know one who could read more than a few letters of any language?'

Ludwig stopped in his tracks and stared at me.

'What are you saying, Gretl?'

'I'm saying the culprit is one who knows the house, who is familiar with the contents of the laboratory, and understands something of herbs and their uses; someone who has been taught to read and write; someone who knows the difference between a healing potion and a deadly poison, and while he may have no use for the former, would not hesitate to use the latter if it served his own perverted ends; someone who has no longer any cause to love this household, and who hates you with all his heart.'

'Andreas!' He uttered the name with a groan.

'Akhtar!' I said. 'Or someone in his pay.'

'But why would Akhtar ... Andreas steal the bottle? He cannot have known it was there.'

'It wasn't for that he disturbed your bedroom and my wardrobe. Akhtar wants the fylfot - Opa's gammadion! He saw the dispensary key by chance, and your book, and took advantage of his opportunity.'

'Why did the Duke's men not kill him?' muttered Ludwig, half to himself.

I recalled my grandfather's last words to me.

'Akhtar will answer to the law for his crimes,' I said.

'How will the law find him when he is nowhere to be found? He arrives from nowhere, does his work, and vanishes into thin air.'

'He'll come again, for he doesn't have what he wants,' I said. Again the vision of the Singari woman was in my mind's eye. Again, in my imagination, I was looking into her clouded mirror to see the face that had often haunted my nightmares since. Again I heard her words: *beware the one who wears the fylfot of the moon, the emblem of Angra Mainyu.*

Now I fully understood, and shuddered.

iii

The rats became more of a nuisance and we knew something had to be done. Even without the knowledge that their bodies were a harbour for the Black Death, we saw their presence in our stores and in the dark corners of our dwellings as an abomination. Even those who scoffed at my father's science - and many did so, either through ignorance or fear of sorcery - were disposed to follow his recommendations that the vermin be driven out or slaughtered.

But how? Many had tried. There were rumours from the towns that travellers, mendicants, Gypsies, priests and rogues pretended to answers in the expectation of reward, and that the townsmen in their desperation were duped into parting with gold in exchange for worthless elixirs, charms, amulets and snares. Of the more fanciful tales that reached us were those of the magic pipes with notes so sweet that any creature on earth would be enchanted and follow the musician wherever he went; and of the magic cat with an appetite so huge that it could devour a thousand rats in one meal.

The peasantry suffered both plague and rats in silence. Their traps were ineffective because the rats climbed out. At the manor house, our animals provided less protection than before because the rats were no longer afraid of them. The dogs were bitten in the legs, the cats found their adversaries more formidable than ever. Seeing the pestilence strike at their families, the country people again migrated to the towns, less crowded now because of the hundreds who had died thirteen years before.

By winter of that year, the bodies mounted in the streets and outside the walls awaiting burial. Poor weather meant more coughing and bad throats, and just as Ludwig had indicated, these symptoms seemed to spread the deadly sickness all the more, especially the kind which had killed my mother, in which the black boils had no time to appear. By good fortune, we ourselves remained free of it.

One grey day in February Ludwig returned home in surprising good spirits.

'I have an idea,' he told me when we were alone, 'that out of the unspeakable suffering and horror I've witnessed today some good may come. As I watched the death carts deliver their loads to the waiting pits, I saw how we might rid ourselves of the rats in great numbers. I can't say with certainty that it'll work but it's worth trying. If we do not act there will soon be no grain.'

We summoned family and servants to a conference.

'We'll dig two large trenches at front and back of the house,' Ludwig said.

'We've tried that already,' said Freddy. 'You know how easily the rats escaped.'

'I don't intend to let them escape this time,' said Ludwig. 'We'll destroy them while they lie helpless in the trenches. I'll need the help of men with spades, of women with long sticks and brooms, some dry hay and straw, and as much lamp oil as we can lay our hands on.'

I watched him supervise the digging. The trenches were about thirty paces in length, deep enough to cover a man's head if he knelt on the bottom, the sides as sheer as the diggers could make them. Only at one end was there a gradual slope. When the task was complete, Ludwig expressed satisfaction.

'Now,' he said to the labourers, 'we line the pits with hay and straw and pray it does not rain in the night, for that'll spoil the plan. Save all your scraps. In the morning we'll lay the bait. If necessary, we'll use surpluses from the larder.'

The setting of the traps was completed early the following day. The domestic animals, or such of them as could be found, were shut up in the barns. Scraps of meat, rotting apples, cheese rinds, the remains of our supper and any unwanted food we could find were placed at intervals on top of the thick matting. Heaps of grain, slices of fresh ham, cole, and other vegetables were added. More hay and straw was laid in bundles along the edges of the holes beside pitchforks.

'What now?' asked Freddy when this was all done, for until that moment my father had not explained his exact purpose.

'As to that,' said Ludwig, 'we may have a long wait ahead. The time can be used profitably in making torches. Prepare them well and use as much oil as you need.'

I began to have an inkling of what he intended. 'And the brooms, Father? And the long poles?'

'Take the women, Gretl. Comb the attics and cellars, under the stairs, and anywhere else that rats may be found. Drive them into the open with the poles. Poke out the holes in the walls where they nest. Brush them from the roofs of the storehouses and from the rafters of the barns. The dogs may have done some of the work for us, but let us further assist them in the task. Be sure to stay at more than arms length.'

His instructions were carried out. Soon, little groups of rats were seen scuttling across the garden, over the stones of the courtyard, and along the wall that encircled the pond.

'They're making for the fields,' I said, fearing that all our efforts had been for nothing. I knew now for certain that he hoped to lure the vermin into the trenches then fire the hay to prevent their escape. 'They have ignored the ditches and haven't taken the bait.'

'Be patient, Gretl,' said Ludwig. 'They'll return.'

For what seemed an age, we waited. The men stood at the sides of the pits, but not too close. In their hands they held torches and flints. They knew what they were be expected to do. Though the day was cold, I saw sweat on some of the faces. They were tense with anticipation; some feared they were about to see sorcery at work. It had been decided that Freddy would oversee the springing of the trap at the front of the house, Ludwig at the rear, and I sat on the ground, clutching my shoulders for warmth, not far from where my father squatted, overlooking the sloping end of the second ditch.

Still we waited. Then I saw two small whiskered noses emerge from the grass, and two sleek black bodies followed by their long tails crept warily towards the trench. Although I had often seen rats, I had never before studied them so calmly and at such close quarters. Compared to their tails, their bodies were short, scarcely as large as a man's foot. The sharp ears stood erect and seemed to be out of proportion with the narrow pointed snouts.

The two creatures reached the edge of the hole. They sat back on their hind feet, lifted their heads, and sniffed the air. With their front paws they stroked their whiskers as if to sharpen their senses to the smell of the tasty meal below. They peered down, then ran along the lip of the trench looking for the most suitable means of descent. Finding themselves at the sloping end, and being meantime joined by four others, they scurried away in the direction of the waiting banquet and disappeared from my view. For a moment I hated myself. The rats were God's creatures too and we were about to destroy them.

This feeling did not last. Many more rats appeared, crawling out from cover of the walls or from clumps of weed, drawn by their hunger and the scent of the food we had laid before them. They made for the sloping pathway, a trickle, then a stream of excited, squealing, creeping things, vying with each other to be first to reach the promised supper. Some could not wait, but leapt from the edge of the pit on top of their cousins feeding below. From where I sat, I could not see them, and rose to get a better view.

I shivered with horror and relived my worst childish nightmare. The trench was full of rats, hundreds of rats, squirming, squeaking, snapping at each other, snatching and gnawing at the meat, devouring the rotting fruit and wholesome grain. Ludwig had risen with me and beckoned to the womenfolk to approach.

'I'll need your brooms and poles again,' he said. 'Don't be afraid. Stand fast at the end here. As you see, this is the only point at which the rats can easily leave the trap. Whatever happens, you mustn't let them. Beat them back if they try.'

'Now light the torches and fire the grass!' he roared suddenly. He leapt into action himself and seized two pitchforks that lay close by.

Flint struck steel and, from the sparks, the torches, dampened by just the right amount of oil, burst into flames. The hay and straw left overnight was slower to kindle, but once it caught it burned brightly, great tongues of yellow shooting into the air and warming all who stood by. There was much scuttling in the trench. In terror of the flames, the rats left their repast and tried to escape. Those that reached the end were brushed back by the brooms, clubbed to death by the long sticks or impaled on the pitchforks. The remainder swarmed in a frenzy as the fire took hold in the pit.

'Pitch the burning grass into the hole,' shouted Ludwig above the noise of slaughter and the crackle of the flames. He took up the pitchforks again and fitted action to his words. Another five fellows, having drawn back when the fire took hold, ran forward again to obey his orders.

Without thinking, I seized a broom handle and began to sweep. Sparks flew into my face and scorched my clothes. I coughed and my eyes smarted as the hot smoke swirled all around. Worse still was the stench of burning flesh as the rats were consumed by the flames. Overcome by it, I vomited, and might have tumbled into the ditch myself had not my father's strong hands caught me and pulled me away.

It was over. The smoke cleared to reveal the men with spades, scooping up the earth and tossing it back from whence it had come. The house was free of rats. We had no doubt more would come, but with extra vigilance and some good fortune our grain supplies might last until next harvest. The barns and storehouses were repaired yet again, the stone crevices were plastered up, and we sat back to await the first signs of spring.

Hameln

i

One morning after breakfast, as soon as weather and daylight permitted, I saddled Princess, intending to ride the forest way to Hameln. This was not the Princess that Ennia had given me, of course, but a fully-grown filly, the second animal to be so named.

I had not visited my maternal grandparents for several months and my conscience was pricking me. They were elderly now. Opa Johann had long since handed over the running of his business to my uncle Leo, though he still managed the accounts himself; Oma Anna suffered crippling pains in her bones and muscles that made travelling difficult for her.

My father had an errand that day but he had promised to join me in Hameln by afternoon. He would travel by the high road, which was much quicker. On the other hand, I loved the forest and would take that way even in winter, though it meant an extra hour of travelling. Matti nagged me about the dangers but as we had never been troubled by robbers, I ignored her. Anyhow, I always fastened a belt and scabbard to Princess's saddle, and the hilt of my short sword was well within reach should anyone be foolish enough to attack me.

I had travelled a mere ten minutes and had not reached the edge of the forest when I met my grandparents' old servant Jonas coming in the opposite direction. He was pale and haggard and begged me to stop and accompany him back to the manor house.

'There's no cause for concern, Mistress Gretl,' he was quick to assure me. 'Our household has escaped the worst of the plague, God be thanked, and Master Leo's little ones are well. But the town is desperately in need of help.'

'Are the people suffering much?'

'As badly as any town in the Empire, I think. Every day the death carts roll past our windows, the bodies covered in black sores. An' more are struck down by the lung fever that killed Mistress Greta, your mother.

But in some ways we are worse off than any city.'

'You mean the rats?'

'The master is frantic lest they destroy Hameln's whole supply, an' there's little enough of that. They nest everywhere, though more in the poor quarter than among we richer folk. If people were mindful of your father's advice like the master and mistress it wouldn't be so bad. They'll tell you that! I only wish I could be sure it's not God's judgement.'

The old man crossed himself, cleared his throat and shook his head wearily.

'If only the rats were all.'

'There's more?'

'More an' worse! Hameln is cursed. The milk turns sour as soon as it's in the pails. Domestic animals die. Horses go lame, ewes miscarry their lambs, and some of last year's wine harvest is spoiled. It's all the fault of a 'Gyptian we drove from the town square.'

' 'Gyptian?' I echoed. 'You mean one of the Singari.'

'Aye. That's the word. Singari – what your other gran'father used to call 'em.'

'I fear I've no remedy for curses, Jonas,' I said lightly as I rode beside him back along the route I had come. 'But maybe Father can devise a plot to rid Hameln of its rats. Or of enough of them! We did it here and should be able to do it there.'

Our table was still laid for breakfast but I had already eaten and watched while Jonas helped himself to some meat and cheese. It always amused my father that this old man, so subservient and obliging in the Queck household should make free with our food and drink, and he never reprimanded him.

'What about this curse, Jonas?' I said when he had finished and was wiping his lips with the back of his hand.

I must have spoken lightly again for he glanced sharply at me. There was too much of Opa in me for me to believe in curses and my scepticism must have shown. In Jonas's eyes, I suppose, I was forward and too like a youth in my habits. My grandmother thought the same and was ever trying to discourage me from meddling in affairs she believed belonged to the men.

It was not the first time I had encountered Hameln superstitions. The truth was, I think, that there being so little going on in the town to disturb the daily humdrum of life, anything out of the ordinary stirred the popular imagination. It was told that, about a hundred years ago, an itinerant cleric had stolen the youth of the town and had spirited them away to a magic land beyond human knowledge. Truly, many young men - and women too, I do not doubt - had given up their lives in the Crusades of Palestine, and the population had suffered as a result. However, the gossips of Hameln had woven around this circumstance tales of magic and mystery to tell to their grandchildren.

I had expected Jonas to begin a new tale of this kind. Spoiled wine, soured milk and lame animals are so unremarkable as to be unworthy of mention. However, it became clear soon that there was more to this supposed curse than I had believed.

'It began in January,' he told me. 'Master Gottlieb was heard to offer a reward of twenty gold coins to anyone who could drive the rats from his grain stores. I don't doubt he would have paid as much for, without grain, he'd be ruined. The others laughed, not at Gottlieb's misfortune, but on account of the tales. Many tricksters have taken gold without being able to reduce the rat population by one. If Gottlieb were foolish enough to part with his money to a knave, the other merchants could not help it.

'Then the Gypsy came. It was after roll call. They were all in the town square – the master, Gottlieb, Baurr, Vogelweise the tailor and some others, arguing as they always do. This fellow came right up and asked if he could claim the reward. He was small and crooked. No one could see his face because he wore a hood like a cleric, but they judged him old from the sound of his voice an' from the fact that he leant on a stick.'

'He had a magic pipe too, I suppose?'

It was an unkind jest but I couldn't resist. The old man flashed me another look as if deciding whether or not I was mocking him.

'I'm sorry, Jonas,' I said. 'Please go on.'

'He did have a pipe, Mistress Gretl. A little one of beaten tin, hanging on a leather thong round his neck.

' 'How do we know you'll not merely take our friend's gold and run off?' asks Baurr.

284

' 'Were I to try,' says the Gypsy dryly, 'would you not easily catch me? As you see, my back is crooked, and I can walk only with the aid of a stick. Besides, I'm able to offer you proof of my talent.'

'He blew on his pipe and, to the surprise of everyone, four or five hideous rats appeared and crept obediently to his feet.

' 'If you can drive all the rats from the town as easily,' says Gottlieb, 'you shall indeed receive twenty gold pieces.'

''Nay,' says the Gypsy, 'the contract was for your storehouses. Nothing was said about the whole town!'

'Just then, Master Leo arrived on the scene. For a moment it seemed the piper straightened his back and stared at him keenly.'

'Leo recognised him?' I asked.

'I don't believe so, but he knew Master Leo all right, as you will hear.

'The master was angry. 'He's a rascal like all the others,' he says, 'an' you are all fools to be taken in by him. And you are doubly the fool to make rash promises, Gottlieb. I don't know how the trick was performed, but trick it was.'

'Then Leo kicked one of the rats and they all fled. The Gypsy turned on him. 'You'll soon learn whether 'twas trick or no,' he growls. 'From now on your town is cursed - and you, Master Queck most of all!'

'He tapped his stick on the cobbles and shuffled away before anyone could recover from their surprise. At the edge of the square he looked round once then disappeared down one of the dark lanes.'

I did not jest again. The matter was more serious than I had imagined. On the morning of the day on which Ludwig's bottle of poison was stolen, I had seen such a Gypsy from my casement. He was shuffling among the tents and carts encamped in our lower meadow.

I knew it was Akhtar who had struck at us by stealing my father's writing and the poison made from rats' blood. The feeling that I was being watched, the evidence of the disordered closets, and the final realisation that only he had the knowledge to carry out the deed, left me in no doubt. Such were his powers that he might easily deceive the picket, penetrate our meagre defences, and by dulling the mind of any servant who stood in his path, pass unnoticed into the house. I always carried Sigmund's dagger in my bodice. I had not previously thought of it as a weapon, merely a solace, but had lately taken to fingering it to calm my lurking disquiet.

I had never considered that Akhtar might adopt a simple disguise to make his task the easier but Jonas, without being aware, had told me my evil cousin had done just that. I was sure that the crooked old Gypsy with the stick and the hood to cover his face was Akhtar. I would have needed no convincing to acknowledge that honest Singari feared him and would be reluctant to incur his anger.

Now, by cursing Hameln, Akhtar had struck at us yet again, not only at my grandfather and Leo on whom he had sworn revenge, but at Ludwig, the brother he had wronged; for he must have known that my father would not refuse help to the town if he were asked. It came to me that we were being lured to Hameln for a reckoning - a final confrontation with this madman who would still, if he could, take by force what he could not possess by right of inheritance; who would learn, by whatever means, the whereabouts of the fylfot.

I knew with certainty it was on account of the fylfot that I had been watched, that my apartments and those of Ludwig had been searched. Akhtar would not rest until he knew its hiding-place. By forgetting the Singari woman's words and secreting the cross in my grandfather's tomb I had made a grave error. Although reason denied it, my heart told me that by wearing the fylfot as Opa intended I would have been protected from harm. Now, my mistake had exposed the innocent people of Hameln to Akhtar's vengeance.

These were my thoughts, yet I said nothing of them to my father. I had no proof that Akhtar and the hooded Singar were one and the same. I reproached myself later that I did not speak out, but how would that have changed things? It was vanity that sealed my lips. Akhtar had not known me. He had not recognised in Gretl von Hasenbach the innocent maiden Lisa he had ravished. He had remarked on my looks, but his eyes had been on the gold talisman.

It was not enough that he should deprive me of my childhood. He had not known me, and for that I hated him as much as I despised and loathed him for the deed itself.

ii

My plans were now awry. I had meant to go to Hameln and still needed
to meet my father there. Jonas's pony was rested but he was tired and
could not match my pace. So I left him to return home at his leisure while
I rode hell for leather through the forest.

The death cart met me at the east gate. The walking corpses who
pulled it were from the very lowest station of life, the poor who lived in
the shadow of the walls, or in hovels on the south bank of the Weser. Sick
beyond hope, the four men would soon find a place at the bottom of the
wagons they struggled to haul the few final paces, to where the gaping
pits stood ready to accept the remains. These four might once have been
country folk, driven by fear to take shelter in the town. I could scarcely
tell whether they were young or old.

The cart contained six corpses, and I saw by the size of the bundles
that at least three of them were children. Soon they'll be unable to replace
the porters and diggers, I thought. If this plague lasted much longer, there
would be no one left in Hameln. The streets were already quiet. Those
people who were about glanced suspiciously at me as I passed.

When I reached my destination, my father was already there. My
grandparents welcomed me warmly, but they seemed distracted. Johann
was thinner than he had once been and his blue eyes were tired. Anna was
gaunt, the rosiness in her face gone, and there was more grey in her hair
than at our last meeting. Only Leo's three children seemed unconcerned
by the town's plight. They played happily round the fire on which a pot
of stew sizzled.

'The day before yesterday there were eight taken, and last Sabbath
ten,' my grandfather was saying as I entered the parlour.

'Is it mostly the poor and migrants who suffer?' my father asked.

'Indeed, Lou. But there have been deaths among the wealthier
families too. Since Yuletide, Baurr has lost a son, the candlemaker two,
and Vogelweise a daughter, to mention only a few.'

'And this curse, does it affect only the merchant families?'

'I can't say for sure. It seems so, but how can we tell if the poor are
affected? They have no animals, and few possessions. These are wretched
times, Lou, and will get worse before they get better. Truly, I don't know

what to do.'

'First things first,' said my father. 'Tell me more of these happenings. The milk? The lame animals? We know enough about the rats already.'

'We'll come to the rats later,' said Johann. 'I have other grave news for you, Lou. Your brother was here in Hameln.'

'Andreas! How would he dare come here when the Duke's forces are still on the lookout for him?'

'He was here, I assure you. Listen and I'll tell you. Until now, only Leo and I knew.

'I told you about Gottlieb and his reward, and about the old Gypsy. Well, something about his voice seemed familiar. I couldn't let Gottlieb and the others make fools of themselves so I spoke out. As the rascal uttered his curse, his hood slipped back from his brow and I caught a glimpse of his face. He quickly pulled the hood down but I had seen enough. It was Andreas for certain. I should have raised the alarm but did not, and so have condemned the town to suffer.'

'Don't blame yourself too harshly,' said Ludwig. 'Let's instead examine the nature of this curse and its effects. Do I have your permission to visit your stables and question your servants?'

'We have lost two to the Mortality. But question the others if you think it'll serve any purpose. As for the house and stables, you're free to treat them as your own.'

Having examined the stables and horses, my father left on a tour of the town, in order to inspect the dairy, the wine cellars and the butcher's shop, and to talk to the chief citizens. He was gone a long time, during which I related what we had discovered concerning the plague's origins, about my father's hope for an antidote, and how we had rid the Bachhagen manor of its rats. I did not mention the poison, nor its theft, for fear of adding to my grandparents' distress. As it was, Anna's face paled with horror as I told how we had enticed the rats into ditches and set fire to them.

When Ludwig returned he was shaking his head and muttering to himself.

'Is there no hope for us?' Johann asked him.

'The situation is desperate, though not beyond hope. The real enemy of Hameln is not my brother but is, as I suspected, something far worse. We must act quickly, before the malady becomes more deep-rooted.'

'The Great Mortality!' I cried.

'God knows that is bad enough, Gretl, though I speak of another malady. You are a man of influence here, Goodfather. Give me leave to address your friends here in your house. I can't guarantee to deliver them from their wretchedness but I can at least tell them the truth about this so-called curse.'

Within the hour, Baurr, Gottlieb, Vogelweise, and half-a-dozen others had assembled in the main room. They were greeted solemnly. Every face bore signs of the misfortunes they had endured, the sorrow of losing loved ones, the blow inflicted by the loss of their trade, or the despair of facing a future blighted by the terrible curse they believed had been laid upon them. There was an air of expectation too as they waited for the silence to be broken. Ludwig sat thoughtfully, his chin on his chest, as if trying to gather his strength for a coming battle. At last he rose. I wondered what he was going to say.

'You know me, tradespeople of Hameln,' he began. 'Most of you came to celebrate my wedding here, and you know I lost my wife to the Mortality fourteen years ago.' His voice shook, but he went on. 'I'm no shopkeeper, yet I understand the principles of your trade because I have managed land, and farms. I have studied physic too, as you know. But though I can treat coughs and fevers, aching limbs, wounds and festering sores, I can't deliver you unaided from the sickness that runs riot in your town.'

There were murmurs of disappointment.

'I've seen the death carts,' continued my father. 'I've watched the rats scurry in and out of your warehouses. You've told me of soured milk, of polluted and rotting food, of dying animals, and I have been a witness to some of these things myself. But I tell you, even within your own town, there are many who are worse off than you. You still have your stores, your horses, your homes and your fine clothes. The poor of Hameln have no such possessions. They have one main enemy - the black plague itself - and they have nothing to lose but their lives.'

The faces of the merchants lost their expressions of eager anticipation.

Instead they wore perplexed frowns.

'This isn't what we came to hear, Master Queck,' said one. 'It's not only the poor who suffer the plague. Your goodson speaks no comfort at all.'

'Is it not our children too who are buried with indecent haste in communal graves?' said Vogelweise. 'You have a beautiful daughter, Master von Hasenbach. Would that I could have seen mine grow to be half her age.'

'Forgive me if I seemed unfeeling,' Ludwig answered back. 'If I speak harshly it's because I see you suffer needlessly. I know the Great Mortality is your enemy, though even that may be fought and conquered. However, it's not of the Great Mortality that I speak.'

There were cries of the Curse from several of the audience.

'The curse in truth!' cried my father, scarcely paused for breath. 'Hameln is indeed under a curse, but it's a curse of your own making; every one of you must bear some responsibility for it. Hameln is a victim of its own fear, of its own indifference. Listen to me! You are so afraid of the plague that you forget the simple rules by which you live your lives in normal times. Your minds are so preoccupied with your trade, your cellars, your shops and smithies, that you fail to see what is going on around you.'

This outburst brought forth some angry shouts. Johann laid a hand on my father's arm.

'Do not go too far,' he said.

'They want my help, so they should hear the truth,' Ludwig said. 'I'll go only so far as I need.'

He appealed to the citizens in turn. 'Listen to me, my friends. I don't mean to insult you. It is only that, as an outsider, I see things you do not. You are cursed, you tell me; your milk sours in the pails. So it does, and will continue to do so if you do not clean out these pails and rid the dairy of the rats that are allowed to run about unchecked.

'You are cursed, you tell me; the horses are lame. So they are, and will continue so as long as you ride and work them without tending and re-shoeing their hooves.

'Again, you tell me you are cursed. Animals die and abort their young. So they will if they are deprived of proper feeding, if they are kept in vile conditions, and if you continue to slaughter your meat in the same quarters that house healthy ewes.

'As for wine spoilage, am I not right in thinking wine will turn to vinegar if left too long exposed to the air, if you seal the casks with dirty broken corks, or if you empty it into old flagons?'

'Even if what you say is true, Master von Hasenbach,' said the wine merchant, 'how can I and my fellow citizens see to all these things when our labourers have the fever, when the apprentices are being carried out, half-a-dozen in one week, and when all others on whom we depend for our living are either dead, or too afraid to leave their homes?'

'I cannot direct you in that, sir,' said Ludwig. 'I only tell you what needs to be done. But you can count on my help.'

'Louey is right,' said Leo, who had sat in silence throughout the meeting. 'I see now how we neglect our duties, and I'm as guilty as any. Most of us have wives, and a few have sons and daughters capable of wielding a broom. Let's attend to the things we have put off too long. Above all, let's devise a means of driving out the rats, for they are the principle cause of our misery.'

'What of the Gypsy?' said Gottlieb. 'I acknowledge my foolishness in offering twenty gold marks to be rid of the vermin, but surely a curse cannot be lifted so easily.'

'Did you not hear Master von Hasenbach?' laughed Baurr. 'There is no curse. Are your ears so full of rat droppings that you missed the whole of the physician's pretty speech?'

Gottlieb fell silent with embarrassment. My father came to his aid.

'The Singar had his part to play just the same,' he said. 'The curse, if I may continue to call it that, began long before he set foot in Hameln, but it needed only one word from the fellow to rekindle your fears. If I could diagnose the malady afflicting your town so easily, do you not think others might do so too? The stranger had only to play upon your superstition.'

'From whence does a hunchback traveller who relies on a stick to support his legs acquire such wisdom? And why should he wish us harm for so small a slight?' asked Baurr.

'Since I know the answers to that, I will not lie to you,' said Ludwig. 'Your hunchback was no Singar. No Gypsy. Indeed he was no hunchback at all. The mysterious piper and would-be ratcatcher was none other than my brother Andreas.'

A number of citizens had not been convinced by my father's arguments, and at this declaration there were gasps of dismay.

'The man who calls himself Akhtar?' said the blacksmith.

'We know of this brother,' said Gottlieb. 'We've heard he is a powerful sorcerer.'

'What if the pails can't be washed out and the floors can't be swept?' asked a man who had not spoken before. 'How do we know it was not this Andreas – this Akhtar - who brought the rats among us, and caused the Great Mortality to strike at our children?'

'Because it is not so,' said my father. 'The plague rages throughout Saxony, and across the empire, as it did fourteen years ago. And I have told you what you must do. Leave my brother to me and to the law. He has no interest in you. He seeks only revenge on Master Queck and his family and, through them, to strike at me and my daughter.'

'I for one am convinced that the remedy lies with ourselves,' said Vogelweise. 'We should begin straightway.'

'I agree,' said the blacksmith, 'but can Master von Hasenbach suggest how we might be rid of the rats? If he's to be believed, they are the cause of the Black Death itself.'

'There are many ways,' said Ludwig. 'Poke out their holes with long sticks. Block up their nests and set the cats on them. Chase them from your shops and storehouses and drive them into the river. Build traps, and use the scraps from your table to ensnare them. I'm no wiser than you in such matters and maybe you can think of better schemes. But you must all act together.'

'If we are to go among the rats, how are we to be protected from the sickness you say they carry?' asked Gottlieb doubtfully. 'What is it that we should fear? Is it their bite?'

'No, it is their fleas!' said Leo. 'I do not understand the reasons, but it is of the fleas that we must be wary.'

There was general laughter. I had been sitting with my grandmother in the chimney-corner, listening proudly to my father as he delivered his oration. Now I now sprang to my feet angrily.

'How dare you laugh at the truth,' I said. The laughter stopped and several men turned to stare at me. My grandmother tugged at the hem of my dress. Leo flushed and bit his lip. But forward I was and forward I would continue to be.

'Tell them of the antidote, Father,' I said over hastily. 'Don't let them mock your discoveries.'

'What antidote does your daughter speak of, Master Ludwig?' asked Gottlieb with the rashness for which he was noted. 'If you've found a cure for the black plague, I'll gladly give forty gold pieces for half a jar of the potion.'

'Gretl speaks of a formula I discovered among the physicians of Asia Minor,' answered Ludwig. 'I carry a bottle of the substance with me even now. But it's untested.'

'Then test it,' demanded the blacksmith. 'There is one lying sick in my house who would be glad of it. It can't do more harm than the fever has already done.'

'It is no cure,' said my father, shaking his head. 'This substance will bring on symptoms of the plague, but to a minor extent, so as to give immunity to further attacks.'

'I don't understand this physic,' said Gottlieb, 'but you'll have a gold piece for just a taste of the salve. I'll risk it!'

'So shall we,' echoed some other voices.

'I'll try it too,' said Baurr, 'and if I'm not dead by tomorrow, I'll give it to my wife and children. At least there'll be hope for them.'

'You're welcome to try my prescription,' said Ludwig, 'and I'll take no money for it. But you misunderstand the treatment, I think. To be effective, the medicine must reach the veins. It is applied through a cut in the arm.'

Those who had crowded forward to see my father's bottle and to sample the fluid drew back. Even Gottlieb shook his head.

'I'll not try that if you pay me twenty gold marks,' said he, making the sign of the Cross. 'It's devilry.'

Most of those present shook their heads. Even Leo looked doubtful.

'You are all cowards!' I shouted, breaking through the half-circle they had formed. 'Look - there is nothing to it!'

I snatched Sigmund's silver dagger from my bodice and, before Ludwig could stop me, unsheathed it and pressed the point into my forearm. A trickle of blood flowed from the neat wound over my wrist and into the palm of my hand. A spot or two fell on my gown and onto the floor.

'You cannot deny me now, Father,' said I. 'Let me be the one to test your antidote.'

He hesitated, but seeing that all eyes were on him, he removed the stopper from the bottle and, taking his own dagger, he poured a little of the fluid onto the blade. It was thick like molasses. He applied it to the cut and massaged it into the wound.

Then Leo stepped forward.

'Gretl will not be alone,' said he. 'I'll test the medicine too. Surely it can't do any harm, and if it protects from the Great Mortality ...'

He held out his arm. There were some whispers of approval among the crowd as Ludwig made the incision and held the prescription to the wound. However, no one else offered themselves.

'Now bind your arms with clean cloth,' my father said, resealing the bottle and replacing it in the pouch at his belt.

As Leo and I hurried away to find some bandages, my grandfather rose.

'We all have work to do,' said he to his fellow townsmen, 'and the day will soon be over. Tomorrow we'll meet in the square as usual to decide what to do about the rats.'

I awoke in the night with a raging thirst. I reached out in the darkness and grasped the goblet on the table by my bed, hoping that I had not drunk all the wine. Fortunately there was a little remaining and I swallowed it hastily. It refreshed me for the time being, and I drifted into a sleep disturbed by awful dreams.

I was alone on a bare hillside. Although the sun shone brightly, the sky was black and the stars had come out. As I watched, the twinkling points of light began to take shape. One became my father, riding a white horse. Another was Akhtar, flying on the wind, his black cloak streaming behind. He had a tail, and I knew if I could only reach and cut it off I would be free of him forever. Just as I lunged with my dagger however, he changed, his head became a rat's head, and I fled, screaming soundlessly as this monstrosity pursued me, gnashing its teeth and flailing the empty air with the tail that had grown to twice its original length. The next instant the head was Akhtar's head again, this time perched obscenely on a rat's body. He leapt, pinning me to the earth, and I awoke gasping for breath and soaked in perspiration. At first I dared not sleep again, but eventually tiredness overcame me and I slumbered soundly, dreaming only of my lover's embrace.

iii

When I rose next morning, I felt light-headed but otherwise well enough. I could hear hammering and the sounds of bustle from the high street below my window, as the townspeople resumed the tasks my father had recommended. After a hasty breakfast, I joined the company, collecting water, sweeping floors and driving penned animals to pasture outside the walls. The weather was warm for the time of year and I perspired as I worked.

There were three deaths in Hameln that day and four new cases of the plague. Ludwig visited as many of the sufferers as he could and I helped him, holding patients' heads while he fed them draughts prepared from the fungi he had gathered. I applied wet cloths to their brows and did my best to comfort them. By early afternoon I was feeling tired. Whether this was due to the effects of the antidote or to the labours of the morning I could not tell. I was unused to heavy work and my arm throbbed painfully.

In every quarter of town, the war against the rats was waged in earnest. The citizens of Hameln, rich and poor alike, chased them from their lofts and cellars into the lanes. As the creatures fled, women stood in the doorways of their homes beating cooking utensils against pails and pots to encourage them in their headlong retreat and bar them from re-entering. Carpenters and smiths built all kinds of traps. They succeeded in ensnaring only a few rats. Many more were driven into the river.

It was not enough. Though many houses were free of vermin, the rats that escaped ran off down the dark alleys to look for new lodgings. Those that had made their nests in the high walls could not be enticed down, and for every one that perished in the Weser another struggled ashore to plague us again.

By evening my head ached. At supper, I drank only wine mixed with water. Leo too did not have his customary appetite. I noticed him push food away.

My father questioned us both keenly about our symptoms.

'They will pass,' he said, but I saw he was tense and anxious.

We renewed the battle the following day. All through the night I had tossed and turned. Never before had I feared the darkness but I did now as visions of death tormented my fevered mind. My temples and forearm throbbed, my back ached and I thought I could feel swellings in my armpit. Dawn brought relief from the nightmares and to my tortured body so, putting on a brave face, I ventured out.

My father was with a gang of townsfolk in the square. The men had brought hand-carts. They were carrying coils of rope and long planks, the women baskets filled with titbits, scraps from the table, apples, and cheese rind. Some of the food was bad and smelled terribly. One cart was full of grain, two more were heaped with hay and straw, while the remainder were empty.

'We will trap the rats as we did at Bachhagen,' Ludwig told me. 'The carts will serve instead of trenches. You'll see what I have in mind if you come along, Gretl. That is, if you're well enough.'

I assured him that nothing would make me stay behind and we set off together towards the river. There, he issued his orders, divided the workforce and sent the groups to different points along the bank.

'Remember! It's a question of mathematics,' he said. 'The wood has been cut to just the right length. If too short, the angle of ascent would be too steep, and the rats, although good climbers, would be discouraged. If too long, the weight of the wood might upset the carts before we are ready.'

We lined up the carts as close to the water as we could. Then we prepared the traps - first a lining of the dry grasses, followed by the grain, and finally the scraps. We laid the planks of wood so that one of their ends just overlapped the rear lip of the carts, forming a gently-sloping gangway. More of the bait we sprinkled on the ground nearby and along the plank. Every cart now stood level on its two wheels, balanced between the weight of its handles at the front and pressure from the plank at its opposite end.

Word was sent round the town to redouble efforts to drive the remaining rats into the open. Apprentices scaled the walls at great risk to their lives and tried to dislodge the creatures from the ledges and crevices. Only a few animals fell to their deaths. The clamour of ladles striking saucepans and pails produced better results. Packs of rats scurried hell-for-leather along the cobbles in our direction. At first, they ignored the carts and made for the bridge or the muddy banks of the Weser, still high and treacherous from the winter's rain. Many were pitched into the flood by waiting citizens.

I had played this game before and sat patiently on a smooth boulder, trying to puzzle out what would happen when the rats were attracted to our bait. None of our party carried torches, and I knew that unless we fired the hay, or found some other means of imprisoning our quarry, it would escape. The rotting meat and leavings would satisfy the rats only for so long. I had often seen them jump and did not think the carts could hold them.

As if in answer to my concern, I spied Leo and Baurr with a group of townsfolk by the east gate. My uncle and the merchant each carried two unlit torches. The others wielded their brooms and poles to encourage the rats away from the dwellings and shops, and towards the traps.

My father took his seat beside me and we continued to wait.

The first rats emerged from a hole in the wall not far from where we sat. Cautiously they sniffed the bait. One placed its forepaws on the nearest plank as if testing the wood's strength. Another leapt onto the wheel of the second cart and tried to clamber over the rim, but lost its balance. Before long, several of the beasts had crawled along the gangways and disappeared from view. We could hear them squeaking with delight as they sampled the meal we had prepared. No one dared move. The slightest distraction would have sent the uncommitted scurrying away.

Still we waited. More rats appeared. They climbed in and out of the spokes of the wheels, devoured the grain and, sensing more was to be had nearby, looked about for a means of access to it. Some ran off but returned as they met others arriving for a share of the pickings. The carts were soon alive with vermin, scratching and screeching as they fought for the remaining scraps.

Suddenly the wheels of one cart rolled forward, and the plank fell to the ground. The cart tipped forward on its handles. As the others followed suit, Ludwig gave the signal to light the torches and fire the hay. Sparks flew as the tinder caught. Fuelled by the oil, flames leapt high round the rim of the carts. Once again I caught the horrid, suffocating stench of cooking flesh as the fire spread, devouring the frenzied creatures in the traps, taking hold of the wooden slats, and turning from yellow to scarlet as the carts themselves began to burn. A few rats managed to jump clear and the men struck at them with the still-glowing brands.

For a while the heat was intense and there was little we could do but watch. Once the flames began to die, Ludwig rushed forward, seized hold of a plank, and applied it as a lever to the wheels. I ran to assist, and this served as an example to others who hastened to employ their planks in the same way. The wood of the wheels was already alight, but was not consumed sufficiently to thwart our purpose. We heaved. The axles groaned, and the wheels turned, propelling the smouldering carts off the path into the soft mud of the riverbank. We heaved again, and this time the axles gave way, what was left of the carts and their gruesome contents pitched over, and the whole structures crumbled and sank silently in the waters of the Weser.

As the smoke and steam cleared, something caught my eye and I glanced over in the direction of the bridge. A solitary figure stood half-concealed by the parapet and close to the far bank, apparently watching us with great interest. He was of slight build, with a crooked back, and dressed in dark clothing. His head and face were hidden in a hood, and he leaned on a stick for support. I blinked to be sure of what I had seen, and when I looked again he had disappeared.

iv

Was it my imagination or had I really seen Akhtar on the bridge? Did I suffer still from the weak poison that flowed in my veins - for such I supposed it to be - or had he continued to spy on me since the day he stole my father's manuscript? He would not, I was sure, risk taking lodging in Hameln as his normal self nor, having once appeared in such dramatic fashion as the crippled piper, would he wish to linger in the town. However, there were many places in the hills or forest where a man might hide.

I thought of the irony of the situation. The place where I had seen the apparition stand was the very spot where by accident Andreas's natural father, the priest, must have met his end. Was that Fate, and was it delivering a message for me? Or had I in reality seen nothing at all?

Illusion or not, I could not dismiss it from my mind. Nor could I be free of the fear that many happenings of recent weeks - the search of my apartments, the theft of the poison, the cursing of Hameln - were part of Akhtar's twisted scheme to entice us into a trap.

Did he plan to be rid of us, perhaps poison us as we slept, Johann and Leo as revenge for their part in the failure of his earlier scheme, my father and I so that he might be unopposed in his bid to take the Bachhagen estates for himself? No doubt too he planned to steal the fylfot, if he could find it. Akhtar had meant to be recognised by my grandfather in the town square. That too was part of his plan to draw us away from the safety of our own manor and bring us to a place where he might more easily strike at us.

I was distracted from these fearful thoughts by the sound of laughter and running footsteps. A group of children were coming down the high street, skipping from side to side, clapping their hands and chanting rhymes.

There was a mixture of ages, boys and girls, rich and poor. The girls had donned their best dresses and wore ribbons in their hair. Even the lads carried ribbons that they waved excitedly in the air. Some had toy drums, others wood whistles.

Behind came a band of older citizens. I could see my grandfather and grandmother, Gottlieb, Baurr, Vogelweise, and a number of the men who, earlier, had wheeled their carts along the river bank. Their faces were blackened with smoke as I knew mine must be, but they bore none of the signs of tension and despair evident two days before. Hameln was not free of the plague, yet its people, scornful of my father's theory concerning the fleas, had nevertheless overcome their superstition, and now had cause to hope their future would be brighter. They had learned how to fight back.

I forgot the stiffness in my body as the children crowded round, took my hands in theirs, and drew me into their circle:

'One, two, three and four,
Soon the plague will be no more.
Five, six, seven and eight,
Now the Devil will have to wait.'

They chanted and danced round and round, making me quite dizzy in the process. My father was surrounded by smiling merchants and tradesmen, eager to press his hand or to clap him on the shoulders. Gottlieb was among the first.

'Here's my purse with the twenty gold coins I promised. They belong to you.'

'Keep your money,' said my father. 'If Hameln is rid of rats, it's through your own efforts.'

'Nay, Master Ludwig, the gold is yours. I confess I don't believe in your fleas, but had you not spoken as you did we would still be living under a curse brought about by our own foolishness.'

'Well said, Gottlieb,' said my grandfather. 'Lou has earned your reward and can accept it with a clear conscience. It's little enough payment for his help.'

'I'll not take it,' said my father, 'but perhaps I might suggest how it be spent. Re-house the poor within the walls of Hameln. There is room to build. Employ labourers to tear down the shacks where they live. I fear the rats will continue to breed there unless something is done. Have masons put up new dwellings and, if any gold is left over, give it to the Church to be used for charitable works.'

Gottlieb agreed and Opa Johann promised to see the project through to completion. There was a great deal of cheering as my father was hoisted on shoulders and carried in a procession to the town square.

I think half the population was already there. The news had travelled and the celebrations had begun. Some folk carried flagons of wine, others baskets of fresh food. Many had brought musical instruments and they struck up in chorus, though not always with the same tune. Friendships were renewed and old enmities forgotten as neighbours greeted neighbours and shared with them their supper.

No one was willing to spoil the fun and, despite the coolness of the evening, the dancing and merrymaking continued by torchlight well into the early hours.

Akhtar

i

Next day, I wakened later than usual. The sun was already up. It shone through the lattices of my window, warming my feet through the blanket. My arm still hurt where I had inflicted the knife wound and applied Ludwig's potion, but my head no longer ached, and there was no sign of unpleasant swellings on any part of my body.

My recollections on waking, and the events of that day are fresh in my memory. At first, I thought my father must have added a sleeping draught to the wine I had supped at bedtime but, almost immediately, I begged his pardon for my suspicions. My senses fully alert, I reached over and took up the goblet. It was full and I remembered I had not touched it. Drugged or not, it was not wine that had caused me to sleep past the usual hour, but some other circumstance.

Always, when staying with Opa Johann, I had been served by Angelika, the girl he retained to prepare food and see to the other needs of his guests. She was about thirteen years old, plump and rosy-cheeked, the daughter of Jonas Graube and his wife, the housekeeper. Angelika would enter the room at first light with a board of bread and cheese and a pitcher of water. She would lay them on a table then, treading carefully so as not to wake me, cross the room and throw open the casement to let in the morning air. Being of a larger than normal figure, the poor girl could not perform these tasks without drawing forth from the slats a plaintive creak that immediately caused me to sit up, rub my eyes, and wish her good morning in a tone of mock chastisement. We had often played this game, and during my visits it became a routine.

That morning, there was no groan from the boards and no food placed by the bed. The air in the room was stale. I rose and went to the window, opened the shutter and drew several deep breaths. Something else was wrong. Not only was there no Angelika, but the street below was empty, save for a pedlar hauling his cart over the cobbles, and a group of men in the square, huddled together in conversation.

From the hall below came the sound of raised voices. I ran to the stairs and looked down. Mistress Graube was talking and gesturing excitedly to my father.

'I swear to you, Master Ludwig,' she was saying, 'the maid is nowhere to be found! We called her to no avail.'

'That's not possible,' retorted Ludwig. 'Children do not just disappear. Perhaps she has gone with the Queck children to play in the next street.'

'Angelika takes her duties seriously. She wouldn't go from the house without my leave. And, besides, the master's grandchildren are not in the street.'

'What!' My father sounded uneasy. 'Are they missing too? Wait, I'll fetch my cloak ...'

He got no further. There was a loud banging on the outer door and Jonas rushed in, accompanied by two of my grandfather's fellow merchants.

'What's amiss,' demanded my father. 'Is everyone mad this morning?'

'The children are amiss, sir,' Jonas said, quite breathless. 'Master Gottlieb's son and the wine merchant's two daughters are nowhere to be found. Master Baurr here vows his entire family has disappeared!'

'The town's empty,' said Baurr. His face was pale and his brow moist with perspiration.

Something was very wrong. By this hour the apprentices should have been at their trade and the maidens playing their sinister game in the square. It was strange how, in these dark days, death and the marks of the Great Mortality should play such a prominent part in the play of children:

A-t-ishoo! A-t-ishoo! We all fall down!

Would that harmless chanting could have protected them from Akhtar's scheming.

I freshened my face and arms with water in the tub by the window, left from the previous day, and dressed hurriedly. When I was half-way down the stairs, I heard a dreadful scream. It came from my grandfather's counting-room on the floor below mine. In three bounds, my father had mounted the steps and reached the door, just ahead of me. Opa Johann lay on the floor in his shift. His face was twisted like an awful mask. Protruding eyes stared sightlessly up at us from their sockets.

Anna leapt at Ludwig, screaming and beating him about the face and head with clenched fists.

'You've killed him, you murderer! What use was your science here? All your physic, potions and vapours could not save him. Your promises even less! First my son, then my dear Greta, while you stood idly by! You could do nothing then and you can do nothing now.'

She broke down in tears. Ludwig gently but firmly removed her hands from his neck.

'Take care of your grandmother, Gretl,' he said.

He bent over the body and lifted the arms to examine the cold skin for tell-tale signs. He raised the shift and peered at the private parts, seeking confirmation for the diagnosis he had already made. But no black blemishes were visible. If it were plague that killed him it must be the rarest and deadliest variety of all. It eats at the brain of its victim and drives him to madness before other symptoms have time to appear.

Ludwig closed the staring eyes and, as he did so, the head fell to one side revealing a red scar on the neck. It was a fresh wound, drawing little blood but leaving the flesh swollen and ugly.

'This is no natural death,' he said. 'I'll swear this is murder.'

My grandmother did not seem to hear him. She had stopped crying and was wiping the tears with the sleeve of her dress.

'When I awoke he wasn't in the bed,' she said. 'What was he doing in the counting-room? He was in good health yesterday. Never a sneeze.'

'He's cold,' my father said. 'But this cut is no more than an hour or two old. If it was poison, it took effect quickly.'

Fear began to take hold of me. I felt a tingling in my neck. 'Akhtar! It's Akhtar who has done this,' I said. 'He has taken the children and murdered grandfather when he tried to stop him. He has used a signet ring, smeared with the poison he stole, to make that wound. Is this how he takes revenge on our family?'

'We can't know that for sure.'

'You defend him!' I retorted.

'There's no proof that Andreas is the culprit.'

'We don't need it,' I said, clasping my hand to my forehead. My strange power of foresight was getting stronger and I could almost see the deed being done. 'I know it and feel it in here!'

Turning from that dreadful scene, I fled from the room, down the steps, across the hall, and out through the open door into the street. I ran across the square, past the church, heading for the river and the spot where we had destroyed the rats along with their deadly parasites. I do not know what I hoped to find. The sounds of innocent laughter, the screeches of delight, the simple music of whistle and drum, so evident the day before, were now absent from the town.

Hameln was silent. There were no rats to be seen. The charred remains of yesterday's fires were dampened by the dew. Anxious fathers stood in doorways. Mothers with babes in arms retreated behind them. Youths and maids there were, fifteen years old or more, but few in number for the black plague had touched most families. Yet I saw none younger.

Across the river I ran, into the narrow, dark passageways between shabby shacks in which the poor lodged, pausing for only a moment to stare at the black water. There were a few children here - poor, crippled and sick children, the children of beggars and thieves who had to steal a crust to stay alive. Dirty shrivelled faces stared out through rude slits in the walls of their hovels. Three tots playing in the muddy, unpaved alleys ran off as I approached. Since the rats had come, fear ruled the lives of everyone, but the plague, no respecter of rank or privilege, had exacted a terrible penalty from these poor creatures above all. Small wonder my father wished to tear down the whole neighbourhood with its filthy, vermin-ridden dwellings of wood and mud, and to re-house its inhabitants in Hameln itself. These people were cursed already and Akhtar had left them alone, reserving his magic, if magic it was, for the children of the more fortunate.

I retraced my steps, past St Boniface's tower once more, and made for the east gate. There was a face or two I knew - childish faces I had seen among the happy crowds of the previous afternoon. So it was only the merchants' children he had taken, those belonging to the families of the chief citizens, who had chased him from the town square. And it was on my account that he had done it.

As I stood in the shadow of the walls for a moment to catch my breath, I fancied I heard a child sobbing. At first, I could not see him but then a movement caught my eye. Crouched there under the wooden staircase leading to one of the houses was a small boy of eight or nine years of age. I bent towards him and he cringed from me. His face and hands, as well as the rags he wore, were covered in grime.

'Stay back if tha values thy life, mistress,' he cried weakly, and, to add more meaning to his utterance, he sneezed twice.

'Do not fear for me,' I said. 'Come out and tell me your name.'

He hesitated.

'Come out,' I called again. 'My name is Gretl, and I truly would learn yours.'

He dragged himself out into the street and stood against the wall, breathing heavily, his forehead bathed in filthy sweat. 'I'm Hanni, mistress,' he said hoarsely, 'and I know thee. Th'are daughter of the rat catcher.'

'Have you no parents?'

The boy shook his head.

'Where do you live?' I coaxed.

He gestured towards the hole under the stair.

'Have you seen any of the merchants' children, Hanni?' The decay and despair of the child's existence had me trembling with emotion. 'The children who played and danced yesterday in the streets?'

His little frame shivered and a look of terror overcame his sick countenance.

' 'Twere the Devil, Mistress,' he muttered and pointed beyond the high road towards the heath.'The Devil took 'em. More than I ha' fingers. Dancin' an' singin'.'

'Is it long since?' My heart was pounding. Ten children or more - that could only be Leo's little ones and their playmates. And Angelika would be there too!

'Aye, the Devil. Dancin' an' singin',' said little Hanni again. The plague had taken hold of him and his life was slipping away. 'I saw him, Mistress.'

I pitied him but there was nothing I could do to relieve his suffering.

Later, I would bring him food, I decided, but first I had to speak with my father. Akhtar and the children had a good start but they were on foot. We could overtake them on horseback.

Ludwig met me in the road outside my grandfather's house. He held his horse, already saddled.

'Is it true?' he asked. 'Have all the children gone?'

'Only the children of the merchants. He has left the urchins in peace. I know the direction they have taken. If we hurry we can catch them.'

'Not you, Gretl,' he said, and I could see he meant it.

'What will you do, Father?'

'We tried to bring Andreas to justice before and failed. Now he has brought tragedy again to our household. Though he is my brother, I know I must kill him, or he me.'

He embraced me and I looked up into his face. There was no anger there, only sadness. He was not yet forty years old. His eyes were Brunswick blue, and there were no signs of grey in his fair hair, which, against the fashion of the day, was cut short. Though the blood of Persia flowed in his veins, he had inherited none of Opa's features, and nothing of the mystical side of his character.

And he did not know, I told myself! He did not know that Andreas was not his true brother, but the son of his sister Hypatia. Opa had never breathed a word of it to him. That was what my grandfather had tried to say on his deathbed. He had not wanted me to tell Ludwig the truth, but to keep it from him.

I recalled something else Opa had said: Brother should not destroy brother. Were his words prophetic, I wondered? Prophetic or not, I was certain now of what I had long suspected. Hassan's duel with his half-brother Oljeitu had been a struggle against the darker side of his heart. Against the dark side of the fylfot, his inheritance. The purer, nobler side had won. The impure had survived to be born again through an evil deed. Through the priest, Father Walther. In Andreas, his grandson. In Akhtar.

In my father was nothing of the Dark Path. I had always known it. He was a good man with a pure soul and could never take a life in cold blood, whatever the offence. I knew he had spoken a lie and would never bring about Akhtar's destruction alone.

But I had inherited a share of both halves of my grandfather's heart. Born with my mother's nose, they said, I was in every other respect a child of the Orient. Like my mother and father, I had always tried to follow the teachings of Jesus but, unlike them, I had loved other gods too, Ormazd, Jehovah and Mahommet. I always gained simple pleasure from the tales from Persia, the stories of the Caliph of Baghdad, Shahrazade and many more. Opa had told me of the myths of creation, of life and death, of light and darkness, and I had hung on his every word.

My childish dreams had been filled by the heroic deeds of the valiant Zal and Rustem. I had imagined myself as the princess Rudabeh, more beautiful than the sun, loosing my long tresses from the terrace above my secret palace to allow the hero to climb up; and I had thought of his kisses and of his golden limbs as no pious Christian maiden should.

I had Ennia's teaching too, that a woman could be a man's equal in all but physical strength. What she could not accomplish by brute force could be achieved by skill and guile.

I released myself from Ludwig's embrace, my resolve firm, my destiny clear. I must strike the blow that my father could not. My injury was greater than his. Though I had never disobeyed him before, I would do so now if I could not persuade him.

'Father,' I said, 'if you had a son, you would want him to ride at your side. I'm both son and daughter to you. Let me come with you.'

He shook his head. 'No. I have made my decision. Your grandmother is in need of female company. What I have to do is my task alone. It's for a grown man to do and not for a mere child.'

I bit my tongue and said nothing. Never before had he spoken to me like that. I pointed him towards the heath and watched him ride off, his horse's hooves resounding on the cobblestones.

I dismissed the groom. Having filled a sack with some bread and ham for the sick boy and myself, I ran to where Princess was tethered. She was already saddled for the day's ride. My short sword and baldric hung on a hook in her stall and I took them down. I patted the filly gently and led her from the stable. There was no time to don a pair of breeches so I rent my dress on one side to make it easier for me to mount. I tied the sack to the filly's neck with a leather thong and added to it some other provisions I thought it prudent to take. These were a water bottle, a jar of oil, tinder and some flints. Sigmund's token, the silver dagger in its jewelled sheath, lay as always at my bosom. The baldric I looped over my shoulder.

Hanni was still by his hole under the steps. I stopped just long enough to unpack some food and to check again that the other items were secure. Satisfied, I prodded Princess forward into a steady canter and headed for the forest path.

Less than an hour had passed since I wakened. It was still early, but the sky was clear and the morning had warmed. The sun had dried the dew and the air was rather heavy, more like summer than the beginning of spring.

The ground was soft in places and, though he was not in view, new hoof prints on the track showed me which way Ludwig had taken. They crossed the main highway and cut through the forest, at a place where the trees were sparser and the ground rougher. Here the hilly country began. Scattered around were smooth, moss-covered rocks and puny shrubs growing in the crevices between. The hoof prints were fewer now, but there was no doubt that a rider had recently passed that way. I followed the tracks until the ground became hard. Loose stones and thorns covered the path. Now I could not tell for sure which way Ludwig and his quarry were headed. Still, hoping to pick up the trail, I went on in the same direction.

The ground fell suddenly into a gorge, formed on one side by a carpet of sharp stones through which my mount scraped and slithered, on the other by an almost sheer rocky incline. From several points on this slope, trickles of water fell over green, slimy boulders, to disappear into cavities leading to some underground stream. Small amounts of liquid had splashed out over a patch of bare soil and there, to my joy and apprehension, I espied human footprints. Not only that, but fifty paces from where I had halted, something bright hung from a clump of thorns. It fluttered like a flag in the breeze.

I slipped from the filly's back, my legs chafed from contact with her coarse hair, and led her by the mane until we reached the object that had caught my attention. My heart gave a great leap for it was a blue ribbon.

Akhtar and the children must have passed this way. Encouraged, I pressed forward. The sun had gone in behind a grey cloud, and there were more on the horizon, dark and brooding.

Though I told myself this wild country was no place to be if a storm were brewing, I was now committed to tracking the kidnapper to his lair, for such I supposed was his destination. There was little else to do but follow the gorge. Having come this far, I could not go back, and to climb out was, for the present, impossible.

I had travelled a thousand paces along the path without seeing any further prints when Princess snorted and planted her forelegs firmly in the ground. My first thought was that she had picked up the scent of a wild beast but I could hear no sound other than the wind. The landscape was as deserted as ever. Yet my instincts told me that something must have startled her. Was I the pursuer, I wondered, or was someone – something - watching and tracking me?

Looking around for signs that I was still on the right track, or to discover a landmark I recognised, I saw between two jutting rocks what appeared to be the mouth of a cave. Fearful of what I might discover, I gripped the hilt of my sword and went forward to explore.

The air inside was musty but the earth was dry. Just enough light came through the opening for me to see that the walls were smooth, and that the floor sloped upwards at the rear. I took a few hesitant steps but the slope ended in a solid wall. It was only a cave.

I scrambled back through the opening. Princess nuzzled my arm and I patted her mane to reassure her. After sniffing the air for a moment, she allowed me to lead her forward by the halter. The ground had become firmer again and I was able to remount and resume a trotting pace.

We came to the end of the gorge and I was in the open again. In front of me, the ground was strewn with moss-covered boulders, and in the soft earth grew clumps of coarse grass and more thorny vegetation. If I had anticipated finding evidence that my cousins and the other children had come this way, I was disappointed. There was no sign of life.

Again I stopped and dismounted. I bent absent-mindedly to pick up what I took to be a small stone, and threw it down again in disgust. It was the skull bone of a rat. Then I saw a complete skeleton, and another skull.

The way ahead was littered with the bones of animals that must have lived among the rocks before they fell victim to the deadly fleas. What kind of place was this bleak mountainside that I had stumbled upon?

I began to think about my situation. What was I to do next? I had been rash to pursue Akhtar alone and wished now I had not disobeyed my father's wishes. Would that he were with me at that moment! I had to continue my quest, but for how long? It was scarce midday but dusk would surely come. Though darkness in itself held no terrors for me, there were real dangers lurking on the heath after nightfall. It seemed to me that the worst Akhtar could do was to be preferred to the sharp teeth of a bear or a timber wolf. I still had the oil and the flints, and could make a fire with some dry vegetation to warm myself and drive off wild animals. However, without a plentiful supply of wood, I would be unable to keep the flames alive through the night.

I looked around to see if there was a path. There was none but there had been once, a winding track where the vegetation was less abundant. Moreover, to my surprise and momentary alarm, not far from where I stood was a ruined cottage. Then I spied another, and another. I was in what remained of a deserted village. Since the plague of 1348, there were many in the province but I had never visited one. Sometimes, whole populations had died out; elsewhere, the few survivors abandoned their home and went, God knows where, to rebuild their lives. I surmised that, being so exposed, these hovels would be in a worse state of dereliction than in other places.

And so it proved. There were eight dwellings altogether and not a single one remained whole. Their rafters, where there were any, were exposed and rotting, their stonework crumbling. I climbed over some stones into the shell of one of the cottages. Animal skeletons were everywhere. My pulse was racing but seeing nothing to fear in my present surroundings, I suppressed a shudder and sat on the remains of a wall to think. If Akhtar had come this far, he could not have walked, not with ten children in tow. Just one horseman would have left prints or at least have disturbed the vegetation. Yet there was nothing to indicate that any human being had been here recently. I was deceived and on quite the wrong track.

I considered what to do next. What would Ennia have done? Or Opa? And it was as I thought of them that the answer came to me, and I sprang up as if the stone were red hot. Suddenly, I was seven years old again and riding with Opa across the meadow towards the Singari encampment. Rising above me was the old tower and there again at an upper window was the face. It had haunted me then. It had frightened me when I saw it in the Singari woman's mirror. And it haunted me still. The face of Akhtar. I knew his lair. Gifted or cursed with foresight, I knew exactly where the madman had gone.

We had been climbing again and I could see that we were now high above the Weser valley. Some way below were the tree-covered slopes above the river but separating me from them was an escarpment of rotted tree-stumps, stones and other debris. I started down the slope. Princess was sure-footed enough but I was impatient and clumsy. I lost my balance twice, and bruised my legs and arms falling against the rough stone. By the time I had reached the bottom, I was badly shaken and sore. My forearm was bleeding. The simple incision I had inflicted on myself had become an ugly gash.

I was angry too. Akhtar had known my father and I were following him and had been playing with us. Was he cursed as I was and did he know therefore that I had divined his destination? I did not care. I fingered the coiled snake on my sword hilt. If indeed it were Fate's purpose to bring us together for a final reckoning, it would be all the worse for him. He would pay for his infamy, past and present, and for his trickery.

Princess was eager to be on her way. I gave her the reins to see which direction she took, and it was no surprise when she pulled me forward, and down into the river valley below. I had no intention of returning to Hameln but, having regained the familiar forest paths, I turned to the north-east and spurred my mount towards the high road to Hannover.

I had never approached the old tower from the west. Seen from this side, its aspect was different. The birch-covered mound fell less steeply to the rear and I saw that the tower did not sit on the summit as it appeared to do from the east but was built into the mound itself. Here, it was taller by two storeys and was supported at ground level by two stone buttresses.

The river must have been higher once for not only were there no trees growing at the base but an apron of discoloration ran the full length of the rear wall.

In other respects, the appearance of the building was the same as from the front. The aura surrounding it was just as sinister. Creeping green vegetation grew in the gaps between the stones, round the embrasures and over the broken turrets. There was no door or gate but just above what had once been the water line was a single barred window.

I urged Princess up the slope and into the trees. There was no sign of a horse or pony, or of a cart. Nevertheless, I approached the front entrance arch warily. I dismounted, unhooked the sack with my provisions and with my hand feeling the comfort of the sword hilt, went inside. The courtyard was strewn with moss-covered rubble, rotted timber and rat bones. There were broken branches and twigs too that, over the years, the winter winds had blown through the openings. The place had a smell of its own too, of neglect and decay.

Ahead of me was a sealed-up doorway. On my left, a crumbling stone staircase fixed to the inner wall led upwards to a gallery, then to another, and beyond that to a platform at the top of the tower. At the foot of the stairs was another opening, dark and uninviting. I looked up. The turreted rim was framed black against the sky. The whole edifice seemed to tilt and sway, and threaten to collapse on top of me. Several windows overlooked me from the lower gallery but they were mere empty frames, scarred and overgrown with creeping vines.

Could I have been mistaken? Had my mysterious sixth sense betrayed me after all? In my childish innocence, I had once thought this place unfit for royalty. A century ago, it had been grand perhaps, its walls hung with tapestries, its chill walls warmed by fires. Now, it was no habitation for any human soul. To the rats in the dungeon, the spiders in the crevices, the weevils and maggots in the rotting wood, it might be sanctuary but surely even a madman such as Akhtar would not choose to live among such corruption. Yet, beside my growing doubt was a small, nagging conviction that he was here. Although my courage was waning, I set a foot on the first stone step, drew my short sword and began to climb.

The gallery was just wide enough to allow two people to pass. Much of the stonework had collapsed and the beams had rotted away. I edged along the inner wall carefully, stepping over gaps and peering into gloomy openings into what must once have been individual rooms. With my heart thumping in my chest, I inspected each dim chamber as best I could before moving on to the next. In this manner, I encircled the courtyard and found myself approaching once more the top of the staircase.

There were two more doorways. The furthest from me lay directly behind a column at the head of the steps, the nearest but a pace or two away. Unlike every other opening I had passed, both of these were closed by plain doors.

I had seen no one and had heard nothing but the whistling of the wind. Now, as I drew level with the first door, the third of my normal senses told a different story. I detected in the air the unmistakeable odour of burnt tallow. In any other situation I might not have noticed but here, amid the smells of damp and decay, it was out of place.

Someone had been in the tower and had been here recently.

The door was slightly ajar. I grasped the latch with my left hand and pulled it. It swung open with a creak. Holding my breath, I stepped inside.

There was a window but it was too high in the wall to afford a view and too small to give much light. However, there was enough coming through the open doorway for me to see that the room was plainly furnished. A makeshift bed sat in one corner, beside it a chest, on which had been placed two candles. There were no holders, only the tallow had been melted to give adhesion to the surface. Both candles were more than half consumed as I could tell from the quantity of grease that had gathered in the coarse grooves in the wood.

I walked round the room, examining the bed and looking for clues which might confirm my suspicion that Akhtar had been using this place as his hideaway.

Thus preoccupied, I was startled by a sound from outside, followed by the patter of light debris falling on stone. I had no wish to be trapped in a corner and made for the door. I was too late. My only way of escape was blocked. A man enveloped in a cloak stood in the doorway. Most of the light was behind him and I could not see any features but I knew without doubt that it was Akhtar. What little bravery I had left froze within me.

Akhtar bowed.

'Welcome to my humble castle, little niece,' he said. 'I am obliged to the Singari for a few repairs and it has suited my purpose well enough.'

I did not disillusion him as to our relationship.

'What have you done with the children?' I demanded.

He ignored the question, took a step in my direction and stopped when he saw my sword. He fixed me with his black eyes. His voice was silkier than I had heard before.

'Here you are, Gretl. That should surprise me but it does not. You did not find the first trail too difficult, I hope.' He laughed. 'A footprint here, a ribbon there, and my poor brother has gone off in an entirely different direction. Or has he sent a daughter to do his business?'

He had deceived us and I had walked into his trap. I backed away from him, holding my sword in front of me. I could see no weapon but that did not mean he had none. His cloak could have hidden a multitude of swords and daggers and I would not have noticed them. I remember how he had confused his captors after the battle of the manor house and I gripped the coiled snake hilt all the tighter.

Akhtar seated himself on the edge of the chest and continued staring at me. I was perplexed. Whatever I had expected, it was not this. He had plotted, kidnapped, murdered, yet he sat before me as if I were a guest at his table.

'You would not kill an unarmed man, Gretl?' he said. 'Put down that sharp plaything and we can talk.'

'What have you done with the children?' I repeated, trying to avoiding his stare.

'They're safe enough,' said Akhtar. 'I have not harmed them.'

'I don't believe you,' I retorted. 'You've cast a spell on them, and made them prisoners in the cellar below this gallery. To what depths of evil have you sunk that you should drag my cousins here, and strike down my grandfather when he stood in your way?'

'You will not believe me either when I tell you that was not intended

- that I meant only to use the children to bring you to me.'

I almost took his word. If he hated me as I believed, and wished only for revenge, and to possess the fylfot, why was he treating me like this? The coldness I had seen formerly in his eyes, the iciness I had heard in his voice, were no longer present. The eyes were passionate, the voice held a tinge of regret. Once again, I felt myself drawn into his spell

'For months I have watched you, Gretl,' Akhtar went on. 'Your beauty and your courage bewitched me when I first saw you at Bachhagen, and ever since then I have longed for the day when we would meet again.'

His gaze never left my face. Now, two voices argued within my head, the one telling me to strike him down before it was too late, the other that here was no threat and that I should listen to his explanation. And the second of these was the stronger.

'Longed and waited,' he said. 'Waited and hoped that one day we might get to know one another better. That one day I might be reconciled to the family. So many years. So many regrets, Gretl.'

I said nothing but my hand relaxed on the sword hilt. Here was no threat – no monster, I said to myself. No sorcerer – no devil faced me, but a mere man. One who had made mistakes and wanted to make amends. I was as deceived as before and did not yet realise to what extent.

Suddenly, everything changed. Akhtar leapt to his feet and seized my right wrist. A simple twist caused my fingers to open and the sword fell with a clatter on the stone. Even then, I did not fully recover my wits, so fascinated had I become by his aura. However, at the same moment, he reached out to grasp my left arm. Had he taken it above the elbow, I might have remained in his power forever, but Fate decreed otherwise. His hand encircled the spot where I had cut myself with my silver blade and which had so recently been opened by my fall.

I cried out in pain and in horror of the earlier memory. It was as if I was again in the tent at the Brunswick fair, the evil face bent over mine, the hot breath on my cheek, and the hands fondling my breasts and limbs. I shook myself free and struck him across the face.

'Do you forget all those you violate so easily?' said I, raging at having been prey of his cunning a second time. 'How could I be fool enough to

316

believe that the fiend who ravished the maiden Lisa in a Singari tent three years since is capable of truly loving anyone but himself?'

Akhtar took a pace backward, rubbing his cheekbone where I had marked him. He stared at me in disbelief.

'That was you? All those years ago it was you who resisted me with such spirit. And I am the fool not to have seen it. I am the fool not to have seen that only the blood of Hassan could defy the blood of Hassan. So be it. I took you forcibly then and I'll do so again. By the time I have finished you'll give me what I want.'

The mask had slipped, and I saw him again for the vile creature he was. My anger grew. I had forgotten the children. I reached for Sigmund's dagger, drew it from its sheath and rushed at him, aiming a blow at his heart. The sharp blade rent his cloak, but he caught my wrist for the second time in his vice-like grip and twisted the weapon from my fingers. I knew how to injure him and aimed a kick at his private parts. Guessing my intention, he evaded the assault, took hold of my hair and threw me to the ground. I landed roughly, striking my shoulder on a corner of the chest. A numbness overtook my whole body. I lay there, gasping in agony, my head buzzing from the shock, while Akhtar stood over me, regarding me with evident lust.

'So, you would stick me with your needle, my brave Margaretha,' he taunted. 'We're even more alike than I had thought. Anger becomes you well, and only increases my desire to make you mine.'

'I will never be yours!' I cried. 'You will not escape justice. When my father discovers ...'

He interrupted me with a contemptuous laugh.

'What do I care for your justice!' he sneered. 'So long as I have the children you dare not harm me. You were not thinking, little Gretl! If I die, you may search until the sun grows cold but you'll not find them. Moreover, if you do not hand over my father's gold cross to me, it may be their pretty little bones, and yours, that Lou finds in this place.'

'I'll never give you the fylfot,' I said, knowing full well that he had the advantage. 'Kill me as you did my grandfather Queck with poison and a scratch on the neck. I'll never tell you where it is.'

'You will, Gretl, believe me!' He held up the hand on which he wore the signet ring. 'Since you have guessed the means I shall tell you. I have here enough poison to kill twenty. You should know, for it is Lou's own formula. But it is not to your neck that I shall hold it, but to the tender throat of the youngest of your cousins.'

He had won. Even Opa would not have wished me to risk one innocent life.

'The fylfot is buried with your father in his tomb,' I said savagely. 'May you be forever cursed if you take it. Now tell me what you have done with the children, so that I might return them to their families.'

'Not so fast, little niece,' said Akhtar. 'You'll have them only when I have the cross. Stay meantime and keep company with some of my friends!'

He pulled a bottle from the folds of his torn cloak, opened it and sprinkled a few drops of fluid on the floor. A sweet sickly odour filled the air. Next, he produced a tiny flute and putting it to his lips blew a few notes. Just as the sound died away, there was a rustling and scratching in the darkness of the corners and a rat emerged from an invisible opening into the feeble light.

I tried to get up but was still dazed and sore from the fall and managed only to prop myself on one elbow. More rats had appeared, scratching and squeaking as they rushed to sample whatever it was that Akhtar had shaken from the bottle. Meanwhile, Akhtar himself had already reached the door and disappeared from my sight into the gallery.

I had only a few moments before I was surrounded and could think only of fire as a means to delay the rats long enough for me to scramble to safety. Despite my confidence in Ludwig's prescription, among such numbers of the vermin, and so close to my person, I still feared their fleas.

My sack had fallen in the struggle and, as I stretched out for it, one of the pack advanced towards me and tried to bite my hand. I snatched the bag away and landed him a kick that sent him sprawling among his less adventurous fellows. The jar containing the oil had broken and its contents had spilled out over the canvas and on to the stones. Fortunately the tinder and flints were dry. I struck a spark, watched the flame take hold, then hurled the sack with the broken jar inside at the foremost rats. They retreated hastily. I managed to get to my feet just as my little flame flickered and died.

There was no feeling in my left arm and I wondered if my shoulder was broken. However, I had no time to dwell on it. My sword lay among the rats. I retrieved my dagger, stumbled to the door and slammed it shut. There was no one in the gallery or in the courtyard below. Akhtar had already quit the building.

I said a silent prayer and, half running, half staggering, set off in pursuit.

ii

I saw it all plainly.

The children were not in the tower and never had been there. How could they be? It was impossible. I had ridden hard; though I had not seen his horse, Akhtar must have ridden hard too. Had he sold them into slavery, or did they lie in some other damp prison, hungry and afraid? Could it even be that they had been transformed by sorcery into …?

No, such things did not happen. These things were legend, tales to frighten simple, uneducated folk. I knew that with my mind yet, at that moment, I doubted with my heart. My science counted for nothing and I was like any other mortal: humble, fearful and gullible.

One thing I did know. Whatever evil scheme Akhtar had executed, whatever trick or illusion he had performed, I had to follow him to the end. I had to discover where the children had gone. I had to rescue them from his clutches.

I steeled my resolve. My only hope of success was to be no more than a few steps behind him at any given moment. He would make for Bachhagen now, that was certain, to plunder my grandfather's tomb and take the fylfot for himself. There I would destroy him. The cross of Shahrinaz was no more magic than the rat bones that littered the courtyard of the tower. Akhtar was mad. And his great folly in believing it to be other than a symbol would be his undoing, if the gods did not strike him down for his profanation.

By the time I reached the bottom of the staircase, feeling had returned to my arm. It hurt, but I could tell it was bruised and no worse. I stumbled across the debris to the exit. Outside, the sky was dull. Angry clouds had gathered overhead and on the horizon.

I called to Princess and she came to me. She seemed to understand that haste was needed and stamped impatiently as I mounted her. I urged her through the birch wood, down the stony slope towards the river and on into a gallop. The pasture where I had first seen the Singari was deserted now and we soon left it far behind. It began to rain, large spots that stung my face and obscured my vision. My left arm and shoulder ached.

When I drew rein within sight of our lands, the sun, on those occasions when it was visible, was low in the sky. The rain had eased but that was small comfort as I was already wet through. I had kept hope alive that I would gain on Akhtar and pass him unseen. Or that he, believing he had nothing to fear, would slow his pace and allow me to surprise him. Still, we had not caught up with him. My hope was turning to despair.

The manor house was in shadow as I rode into the valley. The thunderclouds had settled over the estate. Now and again, there was a low rumble from the heavens. Suddenly, a crash of thunder caused Princess to buck violently and pitch me to the ground. I lay still for several minutes, stunned by the fall and unable to move, while the frightened animal cantered off toward familiar pastures.

I rose to my knees and glanced up. In the west, the cloud had shifted and a large patch of blue had appeared. The sun was visible again but I saw in horror that a murky shadow had fallen across it. That life-giving ball of fire was being eaten up by a round black shape that, by slow degrees, was shutting off the light from the world.

I cowered to the earth.

Mary protect me!

My prayer was greeted with another peal of thunder. It grew darker. The black shape now covered a quarter of the sun's disc. In the retreating clouds, I imagined the outline of the Singari woman who had so frightened me at the Brunswick fair.

You will go on a journey, I heard her say, and her prophecy took on new meaning. *A journey where day will become as night*!

As a child, I had spent many hours studying Opa's star charts. I knew there were rare times when the path of the moon crosses that of the sun. I had never doubted such wonders existed, and allow that what I witnessed then was a natural meeting of the great lights that rule day and night. But such was my terror that I thought of none of that.

Opa had told me of a time when he had seen the sun blotted out all but a ring of fire. I had not believed him, taking it to be just another of the tales he told for our amusement. I did not believe it now and could think only of his awesome words the day we sat together in the herb garden.

Virtue will be despised, sorcery honoured, and the creatures of the night released upon the world.

What had I done?

My mother was dead. Opa was dead.

My grandfather Johann was dead, the children abducted, and my dearest love would never return to claim me, all because I had secreted Opa's fylfot in the darkness of a tomb. Now the bright, shining symbol at its centre would be dulled forever. In Akhtar's hands, it would become the lost fylfot of the moon. Daylight would be banished. Angra Mainyu - Satan, Iblis, the Evil One - would rule the Earth.

'Sigmund!'

I spoke his name aloud but there was no one to hear it. Another cloud burst overhead. The rain fell in torrents. The sun and its black shadow remained hovering in the western sky.

Shahrinaz remained faithful to the truth!

This memory shed a ray of hope on my guilt-ridden soul. Light was stronger than darkness, love stronger than hate. The sun would shine again tomorrow. The two crosses of Jemshid were symbols, nothing more. Perhaps I could still undo some of the evil my action had brought about.

Without truly knowing what I was doing, I got to my feet and began walking up the hill past the church. My clothing was saturated. The rain trickled down my back and arms. Blood mixed with water, pink in colour, dripped from my hand.

A horse was grazing at the edge of the coppice and the iron gate to the tombs was wide open. As I walked unsteadily towards the gate, a bolt of lightning struck a tree less than fifty paces away. At almost the same moment, there was a crash of thunder and the very ground shook. Still in a daze, I passed through the first chamber where my mother's coffin lay and stood overlooking the lower vault that contained the mortal remains of my grandparents.

The lid of Opa's coffin had been raised and moved aside. The body in its winding-sheet was clearly visible, its head and shoulders fully exposed. I was too late, as I had feared I would be. The damage had been done, the sacrilege committed. The fylfot was no longer where I had left it.

There was no sign of Akhtar. Fearing he had hidden himself in some pitch-black corner of that vault, I retreated and sat dejectedly on the flagstones by my mother's tomb.

I do not know whether he had been in the chamber all along, or having seen me enter had followed from the outside, but I looked up and saw his dark shape framed in the arched tunnel to the daylight. Behind him and beyond the gate the lightning still flashed. It illuminated the chamber eerily and glinted from time to time on the gold at his throat.

'So, my brave Gretl,' he crooned, 'you have followed me again. Perhaps after all you don't find my company so unpleasing.'

'Monster!' I threw back at him. 'I have nothing but contempt for you. For this desecration, God's curse is already upon you. I'll not rest until the earth swallows you up.'

Akhtar laughed softly - a foul loathsome laugh.

'What is one curse more or less to me, who am cursed tenfold? The earth will swallow us all, eventually. Meantime, life is pleasant. Why should we not enjoy it together? I will make you a bargain, Margaretha.'

'A bargain! What kind of bargain can you make – *Uncle*?'

Akhtar moved closer. If the word *uncle* was bait, he did not take it. What did it matter anyway? Uncle or cousin, I meant to kill him if I could.

'The kind of bargain that binds us together,' he said. 'I've told you we are alike. You have the blood of Hassan in full measure though only one quarter of his seed. I have the fylfot. Why should we not rule Brunswick together?'

'You are deluded. The fylfot has no power of its own.'

'How wrong you are, little niece,' sneered Akhtar. 'I can already gather the mists around my person and move as freely as the wind.'

'Deluded!' I spat. 'There is no magic.'

His mood changed suddenly and he almost caught me off guard.

'Yet I have a skill,' he countered and I wondered that such an engaging smile could hide his lascivious thoughts. 'You have seen it for yourself.'

'I have seen. You use it for evil when you might use it for good.'

'You know me too well, Gretl,' said Akhtar. 'I cannot fool you with talk of magic. That is why as a pair we would be invincible.'

'I have no desire to be your consort,' said I hotly. 'And you can never be prince here. The whole country knows you. You'll be taken if you set foot again in Brunswick town.'

The smile vanished. 'Wrong again! I have friends, and they will help …'

'Friends!' I rejoined scornfully. 'When did you ever have friends, *Andreas*?'

He scowled at the sound of the name but otherwise ignored my taunt.

'Nevertheless,' he continued, 'there are those who need me for their purpose, as I use them for mine. One day you'll remember my offer. Then, what is not given willingly I shall take again. Even you, brave niece. Your little rosebud will be riper now; my pleasure will be all the greater. Yes, I'll take you, Margaretha, just as I took the maid Lisa three years ago at the Midsummer fair.'

I shrank from him, looking for a means of escape.

'Never,' I breathed. 'Your foul member will never defile my body again. Rather than give you satisfaction I would take my own life. But beware, Andreas von Hasenbach! You can no longer harm me with your tricks, fylfot or no. Take care lest I put an end to you with a dagger in the back.'

'We shall see,' he snarled, leaping towards me and seizing me by the hair. 'There are only two of us now. The maid and the madman! Perhaps I've learned new tricks since we last met.'

He slid his hands over my neck. His groping fingers tore my bodice at the shoulder. He probed the flesh beneath. His repulsive mouth touched my cheek. His lust was already high and his swollen member pressed against my belly. Rage welled up inside me but I could not reach my knife. I bit his ear and clawed his face with my nails. He screamed and reeled back, but did not release his hold. In desperation, I grasped the fylfot and twisted savagely. I was strong and might have choked him had he not thrown me to the ground with a wrestling move. In an instant, he was on me. His signet ring was at my throat and his knees pinned me to the hard floor.

'There's no one to help you now,' he hissed. 'When you might have shared my good fortune, you've chosen to incur my malice. You were a fool to follow me to the tower, and you are the bigger fool for pursuing me here.'

'It was for the children's sake that I followed you,' I gasped, not daring to struggle lest the stone in his ring tear the vein in my neck. 'Kill me if you like but, I beg you, return my cousins to their homes.'

Akhtar released his hold. The anger left his face.

'My poor Gretl,' he mocked. 'Still so proud, yet so vulnerable! I thought you had learned that all magic is in the mind. My father knew it, and before that the princess who bore him. I told you already that I'd set a trap for you. My plan was well laid, and now the circle is complete. I needed only to convince others, and I was sure you too would be convinced, my proud niece. The fylfot was always the prize and you led me to it. My inheritance! What need had I of children? I'll wager the brats never left Hameln, and were already at their play by the time my false clues led you to me!'

I stared at him in disbelief. 'That cannot be! They were seen heading for the heath. You yourself threatened... I myself saw...'

'What did you see, Gretl: some anxious fathers; a frantic mother or two; some filthy beggar boy with the mark of death on his face? I lied to you! Think back. What a day you had. Such sport and dancing! And so much wine. So late into the night too!

'Only the old man stood in my way. When I came early to the house ... when I had sown seeds of confusion in his servant's mind, he tried to stop me. I would have entranced him too but there was no time. He fought. My ring tore the flesh of his neck by accident and he had a seizure. There was no poison.'

'I don't believe you. You killed my grandfather. You killed the children or sold them into slavery.'

'And when would I have done that?' asked Akhtar coldly. 'And why would I lie to you now? Think, Gretl! Tired by the games, too sleepy for a short walk home, they slept at the houses of their kinfolk, or with neighbours. That old fool Graube and the other proud citizens who defied me, they all believed. Even poor Lou was duped by their conviction that I had stolen their precious offspring.

'Now the time for pretence is over. You refuse my bargain. So be it. You'll never see family or friends again.'

I have often wondered if he would indeed have killed me or would, having ravished me a second time, cast me aside in his vanity and contempt. Fate decreed he should do neither.

Outside the storm was in progress. The lightning and thunder raged. The rain had become a deluge. The flagstones on which we had been struggling were wet and slippery from water cascading down the hillside and flooding the chamber through the tunnel.

So sure was Akhtar of victory that he leant too close and allowed the hilt of a poniard in his belt to come within reach of my free hand. I gripped the weapon and slashed, aiming at his groin. The blade missed its target but it pierced his breeches and sank into his flesh. Akhtar howled in agony. He clutched a bloody gash in his upper thigh. I broke free and scrambled to my feet, drawing my own dagger - Sigmund's gift - as I did so. Holding both weapons in front of me, I edged towards the exit.

Akhtar had also risen, his face contorted with pain and hate. His wound was far from mortal. He came at me. I lunged with both blades at his sound leg. Akhtar swerved to avoid the deadly steel, slipped on the wet flagstones, and fell backwards through the gateway. Taking full advantage, I leapt over him and took to my heels into the open.

I had scarcely gone a dozen paces when there was an ear-rending crash. I was picked up bodily by an invisible hand and hurled through the air to land heavily in a sodden clump of grass. Both dagger and poniard were torn from me.

Breathless, and with a strange numbness in my limbs, I rose. A bolt of lightning had struck the iron gate, ripping it from its hinges. Akhtar lay on his back in a pool of water. His body was lifeless, his eyes staring, his whole face distorted by a look of utter surprise and horror. He had reached for the gate in an effort to rise. Even in death, his scorched hands had not released their grip of the twisted metal.

Drenched to the skin, I approached the tomb and its grim relic. After a moment or two, I plucked up courage and, bending down, unfastened the fylfot from the neck of the corpse. I held it in my palm so that the fastenings were hidden and the engraving of the sun uppermost. The hooks of the cross bent always to the right. I turned it over, half expecting to see the emblem of Angra Mainyu on the other side but - no; the fylfot was as it had always been.

Solemnly, I returned to my grandfather's open coffin and made to lay the cross once more on his breast. Then I remembered the Gypsy woman's words and, looking for some other sign, fancied that Opa's head moved in dissent.

Guard it well, she had said.

Guard it well, he had instructed. Akhtar must not have it.

I placed the fylfot about my own neck, said the benediction and pushed the heavy coffin lid back into position. The rain had stopped. The storm had passed over and the valley was bathed in the orange glow of the setting sun, whole once more. It was probably my fancy but there seemed to be a glow too around the chapel. I smelled the pure air, laden with scents of grass, the bark of trees, the carpet of pine needles and early spring flowers. Everything was as it should be.

In my heart, I knew Akhtar had not lied. The children were safe. It had been an illusion, easily performed. When the deception was discovered, the merchants would send after Ludwig. He would return to Hameln, thence to our home. We would embrace, harsh words forgotten. They would bury Hypatia's child in an unmarked grave. All this I saw clearly. Did the fylfot after all have a power of its own?

Akhtar's dead hand still grasped the iron gate. I gave the corpse one final glance and shivered in the cool breeze of the March evening.

Perhaps a priest can be found who will pray for you, I thought, for I cannot.

Epilogue
1366 C.E.

Sigmund came back to me. He had seen war and had survived. We were true to our promises and wed in the autumn of 1362 in the chapel at Bachhagen.

'I shall find a peaceful occupation,' he said as we lay together on the marriage bed, our passion cooled. 'A merchant's life might be interesting, and there are no Brunswick laws that prevent a wife travelling with her husband. If that's not to your liking, perhaps Lou can teach me physic.'

'I have always wanted to travel,' I said. 'But whether you be merchant, physician or farmer, I'll be content to be your wife.'

Already, in the countryside, the tales are beginning to spread. Another legend is being born.

'Folk memories are short,' says my father. He dandles his first grandchild proudly on his knee. 'One day soon they'll forget the truth altogether.'

He wrinkles his brow until his thick blond eyebrows come together. He often frowns when he is worried or thinking deeply. There is something mystical about that frown, the one mannerism he has not inherited from any descendant of the Lion of Saxony.

I think he worries needlessly. Never once have I heard our name linked to the gossip. It is better so. None of us is beyond the reach of the Bishops' Inquisition, and it is no respecter of truth, except its own version of it. I ask him whether the truth matters.

'He will want to know, Greta,' he says. He always calls me that now and I am glad. My mother is gone and it is his way of sharing her memory with me.

I follow his gaze until my eye rests on the bubbling infant. My little boy. He is nearly three now and every inch a Persian child, with dusky complexion, large brown eyes and tufts of raven hair. I wonder what he will make of his inheritance.

'You must tell him when he's older,' I tease. 'It's a grandfather's duty!'

'Not I, Grela!' I can see he is on the verge of laughing at my impudence, but he stifles his amusement. 'I'm no storyteller.'

My eye is caught by my reflection in a nearby glass. A pleasing enough image, even if the complexion has none of the Brunswick colouring and if, of the features, only the nose betrays my Saxon parentage. But I am Margaretha of Wolfenbüttel now and must at least pretend.

My memories confuse me sometimes. Are they real or are they dreams conjured up by my fertile imagination? On balmy summer days, when the river runs low, the fruit swells in the orchard and insects chirp lazily in the long grass, it is easy to believe it a grim nightmare: the rat-infested barns; the black boils; the Dance of Death. It is easy to listen to the gossips of Hannover, and to laugh at their fanciful tales of magic and mystery.

It all happened. I have only to glance at the white scar on my left forearm to know that my nightmare was real. But it is over now. I have my life to lead and will try to forget.

I take my son from his grandfather, fondle him and press his head against the swelling in my body, where a second life has begun. He is nearly asleep. He has grasped the fylfot in his tiny hand and is twisting it to and fro so that the light from the lattice, reflecting on the gold, makes colour patterns on the wall. They flicker and dart, whimsical and elusive, like damselflies over sunlit water.

After only three years, Sigmund's business in the Hansa is successful and he has ships at Lübeck and Rostock. For now, he is helping Freddy on the estate, until my time is due. I am hoping for a daughter. Afterwards, he has promised me that we will go to Venice and Constantinople.

Today, we plan to visit their graves: my mother's; my grandparents; Ennia's. I recovered the sword she gave me and will carry it with me.

Later, we will stop in the little hollow by the beech tree that holds a special place in our hearts.

My son is now fast asleep in my arms. I release the fylfot from his grasp, lay him in his crib and make my way to the stables to saddle the black Arab mare, a wedding gift from Freddy. Kati Langenfurth slipped through his fingers but he lost no time in wooing her sister Maria. She is of a serious disposition and we have become good friends. Soon the manor house at Bachhagen will be full of children again.

Sigmund is waiting for me and we ride together towards the coppice. Neither of us speaks as we stand for a moment by the tombs. The wrought-iron gate to the vault has been repaired now and, as we leave, I fasten three bunches of summer flowers to it.

We ride on to the brow of the hill that overlooks the valley. A little way down is the plain stone that marks the last resting-place of Doquz, who became Ennia. I touch the stone reverently with my sword and we leave her the remaining flowers.

Below us lie open fields and, in the distance, forest as far as the eye can see. Nestling by the river, in the middle ground, are the turrets of the manor house. Just to our left stands the stone church. Everything is as it should be.

Truly, I tell myself, this is only the beginning. The Singari woman's prophecy has not yet been fulfilled.

END

Afterword

Readers of my original novel, published in paperback, criticised it on two levels: First, there was the language, considered by some critics to be out-of-date. For that, I make no apology. It was my intention to recreate a legendary past and both narrative and dialogue were designed with that objective in mind.

Although marketed as historical fiction, the story doesn't belong in that genre because none of the events portrayed are truly historical. Readers who said this do have a point. The main storyline is fantasy and was never intended to be anything else. I have therefore tried to address this criticism by reissuing in a new edition, as a mediaeval fantasy.

However, there are elements of *The Dark Side of the Fylfot* which do belong to history, grim facts of which I am continually reminded as I write this Afterword. The Black Death of 1348 and its recurrence in the next decade or two killed up to fifty percent of the population of Europe. There was no cure. No one in that era understood the disease; no one had the least idea how to stop it. We should be thankful today that medical science takes a less superstitious stance when faced with a worldwide epidemic.

Myth plays a big part in this novel. The legend of Jemshid and his daughters comes, with a few tweaks, from Omar Kayyam's Rubaiyat, Firdausi's Shahnama and various Zoroastrian texts. For the reinvention of the Ratcatcher (or Pied Piper) of Hameln in a new persona, I am entirely to blame.

Whilst the von Hasenbach family is fictional, several other characters who play minor parts in my story, or who are referred to in it, were real people:

Duke Albert II of Brunswick (1268-1318), known to posterity as Albert the Stout (Albrecht der Feiste), and his wife Richsa had thirteen children, of whom Magnus was the twelfth. Albert inherited territories in the province from his father Albert the Great in 1291/1294. The latter and his sister

Helena were great-grandchildren of Henry the Lion, Duke of Saxony and Bavaria.

Duke Magnus I (1304-1369), known as Magnus the Pious, ruled Brunswick and Göttingen jointly with two of his brothers, Otto and Ernst. Henry the Lion had married Matilda, daughter of Henry I of England, so Matilda, or Matthilde, was a popular name in the family. My Matthilde is wholly fictional.

Oljeitu and Abu Sa'id, mentioned in the middle section of the story, were rulers (Il-khans) of Persia between 1304 and 1335. Suleiman was one of several puppet khans who ruled briefly thereafter.

My *Singari* are the people, whom today in Britain we usually call the *Roma* (- the term *gypsy* is pejorative -). They have been in Europe for a long time and are widely thought to have come from India. Throughout history, they have been continually regarded with suspicion and prejudice. In his trilogy *His Dark Materials*, the author Philip Pullman made them into heroes. *I could not follow a better example.*

For any readers who prefer a more history-based approach, and who would like more about Prince Hassan of Persia, and Doquz (who became Ennia), I recommend my novels **The Il-khan's Wife** and **The Tiger and the Cauldron**. Both are available as digital books on Amazon!

And finally, if you enjoyed reading *The Dark Side of the Fylfot*, please leave a short review on the Amazon website. I would love to know your opinion.

Andrew G. Lockhart
May 2021

Other works by the same author:

Adult Romance (*writing as Drew Greenfield*)

Sweeter Than Wine (May 2018)

a contemporary adult romance, set among the lush, green vineyards of the Garonne Valley.

Sweet Entanglement (April 2021)

a spicy tale of wine, chocolate and sex in academia.

Printed in Great Britain
by Amazon